Tara Pammi can't remember when she wasn't lost in a bo... romance, which was much more exciting than a mathematics textbook at school. Years later, Tara's wild imagination and love for the written word revealed what she really wanted to do. Now she pairs alpha males who think they know everything with strong women who knock that theory *and* them off their feet!

Lorraine Hall is a part-time hermit and full-time writer. She was born with an old soul and her head in the clouds—which, it turns out, is the perfect combination for spending her days creating thunderous alpha heroes and the fierce, determined heroines who win their hearts. She lives in a potentially haunted house with her soulmate and a rumbustious band of hermits in training. When she's not writing romance, she's reading it.

SAYING 'I DO' TO THE WRONG GREEK

TARA PAMMI

A DIAMOND FOR HIS DEFIANT CINDERELLA

LORRAINE HALL

MILLS & BOON

First published in Great Britain 2024
by Mills & Boon, an imprint of HarperCollins*Publishers* Ltd,
1 London Bridge Street, London, SE1 9GF

www.harpercollins.co.uk

HarperCollins*Publishers*, Macken House, 39/40 Mayor Street Upper, Dublin 1, D01 C9W8, Ireland

ISBN: 978-0-263-32001-5

03/24

SAYING 'I DO' TO THE WRONG GREEK

TARA PAMMI

MILLS & BOON

CHAPTER ONE

SOMETHING WAS WRONG.

Terribly, horribly wrong in the tableau before Annika Sax-ena-Mackenzie as she stood at the other end of the altar of the centuries-old church, her arm wound through her stepfa-ther's, her lace-and-tulle designer dress weighing her down.

Her gut, her instincts, her heart knew it before her mind, her rationale, seemed to catch up. Or pin it down.

It wasn't the gorgeous smattering of lilies and night jas-mines, scattered about randomly to achieve perfection, that made the church look like it was floating on dreamy white flowers.

It wasn't the suitably awed guests, grateful to be invited to the wedding of the century on the East Coast, staring back at her playing her role perfectly—an heiress worth billions.

It wasn't the string quartet she'd hired after dozens and dozens of auditions and which she'd had flown in specially for this occasion from Vienna.

It wasn't her three young half brothers, who were dressed in matching black suits and trying to behave like perfect gentlemen for their older sister even though they were fidg-eting rascals who couldn't sit still for breakfast.

It wasn't the officiant standing at the altar and gazing at her with an affected kindness that had cost her a pretty penny.

The setting of her extravagant, storybook, fairy-tale wedding was perfect.

Her stepfather, Killian, looking down at her with pride and joy, always on her side, always loving her unconditionally, was perfect.

She was looking perfect.

It was the man waiting for her that was the problem.

Her bridegroom.

Something was wrong. Something was different—strange—*about him.*

Ani wondered if she should stop walking, tell Killian that she wasn't feeling well. Or excuse herself for just a minute while she put her finger on it.

It had taken her months of strategic planning and cunning scheming and secret meetings with a lawyer and roping in her accessory with pleas and demands and threats to finally get here. She couldn't back out now. Not until…

And then finally, it came to her, halfway through the torturous walk toward her destination, leaving her rational mind horrorstruck.

He was wrong.

Dizziness overtook her as realization landed, the tight corset of her dress making it hard to breathe.

He'd fooled the crowd and the media outside, the awed guests and her stepfather who'd only met him twice. But not her.

Ani had always been able to tell them apart, even when she'd been a four-year-old, forever chasing after the Skalas teens during long, hot Greek summers, when their father couldn't, much less the media.

When she'd been a teen, it had been a point of pride that she was only one of two people who could tell them apart when they didn't want the world to know: their grandmother, Thea, who'd raised them, and her.

Now Ani knew why her heart was ratcheting so hard in her chest, why her belly rolled the moment she passed the grand archway and caught sight of him standing there.

This was the wrong twin.

This was not Sebastian Skalas, the playboy billionaire/friend/fellow hell-raiser she'd roped into marrying her after months and months of wearing him down.

This was Alexandros Skalas, the exact opposite of the laid-back, glib charmer that was his twin.

Xander was arrogant, egotistical, ruthless, controlling. The one man who got under her skin with no effort. The one man she'd never been able to win over. The one man who could turn her brilliant plan upside down.

Her stepfather nudged her forward, the weight of his palm at her back, inquiring without letting on. Killian's kindness was a potent reminder that she couldn't turn back on her scheme at this crucial point. Not if Xander was playing along.

But why was Xander here? Had Sebastian talked him into it somehow?

However much they butted heads, Xander and Sebastian loved each other. It was a very contentious, competitive kind of affection, but at the end of the day it was love—a sentiment they both considered a weakness.

Two more steps and Killian would hand her over.

Feeling a helplessness she hated, Ani lifted her chin and faced reality head-on. In a black tuxedo that hugged his lean, wiry strength, her bridegroom was quintessentially masculine, so effortlessly sensual that it drew her and then repelled her for the power it had over her. The patrician nose, the high forehead, the neatly slicked-back hair and that mouth, with its tiny, infinitesimal scar...everything about him was magnetizing, turning her from her rational plans and hard goals and a strong survivor into a mass of feelings and sensations over which she had no control.

One dark brow rose.

This *was* Xander. And with that raised brow, he was asking her if she was going through with it, taunting her to run away, daring her to admit her fear and turn around.

A soft exhale escaped from her mouth, making the lacy veil flutter.

He seemed to think she had a choice. But she had none—not when it came to saving her family. She needed a husband to take hold of her father's wealth that had been left in trust for her—a stupid, archaic condition imposed by her dear departed father and enforced with casual malice by her stepbrother, Niven.

She'd begged and cajoled Sebastian, threatened and cursed in turns, because he was the one man she could trust to not control her once she had her fortune, to not want even a dime of it. For all he was a charmer and a playboy, Sebastian had a hidden core of integrity that had cemented their friendship for almost two decades.

Maybe Xander was going to pretend he was Sebastian and then Sebastian would come back and they could move forward with all that they'd agreed. Which wasn't really much, since she'd asked so little of him as a husband.

Her thoughts in a whirl, Ani took the last two steps and smiled beatifically when Killian kissed her cheek and asked her a question with those perpetually kind eyes. And then she was standing in front of the man who, it seemed, had decided to see this through.

And that was what rankled the most: that she had to be saved by Xander.

She was going to kill Sebastian with her own bare hands for leaving her to Xander's ruthless ego! Because if there was one thing that she knew for sure in this maelstrom of confusion, it was that Xander disliked her as much as she disliked him.

Very few things in life made Alexandros Skalas curious.

Most things, and most people in life, were predictable and the few variables that he did encounter, Xander made sure fell into easy, predictable patterns, so he rarely encountered surprises or shocks. At only thirty-four, he had already turned into a crotchety, grumpy sort of man who liked his things, his businesses, his routines, the people around him, and his life just so.

And given that he was a billionaire a hundred times over, he could care and not care as he pleased. Mostly he didn't.

But there had always been one variable, one person, he had never been able to fathom or put into a box or…dammit, control. The last thing sounded wrong because he wasn't a person who usually wanted to control others, especially when they existed on the periphery of his life.

Annika Saxena-Mackenzie was that variable that kept surprising him and shocking him. His grandmother's goddaughter, she had always been a part of Xander's life in one way or another. He repeatedly pushed her to the margins, and yet, she kept taking center stage in his life. First as a cute, chubby toddler who had stolen his grandmama's attention and care from him and Sebastian when they'd needed her more, then as an intrusive, irritating teenager who forever dogged his twin's steps during summers, making him laugh and howl and generally participating in his escapades and egging him on to more. Then in the last few years, by suddenly morphing into one of the most beautiful women he'd ever set eyes on.

As if it wasn't enough that his grandmama was excessively fond of Annika, Sebastian had a firm friendship with her. Over the years, Xander had waited for a break to appear, as it usually did in all of Sebastian's relationships.

It didn't. Again, that annoying variable.

Somehow, Annika and Sebastian's friendship had not only lasted for two decades, but it had resulted in a shocking engagement announcement not four months ago.

If Xander told himself that the engagement didn't bother him one bit it would be a lie.

It *had* bothered him. It had been bothering him for all of one hundred and twenty-eight days and twenty-two hours.

Being the deliberate, strategic, non-impulsive Skalas twin—the only one with a sensible head on his shoulders among his entire demented family—Xander had waited, with growing impatience, to see the engagement crash and burn.

It was impossible to imagine two such people—rich, privileged, petty hell-raisers—living together in peaceful matrimony. It was like mixing two explosive chemicals, and all that would follow was destruction. But his twin had surprised him yet again.

Sebastian had not only kept up appearances, plastering himself to Annika's side at every charity gala and society event, he had also cleaned up his act. There hadn't been any scandalous affairs with ministers' wives, or getting drunk in nightclubs and getting into fights. Basically, for the first time in their lives, Xander hadn't had to clean up a single mess that Sebastian had left behind.

In one of those weak moments that seemed to come up on him after three glasses of whiskey, Xander had wondered if Annika was indeed the magic pill to fix whatever ailed Sebastian. The thought had brought the truth into sharp relief followed by blistering distaste.

He did not want Annika as his sister-in-law.

For all the media reported that he and Sebastian hated each other—and they let that rumor feed itself—whoever Sebastian married would be center stage in Xander's life.

Even that was only half the truth.

Cloaked in the darkness of the night, his usual control blunted by alcohol, Xander had finally admitted the truth to himself: he did not want Sebastian to marry Annika *because he wanted Annika for himself.*

With a confounding depth and breadth. With a fierce, possessive, almost savage force.

He had always wanted her. Even though she'd always been attached at the hip to Sebastian. Even though she'd always preferred his charming, easygoing, funny twin over Xander himself. He'd wanted her even when he didn't understand her sudden metamorphosis from a sunny, painfully awkward teenager to a brazen flirt and shameless thief.

Even when she got herself into scandals that led to two broken engagements, and ran with the wrong crowd, and got up in his face about his grandmother's failing health in the last year. Even when he'd discovered that she was siphoning funds from his grandmama. Even when he'd discovered his mother's favorite sapphire ring had disappeared on one of her summer visits.

He had wanted her when he'd kissed her in the gazebo at his estate, under the cover of dark, at her twenty-first birthday party not two years ago. He wanted her, more than anything he had ever wanted in his life, when she had pressed her lithe body up against him and moaned her eagerness and greed for more.

He'd wanted her when he'd whispered, "I have finally figured out how to make you behave." He'd wanted her when she'd jerked away from him, a flash of vulnerability in her eyes before she faked shock. He'd wanted her when she pressed trembling fingers to her swollen mouth, and claimed she'd mistaken him for Sebastian.

He had wanted her even when she'd lied to his face that if she'd known that it was him, she would never have touched him, much less let him kiss her. He had wanted her when her lies had kept him up all night.

Far too invested, he had waited and waited and waited for the engagement to fall apart. But it had not. Not two months ago, not a month ago, not two weeks ago, not a few days ago.

Imagining his dislike for Annika had brought about his absence at the wedding, his grandmother Thea had read him the riot act about what it meant to be a Skalas. Especially since her frail health forbade her traveling to see her favorite grandson marry the apple of her eye. For reasons only known to her, Annika had to get married here, instead of at their ancestral estate.

Xander couldn't reveal to his grandmama that he'd been planning to attend all along. That while he didn't know how, he was going to do his level best to stop the wedding.

Pining for his twin's wife from a distance was an affliction he refused to be struck down with for the foreseeable future. He wouldn't have stolen her for himself like some uncivilized brute being thrashed around by his desires, but he was absolutely going to make sure the wedding couldn't go ahead.

He simply needed to be sure that Sebastian's heart hadn't been engaged. And he was right. His brother was fond of Annika but nothing more.

Because despite their cruel, tyrannical father's countless

attempts to pit them against each other, he and Sebastian did care for each other. It was not a traditional sort of affection, but more of a tolerance of each other's flaws and foibles, an understanding of each other's capacity for cruelty that was rooted in their childhood.

Until yesterday morning, Sebastian had been in a high mood. And then, right after the rehearsal dinner last night, he had vanished.

Xander did not worry about his brother, not then, not now. For all he liked to present himself to the world as a useless, charming playboy who only knew how to spend money and waste himself on the wrong women, Sebastian was razor-sharp and just as ruthless as Xander, only he hid his true nature.

They each had their own ways of rebelling against the tight fist of their cruel father. They'd both survived and, even better, they'd both succeeded in their own ways. If that wasn't a big middle finger raised to Konstantin Skalas, Xander did not know what was.

Within half an hour of his brother disappearing, Xander had received Sebastian's call. And what he had been expecting had come true.

Sebastian was unable to marry Annika the next morning.

Xander did not ask why and Sebastian did not venture an explanation. Only that he was caught up in something he could not get out of, for a while. From the rough impatience in his words, Xander wondered if someone had outplayed his devilish twin.

"So you want me to do your dirty work for you? Tell her that you're dumping her at the altar? Can I wait until tomorrow morning at the church to do it? Let me, Sebastian," he said, letting that cruel thread that they'd both inherited come out to play, "let me have the pleasure of telling Annika that her precious bridegroom isn't coming. This could be your birthday gift to me."

"And I thought you hid your cruelty better, brother."

Xander considered his reaction to the news of his brother absconding: relief and delight and something else—an insidious vein of poison he hadn't known was there. "We each have our weaknesses, Sebastian. You very bravely and publicly delight in yours. I shame and beat mine to death before they become a problem."

His twin, showing uncharacteristic wisdom, remained silent. The empty space and spiraling seconds made Xander turn his words over and over in his head. He wasn't impulsive and yet sometimes, there was freedom in lack of control. In the dark, delicious things that emerged when he wasn't actively suppressing every emotion. Damn his brother.

"What is that you want from me?" he finally asked, incensed with himself. He had clearly not been at his best for this…to become such a problem. Maybe ignoring it instead of tackling it head-on had been the fault.

"Marry Ani tomorrow morning."

Ani… The pet name that fell so easily from his twin's lips worked him up into a lather. The fact that he hadn't immediately refused Sebastian's ridiculous, crazy plan was a fact neither of them missed.

"And why would I do that?" he asked, holding at bay a torrent of images coming at him. When had he ever found himself this badly prepared, this out of touch with a situation, that there were this many revelations?

Never.

And yet, in the case of the unruly heiress, as he called her in his head, he was like a green teenage boy who had no control over his body and what it wanted.

"You and I both know you're actively searching for a bride, Xander."

"No."

"Then how do I know that you terrify half the young, eligible women in society?" Now Sebastian was enjoying this. "They come crying to me after you find them not good enough, after you scare them away with your ridiculous, outdated standards and terrifying expectations. All the business-minded papas want you, Xander, yes, but the young women…it's me they want."

Every word out of his twin's mouth was true and Xander kept quiet. He'd thought he'd successfully hidden from Sebastian his efforts at finding a suitable wife but clearly, he'd been no good at it.

"Poor Xander, tasked with carrying on the great Skalas name and legacy. Cursed to follow in Papa's footsteps and create little pyscho Skalases for the next generation."

"Skalas Bank is a four-hundred-year-old institution that has only ever been headed by a Skalas family member and we kicked out the rotten apple at great personal cost. Why should I give up everything I've worked for so relentlessly since I was sixteen because Grandmama has decided to have a tantrum all of a sudden?"

"Tantrum or not, she's the majority shareholder, Xander. Unless she transfers her shares to you, you will not be named president. Did you know that she's been having clandestine meetings with dear cousin Bruno?"

Xander cursed. Obsessed with this farce of an upcoming wedding, he'd missed that too. Bruno was another rotten apple in the family tree who would raze the bank to ashes if given even a little control. "She's too fond of the family name and the *sacred institution* to let him in."

"Her sisters all have a multitude of grandchildren, Xander. And she just had that heart scare. You're not at your best if you can't see what's going on with her. She hates Bruno just as much as you and I do, which is why this has become a crisis for her. And you know she won't relent. She's like a dog with a bone when she sets her mind to something."

"Be respectful, Sebastian."

His brother laughed again, and Xander was surprised to hear the sound of shackles. Actual metal shackles. Somehow, Xander overcame the impulse to ask Sebastian what the hell was going on with him.

"Oh, I respect the old biddy as much as you do, Xander. If it wasn't for her, God knows where we would have ended up, thanks to our dear psychotic father. She will wear you down until you accept someone of her choice. This way, you are taking proactive action, and you, my dear twin, are the most proactive man I know. And, ta-da, here's a ready-made bride for you. With a shelf life of no more than two years."

"As sweet as your sacrifice is, I intensely dislike the idea of your hand-me-downs."

His brother cursed and Xander wondered at how their roles seemed to have suddenly changed. Where were these pathetic, childish taunts coming from? How resentful had he grown?

"I know you think I planned this but I didn't, Xander. I didn't mean to be...incapable of showing up tomorrow." His tone softened. "I am asking you for a favor. I don't want Ani to be humiliated. And there's more than just humiliation at stake for her. She's my friend, she asked me for help and I'm letting her down."

"She asked you for help?" Suddenly, Xander felt like he had a key to the complex mystery that was Annika Saxena-Mackenzie. He'd never have been attracted to an empty-headed twit and even that...had been a recent development. It wasn't the girl he'd known in her teens.

Sebastian hesitated and it spoke more clearly than if he'd given a straight answer.

"How?" Xander persisted. "If you want me to step into your shoes, you'd better answer my questions."

"Ani asked me."

"Asked you what?"

"To marry her." Before he could pounce another question on him, his twin muttered, "I can't tell you more, Xander. I won't betray her confidence."

"You're asking me to marry a woman who asked *you* to marry her, Sebastian. I've pretended to be you when father's rage was high, but this is too much. Too tacky even for you."

"It's not… Ani and I…it's not a real thing, okay? Just do this. For me. For her."

Xander laughed. "She knows you better than anybody. Better than even I do, probably. She should've known what she was getting into."

"Damn it, Xander! You're going to let your bruised ego stop you from helping her?"

Xander let out a soft curse. His brother was in fine form today.

Had it bruised his ego that Annika had asked his twin for help instead of him? It angered him even as he understood the unformed, raw emotion: this expectation of being needed by her. And the longer he thought about it, the more it perturbed him. He should walk away now, let her face what she alone had brought on herself. It was the kind of ruthless thinking that had made him who he was today.

Sebastian sighed. "Listen, Xander, I'm not sure how long I can talk for but I made a guess about you and—"

"Enough, Seb," Xander muttered, steel in his voice. He hated being manipulated and his brother knew that better than anyone else on the earth.

"Don't punish her for my games, okay! That's not you, Xander. Don't leave her standing there."

"I'm not handing her back to you when you return."

Sebastian cursed. "What? Listen, Xander! She and I—"

Xander had cut the call then. He didn't want to hear more. What was the point in stretching out the string of weird confidences?

Both he and Sebastian had known that he would step in from the moment he'd asked. Whether he was doing it for his twin or for Annika was a question he refused to speculate on. The third choice was the right answer: he was doing it for himself.

And now here he was, waiting to see if she'd walk the last few steps. Because she knew.

Annika had always known when it was him.

And if she wanted to marry him, if she was that desperate for a husband, then she'd have to acknowledge it was him she was marrying, that he was the one who was rescuing her. He refused to pretend to be anyone else at his own damned wedding.

CHAPTER TWO

ANNIKA THOUGHT SHE'D made her peace with the situation, but she fared no better by the time she stepped up to *him*.

It would help so much to think of him as a placeholder—whatever the reason he was holding his twin's place. It would be so much better if she could view Alexandros Skalas as just any man who was coming to her aid, would help so much if she didn't feel this combination of shuddering relief and begrudging gratitude, and the inexplicable fury that *he* was the one standing there.

And the gut-level conviction that now, with him in charge, everything would be all right. *That* stung her throat like bile.

For all she'd cultivated a persona as an inveterate flirt—an empty-headed, fun-loving, spoilt heiress who jumped from man to man, who had the slight problem of sticky fingers when it came to shiny baubles, who had two broken engagements behind her—it was impossible to continue that act with him.

It had always been impossible to pretend that Alexandros Skalas was any other man that had come into her life's narrow purview. She was used to men and their fragile egos and their petty demands and their near manic need to control her and chain her and bind her and yet it seemed that a lifetime wasn't enough to get used to him.

She was shaking when he lifted her veil.

If she could kick herself right now for going with a traditional lace veil, she would. Because this...unveiling at his hands felt too much like her undoing, the beginning of her unraveling.

A full-body shiver took hold of her. As if her humiliation wasn't complete, it took his large hands gently resting on her bare shoulders for her racing pulse to slow down. Even that—the kindness that her body seemed to crave from him—she hated. It was a betraying weakness, and like a predator, Xander would catalog them all.

She lifted her chin and looked into his eyes.

Once again, she was hit by the striking distinction between the twins. How could everyone not sense the difference in their energies, in their personalities?

Sebastian was all easy charm, smooth smiles and sneaky, dry humor.

This man in front of her was built in a different way on a cellular level. If his brother made his way through life mocking and taunting, and making fun of everything sacred, Xander was the one who made the rules by which most of that Greek society functioned. He was considered to be one of the most ruthless and brilliant bankers in a crumbling economy, held the loyalty of every employee and commanded great respect even among his enemies. And to top it all off, he was extremely private.

He was like this...big, mysterious, magically foolproof treasure box that Annika had always desperately wanted to crack open, especially when she was younger and hadn't taken on the burden of protecting her family from her psycho stepbrother.

With the reckless courage of a young woman believing her own hype, she'd even tried to crack the code of what made Xander tick.

Now, standing there, she was surprised by her own daring. How reckless and self-destructive she had to have been to kiss this man, to lose herself in it, and then pretend that she'd thought all along that it was his twin? She'd been burned by his kiss, and then by his blistering contempt. Only, the scars were invisible, like all the others.

The pad of one thumb climbed up to her bare shoulder and, to her shame, Ani found herself leaning into the touch. Dark gray eyes watched her, and she wondered if there was a laser built into his mind—his eyes on her felt like he was forever probing her.

Once, she'd made the mistake of thinking that it was curiosity that Xander held for her. Because curiosity meant interest, right? And that had led her silly self into thinking it meant her interest—her fascination with him—might be returned.

But Xander had very effectively put paid to that foolish hope, reminding her why she'd always felt such a strange, dangerous awareness near him: it was what prey felt near a camouflaged predator.

He thrived on control. He thrived on order and discipline and that brittle self-sufficiency that made powerful men start to believe in their superiority over everyone else, that made them want to turn people into puppets.

Her stepbrother from her father's second marriage was a control freak too and until Killian had rescued her from him, Ani had barely kept her spirit intact under the boot of his cruelty, which masqueraded as care and concern.

Xander was a thousand times more powerful, more tightly wired, and seemed to hold an infinite capacity for that same casual cruelty. Annika reminded herself of those crystal-clear words she'd heard him say to his grandmother not a year ago.

"I don't understand why you're so fond of that…frivolous, empty-headed twit. Why are you so supportive of her when she can't be loyal to anyone? When she's got nothing to recommend her except a fortune that might never truly be hers? In case you forgot, she stole from you. She stole my mother's ring."

"She's my goddaughter, Xander. And whatever she is, she deserves my care and protection." Thea's defense of her had tears falling down her cheeks. Because even without Ani confiding in her, Thea had known the utter hell she'd been living in back then, before Killian had won custody of her; before she'd been allowed to go live with her stepfather and her three young brothers.

"She's a thief and a flirt and a—"

"Enough, Xander. It is *my* fortune I wish to share with her. Not yours."

"She's a manipulative gold digger, Grandmama. If you can't see that, if you want to lose your money on her, then so be it."

It was exactly the face she'd always presented to the world—this persona that would keep her away from her stepbrother's controlling nature, keen eye and utter greed to take hold of her fortune too.

But she'd expected that Xander would see through her deception, or at least have a little affection for the girl that had once hero-worshipped him. Thea had never asked her to explain her sudden shenanigans and loved her the same. Sebastian had probed gently but retreated when she'd told him that she had to fight her demons herself, that try as she might, she couldn't get used to his support.

Only Xander had written her off. Only Xander had decided, by his damned impossible standards, that she wasn't good enough to even look in the eye.

The slap to her face had come from her own expectations. From her own foolish heart's naive hopes.

She had to remember that. She had to remember that Alexandros Skalas did nothing without expecting something in return and she must brace herself for the price she'd have to pay soon.

But even in this, he made her give her assent. Made her agree that yes, she wanted to court *this* destruction—that she wanted to marry him—instead of the kind that awaited her if he walked away.

Annika gave him her answer with a slight tilt of her chin. The horde of captivated guests would love to see her fall apart, and she had no doubt that her stepbrother had planted his spies everywhere.

And she was damned if she would let him win, damned if she would let down the only man who had ever been kind to her.

To remind herself what was at stake, she cast a quick sideways glance to that first row where Killian and her three half brothers were sitting, watching her with pride and joy and love. Xander's brow tied into a tiny scowl as he caught the quick exchange.

She somehow got through the beginning of the service, feeling nothing but contempt for an institution that had made a prisoner of her mother before she'd met Killian.

Suddenly, the pitch of the priest's tone changed and she was startled, coming out of her trance. She could hear soft, buzzing gasps behind her as if a whole hive of bees had been released, like a cresting wave reaching its peak. Something knotted hard in her stomach and she knew she wasn't going to like this new development. The priest seemed to recover and addressed her bridegroom again.

"Sebastian Skalas, do you take this woman, Annika Saxena-Mackenzie, as—"

"It is *Alexandros* Skalas. If I have to repeat myself one more time…"

Sharp color rose in Xander's cheeks and her breath was stuck somewhere in her lungs as Annika tried not to look like a gaping fish. But her instinctive, almost visceral horror at his words couldn't be arrested or hidden. She turned her face toward him, aware that her body language, every nuance on her face, even the polite tilt of her eyebrows was being noted, and captured, and would immediately be dissected.

The uncaring beast at her side raised his brows and his mouth twitched. It might have been a smile but who knew if Xander Skalas ever smiled? Could one tell when a great fire-spewing dragon was smiling and when it was baring its fangs at you?

Once again, his fingers landed on her cheek, featherlight. She was aware of the silkiness of her own skin by the abrasive pads of his fingers. Another distinction, another separation that only she knew about. Another small but intimate detail that Annika wished she could delete from her brain.

For the entire world watching them, it would look like a lover's tender gesture.

Only Annika knew the truth. He had declared himself to be Alexandros Skalas, and if she was not in agreement, he would walk away.

It was a laying down of terms, she realized, all those little shivers having returned to dance across her body. He was telling her that this was how it would be if she wanted him as a husband.

How Annika wished she could scream in his face! She didn't want to want him. She just needed a husband for two years in order to beat her abusive brother at his own game.

But whatever it was that Sebastian had told Xander, it was clear that he would only do it on his terms.

Take it or leave it, his eyes said, watching her with that intensity that had always made her feel like a pinned butterfly. A butterfly whose colors were all false camouflage and who beneath it all was nothing but a scared, flawed, maybe even a broken, bird.

She turned away from him, from his touch, making sure to paste on a wide smile that could be caught in the periphery just before she did. The priest repeated his question, and Xander said yes.

Then that booming voice turned to her. "Annika Saxena-Mackenzie, do you take this man, Alexandros Skalas, to be your wedded husband?"

Annika's hurried affirmative cut off the priest and a gurgle of laughter broke out behind her.

Already, she could feel the crowd lapping up whatever it was that Xander served. Even she could see the draw of him despite being a reluctant pawn he was moving about on the board that she'd thought was under her control.

This was Alexandros Skalas, a man who found fault with everything and everyone. A man who conducted his affairs—all kinds of affairs—with utmost privacy. The man who, in contrast to his twin who shockingly revealed every *passage* of his life, played his cards very close to his heart. And she knew what the narrative would look like.

Here was Xander Skalas, in his twin's place, a victor once again, having maneuvered his twin's fiancée into being his wife instead.

As if her waking nightmare wasn't entertaining enough, Xander bent down from his great height and nudged her shoulder with his. It was such a playful, completely uncharacteristic move from him that she looked up.

"I would prefer your 'yes' a little louder, *yineka mou*. We do not want our guests to think that this was a shock to you too, do we?"

"What?" she said, the single word vibrating with a belligerence that she could not quite control. A long time ago, Annika had decided that her wedding was going to be a farce. But she'd never imagined that it would come about with such brutal reality and in such Technicolor, because what was this if not a farce of the worst kind?

His gray eyes gleamed. "As appetizing and juicy as all this gossip would be to Sebastian, *I* do not wish to be known as the man who stole his twin's bride. So I suggest that whatever your reason for acting out this farce, you had better do it with a lot more enthusiasm than you're showing. I would prefer not to be a source of gossip at my own wedding."

"And how is that my fault?" she whispered, regretting the words the minute she said them. Like it or not, Xander was saving her hide, giving her a chance to save her entire family. She could not afford to annoy him.

She faced the priest and declared in her usual naive, blundering way that yes, she would very much like to and was quite eager to marry Alexandros Skalas.

And then it was over and she wanted to rip the stupid veil off her head and tear the dress from her body so she could breathe. Months of planning and sneaking about, and riveting herself to Sebastian's side in tacky, public displays of affection… All of her act had reached its ending.

"You may now kiss the bride," the priest announced, as if he were the avenging angel come to make sure every one of her punishments was meted out.

"Shall I, *matia mou*?" Xander asked, the perfect gentleman.

If she said no, he wouldn't touch her. She knew that. But if she said no, her farce wouldn't be complete. And the worst part was that she wanted to say yes. She wanted to use the occasion to fulfill her darkest wish.

She nodded, unable to voice her assent.

Something dark glittered in his eyes as his long fingers circled her nape, and then she was being kissed to within an inch of her life. It was such a skillful kiss that it made her forget to breathe within two seconds. It was also an assault.

A call to arms.

A declaration of war.

It was also revenge for how she'd taunted him after that kiss all those years ago. Revenge for how she'd blatantly lied that she had mistaken him for Sebastian.

Stars exploded behind her eyes and Ani clutched him, afraid she'd fly away if she didn't. His mouth was rough and firm, and when she gasped, he stole into her mouth, ravishing her very will away from her.

It was the right kiss, the best kiss she'd ever had, and she'd kissed enough men to know that. But for all the wrong reasons.

It made her breath flutter about all over her body like a butterfly. It made her rise to her toes and sink into him, forgetting all her inhibitions, forgetting that this was a man she shouldn't kiss with such eager greed. It was a kiss that made a mockery of the months of worrying and fears and doubts that she wouldn't be able to protect her family. Everything misted away under the onslaught of his firm lips and wicked tongue and utter control of her.

There was pleasure in giving up control, Annika thought then, clinging to his tall, lean, firm body like a puppet, in surrender to someone who'd take away her will, yes, but also her worries.

And suddenly the tenor of the kiss shifted from an assault to something tender and infinitely sweeter and achingly perfect. Her heart thudded against her rib cage. One hand clasped her cheek while the other stroked over her back, gentling her. Now she was the one nipping and chasing and demanding and…

It was the tenderness that broke her. It was always the tenderness that broke her and reminded her that she was being a needy, naive fool once again.

She, who had molded herself, who had trained herself to expect only cruelty in this life. Tenderness was not to be trusted, not to be welcomed and definitely not to be reveled in, as she was doing now, drinking it up like a fool who didn't know the bitter taste of hope.

It was a habit Killian had tried to break her of but she wasn't sure if she would ever be separated from it.

And suddenly, she hated Xander with a surge of fury fueled by old wounds, for making the kiss into something they both knew wasn't true. She'd take his raised brows and twitching mouth and silky threats over false sweetness.

She broke away from the kiss, but before she did, she bit his lower lip. Hard. His fingers tightened over her back and his hips—that had maintained a respectable distance until then—chased hers and for a second, Annika felt the shocking, scalding weight and shape of his erection against her lower belly. An action and its reaction. For a second, just for a second, she wasn't sure if she had the strength to pull back.

She did, by sheer force of will.

On instinct she couldn't fight at a conscious level, she hid her face in his chest.

Nothing like running toward the storm that was determined to drown you, she thought, and still, she couldn't detach from the solid, hard haven his chest offered. At least she'd look like a blushing bride hiding her tremulous smiles and swollen lips and scalding arousal from the world. Like she'd been cajoled into a sweet kiss instead of being ravished into surrender.

CHAPTER THREE

ANNIKA RUSHED INTO the bridal suite that her stepfather had booked for her as a treat—something he couldn't afford—escaping the already short reception that she and Sebastian had planned to the last minute.

Since his reputation was that he was unconventional, he'd have it put about that he was eager to get away with his gorgeous bride before they had to show up at the Skalas mansion in Greece. And she, not only needing a breather from the circus act she'd put on for the last few months, but also to visit Thea, had agreed readily.

Being introduced to the very extensive and very greedy Skalas family by the matriarch Thea was a rite every new bride must get through, Sebastian had announced loudly when Niven had been about to invite her and Sebastian to his own estate in the Hamptons.

She had no doubt that Niven would use the flimsiest excuse he could find to deny Ani access to her trust fund. She knew the extreme necessity of showing to the world that her marriage was very much a match for the ages. It was imperative that she and her husband reflect matrimonial bliss.

And yet, she hadn't been able to stand next to Xander and pretend that she was a blissfully-in-love bride. If she had to take his beatific smile any longer or dance with him or eat a piece of cake from his bare fingers one more time, she'd explode. Or was it implode with her own desires?

Somehow, she'd managed to evade Killian. Either she'd burst into tears or admit to the whole farce. She needed a moment to think, to catch her breath, to not be drowned in the scent of a man she couldn't resist and couldn't trust.

What had felt like a cunning farce with Sebastian now felt all too real. As if to remind her, the beautiful princess-cut diamond and the simple platinum band felt unbearably heavy on her finger.

With a soundless scream, she tugged the veil off roughly, uncaring that pins went flying and she was plucking her hair out by the roots. She kicked off her heels, and was twisting herself inside out to get to the hundreds of tiny eyelet buttons studded with pearls at the back when the doors to the suite opened. She stilled, wondering if Xander knew he was playing with a cornered feral animal who would bite, kick and fight for what was hers.

Xander tucked his hands into his trouser pockets and eyed the rabid chaos of the suite. Makeup tubes and pots, designer handbags, at least ten pairs of heels strewn about, expensive lingerie, and a pile of unopened gifts on every surface…his new wife stood in the eye of a storm, her expression a heady combination of outrage and helplessness.

Then there was the way the lace of the dress kissed her bare shoulders and gleaming, golden-brown skin. Slender shoulders and a tiny frame, with lush curves in between. The flimsy fabric clung to her breasts and her hips, somehow bringing out all of that elegant voluptuousness into striking relief. Her dark golden hair fell in thick waves, the ends grazing her breasts.

In a nervous gesture he remembered from when she'd

been all gawky limbs, her fingers played with the dark ends. Even that served to heighten his awareness of her as the movement flashed her ring finger at him.

Satisfaction swirled through him when he'd caught her surprise in the moment he'd removed Sebastian's ring—a gaudy, flashy diamond—and replaced it with an elegant sapphire sitting amid a cluster of tiny diamonds. For a man whose only example of marriage had been the disastrous one between his abusive father and his alcoholic mother, he felt quite the possessive rush at seeing her branded with jewelry he'd personally picked.

Branded...

Imagining her outrage at the term made the high he was riding even sweeter. *She was his*...for as long as she needed him. For as long as they needed to work each other out of their systems.

Because for all her lies and playacting—and he was beginning to realize the real Annika was buried beneath a heap of it—she wanted him. That kiss had betrayed both of them. Christos, he'd never been revved up so fast.

Whatever her reason for asking Sebastian to marry her, he would see it through. Being a natural and brilliant problem solver, he could present her with a solution that was a thousand times better than anything Sebastian could have cobbled together. Now he just had to convince his prickly bride that he'd done her a favor.

"What are you doing here?" she asked, tilting her chin up.

She was the sexiest woman he'd ever met and yet, Xander knew without doubt, it was her spirit that provoked his baser instincts, her spirit he wanted to conquer. He wondered if Konstantin's madness had been passed on to him, despite his every effort not to be the cruel monster his father had been.

"You escaped the reception without your usual flair for drama. I thought it a good idea to follow since we want to create the impression that I can't keep away from my...luscious bride. Especially after saving her from the horrible fate of being left at the altar."

"I didn't ask to be saved by you, Xander. I'd rather—"

"An annulment won't be that hard to achieve, then," he said smoothly, flashing his cell phone at her. "Shall I call my lawyer?"

"No, wait!" Her chest rose and fell with a long inhale of air and a boatload of pride, no doubt, which had always been like a live flame. "I need this marriage. And I...appreciate you stepping in."

"Glad you didn't choke on that."

Her eyes gleamed with challenge. "I guess that's one thing you can provide better than Sebastian—brutal honesty."

"You know very well that there are a lot of things I can do better than my rascal twin."

The pulse at her neck fluttered like a trapped butterfly's wings as she bit out, "That's...a disgusting thing to say."

"I'm a better financial provider, better at sticking to commitments, better at giving you security. Why, dear wife, which scandalous place did your mind go to?"

Pink dusted her cheeks as she resolutely held his gaze. "Point to Alexandros Skalas. But you'd better remember I'm not a wind-up toy you stole from Sebastian because you suddenly decided you fancy it."

"Let's not moralize to each other, Annika. After all, you thought nothing of lusting after one brother and scheming to marry the other."

She flinched but recovered with a refreshing verve he found in very few adversaries. Was that her appeal? Most women were intimidated by him, his standards, his demands. Annika's stubbornness, willfulness and recklessness, on the other hand, seemed to grow inversely at his censure.

A dangerous smile wreathed her lips. "How do you know I don't lust after you both? Or that I don't consider you interchangeable? Or that I don't care whose bed I hop into or whose ring I wear as long as I reach my destination?"

Ugly jealousy such as he'd never known before struck Xander like a punch to his solar plexus. There was no earthly reason for him to be jealous of his twin, he who'd borne the brunt of their cruel father's brutality growing up, who hid his scars even from his brother. It wasn't that he considered himself superior to Sebastian—they just had different personalities and different priorities. They went about beating their demons into submission in different ways. And somehow his had led him to…the woman staring at him, challenge pouring out of every delicious inch of her. The awareness that she very much knew the competitive streak and its origins between him and Sebastian and still chose to deploy it as a tactic didn't dim the effect one bit.

He wanted to be the victor with her, even when he didn't know what the spoils were.

He swallowed down the dark, unwieldy jealousy coating his throat. Taking her bait was beneath him, especially when she was only responding to his provocation. "Point to Annika Skalas," he said, going for a soft thrust.

It struck harder and truer than he'd expected because her entire body seemed to bow and bend. "Actually, strike that," she said, rubbing a hand over her face wearily. "I wanted Sebastian. I chose Sebastian. I…needed Sebastian. But when has life ever been fair, right? So I'll make do with you."

"I'm sure it's extra frustrating because you can't manipulate me like you do Grandmama and Sebastian. Grand-mama, I still see it, but Sebastian…he's never struck me as gullible."

"At least I'm aware of the shallowness of my life, Xander, that I'm willing to do whatever it takes. You, on the other hand, sit on your high horse, sneering down at us. You forget that I know you. You didn't do this out of the goodness of your heart. So please, enough of this mudslinging. I thought, with you, we could get down to business without catering to your masculine ego. Or am I mistaken in that too?"

"How refreshing, Annika," Xander said, honest for once. In all his search for a potential bride, he hadn't met one woman half as gutsy or half as honest. Or half as self-aware, he added to himself. Again, the disparity between the image she presented and the real woman was disarming. "What are your requirements?"

"I need this marriage to last at least a year. I need my stepbrother to believe that we're the very definition of matrimonial bliss. I need you to blatantly advertise your abiding love and loyalty to me at every public opportunity so that the antiquated conditions my father set in the will are met."

"And what does that get you?" he asked, showing his apparent distaste for the sort of PDA in which his twin specialized.

"My trust fund," she said unflinchingly. "My father, for some godforsaken reason, decided to appoint his stepson, Niven Shah, as the trustee."

"This is the stepbrother Killian Mackenzie fought for custody of you?" Thea had mentioned that Annika was caught in a custody battle between her dead father's stepson and her stepfather, Killian. After years, Killian had won. "Didn't Killian know he wouldn't be getting his hands on your fortune?"

Rage licked into her eyes and her voice went low. Her face was a map of her loyalties, her dreams. "Killian has no—"

She breathed in deeply, and he could see her picking up the shards of her armor and putting them back in place.

"This is about me and my money. I'm sick of living on handouts from Thea, Killian and even Sebastian. Sick of having to watch every penny, of living in a crummy house with my three half brothers, sick of shopping at discount stores. I want the life I was born to."

"Today's wedding was anything but cheap."

"Sebastian paid for it," she said with that careless shrug. "I want a carefree, easy, luxurious lifestyle and it is my birthright, just as the Skalas throne is yours."

"My right to the Skalas throne has been won through almost two decades of hard work. Or there would only have been rubble to sit on."

"Oh, and my right to my father's wealth is unearned?" Anguish flared in those gorgeous eyes, then disappeared in a flash, making him wonder if he'd imagined it. "Enough games, Xander," she said, sounding exhausted. "Why did you show up? I'd think seeing me humiliated would have been your greatest joy."

"The idea of you owing me a favor was too delicious to pass up."

"You don't do kindness. You don't do anything for your own pleasure even. *Why did you step in?*"

He stared at her and wondered at how well she knew him, and at the shrewdness with which she parried words. There was more to her than the empty-headed, grasping, greedy woman he'd thought her. "I need a wife, just as you need a husband."

She laughed then, a genuine thousand-watt smile on her face that made every inch of her light up. The sound was…

husky and arousing and magnetic. His head felt as if he was suddenly swimming in blinding sunshine, the sensation both pleasurable and painful. Her body undulated with her laughter, a shimmering, sensual vision in white whose layers he wanted to peel back one by one.

"This is too good. Are you telling me the hot, brooding, ruthless billionaire banker Alexandros Skalas couldn't find a woman to marry him? Is Sebastian really unavailable or did you have a hand in detaining him so that you could swoop in and steal me?"

What would she do if she knew how close she was to the vague plan in the back of his head if Sebastian hadn't called him? "I find pale, quivering, half-terrified women with zero wit loathsome and boring. My requirements, if you must know, are few, the most important being that I should at least get an intelligent reply back in a conversation."

Her eyes widened, that pink cresting her cheeks again. He had the most insane urge to lick her up, as if it were hot summer and she the cold drink that would satiate his thirst. *The only drink.* "You've got to be joking."

"That's Sebastian's arena, *ne*, and apparently that inane humor of his is what makes him popular. I can count on one hand the number of women, and men, who will look me in the eye. Even fewer who stand up to me. Who challenge me. Who provoke me." *Who make me lose control.* "The hunt for a bride became as taxing as pretending to like all my various greedy cousins."

She swallowed and he thought she understood what drew him to her. What had always drawn him to her, even when he loathed her for having no integrity or standards or... boundaries.

Looking down, she tugged at the lace on her sleeve. "Here I thought you'd want a biddable wife, Xander. Someone who follows your instructions from dawn to dusk without question. Someone you can review and rate based on pedigree and performance, someone who would bend and bow to satisfy your robotic need for control."

"Where is the challenge with someone who's already cowering and admitting defeat?" he said silkily, and had the reward of seeing her breasts rise and fall. What he wouldn't give to have her beg him to rip that dress off her, to turn all of that aggression and animosity into passion, to have her on her knees, giving him her surrender. What he wouldn't give her in return. "It's gratifying to know you've thought, at length, about my preferences in a wife, *yineka mou*."

"It's not like I have to sit and think about it. You're just so infuriating and calculating that—"

He raised a brow and waited.

"Oh, go to hell!" she bit out. She rubbed long fingers over her temple. "Two hours of being married to you and I already have a headache."

"I, on the other hand, am already enjoying the state of matrimony. Grandmama is right. The right partner makes all the difference."

She cursed. Long and colorfully. Grabbing a water bottle, she chugged half and poured half over her head. Like her, nothing could contain her unruly hair, and most of the water pooled down over her impressive chest. Her nipples jutted against the lace and lust hit him hard. If she'd done it on purpose, he'd have reacted. With the mascara running down her sunken cheeks, he knew she was exhausted.

"Grandmama refuses to pass on the presidency of Skalas Bank to me if I don't marry."

Annika frowned, tension bracketing her lush mouth. "Thea expects your marriage to be fruitful. She wants heirs for the Skalas legacy, not some ridiculous farce of a wedding."

"That's not on offer, then?" he said, unable to resist the taunt. "I haven't been through the Ts & Cs yet."

"What, sleep with you *and* give birth to little Skalas devils like you?" she scoffed. "No thanks. I want a free, easy life. Not one of obligation and duties."

"It would be anything but obligation between us."

"I'm not attracted to you, Xander."

"Are you trying to convince me or yourself?"

"I'm not. And even if I were, I wouldn't act on it. For all the trust funds in the world."

"And yet I'm sure your prenup with Sebastian—"

"We didn't sign one."

He stilled. So much was at stake and Sebastian did this? "My brother is many things but he's not foolish."

"Something we agree on finally."

"Then why?"

"It's unfathomable to you, isn't it? Sebastian trusts me."

"It's sheer foolishness."

"Forget Sebastian. I'm stuck with you and, believe me, I'd beg on the streets before I take a penny from you."

"This marriage is becoming more and more interesting by the minute, Annika. A year, then. You behave as the perfect, doting wife, and convince Thea—"

For the first time that day—or ever—she looked defeated. "I don't think you've thought this through. I can fool any number of people, the entire damned world, but not Thea. She knows me too well."

"And despite that, she's inordinately fond of you. I've never understood it. She was elated that her favorite outrageous grandson was marrying you. That you'll truly be part of the family now. That she'll never have to part from you." It was only as he said it that Xander wondered how his grandmother would react to the news that he had married her precious goddaughter.

It wouldn't be favorable, but he would overcome her anger as he did everything else.

"By that very same logic, she'll find it impossible to believe that this isn't a farce," Annika argued. "She knows you and I hate each other's guts. She knows I'd never give up on my dream by tying myself to you."

"I thought I was bringing your dreams to fruition, Annika. Is this a different dream?" When she glared at him, he raised his palms. Something about riling her was incredibly energizing, as if he were a device finally thrust into its charging port.

"Thea understands lust, attraction, desire. She'll believe that our mutual hate boiled over into more when necessity struck. We will tell her I was overcome by tenderness for you when I learnt that Sebastian was ditching you at the last minute. Despite the dragon she likes to pretend she is, Thea loves a grand love story."

"Tenderness? You?"

"As believable as loyalty in you."

"I don't like the idea of cheating Thea."

"And what has your entire life been so far?"

"Fine. Fine! I'll slobber all over you and you can pretend as if taking care of me is your greatest wish in life. Just so you know, Niven's...a controlling bastard. He'll try a lot of things to cheat me out of what's rightfully mine. He'll fill your head with any number of disgusting lies about me. He'll do everything he can to make you hate me."

The fear and bitterness in her eyes when she spoke of her stepbrother made Xander's stomach churn. He hated nothing more than a bully picking on weaker people. Why hadn't he ever heard her speak of this man? What was he missing?

"He doesn't know that that my opinion of you can't get any lower," he said, wanting to see her fighting spirit back.

"No, he doesn't," she said, relief shuddering in a long exhale. "That's the one thing to my advantage. He will be a small predator being stalked by a bigger, badder one."

"You think your stepbrother and I are alike?" Xander said, holding his shock back by the skin of his teeth. Did she think him a monster? Did he care? How deep had she dug her hooks into him already?

"Niven's domineering, ruthless, and pounces on others' weaknesses. He thrives on asserting his reach and power. You are a step ahead because you control your own weaknesses with just as much resolve. So, yes, I guess if anyone can take him on, it's you."

"Is that gratitude I hear?"

She glared at him just as a loud knock sounded at the door to the suite, followed by the voices of quarreling boys. "That's my brothers and Killian. Give me half an hour with them and I'll be ready to leave."

Ignoring the chaos she'd created, he ventured farther into the suite, closer to her. With every step he took, she stiffened until he could very well believe that she was a statue. "I'd like to meet them."

"No."

"You've only made me curious."

"Fine. I hope my brothers rub their sticky, chocolate-covered fingers all over your Armani suit."

Xander donned his poker face, even though the picture she painted urged him to leave. How did she know that he was...allergic to children? That whatever legacy Thea wanted would be provided by one of Sebastian's very probably illegitimate children born out of one of his numerous affairs?

"I hope the little one crawls into your lap and barfs in your face," she continued, fascinatingly bloodthirsty. "And the middle one collects worms and ants and bugs and—"

"*Ani? Ani!* Let us in. We want to see you," came a small boy's voice.

"Is it true you married Sebastian's twin?" came another. "I heard someone say he's not fun or cool like Seb. Why'd you have to go and marry him?"

"Ayush Mackenzie, watch your language!" came Killian Mackenzie's gruff voice.

"That's what everyone's saying, Dad," said a fourth voice, almost on the cusp of manhood. This one was truly worried about his sister, painting a different picture than the one Xander had anticipated. "They said Ani's new husband is a horrible, monstrous bully. We can't let her go with him. If he hurts Ani, I'll try my right hook on him. I've gotten really good."

Holding up the train of her dress, a triumphant light in her eyes, his new bride moved to the doors and made a bow. "Your wish is my command, Xander. Here's my family."

CHAPTER FOUR

THE FIRST THING Xander noticed when Annika got on the flight—joining him at the private airstrip a whole ninety minutes later than she'd promised—was that her eyes were swollen and red-rimmed, as if she'd spent the entire three hours after he'd left her to her family sobbing her heart out.

The sight was one he disliked intensely. Even worse was an overwhelming need to…fix it. To fix her. He'd never seen her cry—not even when her mother died.

Frowning, he watched her as she slid into her seat as if her limbs were incapable of independent motion. She was still in her wedding dress, which not only had a tear in the hem but was now wrinkled so thoroughly that it looked like she'd rolled around on the floor—which she probably had, with her brothers. Her hair was a mess and she had dark streaks of mascara smudged under her eyes. She should have looked like a failed participant on one of those horrible survivor-type reality shows that his grandmama was forever watching.

Instead, she looked like a beautiful broken bird that Sebastian had once nursed back to life with a tenderness and conviction that Xander had thoroughly envied because he lacked those qualities himself. He felt the same lack now and resented her for making him aware of it.

The flight attendant announced they were taking off. Unmoving, Annika stared out at the private airstrip, a strange melancholy seeming to take hold of her limbs.

Leaning across the table that separated them, Xander pulled the seat belt across her torso and clicked it into place with a rough jerk that he hoped would startle her out of that fugue. She didn't even blink those long lashes. His muscles tightened at the sweet lemon scent of her filling his nostrils.

"Annika, are you ill?"

Her response was a long, shuddering breath, before she turned away and closed her eyes.

He searched for and discarded words to rile her out of it and found himself without a strategy for the first time in his life. In profile, she looked defeated, and he hated seeing that. He wanted a functioning wife, not some delicate creature he had to console. That was the only reason her melancholy was getting to him.

"You look as though you've been dragged through a bush," he said, filling his words with as much contempt as possible. "Or was it a tussle in the bridal suite with one of your forlorn exes? Should I not have left you alone for so long?"

"How dare you?" she gritted out.

"Your history gives me the daring. You have three broken engagements behind you, the reason for each more colorful and scandalous than the previous. I might wonder if you've already broken your marital vows and—"

"Of course I didn't, you...*beast*." She fairly spat at the words at him.

"Was that the appeal for Sebastian? That you're without morals or boundaries and yet you're honest about all of your vices?"

Like a doll who was being pulled by invisible strings, she flicked those intense eyes open and glared at him. But he didn't miss the red tint flushing her cheeks. "Leave me alone, Xander."

"I'm afraid we haven't reached that stage of marriage

yet, as much as we both wish to be there." Reaching out, he rubbed the pad of his thumb under her eye, further smearing the black streak.

She stiffened so visibly that satisfaction swirled through him. He couldn't wait for the day when she'd sink into his touch, or even invite it. He'd never looked forward to something like that.

He held up his thumb, showing her the smudge.

"Okay, I have raccoon eyes," she said without a sliver of self-consciousness, her folded arms thrusting up her breasts. "What's your point?"

"Looking like you do, flinching at the most innocent touch from me, you'll doom us both within the day. Thea might turn vengeful if she smokes us out."

"If you want me to start slobbering all over you already, no thanks. I've had a rough day as it is."

"And what is the reason for that?" he asked casually, using every weapon in his arsenal to incite her into betraying herself.

"Like I'd tell you." Then she looked at him. "Even if I did, you wouldn't get it."

"Don't tell me you're already admitting defeat in this arrangement. Did you cry at having to marry the big bad monster Alexandros Skalas instead of the man you could wrap around your finger? Or did you bawl your eyes out because you might have to put in some actual work to get to that trust fund of yours?"

Her breaths rapid, she tugged roughly at the ends of her hair. "Underestimate me at your own peril, Xander."

She would not reveal the distress he'd seen in her eyes to him, then. Defeat was a bitter pill in his throat.

"Anyway—" her fingers played with the lace cuff of her sleeve, betraying her nervousness "—we're in your private jet. And I have no doubt your lackeys won't betray you to Thea or the media with a single breath."

"True. But I'm not confident in your acting skills, Annika."

"What does that mean?"

"While Sebastian would have gone along merrily with an empty-headed party girl for his wife, I won't. You're married to the chairman of the world's richest, most prestigious bank."

"You haven't been named yet," she said with a gleeful smile, her bare toe grazing his trouser-clad leg in a childish move that both annoyed and pleased him because his tactic had worked.

"And banks and financial institutions," he continued, as if she hadn't interrupted him, "if you didn't know this already, are traditional structures with conservative values. Which is why they'd never accept Sebastian."

"Yes, but don't forget I know Thea as well as you do and she knows me. If I let you make me over into some elegantly boring, mind-numbingly perfect trophy wife, she won't buy it."

"It's a balancing act, then, *ne*?" he said, feeling more alive than he had in years. It was exhilarating to match wit and words with her. "But you might be finally coming up against the one thing Grandmama holds dear, even dearer than you and Sebastian—the Skalas name and legacy. She'll hate you if you taint it with even a small scandal. Better if we lay down some ground rules."

"You mean you'll lay them down and I'll have to follow like a good little soldier?"

"But this is quid pro quo, *ne*?"

"I can't wait to order you around, then," she said, her eyes gleaming with sudden cunning. "Let's get this clear—you'll act the way I want when it's my turn to show you off?"

"I'll be the big bad wolf and huff and puff at your step-brother if you want me to."

A smile touched the corners of her mouth but not her eyes. And he felt a weird sense of defeat.

"A new wardrobe first."

She shook her head, working herself into a temper. That excited Xander more than another woman's mouth on his most responsive parts. Maybe there was something to indulging one's deepest desires like his twin did. To an extent, at least.

"You have a problem with how I dress? Even you can't be such an uptight, controlling—"

"I have an image to maintain in the banking world and you're part of that now," he interrupted calmly. "None of your boho gowns, and tank tops without bras, and shorts with half your ass hanging out and definitely no—"

She straightened with a jerk. "How long have you been waiting to say that to me?"

"No getting drunk and passing out on someone's couch—"

"I didn't realize what a trip this marriage is going to be for you."

"No meetings with shady exes and definitely no stealing from distinguished guests. That is a complete deal-breaker."

She turned red, her jaw working. Then she swallowed. "What if I—"

"Whatever you need, I can provide it, Annika. As my wife, you'll have access to luxuries you've never imagined."

"And if I can't help myself? What then? Will you return me with the price tag attached? Will you get me fixed so that I can work as you intend for me to?"

"If you need medical help, then you'll get it. But that's not the issue, is it?"

Something about his tone made her go still. She licked her lips. "What...do you mean?"

"It's not a compulsion, I know that much. You do it for some other reason. I used to think it was simple greed. But I'm not—"

"I've had enough of you."

He moved his legs so that she was caught between the seat and him. "You embarrass me in any way in front of the world and become a liability instead of an asset, Annika, and I'll make sure you never see a single cent of your trust fund. And we both know it's very much in my power to do so."

Rage shimmered in her eyes. He waited for the explosion, for her temper to fracture like it used to when her mother had been alive. Instead, like a black hole, she swallowed it all back and tucked it away, though where he had no idea. It was horrific to watch her pull everything inward. And it reminded him of...himself, a long time ago. His heart thumped, with excitement at the mystery she presented and also with a niggling sense of dread.

Slowly, she uncoiled from her seat to her full height. She even managed a smile as she leaned over him, her hands on the armrests, her wide, lush mouth inching closer and closer. Her fingers touched his lower lip, then trailed down to his throat and the V of his shirt. "If I run my finger down, down, down, will I find you hard, Xander?" Her arms pressed her breasts together into a cleavage as she molded her body into a parody of that shallow sensuality most men fell for. Until last night, when he couldn't sleep for wondering how to stop the wedding, he'd been one of that number.

"This is foreplay for you, isn't it? Threatening what someone else holds dear?"

Xander stared into her eyes, and while she could fake the

smile and the languid sensuality and the taunting words, her eyes betrayed her. This close, he could see the entire spectrum of emotions there and the most prominent was fear. And as hard as her nearness got him, it was also like being doused in ice-cold water. "Find out for yourself," he said, calling her bluff, hating himself a little in the moment, for even now he could not show her weakness or mercy, not until she had unraveled completely beneath him. "After all, this is supposed to be our wedding night, *ne*?"

Fire burned in her gaze and she moved her palm down his chest to his abdomen, and further down until the base of her palm rested right above his pubic bone. He arrested her fingers.

There was no relief in her eyes, only stubborn determination. "Why stop me when I'm playing right into your hands?"

"Because you're sullying yourself and me, Annika. Because I want your surrender, not your defeat."

Her mouth flinched, and she pulled away as if burnt. A shuddering exhale left her trembling. "Dress me however you want, parade me like a puppet whose strings you're pulling, mold me into a blow-up doll for all I care, but I'll never surrender to you, Alexandros Skalas."

With a growl, she pushed past his legs and stormed into the rear cabin like a furious wraith.

Xander rubbed a hand over his face, feeling as if he'd won the battle but had made a major blunder in the strategy for the war. Clearly, Annika's armor had a breaking point and he'd pushed her past it.

She'd turned the tables on him as only a worthy adversary would. And yet, he didn't like the taste of her pain in his mouth. A part of him wanted to do what she'd suggested— get an annulment and leave her to whatever fate befell her.

Only a small part, however.

The survivor in him recognized the same quality in her. She enticed him no end. The one thing Annika didn't know was how much he thrived on a challenge. How his best came out when the worst was thrown at him.

His father had tried to destroy him before he'd reached his majority, tried to crush him to the ground when he'd realized his favorite son had been planning his doom behind the scenes all along. With Thea's support, Xander had taken down Konstantin and every one of his cronies, cutting the rot from his family and the bank.

Annika's stubbornness was no barrier.

He'd have her and all her secrets before this farce of a marriage was over, and she was out of his life permanently. Maybe then, he could move on from this madness too. A taste of it *had to be* enough.

Damn it, why had she lost it so spectacularly? What had Xander done except to lay down the law, as was his nature? And worse, why was she taking it personally if he wanted to model her into a dummy Stepford wife when that was what he needed out of their arrangement?

She sat on the luxurious bed and went over what had transpired.

She'd been upset and he'd noticed. And he'd tried to probe. And when she hadn't responded to his demands, he'd needled her. She'd played right into his hands, against her own agenda. She couldn't afford to antagonize him, and it was exactly what she'd done.

After everything she'd planned and executed, bending to Xander's will and transforming herself into some perfect zombie wife was no hardship. God, she'd played so many games and pulled so many cons that she could do it in her sleep. So why was she riling him up when he was the only one who could get her what she needed?

She buried her face in her hands and sighed. She knew exactly why.

She despised it when she was backed into a corner, when she could do nothing but shed tears of rage and powerlessness, and that was how Xander had found her—wounded and hurting and near feral. It had taken him very little to push her over the edge when she'd already been scrambling for a foothold.

It hadn't been easy to say goodbye to the boys, and it hadn't helped to know that she'd be lolling about in luxury for the near future when Killian had admitted—under her forceful questions—that he was close to declaring bankruptcy. He had to sell their house because he couldn't afford mortgage payments.

The very house in which her mother had been happy, the house where her brothers had been born, the house where Annika had hoped to live in the future.

Because of Niven and his damn mind games. He was destroying her stepfather piece by piece because she hadn't toed the line. Because she'd dared find her own bridegroom. Because she was inching closer and closer to getting her hands on her trust fund and to being completely out of his reach.

She needed to wash the day off her and start over. And then she'd apologize to Xander, even if she choked on the words. Somehow, she'd learn to play nice. Five minutes later, she was back to trying to twist herself into unnatural angles to get to the thousand eyelet buttons on the back of her dress.

"I believe that's my duty," Xander said, meeting her gaze in the gleaming chrome of the shower.

"Perks before duties, with me, always," she said, regretting the taunt instantly.

"Let's not forget the reason he gets such an easy rise out of you, my dear Ani," Sebastian had mocked her once. *"You lust after my brother. Always have. Always will."*

Trust that rogue to throw that unpalatable truth in her face.

"If you let me perform my duty first and undress you, the perks will follow. With me, your gratification will not be instant but...long-lasting."

Ani barely managed to hold off her own colorful retort. Turning, she considered him, reaching for the only available strategy. He was right that she couldn't manipulate him. "I agree to all your ridiculous demands."

"Annika—"

"No, let me get this out all at once. The first thing I will do after we land is go hunting for bras. Lock these babies away in a jail," she said, doing a little jiggle of her chest, "even though those horrible underwire thingies bruise my skin like hell. I'll donate my skanky tank tops and ass-baring shorts to charity. I'll cut my cotton boho dresses and make quilts for homeless children. I'll give up drinking and fun and shady exes, and when I feel the urge to steal something, I'll come and tell you so that you can cuff me to your bed. I'll only wear clothes that hide my tats and my belly button ring."

She unraveled the wavy mass of her hair, the bane of her life, and the thick strands fell to her waist. Maybe it was time for a change of image too. It was exhausting to be in a fight against life every single minute of every single day. Maybe she should view this as a short breather in the war she was waging.

"Quite the picture you have painted," Xander said, walking into the room, but leaving the bed in between them. "Shall we address the sudden one-eighty in your attitude?"

Twisting her hair into a knot with a rough tug, she said, "I'll even chop this off and get something sleek and chic and suitable for a rigid banker's perfect, peerless wife."

"No."

"Don't be your perfect wife?"

"Don't cut your hair."

And just like that, it was back in the room again. Electricity hummed in the air, arcing between them, brought in this time by that dark, possessive current in his command.

He hadn't actually praised her hair or said he liked it or written poems to it as one of her poor fiancés had done, and yet, Annika could feel his desire in her own body like the vibrations from some hidden chip whose button lay in his hands. In his words. In his looks.

"I want a change," she said, her protest weak and late and utterly for principle.

"Are we back to arguing, then?" he said, taking a step around the bed.

Ani ran her palms over opposing shoulders in a bid to cover the fact that the innocent scrape of lace against her breasts had them beading with desire. With each step he took toward her, her skin felt two times too small. And the worst part was that she knew he wouldn't touch her. It was her own desires and demons she was up against.

Taking the bull by the horns, she turned around to present him with her back. Her breaths were shallow as she waited. His fingers landed on the nape of her neck and she jerked, like a fish thrown out of water.

His touch became firm, one hand holding her in place, while he deftly began undoing the buttons. With each inch of skin he bared, Ani felt the rough press of his finger pads leaving a searing trail.

"I want a wedding present," she blurted out. That was it.

Stick to your best role. She added a bit of complaint to her tone. "Sebastian promised me one."

His fingers moved relentlessly, reaching the middle of her spine. He moved closer, and with one hand on her shoulder blade, he pressed her down. Her hips hit his thighs and instant dampness bloomed between her own.

Ani pressed her hand onto the bed to support her trembling legs, fighting the urge to push back into his solid hard warmth at her back. How was she going to get through this if her panties melted off whenever he touched her?

"And what was my brother getting in return?"

She heard it then—the thick desire in his voice and how he battled it by bringing Sebastian into this place between them where he didn't belong.

"My delightful company."

Now Xander's fingers were at the dip of her spine, and still the buttons continued. "A wedding present? That's supposed to explain your eager agreement?"

"I'm a woman who has her priorities straight and doesn't let anything get in her way, Xander. You'd admire my single-mindedness if you didn't hate me so much."

For the first time since they'd begun the torturous journey down her back, his fingers stilled. His other hand had moved lower too and lay still between her shoulder blades.

Ani clutched the front of her dress as it came away from her skin, releasing flesh it had tortured for hours. "Xander?"

"I do not hate you, Annika."

"Let's not fight about semantics," she said, shaking now that he was working on the last few buttons, right over her buttocks. "I also want an allowance." And because he could feel her trembling body and she hated that it was betraying her like this, she added, "And I'll even let you undress what's underneath—"

"Don't, Ani."

She turned around, that word on his lips searing through her worse than being undressed by him. Tears gathered at the backs of her eyes and she blinked to fight them off. "Don't call me that."

"Why not?"

"Only people I love get to call me that."

His upper lip rolled and Ani braced herself for whatever he would deal. "You'll have one million euros in your bank account within the week—my wedding present. No conditions attached."

Her breath left her in a sudden gush as relief and gratitude flooded her. Maybe Killian could fight to keep the house, continue to send the boys to good schools, even funnel some money back into the business, cover some of those losses Niven had bamboozled him into... "Why a week?"

He laughed then. "Greedy little thing, aren't you? There will be a lot of paperwork to go through before you have a Swiss bank account and it lands in your account. A lot of tax legalities on your end."

"And the big bad banker can't just make all that go away?" she asked, turning.

"Not if I want to maintain my reputation as..." He stilled and stared at her.

The dress fell away, revealing the virginal white silk bustier and a matching thong and garters holding up sheer thigh-highs. Her friend had teased her mercilessly that she finally understood how Ani had tamed the ultimate playboy, Sebastian Skalas.

Ani had simply smiled, hating that she couldn't share the simplest truth with her friend. The veil and the ridiculously lacy dress and the train...they had all been for show, yes.

Her lingerie, though, had been for herself. Desperate

to claim something in that farce for herself, she'd gone to town, blowing all the money Thea had given her as a wedding gift on lingerie. Now, she felt a giddy heat and intense gratitude for that crazy decision as Xander's gaze moved over her. Her shoulders and the tops of her breasts, which were indecently pushed up by the bustier, and the strip of her flesh above the low thong…every inch of her skin felt his gaze like a brand.

And that too—that flare of hot want in his eyes, the way he'd stilled, the way his nostrils flared—she'd claim that for herself too. While she wouldn't admit it to him, this hot pulse of wanting between them that gathered momentum like a wildfire was one of the few real things in a life she'd filled with artifice and cunning.

"Come here," Xander said, and she went without question.

He reached out and ran a finger along her collarbone, making her pulse flutter like the wings of a bird desperately making a bid for freedom. "I'll give you an allowance if you agree to one more thing."

Ani nodded, her heart pounding in her chest, hating herself just a little.

He clasped her cheek and tilted her chin up until she had nowhere to go except the stormy, raging gray of his eyes. His words were cold, remote. "You will burn every single piece of clothing you bought for this wedding. For him."

Shock swept through her. He really didn't like that she'd been about to marry Sebastian. Because she wasn't good enough for his brother? Because he himself despised her? Or was there another reason?

"You want me to walk into your home naked?"

"A small detail that will be taken care of in mere minutes." Then his hands were in her hair and his mouth was at her temple and he…nuzzled at her cheek. The movement made her chest rub against his muscled side and that was exquisite torment too, and she just wanted to sink into him, to cling to him, to demand he give her one moment of respite and pleasure after a day of war.

With that grip in her hair, he shuffled her backward with a gentleness that threatened to undo her already fragile grip on her senses. Then his gaze was on her mouth and she licked her lips compulsively, begging him to cover the distance without saying the words.

His mouth quirked. "It is nonnegotiable, Annika. Is that clear?"

She nodded like a chastised child and in the next blink of breath he was walking away, while she grappled with a damp, aching core, heavy breasts, and need rippling through her.

Her legs gave out at the loss of him holding her captive and she flopped onto the bed, as if she were already that puppet and he'd cut her strings. Heart pounding, she wondered what else she'd gotten wrong about this man she'd married. Clearly, he felt a great many things: he was possessive, he was jealous of her relationship with Sebastian, and he'd wanted her long before an accident of fate had brought him to the altar.

Under the hot, pounding shower, Ani realized that despite it all, he'd walked away easily. Effortlessly. Meanwhile, she was reduced to touching her damp, aching folds, her mouth pressed against the gleaming chrome knowing that nothing but his touch would bring relief now.

CHAPTER FIVE

FOR THE TWO days since arriving at the villa in Corfu, all Ani had done was eat, sleep and wander down to the private beach every evening. After showing her to the third story—his private wing that had always been forbidden to her before—Xander had disappeared. The rush of the chopper not a half hour after they'd arrived told her that he'd left for Athens.

Two days of reprieve from not only him but Thea too. Two days of wandering through the house, playing her cello in the huge ballroom with fantastic acoustics on the ground floor, chatting with her brothers on the phone and convincing Killian to accept the money she'd send him soon. He'd only agreed when she'd reminded him how Bug, her middle brother, had flipped out at the idea of having to change schools—a fact she'd learned from Ayaan, her oldest brother.

This morning, knowing that Thea was back, Annika took her time getting dressed. She chose a light blue silk camisole and white linen trousers and a bra from her new wardrobe. Then she braided her still-damp hair, while standing on the terrace that stretched out like an overhang directly into the Ionian Sea.

The magnificent three-story villa had been built right into the very edge of the first cliff and had multiple terraces, each with gorgeous views. From the first moment she'd visited the villa as a little girl with her mother, the tranquil view of the sea, the beautiful home and the private strip of beach had meant safety and security. Not that she'd known at the time that her mama had been planning to leave her father soon and abandon Annika to him in the process.

Her mother had already been pregnant with Ayaan and Annika's father wouldn't divorce her. As always, Ani wondered for a moment whether her mother had worried that she might lose Ani, or whether her husband would use Ani to punish his wife's infidelity.

The only constant had been her godmother, Thea. Ani's father's interest in her had faded when he'd married Niven's mother following the divorce.

Any hope she'd nurtured of seeing her mama had been dashed, thanks to the bodyguards dogging her every step. But being here with Thea, following Sebastian as he wandered the island, catching flashes of Xander at dinnertime when he'd show her tricks with numbers—the man was a genius when it came to it—had been a balm to her soul. This villa had been a sanctuary to her. A refuge.

Now, standing on the terrace, Ani raised her face to the sky, the April sun kissing her cheeks. But the gorgeous view didn't calm her frantic mind today.

Coming here as Xander's new bride was unsettling in a way she hadn't foreseen. She'd have been in the second story as Sebastian's wife. So why did this feel so…strange? After all these years, it felt like her relationship to the house was morphing. Things were going to change when this farce was over. Was that the reason she felt such dread in her belly?

She and Sebastian had planned to separate a few years down the line; they'd walk away without causing any lasting harm to their friendship, or to her relationship with Thea.

The older woman knew very well the odds were stacked against Sebastian sticking it out in matrimony, acknowledging that no one but Ani could even *bring* him to the altar.

But being here as Xander's wife was different. Sharing a private suite with him, having to put on a show for Thea and the world, resisting him and then parting ways...it was going to change everything. Of all the turbulence life had thrown at her, this was the hardest. If she lost Thea and the house...

Suddenly, Ani felt scared and alone and rootless.

When her cell chirped with a text from Thea, who was impatiently holding breakfast for her, Ani wiped the wetness from her cheeks and put her game face on.

Xander kissed his grandmama on her cheek and took the seat opposite her. He'd returned from Athens ten minutes ago, and had been ordered to show for breakfast when all he'd wanted to do was to run up to his suite on the third story and...do what? Pant over his new bride like a randy teenager?

He'd spent two days away, to give them both respite. To get his head screwed on straight. Seeing Annika in lingerie she'd chosen for his twin had made him feel like a caveman. Yes, he wanted her, but this...indefinable possessiveness was neither appropriate nor good.

Pouring himself a cup of dark coffee, he raised a brow at Thea. "No congratulations for me? After you pestered me for months to find a bride?"

"I'm not sure if I should congratulate you or disown you for your actions," she said, coming straight to the point as always. "She was Sebastian's intended. God knows no other woman can straighten Sebastian. They have friendship and understanding and similarities that were a good foundation for marriage. And you..." her mouth pursed with disapproval, bordering on distaste "...swooped in and stole her. I taught you better than this. I taught you to watch out for him."

Xander hated disappointing his grandmother, the one responsible adult he'd ever known. But for the first time, he felt extreme resentment toward her. He rubbed a hand over his face. "You have a sharp enough mind not to forget that your favorite grandson went missing minutes before the wedding. He *left* her there."

She harrumphed. "You couldn't stand as a placeholder? Pretend to be him and give her back when he returned?"

"And you couldn't, for once in my life, not ask me to consider Sebastian's needs or this family's needs or the great Skalas name before my own? You couldn't for once think of my wishes, Grandmama?"

A stunned look came into her eyes. "Alexandros—"

"It is done. She is my wife," he said, cutting her off. It continued to be disconcerting how easily he was ruffled when his new wife was the topic. "I'll not explain myself to anyone, not even you."

"Fine. I will put my concerns for Sebastian aside. You... have been voluble in the past about how you can't stand Ani—that she's here every summer, that I am fond of her, that she... You barely tolerate her presence in our lives, Alexandros. What am I to think of this development? How do I know you will not shred that child to pieces with your impossible demands and controlling nature? You are not an easy man to live with."

Xander laughed, the sound full of scornful self-deprecation. "So I am to be molded into a controlling monster to save your family and its fortunes and then be castigated for the very same?"

Thea blanched and her stiff mouth wobbled. She suddenly looked very much like the seventy-eight-year-old woman that they forgot she was, for her will was made of steel. A tired sigh escaped her. "She has fought far too many battles in her short life."

"While I do not know what they are," he said, curiosity gouging a hole through him, "I can reassure you that it has made her fierce enough to take me on."

Thea blinked, opened her mouth and then closed it. "So you do see her," she said with almost savage satisfaction. Then she frowned anew. "Unless you've used her desperation to your own advantage and roped her into—"

"Isn't it interesting that I have more faith in her than you do," Xander interrupted, "for all that you claim to love her?"

"She does not know you like I do."

"On the contrary," Xander said, the words full of a recently discovered conviction. "Annika knows exactly who I am. I will even admit that I have fallen for her act...like every other man out there."

Before Thea could interrogate him more, Annika appeared over the slope, one of those twinkling smiles from her repertoire stitched onto her lips. But Xander saw the vacuous nature of it now. He leaned back in his seat, watching her. Two days spent away from her hadn't dimmed his awareness of her one bit.

In a simple silk camisole and linen pants that flaunted her long legs, she looked every inch the sleek, sophisticated woman he'd demanded she mold herself into. Her makeup, if she wore any, was light. With the dark circles under her eyes gone, she looked rested, even poised, as if she'd simply removed the reckless, flighty party girl filter and put on the perfectly groomed, boring socialite filter. Like they were all just masks for her and the real woman was buried deep beneath. Or even lost, he thought with a vague sense of discontent.

As she came closer, he noted the diamond circle pendant on a gold chain at her neck and the platinum Rolex on her wrist and diamond studs at her ears—every piece chosen by him. For a man who'd never personally bought a gift— his ex-fiancée and current business partner, Diana, was too practical to even expect that he would—he'd enjoyed walking into a jewelry boutique and selecting pieces for Annika.

When she tucked one stray wild lock of hair behind her ear, he saw the last piece on her finger. Different from the rest, it was a large bloodred ruby set in a gold ring—an antique Indian piece from a specialized collection, he'd been informed, that had once belonged to a warrior princess.

He'd bought it on impulse—though it didn't match the dull, almost boring, elegance of the rest of the collection— because it had reminded him of her, of who he was beginning to see she was beneath all the armor she covered herself in. And against all his own rules, he had wanted her to have one thing she'd appreciate.

Shooting to his feet, he gave in to the insane idea of messing up the boring veneer he'd insisted on. "Excuse me, Grandmama, but I'd like to kiss my wife," he announced to a shocked Thea.

My wife...

He liked the sound of that very much.

Annika stumbled on the downward slope, even though she was wearing flat sandals, when she saw Xander prowling toward her, as if he'd set his prey in his sights. He moved like a predator too, all casual grace and economic gait. But instead of being scared, she felt a pulse of excitement, remembering his hands on her back.

In the next blink he was there, catching her with an arm around her waist. Her chest banged into his, knocking the breath out of her. She'd barely taken hold of her senses as she drowned in the rich, ocean scent of him when he pulled her closer.

Palm at the base of her neck, fingers spread upward into her hair, he tilted her face to meet his. The tips of their noses touched, and his exhales teased her lips. "Xander, what—"

"*Kalimera*, Kyria Skalas."

It took her a while to remember how words were made. When she did, they came out all husky. "Good morning, Kyrios Skalas."

"Two days away from each other, *ne*?" he teased, though the amusement didn't reach his gray eyes. "Let's make it look like they have been unbearable."

It was all the warning she received before his mouth found hers.

Ani moaned, the idea of protest not even a passing thought. Tendrils of pleasure shot through her and she grabbed onto him, sending her fingers on a quest. He smelled like dark decadence, like all the sinful desires she'd never let weaken her. Like the deepest, darkest longing she'd hidden away, even from herself.

If he'd punished her again, if he'd tried to assert his dominance over her like he'd done at the wedding, she could have mounted some kind of resistance. She would have. But the cunning, ruthless bastard that he was, he switched strategy.

This kiss was nothing like the last one. This was…a tender exploration, a gentle teasing, an invitation to play. As if they were equals and there were no rules except pleasure and no destination to reach. As if there was no muddled past or murky future, nothing but the heady present.

And she played. Shamelessly. Selfishly. Opening her

mouth for him to sweep into. Tangling her tongue with his. Sucking at the tip of his. Rubbing herself against his chest with an urgency she was beginning to understand only now. She was already addicted to him—his brand of possessiveness, his dares, his mouth. And she knew why. He made her forget her life, her troubles, her self-control, her principles. He made her want to be swept away instead of constantly, relentlessly swimming upstream.

"Xander," she whispered, needing more.

His palms drifted down her back and the pressure of his lips increased in direct proportion to her unspoken demand.

Ani found herself losing her foothold on rationality and reality as the gentle play broke new ground. With hungry nips and eager pants and shallow breaths, she followed him as he funneled more and more pleasure into her until she was pressing herself against him with wanton abandon. She raked her fingernails over the nape of his neck when he stopped and dug her teeth into the pad of his lower lip.

A rough grunt shuddered out of him, his hips jerking against hers, and the shocking press of his arousal made her knees tremble. She felt like she was deep under water, weighed down by sensation, floating along on pure pleasure, without a care.

Hands clasped her cheeks tenderly and she opened her eyes.

Xander looked as ravaged as she felt within. His designer haircut was all mussed and on his lower lip there was an indentation of her teeth.

Ani jerked back, remembering what she'd done. "I'm sorry. I…"

He touched his finger to the mark she'd left on his lip, something hot and slick coming awake in his gray eyes.

"Everything is a lie with us, *ne*? You don't have to apologize for what is not."

She nodded, licking her swollen, sensitive lips and felt the pang somewhere else.

"Especially when we both like it," he said, somehow the words full of both tenderness and raw claiming. "That should go some way toward pacifying Thea," he said.

Ani looked up, heart in her throat. Uncoiling herself from around him, she glanced at Thea, who was watching them without blinking. That shrewd gaze brought her back to reality with a thump. Embarrassment welled up within her—she'd almost climbed him as if he were a tree!—and she tried to step away from him.

Xander's hold tightened. "There's nothing to be ashamed about either."

Ani sighed, knowing it was too late anyway. "Is she angry?"

"With me, yes. Not you," he said, straightening her rumpled blouse with a casual possessiveness she'd never, not in ten lifetimes, expected of him. He took her right hand in his and brought her knuckles to his mouth. "All you need to do is play into the narrative that I'm the big bad wolf that has gobbled you up. Gullible and guileless, upset by Sebastian's abandonment, you were broken up about your future when I swooped in heroically and saved you. Maybe you've been secretly in love with me for years, were distraught you couldn't have me, which is why you settled for second best and—"

"That makes me sound like an awful human being," Ani said, pushing at his chest and stumbling. She didn't know whether to laugh or cry at the tale he was spinning.

He caught her and she saw the unspoken question in his

eyes. The lies in which she'd draped herself were too horrible to let stand. "Xander, about Sebastian and me—"

"Leave it, Annika."

Their gazes held, battling it out, neither willing to give an inch. Until she did, shaking, despite the balmy weather. "Love is too big a lie, especially when it's about you and me. And Thea has never thought me guileless."

"No. And yet, she's so protective of you, *ne*? Grandmama does not suffer—"

"Empty-headed twits like me?" she said, feeding him back his own words.

His expressive mouth flattened. "I'm not the first man to fall for your wiles."

Heart thudding, she scoffed. "You make me sound like a veritable femme fatale."

"Thea not only loves you but respects you," he said, ignoring her jab. "I did not see the distinction until now."

Suddenly, Ani felt like one of those bugs her second brother collected. He never hurt them, he didn't torment them, but he studied them constantly, fascinated. Now she had caught Xander's…interest. Frenzied excitement bubbled over in every cell at that adolescent dream taking shape. This was *so* not her plan!

Tucking her into his side, he shuffled her toward Thea, instantly shifting his stride to match hers. "The one thing you need to convince her of is your commitment to me."

"You said she's angry with you. Why?"

"She thinks I stole you out from under my poor, naive twin's nose."

"Wait," Ani said, forcing him to stop. A strand of her hair got caught in his jacket button, gleaming golden brown against the black fabric. She tugged at it, working through the knot in her head. Looking up, she caught his surprise at how easily she touched him and flushed. "That's not right or fair."

"What?"

"I might not like you or agree with you on most things, but I'll not support this ridiculous theory that you took advantage of me or conned Sebastian—*as if* he can be conned. Does she know him at all?"

Xander shrugged.

"She's always had a soft spot for Sebastian. It makes her blind to his true nature," Ani continued. "And she can't now complain about your ruthlessness and demand for perfection and your brilliant strategic mind when she has employed them to great benefit to protect the Skalas name and legacy."

His shock was a palpable twang in the air around them. He looked away, jaw so tight that she wondered if she'd crossed some invisible line between them. When he turned back to her, his gray eyes gleamed with a dark humor. "Not only a wife who'll follow my every rule but a champion too, Annika?" He ran the tip of his finger over her jaw. "Careful, *matia mou*. I might never give you up."

Ani shivered at the silky claim.

"Right now, you're angry with Sebastian, so your loyalties have shifted," he said, rejecting her impassioned speech in one moment.

For once, his accusation that she was flighty didn't bother her because there was a greater truth she couldn't unsee. Sebastian, for all he'd agreed to help her, was slippery, his motivations a labyrinthine haze that no one could really pierce. Not even his twin. He'd been a good friend to her, to the best of his ability, but Xander...was the opposite.

Once he gave his word, he'd move heaven and earth to keep it. Ruthless as he was, he also claimed intense loyalty in his staff, for he looked after them, donated generously to their children's education and retirement funds and was renowned for his fair and equitable practices in the banking world.

The sudden intimacy of their conversation, the idea of her and Xander together against the world, made warmth blossom in her chest. As if she now had an army at her beck and call. As if she wasn't alone in her fight against Niven anymore.

"I know marrying me suited your needs too," she said, making sure she met his gray gaze. "And you drive a hard bargain. But you didn't have to step in as you did. For that I'm grateful."

Hands tucked into his pockets, he watched her, unblinking and radiating intense dislike. "There's no kindness behind my actions."

"Yes, well, being weighed down in diamonds can go a long way toward making a girl grateful," she said, reaching for that easy flippancy, refusing to give up her conviction that his actions meant more than just a mutually convenient transaction, in a life where there had been very few.

"Why did you propose to Sebastian if you have feelings for Alexandros?" Thea demanded the moment Ani sat down.

Luckily or not, Xander's phone had rung right when they'd had reached Thea and he'd excused himself. Annika took a bite of a buttery croissant, prolonging the moment. "You're the one who suggested I should propose to Sebastian," she said, her hand shaking as she poured herself some thick, dark coffee.

This was what she'd dreaded: lying to the one person who'd always stood by her.

Thea clamped her wrist in a hard grip, forcing Ani to

meet her eyes. "I will forgive you for anything...except playing my grandsons against each other."

Hurt sliced through Ani. "You know me better than that."

"I thought so too. But that kiss looked very real. Why agree to my idea then?" Her gaze was a laser burn on Ani's skin. "Unless you and Xander have made a dangerous deal."

Annika went for as much truth as she could, seeing Thea was dangerously close to it. "Look, Sebastian disappeared at the last minute, despite knowing how much was at stake for me. He left Xander to do his dirty work. Xander...tried to console me and something happened. Something the both of us have ignored for a...long time. It led to...more." When Thea's stare remained unrelenting, Ani let some of her own confusion and tiredness infuse her words. "I'm tired, Thea. Tired of fighting Niven. Tired of seeing my stepfather and my brothers suffer because of me, of...being unrelentingly strong. So, yes, when things went too far with Xander, I told him everything and he offered to marry me. Of course I jumped on the chance. I want a protector, a provider, and even you'll agree, Xander is the best choice. I'll do my best to be the wife he wants."

Thea's anger melted like the last remnant of snow under a suddenly dazzling spring sun. She took Ani's hand in hers, her eyes full of the same affection and compassion that had always nurtured her. "I can see the passion between you two but you're both—"

"We're both willing to do whatever it takes. In that, we're very similar."

Looking thoughtful, her godmother nodded.

"Maybe you think I'm not good enough for the Skalas heir, eh?"

Thea smiled. "Or perhaps you could be the one who brings my stubborn, arrogant grandson to his knees?"

"I can only dream." Ani laughed, knowing she could never. She didn't even want to. Or so she kept telling herself.

Reaching out, Thea palmed Ani's cheek. "But what about you, Ani?"

"You're the one who taught me that practicality is more important than—"

"What about love and freedom and your music and all the dreams you've held on to for so long? What about your longing for a family and children and a big house and a man who adores you? What about not letting your mother's mistakes dictate your own—"

Annika's neck prickled and she felt Xander behind her, like a phantom pulse inside her body. The last thing she wanted was for him to know anything about her real hopes and dreams. He didn't have a right to them.

Tilting her chin up in a playful gesture, she met his gaze upside down.

Questions swirled in his gray eyes, his mouth a taut line of displeasure. Reaching for his jaw, she ran the ruby from her ring against his chin. "This piece..." she said, heart in her throat, "it's different from the rest of the collection. So... unique. I've never seen anything like it. Does it have a history? Where did you find it?"

"Magdalena found it," he said, throwing out his assistant's name with a careless casualness.

Under the guise of holding her hand up and studying it, Ani beat back the prick of hurt. Just because Xander was on her side didn't mean he'd suddenly buy her meaningful gifts.

"That charity gala at Lake Geneva in two weeks' time?" he said to Thea. "Annika and I will attend."

Thea's gaze swept over where his fingers lingered on Annika's shoulder. "It will be the first time in sixteen years that a Skalas will attend. The media attention will be too much for her, Alexandros."

"Is it significant if we attend?" Annika asked.

Grandmother and grandson stared at each other before Xander said, "My father did a lot of damage to our reputation and our business the last time he attended the gala. He lost clients' trust and their hard-earned money. Grandmama has done her best to repair some of it."

Using Xander's genius brain, no doubt. "Why haven't you gone all these years?"

"Only the chairman of the Skalas Bank is invited and while Thea has been managing it as a proxy, there hasn't been one in a while."

"So if you go now, it's like an informal declaration to the world that you'll be the next chairman, *ne*?" Annika pressed the issue shamelessly, wanting to get it over with, both this discussion and the inevitable prize Xander wanted.

Thea shot them both a hard look.

Shaking inside, she clamped her hands over Xander's arms around her neck. "What?" she said, keeping her tone casual and throwing a charming laugh at the end of it. "You've dangled the position in front of Xander for years now, making it conditional. We all know it should be his already."

"I have a fierce champion now, Thea," Xander said, his voice silky smooth and full of suppressed laughter.

Thea bared her teeth in a smile. "I begin to see what you mean when you say you two are very similar." Then she sighed and addressed Xander. "Let me throw you both a reception here first. She can attend next year."

Leaning down, he rubbed his cheek against Ani's, making her shudder from head to toe. "I have waited for this moment for a long time. If you wish to lend her support, you can accompany us. If not, help Ani with her wardrobe and the politics. I have that delegation from Japan to deal with this week."

"What about a honeymoon, Alexandros?" Thea asked, challenge in every regal line of her face. "What about giving your young bride a little of your time before you toss her into a sea of sharks?"

His long fingers cupped Annika's chin from behind and he pressed a soft kiss to her temple. Her senses reeled from all the possessive little touches. For a man who locked away desires and wants and emotions with an inhuman, steely ruthlessness, Xander sure touched her a lot.

"All the years of training you have unknowingly given her have made her perfect for me, Grandmama. Annika does not dwell in silly dreams and naive hopes. And what better way to adjust to each other than this trip?"

So he'd heard Thea's mention of her silly dreams.

His words haunted Annika for the rest of the week as she prepared to present herself to the world as Alexandros Skalas's prized young wife for the first time.

CHAPTER SIX

ANI RAN UP the stairs to the third story, without slowing her pace. Her thigh muscles groaned and her chest felt as if it was gasping for air but she kept going until she reached the vast bedroom with an open layout and a view of the sea on one side.

In the three weeks since they'd arrived at the villa, the constants in her day were running and endless shopping while being tutored in the utterly boring world of finance politics by Thea. Which made for an easy, slow life. But with her mind on how Killian was making out and the utter quiet from Niven since the wedding, plus all the forced intimacy with Xander and her in the same bedroom, tiring herself out by running up and down the cliff and the entire perimeter of the private stretch of beach was the only thing keeping Ani sane.

With Thea watching them like a hawk, it was all Ani could do to spend time on the third story, whose every inch smelled like Xander. Thank goodness the man worked a bazillion hours, mostly out of his Athens headquarters.

Her thighs and quads quaked as she chugged water from her bottle, pouring some over her head. With Xander gone, she'd been able to play her cello to her heart's content.

Kicking her shoes off, Ani tore off the packaging from a new bodywash that Thea had bought her and took a whiff of it. Then she pulled off her sweaty T-shirt, lost her shorts and entered the bathroom in her neon-pink sports bra and matching panties to find Xander stepping out of the shower with a thick white towel around his hips.

Ani stilled, clutching the bottle of bodywash to her chest. But the damage was done because she'd already taken in the taut stretch of olive skin with just the right amount of chest hair; defined pecs and a washboard stomach, with a trail of dark hair disappearing into the towel...

A soft, loose heat lashed through her, making her aware of every inch of her own skin. Hair slicked back with wetness, and water drops clinging to his olive skin, he was the exact teenage fantasy she'd indulged in. Only, he was solid and real this time *and* she had a right to look and touch and do more, if she wanted.

He'd made it more than clear that he was all for working this out of their systems; probably even assumed that it was an easy decision for her. As easy as proposing marriage to Sebastian one day and jumping into bed with him the next. It was exactly the image she'd nurtured. She'd made herself into a number of unsavory things, to make sure the men Niven picked for her would reject her. Nothing in her life had ever been fully her choice.

Unlike her, however, Xander didn't stop and stare. He didn't even blink. It was as if Annika standing there, gaping at him, was no big deal. As if he was used to women strolling through his private bathroom every day.

He wasn't, Ani knew for a fact. For one thing, Thea would not allow either brother to bring their *partners* to this home, which was only for Skalas wives.

For another, Xander—unlike Ani and Sebastian—was extra-extra-protective of his private life. She knew only of one attachment he'd had in all these years and that was only because that woman had been in Xander's life forever as a childhood friend, college mate and business partner, all rolled into one. He'd been engaged to Diana Van Duerson for three years.

Hadn't she spent all three of those summers living in the utmost fear that she'd come across this perfect, mythical woman who met Xander's standards—or worse, see him kiss her or hold her or…something. She'd been a very angsty sixteen-year-old.

Why had the engagement ended? Was that why not one woman that Thea had paraded in front of him had caught his interest?

The thought of him still being in love with Ms. Van Duerson made bile rise up in Ani's throat. Or was that the green smoothie she'd forcibly chugged before the run?

Moving to one of the dual vanity sinks, Xander whipped out his shaving brush and lathered his cheeks and chin with an efficiency he seemed to employ universally in life. "Good run?"

She panted out a *yes*, words refusing to rise to her lips.

"Are you packed?" he asked, meeting her eyes in the large mirror.

"What?" Ani said, stepping further in, captivated by the muscled planes of his back and the divot right above his—

"For what?"

"We fly early tomorrow morning to Geneva."

"Almost."

"The shower is all yours," he said, grabbing a razor.

"That's fine. I'm…"

Covered as his mouth was in shaving cream, Ani couldn't be sure but she thought his mouthed twitched. "I won't peek, Annika. Unless you want me to."

"Stop playing with me, Xander."

"I like playing with you," he said, though there was nothing playful about his tone. Like everything about him, this too was straightforward and ruthless in a way she couldn't hide from. He swiped the razor with practiced ease over his jaw and even that was a thing to watch. "It's the only time I know I'm dealing with the real you."

The bottle of bodywash fell from her hands and Ani's breath turned to shallow pants.

And then he looked at her. And looked. And looked. His gaze lingered nowhere in particular and yet she felt it like a phantom touch on her breasts, her belly and even lower, where she wanted his eyes and fingers and mouth and... more. Desire lapped through her in lazy waves, making her nipples bead behind the thin Lycra of her sports bra and he noticed that too.

Ani clenched her thighs and then flushed bright red. Because he saw that too. He also let her see that her body pleased him, covered as it was in sweat and dust and sand from the beach. Somehow, it wasn't intrusive or invasive. And she knew then that he'd liked her eyes on his body too, that he'd found pleasure in the fact that it aroused her. And it was such a Xander thing too—not letting any emotions or hesitation pollute this.

"I don't know what to say to that. How to fight this," she said, baring her confusion.

He frowned and continued shaving. "You're aware of the draw you hold for men."

She scoffed, feeling as if there were a million sensors set into her skin, every single one of them lighting up anytime he was near. "The draw has always been my fortune. And anyway, you're not most men."

"Is that a good thing or a bad thing?"

"It's a thing," she blurted out, unable to dissemble.

His gaze held hers. A world of questions and answers lobbied back and forth between them. Pulling her gaze away with effort, she bent to pick up the bottle and groaned at a sudden shooting pain at the back of her thigh.

Instantly Xander was shuffling her to the lip of the monstrous bathtub, his hand on her bare hip. Once he was sure she was balanced on the edge, he pulled her leg up with an infinite tenderness that made her shiver. When was the last time anyone had tended to her? Or watched over her with such…gentleness?

Never.

He cursed when he saw the fist-sized muscle bruise on the back of her thigh. "You shouldn't run on this."

"I'll go mad if I don't," she replied, trying to get to her feet.

"Sit down, Annika," he bit out in that low voice, like he used to when he caught her in the middle of some prank Sebastian had instigated.

He returned, clad in loose sweatpants, with a spray and a cold compress. When he gently pressed his fingers around the bruise, she couldn't swallow her grimace. On his knees, he bent closer, his warm breath caressing her skin. "You'll damage the tendon permanently if you don't take care of this."

Ani had the most overwhelming urge to run her hands through his thick hair, to lean forward and press her mouth to his shoulder, to sink into his capable hands.

"How will you run away from me then? And from yourself?"

"You're taking the whole 'protect and cherish' part of our vows too far. There's no one here to watch us."

He leaned back on his haunches, his hand still cupping her knees. "You seem to have forgotten all the scrapes Sebastian got you into which I got you out of, every summer you visited."

Ani smiled, remembering the glorious sun-kissed days when she'd loved to follow Sebastian about, when she'd lived to get a rise out of Xander. "Sebastian set you up every time and still you came. I think, deep down—" she poked a finger at his granite-hard chest "—you loved playing the hero."

She snatched her hand back as the gray of his eyes deepened. She frowned. "Why did you, Xander? You must have known that Sebastian wouldn't have let me get hurt."

"Like the time he left you napping in the branches of an eight-foot tree when you were thirteen? You'd have broken every bone in your body if you'd fallen," he said, shooting to his feet, every inch of him taut with remembered tension.

Ani was stuck in that moment in the past, though, submerged in the hazy sunshine, the strawberries she'd glutted herself on, the thick, pungent smell of roses surrounding her as she'd suddenly startled awake at Xander's gritted calling of her name. "You'd just returned from that big board meeting where you took your father on. In a white shirt with the cuffs rolled back, tie barely loosened, and you came running to that orange grove…and called my name." Even back then, Xander had worked tirelessly against his father to save the bank, while Sebastian had lazed his days away.

"My charming twin doesn't know his limits. Whether it's stupid stunts or pushing our father—" He bit off the rest, turning away from her with a sudden edge to his movements.

Ani stared at his muscled back and the tense shoulders, his body a map to his emotions. It shocked her, this unveiling of what lay beneath his control, his discipline, his ruthlessness. That day too, it had been fear beneath his vibrating anger.

Xander had always possessed an overdeveloped sense of responsibility toward the people in his sphere—something Thea shamelessly exploited to push her own agenda when he was young.

He'd punched Sebastian in the mouth that day, all while cradling Ani against his chest, as if she were precious. Sebastian had grinned through a bloody mouth, as if he was the victor in a game for which only he knew the rules. Xander hated violence in any form and yet, he'd lost control that day. Over her. He'd been worried about her, enough to come running, enough to get into a fight with his twin.

Ani grabbed the edge of the marble tub, not knowing what to do with the realization that Xander had cared about her once upon a time. Until suddenly, he didn't. The loathing of the last few years had been so vehement that it had distorted all the good times.

What had changed? Was it simply her party girl persona that had put him off? Her supposed greed that disgusted his lofty morals? Would he tell her if she asked? Did she want to know?

"Sebastian liked—still likes—provoking you. You must know that."

Xander splashed water onto his face. And then he was in front of her, looking down at her, disdain dripping from each word, flipping the energy in the room to that pulsing contempt. "After the whole wedding fiasco, you still trust Sebastian, but not me?"

Ani wished she could tell him how much she wanted to give herself over to his capable hands, as she'd told Thea. How much she wanted to give in to this…heat between them. She licked her lower lip, suddenly sick of all the lies swirling between them.

You pushed me away, rejected me, looked at me with contempt in your eyes.

She locked the baffled hurt away, as she'd done before too. "I can't."

A bitter twist to his mouth, he was almost out the bathroom when he stopped. "I ran into your stepbrother the other day."

"What? Where?"

"At a charity auction in NYC last week."

Her throat felt like hot coals had been raked through it. "What...what did he say?"

"He walked up to me, introduced himself, and said congratulations. Invited us to his Hamptons estate. Insisted I tell you that he's sad you had the wedding when he was out of town, that you shouldn't spend a minute worrying about Killian or your brothers because he'll make sure they're all okay."

Ani shot to her feet, feeling urgency creep up under her skin. Niven was turning the screws tighter and tighter.

"Annika?" Xander said, turning around.

She shoved past him, her thoughts in a whirl. She wanted so much to tell Xander about the implied threat in the message Niven had conveyed through him, how the mention of Niven triggered a rage and helplessness in her. But she'd fought her battles alone for so long and that memory about Xander holding her to his chest only told her how foolish it was to put her faith in him.

Xander recognized the look in Annika's eyes before she ran. He'd seen the very same in Sebastian's eyes and his own when he'd looked in the mirror a long time ago, before he'd learned that the trick to defeat his father was to not show it.

It was fear.

Seeing Annika's expressive face turn colorless made him want to pound something into a pulp. He stared at himself in the mirror, shocked at the overwhelming intensity of it. He had no prior experience with these swings in emotion, loathed being under the grip of such intense desires as she provoked in him. His expectation that he'd defeat this obsession with her once he had her in his life seemed impossible now.

With each passing day and night, he was more invested in the puzzle that was Annika. The question Thea had asked her when she'd thought him out of earshot had disturbed him enough that he had fled to Athens to drown himself in work.

What about love and family and all your other dreams?

Being a very logical person, he looked for reasons as to why it bothered him so much. Maybe because he'd thought her one thing and, as always, Annika kept turning all his assumptions upside down. Maybe because he'd always been extremely competitive and a stubborn part of him wanted to give her everything she wanted.

He could simply ask Thea about her, but he didn't want to betray his confusion to her hawklike attention. And more importantly, he wanted to hear it all from Annika's mouth. He wanted her to give him her confidences and secrets and fears willingly. He had an inexplicable need to have her come to him, to have her depend on him, to have her... need him.

And he would, too. He would unravel every secret, every fear, until she was bare to him. Then maybe he could kick this as he would any other addiction.

He found her in the expansive closet, pulling and discarding shirts and dresses with a near frenzy. Drawers with expensive lingerie lay open, silky wisps of lace overflowing out of them. Whatever she was looking for was probably lost in the mess.

One side of the closet was intact—his suits and ties and shirts and leather shoes and loafers all kept in their designated place by staff who knew how obsessively particular he was with his things.

The other side of it was a wreckage with Annika at the center of it. Unaware of his arrival, she tugged her sports bra off over her head, giving him glimpses of silky smooth brown skin. Then she grabbed an old T-shirt—his university T-shirt, to be exact—and pulled it on. Something feral sparked inside him as he saw a pile of them had been transferred from his side to hers.

Tall as she was, the T-shirt barely covered her upper thighs. With a rough growl, she pulled free her braid that was stuck in the neckline. Sneaking her hands under its hem, she pulled her panties down. The glimpse of a shapely buttock held him in thrall.

It was like offering a starving man a glimpse of delicious morsels he could only see but not consume. But even more than the arousal flooding through him was the tenderness she provoked. She looked like a wounded animal and he desperately wanted to soothe her. And the only way to do that, it seemed, was to rile her.

"You said you'd finished packing," he said, unable to look away from the chaos she created wherever she went.

She turned around and blinked. "Divorce me for being a last-minute packer."

"Forget packing, this is a…disaster zone! Like the bridal suite. Do you always ransack through your stuff like some deranged raccoon?"

Her mouth twitched, that wicked gleam returning to her eyes. "Wait till you see what I've done to the study."

"My study is a no-go area for anyone," he said, unable to keep the horror out of his voice.

"Not to your wife. Isn't married life fun?" Grabbing a drawer full of makeup, she emptied it out in front of the large, full-length mirror. Tubes of lipstick and eyeliners and mascara rolled around. She pushed the heap to the ground, emptied another bag and started over. Then it was a tiny bag of coins. Then a bag of rocks—actual rocks, still covered in dirt and moss and—

The nerve in his temple started thrumming. "If this is the game you want to play, you should know I will win it."

Smacking her lips, she beckoned him with a finger. The audacity of the gesture made him want to kiss the hell out of her. Or pound it out of her in the best way he knew.

"You know what, Xander? Let's make a bet."

"Sebastian has ruined you."

"And yet, I have the most fun when I play with you," she said, holding his gaze.

"What is the bet?"

"If you can walk through this mess and come to me, I'll pack right now, while you stand there, to your satisfaction. I'll even let you…kiss me again. Just for the fun of it. No audience."

Xander saw the pattern then—the more cornered Annika felt, the harder she came out swinging recklessly at the world. So many of her scandalous actions could be neatly slotted into place then. "That's a dangerous bluff, *pethi mou*. It might mean that our first time together is on that hard marble bench in the middle of a very messy closet when I'd prefer taking my time on a comfortable bed."

She cleared her throat, even as her gaze drew a tantalizing trail down his bare chest. "That's very…cocky of you."

He raised one shoulder even as he considered a strategic

route to get to her through the mess. His right eye twitched at the idea. "You and I both know we won't be able to stop with a kiss one of these days. I have simply accepted the inevitability of it."

A blush ran up her sharp cheekbones. "More steps and fewer words, Xander."

The very thought of entering the center of it made his muscles clench up tight. Even as he fought the trigger, his body—like Pavlov's dog—remembered the punishment such a mess had earned him once.

Shame burned him at his inability to shred the memory, his inability to fight the conditioned response even as a thirty-four-year-old man. He thrived on keeping his cool and control in the most challenging situations at work and in life but this...this threw him.

Whatever Annika saw in his face—and Xander loathed the very thought that she might be privy to his internal fight—she lowered that belligerent chin. "You know what? This is silly. I'll just finish packing."

Without waiting, she marched back around the labyrinthine closet and tried to pull an overnight bag from the top shelf. Reaching her, Xander pulled it down. When she turned around, he raised a brow.

"It was a stupid bet."

"Which I won," he said like a petulant teenager.

She smiled then and it was a soft, sweet one that she used to give him as a kid. The ones that used to feel like a balm to his soul. The ones he'd gotten so addicted to that he—

"I'll make sure I don't create such a mess, moving forward."

His heart gave a thump. It was a very strange feeling that she invoked—her sudden ferocious claims where she championed him, or supported him or, like now, sought somehow to protect him from hurt.

No one had ever done that for him, not even Thea. And it stuck to his skin like something unwanted and sticky and painful. He didn't know how to sit with it. He didn't want it. And the only response he'd taught himself for those occasions—a blistering set-down—rose to his lips but he couldn't release it. There was an earnest sweetness to how she'd made that offer.

"You can create all the mess you want here," he said, putting on an air of condescension that she hated. "No one else will be privy to our personal life, *ne*? Especially since it pushes you to offer me sweet, tantalizing deals in return for my...hardship."

A surprised smile broke through. "A kiss, then?"

"A secret."

"Way to bring down a girl's confidence," she said, looking adorably put out. "What secret?"

"Tell me why you're scared of your stepbrother."

"I'm not," she said automatically. "He's just a...greedy asshole who wants to steal my trust fund." When he simply stared at her, she said, "Even with Papa gone, he continues this twisted legacy of controlling me. You understand not letting someone like that win, don't you?"

"I also understand the confusion left behind by a mother who didn't choose me over her own happiness or her freedom. As does Sebastian, *ne*?"

Ani fell back against the wall.

Konstantin Skalas's cruelty to his sons was not news to her. He had wielded different weapons over them, demanding perfection and ruthlessness and order, and meting out punishment for the smallest flaws.

While Xander had striven for and won his father's approval, Konstantin's treatment of the chaotic, artistic Sebastian had been intolerable. While the brothers had never let Konstantin break them by turning them against each other, he had left invisible scars all the same. And their mother had simply fled, leaving the twins to the mercy of a man she couldn't live with. "You never mention her," she whispered, her mind reeling.

Xander shrugged. "She left. There was nothing to do but make my peace with it. Sebastian is the one who still hopes to find her."

Suddenly, so much about Sebastian made sense. "I understand his hope."

"Do you?" Xander said with a bite. "It is a foolish pursuit to chase someone who does not want to be found. To want someone who does not want you. It is a madness that has consumed him for years."

"And you? Is it easy to write her off, Xander? To forget her? To move forward as if she hadn't been a part of your life once?" Ani didn't know why she was poking at a wound that had to hurt and yet she wanted something from him. An admission that he missed a woman who'd left him two decades ago? A glimpse of his pain? A fracture in his control? When had she turned so bloodthirsty?

"I didn't have the luxury to dwell on what life would have been if she hadn't left. I chose to deal with the monster she left us with, to protect Sebastian from him, to repair the damage he did to the bank, to its staff, to the clients who trusted him. There was no one else to do it. Konstantin left Thea a wreck."

She had known he'd stepped up to help Thea, that he'd once taken a beating meant for Sebastian, that he'd driven Konstantin out of the company, that with the trust of two good men in the company, he'd made millions at the age of twenty-one.

And yet now, after all these years, after all the prejudices and hurt she'd held on to like a shield, she saw Xander with the understanding of a woman who had fought her own monsters. In the process, they had both acquired battle scars. And who was she to say hers were more justified than his?

She felt the most insane urge to throw her arms around him, to hold him, to just be with him in this moment when they could see each other without masks and veils, in all their unbroken glory. But to do so would be to let her guard down, not just in front of him, but for herself.

"Why did you mention her, Xander?" she asked, curious.

He rested one long finger against her temple, while his thumb softly patted her cheek. The tenderness in the gesture floored her. "If you're fighting this battle for yourself, do it. But do not carry out some misunderstood revenge on your mother's behalf. Do not try to champion someone who should have championed you. Do not imagine a different past because all it will do is ruin your future."

"I've already ruined it," she said with a sudden laugh that barely covered her tears. She'd called him emotionally ruthless and yet he had seen into the heart of her so easily.

Yes, she didn't want Niven to win. But a part of her wanted to earn her mother's approval from beyond the grave by saving the sons she had loved. By proving that she was worthy of a love that should have been her right anyway. "By tying myself to you."

He smiled. "One day, I will hear you admit that I saved you, Annika Skalas."

CHAPTER SEVEN

ANNIKA HAD BEEN pretending to be a vacuous airhead for hours, playing into the narrative Xander's ex, Diana Van Duerson, eagerly spun by talking about banking and finance in a way that no layperson could understand. In between the hundred questions she asked Xander at their dinner table, she kept saying "Oh, I'm sorry, this must be over your head," to Ani, followed by a patronizing pat on her arm.

It was their second evening at the charity gala, and Ani was beginning to wonder if this was why Xander had insisted on bringing her—to have his petty revenge on her by thrusting his very accomplished, very smart, very beautiful ex in her face.

Or was he already regretting his decision to *save* Ani, as he put it? Did he wish he'd stuck to Diana instead? Would he ever tell her why he'd so readily jumped in to help her?

She'd never let a man close for this exact reason and it had always worked. But with Xander, all her usual practicality took a flaming jump out the window, leaving her at the mercy of her foolish heart and frisky hormones. Once, she'd been crushed by his sudden remoteness toward her. Even the warning that she couldn't go through that again didn't stop her from reading more into his actions.

In a dark gray suit that made his eyes pop, Xander looked nothing like the rest of the fuddy-duddy old bankers around. And now, there was an extra element to her attraction to him because she knew what pulsed beneath the suave, ruthless exterior. He'd mentioned his mother with that clinical lack of emotion, and yet he'd done it because he wanted her to know that he understood. Somehow, despite Thea and Sebastian knowing her much better, *he* had seen her wound. His kindness had always had a cruelty to it, but it also had a blistering honesty and zero calculation to it that she appreciated in a life full of broken promises.

Her mama had promised to come back for her, hadn't she? It was why Killian had fought Niven for custody of her for so long, because their happiness together had been tainted by how she'd abandoned Ani to her father.

If Xander made a promise, though, he'd keep it. The more time she spent with him, the more she was caught up in her own silly hopes that took the vague shape of a future she couldn't have. It was like living in the shadow of a huge predator's wings, not knowing when you might be gobbled up but kind of looking forward to it anyway, because at least then it was completely out of your hands and you realized too late that you had a thing for monsters who would bare their own underbelly to protect you.

A sudden burst of raucous laughter from the open terrace made her turn. It was exactly her type of people up there— trophy wives and bored heirs sustaining each other—and she'd had enough of hanging on to Xander like an accessory. Throwing back a glass of champagne on a dangerously empty stomach, she tapped on his arm to catch his attention. When he turned, she snuggled into his side and flashed him a smile, hopefully bright enough to blind him. "As Diana has pointed out repeatedly, all this talk of international finances is beyond my tiny brain. May I please be excused?"

Of course, snuggling into him to get a rise out of him was a huge mistake because he smelled of woodsy warmth.

"To do what exactly?" he said, leaning down so that only she could see the warning glint in his eyes.

Ani made a pout of her very red mouth—the unrelenting black of her evening gown needed the perfect red lipstick and it made her look hot and sexy and a little wild. "You don't want me to get bored, Xander. That's when the reckless behavior kicks in."

He tapped his thumb against her chin. "Joining that crowd will rein in these...dangerous impulses?"

"Yes, well," Ani said, including a very curious Diana in her reply, "this is the over-thirty-five crowd and all you talk about is making money, and hiding the money you've already made. Out there is the crowd that likes to spend it, like me." She added her signature airhead laugh.

"For a woman who's fixated on wealth and luxury, you keep forgetting to wear half your jewelry," Xander said, pitching his voice low yet again. He ran his finger over the shell of her ear down, down, down the empty lobe. "You didn't like the diamond earrings?"

Ani shivered at the feathery touch, feeling it all the way between her thighs. She clenched them together, desperate for friction. There was something velvety rich and sinful when he spoke like that to her, something very intimate about how he kept their conversation away from prying ears. It was all a web to lure her in and she was inching closer.

She exhaled roughly. "I don't need more presents, Xander. And those are—" she remembered herself just in time "—ancient in design. No one wears huge clusters like that."

He took her right hand in his, where the ruby ring shone brightly. "And yet you don't take this off."

"There's no big mystery to every little thing I do," she whispered against his cheek, desperate for him to drop his relentless probing.

He turned his face until the corners of their mouths touched just so. Air left her lungs in a choppy exhale and she trembled at the effort it took not to meet his mouth fully.

"And yet the truth is the exact opposite, *ne*? I think everything about you is fake. I won't leave you alone until all of this is stripped off, *matia mou*, and you're gloriously bare in front of me."

And then he was the one melding their mouths together for a quick, filthy little kiss that ravaged her to the very depths of her being. It was over before Ani could sink into it.

Xander fixed her lipstick with his thumb, patted her shoulder and said something that sounded very much like "good girl" and then simply dismissed her. And Annika shivered at the fresh wave of arousal blooming between her thighs at his compliment.

Who knew lusting after one's own husband could be so deliciously tormenting?

Xander found Annika close to midnight.

She'd never returned to their table or even to their suite. His mind had been on her constantly. But he couldn't walk out on important people he'd see only once a year because his reckless little wife had broken her promises and was probably out partying somewhere.

It had been a useless exercise in the end because he'd been distracted and irritable all evening. The cold burn of his resentment—at how much she occupied his thoughts— had morphed into something hotter, changing shape and form as the hours wore away. His temper had simmered hot, especially after the phone call he'd received just when he'd started looking for Annika. Especially after Diana had teased him about misplacing his child bride.

All evening, his ex had tried to embarrass Annika several times, reminding him, perversely, why he'd chosen to walk away from a relationship that had been more than a decade in the making. He hadn't stopped her, though, because he wanted to see Annika's reaction, wondered if she'd put Diana in her place. Annika had disappointed him, perversely, by conducting herself just as he had wanted.

With justifiable bitterness after he'd refused to set a wedding date for four years, Diana had made him face the fact that he hadn't considered, even for a second, not showing up for Annika at that church. He was egotistical enough not to like how it painted him and ruthless enough to want to control the narrative in his head even when it was clear that nothing about his actions regarding Annika made any sense.

Clearly, he'd decided he wanted Annika however he could get her. His obsession had become far too deep-rooted for him to wonder *if* they somehow could make it work.

He wanted to conquer her spirit, craved her surrender, in a way he'd never wanted anything in life. She distracted him no end, made him wonder about things he'd never even considered before, drove him to be at the mercy of his emotions, opened him to a bunch of ridiculous notions he'd done well without for this long in his life.

And yet, all the unpalatable realizations in the world didn't stop him from chasing her down.

He found her in the massive ballroom of the hotel that had been newly renovated but was not open to public yet. No doubt one of the younger men he'd seen flit around her had snuck her in here, hoping to inhale a bit of her wildness.

Huge chandeliers hanging from vaulted ceilings illuminated the vast space, fragments of light caressing the woman sitting in the middle of all of it.

All evening, she'd been a vision in the black velvet dress

with its shoelace straps. It had taken everything he possessed not to stare at how the thick, soft fabric hung in a loose neckline between her breasts. How her brown skin shimmered against the luxurious softness with a radiance he wanted to lick up. And the complicated knot her hair had been fashioned into…with each hour that passed, one stubborn wayward lock would fall out of it to kiss her shoulders in a tantalizing invitation. A potent reminder that Annika herself would only behave for so long.

Now, at the stroke of midnight, all of it was undone. All of it unraveled just the way he wanted.

He stood under the huge archway, stunned by the glorious creature in front of him. His blood pounded with a feral possessiveness that no one else would behold his wife like this.

With the velvet pushed up to reveal toned thighs and long bare legs, the disarray of her hair swaying about with each movement of her head, her body bowed forward and swung back, eyes closed. She was in…a delicious delirium of pleasure. A sight unlike he'd ever seen. And that was before the music reached his ears.

How he suddenly envied Sebastian his artistic soul. Even though he was built of logic and rationality and numbers on a cellular level, Xander could still appreciate the haunting melody of the tune, could hear the longing and the ache and the sudden pulse of hope fracturing the melancholy.

At the center of the vast black-and-white marbled floor, with the cello between her legs, his wife was lost to the world. Lost in the acute pleasure she weaved with her fingers. Here was the real Annika.

He was standing in front of her when she finished with quite the flourish. Musical notes seemed to soar through the air long after she was done, vibrating with a rich intensity he'd never forget.

Slowly, Annika opened her eyes and looked around, like a baby bird waking up from a trance. Tiny dots of sweat pearled over her upper lip and neck. Her slender arms were trembling when she pulled the bow up and away from the instrument. Reaching down, Xander took the bow and put the cello away.

Sudden tension gripped her shoulder blades as she gathered the thick mass of her hair and bound it into a knot at the top of her head. Her chest rose and fell, the soft little pants of her breaths a new beat to which he automatically tuned himself.

Xander sank to his knees in the space the cello had occupied, loath to let her run away. Loath to let her hide all over again.

Her brown eyes widened into large pools, her palms descending to her belly.

"You play beautifully," he said, knowing that his words were inadequate. Knowing that, despite the desire arcing between them, all he wanted was to delve into her mind. Into her heart even.

"Thank you," she whispered, a slight huskiness to her voice. "Is the interminable dinner over?"

"Why do you hide such talent?" he asked, ignoring her second question. "Such passion?"

"Because the music is mine. My own. Not to be…" A defensive note crept into her words. She looked down, and it struck him that he'd never seen her so…unsure of herself. So vulnerable, of all places, in her perfection. "It was my companion when I lost everything. It is my love, my only love. And love becomes weakness in the eyes of men like you."

Hurt was a jagged thrust through his chest. "You think I would use it as a bargaining tool?"

She shrugged, though a sliver of doubt entered her eyes. "Did you know that once women were forbidden from playing the cello?"

He raised a brow, waiting, knowing instinctually that something lay beneath her anger and aggression.

"By men, who else? With the way the instrument sits between your thighs, and the posture when you play…they thought it might do things to us that our tiny little brains and bodies couldn't possibly handle."

"Ahh, of course. Shall I tell you a secret, though?"

"What?"

"I'm glad you don't share it with anyone, then. Maybe I'm as controlling and ruthless as you say."

"What do you mean?"

"Your music, I would share it with everyone, Annika. But the way you look when you play…"

Her hands moved to her bare thighs then, her fingers playing with the hem of that velvet dress. Baring another inch of silky soft brown skin. Tantalizing. Taunting. Tempting. "This is nothing, Xander. I've worn much more scandalous things."

He smiled then, because she had no idea how glorious she was and that too was another revelation. "But it is not your body I wish to hide. It is you in that moment, how you look, how you feel, the heart of you that you bare when you play, that I would not share with another man. You're gloriously lost, as if the music itself was moving through you, pleasuring you, provoking you, pushing you to the edge of…everything."

"That's exactly how I feel," she said, worrying her lower lip between her teeth. Then her gaze touched his features, searching. Frowning. Seeking. "I didn't think you'd understand it."

"We're both full of surprises, *ne*?"

"Pity it's not for you to decide who would see me," she said, the fight returning to her. "Maybe tomorrow night I'll play for everyone. Scandalize everyone and cause you displeasure. That would be a nice break from the monotony."

He refused to react to the bait; it was but another distraction to divert him away from the real her. Every conversation with her was a game and he was determined to win. "Did the young fool who brought you here watch you play?"

"No. He...was disappointed, I think."

"Maybe because you were too tired to keep up your act?"

She raised one shoulder.

"Tell me something more about your music."

Surprise flickered in her eyes. "I learned for myself. I play for myself. It is the one thing that I allow myself to weave dreams around."

He realized, then, how truly similar they were. How they both avoided emotional connections for their own reasons. "Your mother used to play it, *ne*?"

She stilled, as if he'd taken a stick and probed at her deepest wound. The hard swallow at her throat made tenderness sweep through him. "You remember? How?"

He hesitated, just for a second. But if the topic he loathed with a bone-deep aversion was the thing that would build a bridge to Annika in this moment, then he would do it. He'd already done it once. This was madness, this thing between them, and for now, he would let it guide him because he wanted the prize. He wanted her enough to break a lifetime's conditioning. And that realization sent a shiver of dread down his spine. But not enough to stop him. "My mother," he said, and wondered that he hadn't choked on the word when he hadn't said it in more than two decades, "used to be supremely jealous of her talent."

"I probably shouldn't have touched that instrument. But it was...irresistible." She met his gaze, hers filled with some inscrutable emotion he couldn't pin down. That familiar, naughty smile found its way to her mouth again. And he saw it then, the artifice of it. "So be prepared to get thrown out on account of being the one who brought me here."

"They won't dare complain. And if you want to play that instrument again, or if you just want it, you can have it."

She laughed and some of the tension arcing between them scattered. Only some, though. "They won't, Xander. I'm telling you, they might even—"

"I'm telling you that if my wife wants that particular cello, she will have it."

Her laced fingers remained on her belly and Xander saw that for the shackle it was. She wanted to touch him but was fighting it. "I…guess that's one benefit of being married to Alexandros Skalas. Even the starchiest, most powerful bankers bow to you."

He shrugged. Power had only ever been a matter of survival to him. It was the only currency his father had understood and appreciated. Once Xander had had a taste of it, he'd held on to it, though. Just like another suit in his closet or a set of cuff links.

Now it pleased him enormously that he could make every dream of Annika's come true with the flick of a finger. *Most of her dreams*, anyway. Though he still wasn't sure if he believed what she'd told Thea that morning.

"You sent every single dollar of my wedding present to your stepfather," he said, bringing up the little nugget that had been eating away at him for hours.

Her smile disappeared. "You're spying on me now?"

"It's a large amount of money to transfer from a joint account, Annika. An alert would obviously go up."

"As your girlfriend pointed out, I'm close to illiterate in these matters." She straightened, her prickliness returning. "I'll ask Sebastian to teach me a few tricks going forward."

Just like that, his own even temper, which was hanging by a thread, vanished. "You will not ask Sebastian for anything. And I mean *anything*."

"You can't just forbid me, Xander."

"Actually, I can. That's the very basis of our agreement, *ne*?"

"Then what if I demand that you stop exposing me to that...woman? I should win a bloody crown for sitting through her condescending lecture while she batted her eyelashes at you and flirted with you relentlessly."

"You sound jealous, *yineka mou*."

"Even a fake wife would be jealous. If I'd poured that champagne down her cleavage, no one at that table would have found fault with me. I'm supposed to be your young airhead trophy wife, remember?"

"You are no airhead, but yes, you behaved remarkably well despite the provocation tonight. I believe in rewarding good behavior. You will have your diamond-studded crown tomorrow morning."

She gasped and her lovely, lush mouth fell open and Xander felt the most overwhelming urge to press his mouth to hers, to swallow her lies and taste her truths and everything in between.

"Now let's come to the real matter. All these years, the money you took from Thea, from Sebastian, you've been sending it to Killian. Why?"

"You don't know that," she said, shifting restlessly. Ready to push him away.

"I want the truth, Annika."

"And what? I'm supposed to hand it over to you, just like that? Because you demand it?"

"If you insist on perpetuating this...act, you will lose. I always get what I want."

"Fine. If you answer my questions, I will answer yours."

"Ask me then," Xander said, holding her gaze.

CHAPTER EIGHT

"Do you wish you'd married her?"

Ani hated the shape and sound of those words the moment they were released. It wasn't the question she meant to ask at all. She sounded needy and clingy and far too invested in his relationship with his ex, but thinking of her mother always left her a little shaky and vulnerable and unsure of herself. She felt lost in the very games she played and Xander was becoming the solid thing to hold on to.

His gray eyes gleamed perceptively. And ever the ruthless strategist, he withheld his answer for long, unbearable minutes.

Ani tried to shift the tension building up around them, but it was impossible…with him kneeling right in front of her. It was a sight she wouldn't have been able to conjure in her wildest dreams. But now she felt a strange bloodthirstiness she didn't understand.

Here he was now, jacket gone, shirt unbuttoned to his chest, hair rumpled, and on his knees—for her. If it was a weapon he was deploying—the soft charm, the gentle probing, the compliments and the interest—it was working only too well. Every inch of her trembled at his proximity, every cell in her wanted to bow toward his solid, enticing warmth.

For the first time in a long time, Annika wanted to make a choice for herself. Not to fight her stepbrother, not to help

Killian and not to feel connected to a mother who had abandoned her a long time ago. She wanted to know that she could still feel something, to give in to pleasure and oblivion and escape, to indulge herself with him. In the end, this thing between them would win. *Xander* would win.

She'd rather choose the time and venue of her defeat, make it a claiming, not a surrendering. And when it was all over she'd walk away, happily owning her desires and needs. She'd walk away, head held high, knowing she'd taken a chip off Alexandros Skalas's legendary control.

"You agreed to answer my questions," she said, feeling her desire flex its claws with the heady urgency of a decision made. The evening scruff on his jaw, his long fingers, the tiny scar near his upper lip, the corded column of his neck...every little thing about him sharpened into focus.

"I broke it off because I felt no urgency whatsoever to meet her at the altar."

"She clearly still wants you."

"I don't want her, *pethi mou*."

Their gazes met and held, his unspoken declaration lying there between them.

"I have one more," she said, leaning forward, both because she wanted to and because she needed to distract him. Her mouth hovered a few inches over his, their breath meeting and melding.

The gray of his eyes deepened. "You're trying to distract me."

"Is it working?"

"Last question then," he said, tweaking the tip of her nose as he used to do a long time ago.

"I want another wedding present."

He laughed then. Head thrown back, tendons in his neck stretched taut, he was breathtakingly gorgeous. And she wanted a bite of the feast. No, she wanted to glut herself on him.

"One more wedding present for Kyria Skalas," he said, grinning.

Annika stared, because she'd never seen him smile like that. Not even as a teen, when he didn't have the weight of the entire world on his shoulders.

"Don't get shy now."

"I want a kiss. No, I want a thousand kisses and I want you." The words rushed out of her. "I want it now." She dragged the tip of her finger down his Adam's apple, the hollow of his throat, down, down, down to his chest.

He stared at her, shock flickering in his eyes. "If this is part of some *game* to control me, Ani—"

"It's not. Everything else in my life..." She swallowed the words that wanted to rush out too—the bitterness, the loneliness, the grief and the fear. "Yes, but not this, Xander. I wouldn't do this for any other reason." She licked her lips and his eyes tracked the movement. "I want this. With you."

Annika had no idea if he moved forward, or if she'd bowed but their mouths met in a frenzy, like starving animals.

She had no thoughts or enough brain cells left to catalog the assault of his tongue licking into her mouth, his teeth nipping at her lips, or the way his long fingers cupped the base of her neck, tilting her mouth this way and that as he ravaged her. Each kiss they had shared until now had been the tip of an iceberg. No, the tip of a volcano. They were chaste, mere pecks compared to this...explosion.

His hands—his large, abrasive-feeling hands—moved up her thighs, pushing the hem of the velvet dress higher and higher, and his mouth moved from her lips to her jaw to her neck to the pulse fluttering madly there and then he scraped those teeth against her shoulder.

Annika jerked at the jarring pinch of pain and the sweet, sharp pangs of pleasure that followed when he licked the spot. She had no idea how she was breathing. All she could hear was a mad, deafening rush in her ears, a pulsing wave building, one beat at a time, into a torrential tempo, and still, she was left wanting.

"Please, Xander. More."

She felt his laughter like vibrations through her own body, as if she were a tuning fork he operated. His mouth moved from her shoulder, back to her neck and then down her chest. It rankled that he still was in control when she was already in tatters, so Ani grabbed the straps of her dress and tugged the bodice down. A cool breeze kissed her bare breasts.

With her eyes closed, every other sense amplified. The scent of Xander's subtle cologne. The utter stillness of air around him. The rough grunt of his exhale. The tightening dig of his fingers over her inner thighs.

Opening her eyes, Annika reveled in the feral hunger etched on his features, the harsh pants of his breaths. Whatever else he might think of her, this was real between them. Here, they were equals. Here, there was only truth.

His gaze moved from her plump nipples to her aching breasts, to the small tattoo she had gotten under her right breast, to the diamond stud at her belly button, and then back up all over again.

She waited, her heart lodged in her throat, for him to do something. Anything. For a second, she feared that was merely a game for him.

The hard swallow at his throat brought her breath back into her lungs in a shallow rush. She grabbed the edges of the bench and straightened her spine, faking a brazen sexuality that felt instinctual. His words about not letting anyone see her play—both a warning and a claiming—gave her courage.

For she'd never thought much of her body, her face or even her sexuality. She'd barely even understood what womanhood meant before her stepbrother had tried to turn her into a shiny package to sell to the highest bidder. So she'd done what she had to do. She'd turned her beauty, her body, even her sexuality into a tool. "Maybe you don't like what you see, *ne*?" she said, throwing a husky laugh to cover her floundering confidence. "Maybe you want to return the goods you bought for a refund? Maybe all of this is nothing but a powerful man patching up his ego because he lost to his twin for the first time in his life?"

"If you refer to yourself as goods again, I will take you over my lap and give you a spanking." Then he bit her lower lip in sweet punishment. "Same if you mention him again."

Ani leaned closer, her nipples grazing his chest, all of her being pulsing at that grazing contact. "What the hell do you want from me, Xander?"

"More."

She shivered at the resolve in that one word. "What else is left?" She bit back the sob that wanted to break through. "I've stripped myself bare, literally. Do you want me to beg? Is that it?"

"Your body is a weapon, *ne*? I'm beginning to see your patterns now. I want more than all the fools who lost their wits over you."

Ani stared, shaken yet again by his perceptiveness. Shaken by his supreme arrogance that she wouldn't just walk out on him. Did he know her desires better than she herself did? "Spell it out for me, then."

"Admit that you've wanted this." He touched her nipple in a quick lash of his tongue that went straight to her sex. "That you've wanted *me* for a long time."

"So all of this," she said, pulling the shroud of her tattered dignity around her nakedness, "is just an ego game to you?"

"You're the one who made it a game, Ani. I'm just making sure I win it."

"Why isn't this enough?"

"Because I want it all. All of your dirty secrets. All of your deepest wishes."

"Fine. Yes, I've been panting over you like a dog in heat for a long while. I kissed you that day knowing it was you. I've never wanted another man like I want you. I've never been this…" Her breath fluttered in her throat, blocking the confession that would shred the little armor she had left.

"Show me how you like to be touched." Leaning forward yet again, he closed his lips around her nipple, leaving it decadently wet, leaving her wet in more places. "Even better, make yourself come."

A lick of a shiver went down her spine. Of course he wasn't going to make this simple or easy for her. This was Xander. Everything was a challenge to be conquered.

She was a prize to be won, she thought with sudden clarity. And she dared not wonder how he'd throw her away when her surrender rendered her appeal stale.

"I've never made myself come," she said, truth making her voice shiver. "That day on the flight, I tried, but…"

"But your lovers have, *ne*? Show me what you like."

Ani felt a flicker of doubt about the wall of lies she'd surrounded herself with falling away at his feet. But if she spilled the truth now, the magic of the moment would disappear. He'd ask more questions and her courage would be gone and she wanted this…*needed* this for herself. "You're being a bastard."

"Because I want to know what you like? Because I want to make sure you remember no one else's touch but mine?"

"Xander—"

"I don't want an act. I don't want the fake Annika you show the world. I want the real you," he said, all steely command in a velvety voice.

Ani laughed, because the other choice was to cry. She'd spun her lies so well and for so long that her truths were not recognizable anymore. This was the real her—the one that had never had a single sexual experience except the kiss she'd stolen from him. The one who hadn't explored her body or her needs, or wondered about the normal, care-free life she was giving up because to do so would open a floodgate she'd kept tightly locked. Because to do so was to face a fear that maybe her heart had been irrevocably broken and she'd never use it again.

The only man for whom she'd broken all her rules was Xander.

Gray eyes held hers in an all-or-nothing dare.

And maybe this was the freedom Xander would give her, she thought, shaking inside. In this fake relationship, she could explore her desire and provoke his and experience everything she'd denied herself. Even risk whatever it was she'd become when he was done with her because his fascination with her was only temporary.

Under his watchful gaze, she lifted trembling hands and cupped her breasts. They were soft and heavy in her palms and ached for a firmer touch. For a rougher clasp. For the expert graze of teeth.

"You are a good girl here, then," he said, such wicked light in his eyes that she thought she might bare and strip every inch of her pride and vulnerability if he smiled at her like that.

"Only here," she said, determined to match him word to word. "And maybe only for you."

An unholy light dawned in his eyes, morphing the gray from a cold flatness to a shining warmth. And she realized that in his own roundabout way, Xander was giving her back all the power and agency that had been stolen from her. That he was pushing her to make her own choices, and for that alone, she'd adore him for the rest of her life.

"Touch me," she said eagerly and then shook her head. "Kiss me, here," she said, rubbing the pads of her thumbs over her peaked nipples. With his gaze on the movement, fire licked through her. "I want to feel your tongue. Your teeth. Your…stubble rasping against me." She pinched the tight buds and nearly came off the bench at the twang shooting to her pelvis. Her moan was loud and brazen and so very needy.

And just like that, he was there. His mouth was there. Licking and swirling and playing with her nipples with such expert skill that she grabbed his hair to hold on and to keep him. His mouth devoured her, alternating between her breasts, releasing her flesh with a popping sound that was a spark at her core. She rocked into his caresses, writhing on the bench, rubbing her thighs together for friction.

Then his fingers were tracing the tattoo she'd gotten under her breast of a cage and a tiny bird fleeing it. "You're a contradiction I will untangle," he said, almost to himself.

Annika swallowed, her brain figuring out how to make words, anew. "No more questions, Xander." Grabbing his palm, she pressed it to her chest, her heart pounding under it. "Or I'll figure out a reason to stop. And I don't want to stop tonight." A near sob filled her voice. "I don't even want to leave this ballroom."

"More conditions, *pethi mou*?"

"You said you'd grant me whatever I ask for."

"I don't have protection."

"I'm on the pill and I'm clean."

"So am I."

Then he was kissing her and lifting her and whispering filthy promises against her mouth. With a surprised laugh, she wrapped her legs around his waist. The tight clench of his abdomen dug into her pelvis and Ani abandoned herself to it. Her breasts rubbed against the soft nap of his shirt but it wasn't enough.

She needed skin-to-skin contact.

She needed his hands over every inch of her flesh.

She needed everything because she wasn't sure she could have this again. Already, she liked Xander's kisses, his touch, his filthy promises all too much. This was already changing her because she already wanted their next time before this time was even over, before this time had even begun.

She squirmed when her back hit the firm upholstery of the chaise longue. And then he was there, his knees straddling her hips, his saturnine face revealed in full glory as he looked down at her.

Pushing up, she unbuttoned his shirt and ran her palms over the hard contours of his chest, the sprinkling of hair, over the tight pack of muscles in his abdomen, back up, up, up over his shoulders, and still she couldn't get enough. She sobbed, feeling an urgent emptiness between her thighs.

His fingers tightened over her roaming hands, arresting their frenzied exploration. Leaning down, he trailed kisses over her neck, her chest, and then his mouth licked at her breast again, suckling, sending sharp pleasure to pool down in her lower belly. Ani was panting and moaning and whining, begging for more, demanding more.

"What else do you want from me, *agapi*?" he asked, his voice sharp with a frenzied edge.

"I want your mouth," she said, licking her tremulous lip, meeting his dare head-on. Meeting herself head-on for the first time. Holding his gaze, she kicked her dress off. Heat poured through her as his gaze swept over her belly and her sex. She cupped herself over the flimsy thong, the tips of her fingers digging where she needed him. "Here. I want your mouth here. No one's ever gone down on me and—"

He didn't let her finish. With one tug, Xander ripped her thong and he was there, on his knees, his proud head bent, his thick hair tickling her inner thighs. He nuzzled the fold where her thigh met her hip, breathing in her arousal, fingers tracing the shape of her most intimate folds.

Every breath inside Ani stilled. The first stroke of his tongue was a feathery lash, gone before she could process it. And then he notched his nose at the tip and licked her again and again, thrashing a rhythm out of every nerve ending, building her to a frenzy. She pushed herself up onto one elbow, dug her fingers into his hair and tugged his head this way and that, a race car driver exploring a new loop. His laughter against her folds was as arousing as the clever assault of his mouth.

Breath serrated, she watched as he looked up. She pulled his hair harder, saw his nostrils flare, and said, "More. Faster. Harder."

He grinned, and then he was sucking at her clit.

Ani lay back, every inch of her writhing and thrashing at the building frenzy, and then exploded, fragmenting into a million shards, flying up and away from all the things that continued to tether her and bind her and keep her lost, even to herself. She wanted to keep flying away on wings of sensation but all of the shards came back together to remake her. Sobbing, hands searching madly for purchase, she found his steely strength.

Tears on her cheeks, Annika thought maybe being tethered was not a bad thing if she could feel such pleasure, if at the end of that spiral and the flight and the crash, Xander was there, waiting for her.

Holding her through it.

Looking just as he looked right then, his lips damp with her arousal, his hair rumpled, nostrils flaring and his eyes… those gray eyes alight with emotions she'd thought him impossible of feeling.

She pushed up and took his mouth in a hard, fast kiss, tasting herself on his lips. She trailed kisses down his jaw and his throat, licked the hollow of his neck, raked her fingernails down his chest, drew more kisses from his chest down to his abdomen, following the trail of hair thickening and disappearing under the seam of his trousers. She didn't hesitate though this was new ground.

Undoing his trousers, she snuck her hand inside with a confidence she didn't know she had. Her breath stuttered out of her in a sharp hiss as she touched his hard flesh. His entire body stiffened. Gasping, she ran her fingers over the velvety length of him as if he were the instrument now and she was determined to be the virtuoso.

Renewed hunger filled her as she slowly, instinctively, wrapped her fingers around him.

Xander grunted, dipping his head between her breasts in what felt like a prayer.

Pleasure shot through her in thick, dense pools as she swirled her fingertip in the wetness she found at his tip. Her mouth falling open, she rubbed the base of her palm against it. His exhale coated her breasts and he bit down on her flesh. She jerked as the slight pain contrasted lazily up against the pleasure already simmering through her.

His lashes flickered up and down; his breath was rough,

fast pants. She watched every nuance of his reaction to her actions, a strange new power surging through her.

She fisted him, up and down the thick length, feeling fresh dampness at her own core. Leaning into him, she licked the corner of his mouth, feeling a languorous unraveling inside her, as if all boundaries had been broken. She laid open-mouthed kisses over his lips. "I want you inside me, Xander." She bit down on his lower lip, like he'd done to her, intent on marking him. Intent on stealing whatever she could of him. Intent on changing him. "I want to be taken and owned and possessed until I forget how we got here. I want everything you can give me and we'll call this—" another rough stroke of her hands and another grunt from his lips "—the final wedding present?"

He caught her lips with his, with a rough growl that sent fresh tremors curling through her. On the next breath, he was lifting her until she was straddling him on the chaise longue, and for the flicker of a moment, fear shuddered through her.

She trembled violently.

Straightening up, Xander covered her flesh with his hands, stroking her, soothing her, whispering endearments that brought tears to her eyes. With a brazen strength she dredged up from some sweet, naive corner of her heart, she pushed onto her knees and shook out her hair, so that it fell in waves over her shoulders, the ends kissing her breasts.

He played with the thick, silky strands, strumming her breasts and belly and her sex. "You are beautiful, *matia mou*, and I have wanted to see you like this for a long time."

"You hated me," Ani said, fighting the pleasure his words brought, and failing.

"I hated how much I wanted you," he said with brutal honesty.

"And now?"

"Now you're mine to look at. To touch. To kiss. To ravage and ravish."

"And here I thought Sebastian was the artist in the—" With a gasp, she pressed her hand against her mouth.

"Now you're learning my rules."

For the first time in her life, Ani liked the lush voluptuousness of her breasts, the symmetry of her features, the toned length of her thighs, the soft curve of her belly. She liked the pleasure it brought her—and him. She liked who she could be in these mad moments with him. She almost broke at the thought of who she could be in the future with him if this marriage were real. But that way lay nothing but exquisite hope and enormous pain.

"Will you make me wait now too?"

He shook his head and with one arm cupping her hip, he positioned her as he wanted her and then he pushed up into her in one single thrust that almost cleaved her in two.

Ani gasped as pain ricocheted through her, and before she could catch another breath, he'd turned them both over onto the chaise longue with strength she didn't understand. One tear fell over her cheek and a rough thumb wiped it away. Lower in her pelvis, she felt another rough pinch and suddenly, she felt as empty as she'd always been. And as alone.

She opened her eyes to find Xander standing over her, the shape of his thick erection pushing against his undone trousers, his face wreathed in lines of fury, his gray eyes filled with betrayal.

CHAPTER NINE

XANDER HAD NEVER seen a more beautiful sight than Annika lying on the chaise longue. Hair thoroughly rumpled, her eyes full of lust, her skin shimmering with a damp sheen, her limbs and full curves naked, she was a glorious image he'd remember if he lived to be a hundred. Sharp cheekbones dusted with pink carried lone tears into the dip of her throat, and down into the valley between her breasts.

She looked achingly innocent and thoroughly ravished and...unraveled at his hands.

His entire body felt like one shrieking mass of agonizing, pent-up desire, demanding finish. The sensation of velvet heat clutching him before she—

How could she be a virgin? He'd rammed into her like an animal! Already, her cry haunted him.

Fury and betrayal vibrated through him in twin flames. She'd made a villain out of him, a man not unlike his father. But even if he could live with that, he loathed that he'd caused her pain, that he'd hurt her when it could have been avoided, and that even now it took every inch of his tattered self-control not to take what she so foolishly offered.

Her lies, her acts...it felt like the ground had been pulled out from under him and that was a boundary he couldn't let anyone cross. Not even Annika, for whom he was breaking most of the tenets he lived by. This was supposed to be about getting her out of his system, not letting her lies and truths get to him so much that it robbed him of clarity and control.

Still, desire and something that tasted like a dangerous longing muddied his head, and he couldn't allow that. Unlike his twin, Xander didn't dare test where his boundaries lay. He didn't dare let her cross his control, for he was so much more like Konstantin than Sebastian had ever been.

She extended a trembling hand toward him and every cell and sinew in him wanted to reach out and take it. "Xander?"

"Dress yourself," he said, his words coming from some cold place he loathed.

She licked that full bow of her upper lip, confusion clouding her eyes. "You're stopping?"

He scoffed and it hurt every muscle in his face. "The trail of tears running down your cheeks tells me it is the wisest course of action."

"No, please. I want this. More than anything I've ever wanted in my life."

"Then you shouldn't have played games with me. I told you I hate losing."

Her brow cleared. "You can't just…leave me like this. You promised you'd give me whatever I asked for."

"You're so full of lies that even you have forgotten the truth!"

She smiled then, through tears. With her eyes red, her nose blotchy, her mouth trembling, she reminded him of the girl he'd once adored. "You wouldn't have believed me if I told you the truth."

"I wouldn't have touched you if I had known you were—"

"And there's the alternative that I didn't want. But I guess I underestimated how much your control means to you." Something blazed in her eyes and she pushed up to a sitting position. He saw the grimace she tried to hide from the small movement.

Instinctively, he leaned down to pull her up but she jerked away from his touch, her chin set at that stubborn angle he knew so well.

His gaze swept to her thighs and the streak of pink there. Bile rose in his throat. Picking up the dress, he threw it at her. She didn't lift a hand to catch it and the velvet dress pooled near her feet. "For the past few years, you have loathed me. You judged me because you thought I was a greedy, selfish thief, an airhead flirt, a scandalous party girl, and now...you flip the script? Now what, I'm too virginal for you? Too pure and inexperienced for you?"

"I don't care about that. I care that you spin and weave lie upon lie so that I don't know who you are."

"I didn't know you vetted your sexual conquests with such thorough criteria."

He flinched. "You're not just anyone, Annika." The words poured out of him on a wave of emotion he couldn't understand, contradicting the very order of his thoughts.

She smiled but there was no humor or joy in it. "I'm the girl you hated for years and now I am your wife. How does my virginity change anything?"

He thrust a rough hand through his hair, a tightness pressing down on his chest that he could not dislodge. He hadn't cared how many lovers she'd had in the past because their arrangement had made her his in a way he'd needed. What he couldn't tolerate was the guilt that pricked him at how he'd spoken to her for years, how he'd thought her beneath him, how he'd used all her tricks as a reason to dislike her. He'd never thought himself a good man—far from it—but a fair man, yes.

All the scaffolding he'd used to build his opinion of her

was based on her lies and now it had come toppling down. He felt…disturbingly unsure of what he was doing. Of what—and how much—he was feeling. And he hated that kind of uncertainty, which came with not knowing his own mind.

She'd sent every dollar of her money to her stepfather.

She played cello with a depth of feeling and intensity he couldn't fathom.

She'd never been intimate with a man, despite three broken engagements and a host of scandalous rumors attached to her.

What isolation and artifice and loneliness that must have brought…

She dreamed of love and freedom and a life free of men like him.

Acid burned through his throat.

Everything he'd thought about her was a lie. And the truth that was forming from all the little pieces he kept discovering…he didn't want *that* Annika.

He wasn't equipped to deal with *that* Annika because she was all innocence wrapped in brazen confidence, fragility masquerading as strength, dreams and wishes warped into lies and acts, and he was a man who didn't, couldn't, have a woman like her. Even temporarily. Even just to sate his lust.

She wanted him—there was truth in that. But he could never let himself be led around by this unfathomable obsession. He'd never wanted something or someone so much that it tested his control. It made him examine his own flaws and he couldn't start now.

"So that's it? You're going to leave me here like this? After demanding that I give you the real me, you're going to punish me for a truth that makes no difference at all?"

"No difference? You chose to lie, Annika."

"And, what? You deserve all my truths and dreams and

secret desires? Hell no, Xander. We were friends once and you just shoved me aside like distasteful garbage when I didn't measure up to your insufferable standards. Why the hell do you think I owe you anything? This, you and me, all of this, is a convenient arrangement. An itch we're scratching. Why are you suddenly making this bigger than it is?"

Every question that fell out of her lovely mouth was valid. And yet, Xander didn't have an answer that satisfied him, that could stop him from feeling like he was spinning out of control.

"Please Xander. Don't do this." Even her entreaty was a demand and she'd never looked more beautiful.

But he was caught up in his own head and couldn't find the ground under his feet. It took everything he had in him to walk away from the stricken look in her eyes. From *her*. "I don't want you anymore," he said, leaning into that ruthless edge that scared grown men in boardrooms.

She flinched and he thought there would be a special place in hell for him. Nothing new, then, given his genetic makeup.

"This isn't about me," she said, shooting to her feet, looking incredibly weary. "This is all you, the mighty and powerful Alexandros Skalas. You're a control freak and I'm the variable you'll never understand. I refuse to be the pathetic, rejected one here. It's your loss."

"It doesn't change our deal, *agapi*," he said, forcing himself to say the word with a casual cruelty that sickened even him. "I'll make sure you get your hands on your fortune. Just continue…your act and it will work out exactly as we planned."

Ani wished she could board a flight to New York and simply disappear into the night. Run into her stepfather's arms and vent about the bastard who'd rejected her with such cruelty. Confide her confusion about the torrent of feelings her husband had unleashed within her.

She did nothing of the sort.

With a brittle smile in place, she got through the next two days of the damned charity gala and she played by the rules so well that every man and woman fluttered around the "young, beautiful Skalas bride." Impeccable manners, easy small talk and graceful, witty anecdotes—she owned everyone at the gala.

The final evening, she wore a neon pink dress that wrapped around her neck and chest in wide straps, leaving a little gap in the center of her cleavage and showing a little side boob.

It was the most daring dress amid a lot of boring blacks and staid navy blues. Instead of straightening her hair, she'd let it air-dry into thick waves and plopped on it the diamond-studded tiara that had shown up on her pillow the morning after his brutal rejection.

All in all, she looked hot—even she had to admit it. The dress clung to her curves, forbade any kind of underwear and dipped so low in her back, leaving the top bare, that if someone stood behind her and peeked, they would be able to see her ass.

Something had unlocked inside her with Xander's brutal rejection. There was freedom in having taken the leap and falling hard, with colorful bruises to show for it. She wasn't wearing the dress to break his rules or toe his line.

And as much as she hated him for it, she felt as if he'd released her from a cage of her own making. Ani before Xander's rejection was different from Ani after.

She'd done all she could to take care of Killian and her brothers, she'd survived Niven's mind games and soon she would emerge out of this…debacle, with her fortune in hand. Now it was time to look after herself. Because the one thing Xander's rejection had taught her was that she deserved happiness and love and a real chance at life.

And whether she'd find it or be able to trust a man with her heart wasn't certain but it was time to start living for herself.

She hung on to Xander's arm for the first half of the evening, nodding and smiling politely. Once she stopped treating it as a chore, she actually found herself enjoying the conversation and the people.

Particularly the company of a man around her age, who was clearly at the gala under his father's sufferance. They laughed, more than once, at a shared grievance about fitting into the molds people decided for them. The more she spent time with him, the more she liked him, for he didn't come on to her even once. He even teased her about the covert glances she kept sending in Xander's direction from the moment she'd arrived at the ballroom.

He was perceptive, her new friend. Of course, Ani couldn't tell him that her husband had not only not returned to their bed, but he had not returned to their suite for the last two nights. Which was the most un-Xander thing she'd ever seen.

Deciding that it was his loss was one thing.

Curbing her curiosity about where he'd spent the nights was another.

Which then led her to spying on what Diana was up to. Thankfully, Diana had maintained her distance from Ani. Not that it stopped Ani from imagining that the reason Diana was maintaining a tactful distance was because she'd spent the night with Xander.

Thankful that the ordeal would be over tomorrow morning and she could go back to hiding at the villa, she spent the last hour chatting with her new friend when a tap on her shoulder brought her head up. They'd been so busy talking about classical music and maestros with such exuberance that Ani hadn't even noticed Xander striding toward them. The momentary reprieve from consuming thoughts about him had lifted her spirits. Maybe one day, she'd go a whole day without wanting to kiss him or kill him.

"Dance with me, Annika."

The command grated but Ani pasted a sweet smile, excused herself and followed him to the dance floor. As if on cue, the string quartet switched to a slow, soft classical cover of a pop tune. Ani swallowed as Xander's hands landed on her bare back and then spread wide.

Tension sprang from every inch of her skin that he touched, from the soft graze of his thighs against hers to the way he watched her, his gaze lingering on her mouth.

And what was the point of this exercise at the last minute anyway? She'd charmed the pants off most of his colleagues, reassuring various powerful and privileged men that the mighty Skalas dynasty had a new, fresh broodmare guaranteeing heirs to continue the line, establishing Alexandros Skalas once again as the apex predator at the top of the food chain.

"I thought you were too ornery and starchy to dance so well," she said, desperate to deflect the building tension.

To her everlasting shock, he shrugged and smiled. "Sebastian loves dancing. Since our father would not permit him to learn outside, I used to dance with him. We would take turns leading."

The thought of the twins dancing in that ballroom, staid serious Xander with charming, laughing Sebastian, made warmth fill her chest. "You really do care about him." The wonder in her words lingered after the sound of them faded.

He raised a brow. "It's survival more than anything else that binds us."

His answer irritated her. Why was it so important to believe and prove that he couldn't care about anyone? What lay beneath Xander's desperate need for control? He'd discarded her so easily two nights ago—did it prove that he didn't care or the opposite? She was twisting herself inside out pondering the damned question.

"Is this necessary?" she asked, breath hitching in her throat when he swung her with a fluid agility.

"Is what necessary?"

"This. You and me. Dancing." She poked him in the chest. "Continuing this farce. I've done my job and charmed everyone beyond even your expectations. Can't I have one hour to myself instead of dancing attendance on you?"

"Is that what you've been doing for the last two hours, chatting with that young man?"

She glared at him. "We weren't flirting."

"I didn't say that."

"If you must know, he's an interesting guy. I've decided it doesn't hurt to develop friendships with those rare individuals who have integrity. When you and I are through, I'm going to be a very rich heiress and I don't want to keep my life on hold forever."

Irritation flickered in his gaze though he sounded perfectly content. "Long-term planning already, I see."

"I knew you'd appreciate it."

"But the young Neilsen heir knows not to mess with what's mine. Even after."

"That makes me sound like a prized poodle, not a wife.

Would you like me to wag my tail and trot after you when you walk out of here?"

He laughed and her heart flipped in her chest. A lock of his hair fell onto his forehead and she pushed it back without thinking.

He stilled and she jerked her hand back. His fingers wound around her wrist, and he brought her palm to his face in a gentle gesture that punched through her. "You look beautiful, but something is different, *ne*? You're...glowing from inside out."

She stared, stunned anew by his perceptiveness. Just because Xander chose not to indulge in emotions didn't mean he didn't understand them. Annika kept having to learn that truth over and over. "Your rejection taught me a good lesson. It showed me that I was the one who chained myself. The freedom that I could and should be my own woman, free from the past, is...exhilarating."

"Ahh... No wonder then that every man here is jealous of my good fortune."

She swallowed at the sudden surge of longing thrashing through her. "Don't do this, Xander."

"Do what?"

"You've already decided you don't want me. So why play games?" She pulled back and stared. "Or is it about your ego? Must you show all these men that you possess what they desire? That you're the victor?"

He rubbed his face against her palm before letting go with a scornful laugh. "I was so angry with you, with your lies, your...act. But it wasn't about duping me, was it?"

"Of course not. None of this is about you."

Another self-deprecating laugh greeted her. Really, he was in a strange mood and Ani felt herself drawn deeper and deeper all over again. "Once, I imagined and even hoped that you, of all people, would understand the things we do to survive."

His gray eyes flickered with dawning understanding. "I do. I would have if I—" His jaw tightened impossibly. Whatever his reason was, it was swallowed up by his infuriating need for control.

"You didn't earn the right to my secrets, Xander. And just when I was beginning to think you had, you pushed me away."

He frowned. "You think I enjoyed hurting you further by walking away? It was necessary."

He sounded so unsettled—which was so uncharacteristic of Xander—that Ani was speechless for a moment. Did he really care that much that he'd hurt her? Did it bother him so much that he'd bought her act so thoroughly? Or did the truth make him face something else?

But she wouldn't, couldn't, afford to read more into his words than was there. Couldn't let him twist her inside out. This was supposed to be about doing a good thing for herself, not losing herself all over again in this temporary relationship, in *him*.

"You left me high and dry. You gave me pain and no pleasure like every other man I've ever known—"

"Damn, but you wield your words with such efficiency!"

"And then you went to seek yours," she burst out, far too gone in her jealousy to control herself.

His mouth flinched. "What?"

"Did you go to bed with her, Xander?"

"And if I did?" he asked, recovering already, silky challenge thrumming through each word. "Would you go back on our deal? Would you walk out on this fake marriage?"

How Ani wished she could say yes, but she'd worked too long and too hard to get here.

She looked up at him and realized he knew the answer. He knew she wouldn't give up her fortune. The truth certainly hadn't set her free; it had only made her more vulnerable to the one man who could crush her heart into so many pieces.

Because, it seemed, after all this time, she cared about Xander's opinion. She cared about him. Maybe it was the remnant of fond childhood memories, maybe because she kept seeing glimpses of the real Xander she'd once adored in his actions. Maybe because she was beginning to realize that, despite his veneer of control and ruthlessness, he had a heart that was capable of so much.

And it was impossible to unsee all that, to unsee all that they could be. All she could hope for was that she'd walk out of this arrangement richer and freer, but without losing herself to him. "I would politely remind you that Thea would not name you chairman if you stray before even two months are up."

"That is your opinion of me, *ne*? And you wonder why I walked away." Scorn dripped from his every word. "You think I would take your virginity, make you bleed and run into another woman's bed? What an understanding wife you are."

Frustration made her words come out serrated and shaky. "I don't know what to think, Xander. You asked for the truth and I gave it to you, and you walked away from that moment with such easy cruelty."

"Whatever else it was, it was not easy."

"It shouldn't have been possible at all," she bit out, anger scrubbing the pain away. She pulled back, refusing to give him any more of her pain. He hadn't earned that either. "So yeah, thanks for the reminder that you will go to any lengths to maintain your control and keep the upper hand."

"You think it was a power play?"

She sighed. "What else can it be?"

"I don't do well with lies. With surprises. With things being out of my control. With things not conforming to the narrative in my head."

Her eyes wide, Ani took in the flaring nostrils, the tic at his temple, the remote bleakness in his eyes. She wasn't sure if she liked that she'd forced him to explain, that she'd clearly caused him some kind of pain. "Is that an apology? Or an explanation? OMG, has the sky caved in yet?"

A smile barely touched the corners of his mouth. "Shut up and dance with me, Ani."

"Why?" Ani said, bracing herself against what his words did to her. Every time he said her name like that, with that possessive pride, she found herself stripped before him. "Give me one good reason why I shouldn't punch your face in for abandoning me like that, for leaving me to an empty suite for two nights?"

"Because I've been dying all evening to dance with my beautiful wife," he said instantly. "Ever since you walked out in that dress, with that tiara in your hair, looking like a queen. I recognized something about the girl I once knew in that woman tonight."

The husky honesty in his words undid Ani at a new, deeper level. He was telling her he saw her finally without saying it. That he saw her battles, her struggles, her flaws, her acts, that he saw...*her*. Her already flimsy resistance to him crumbled.

Ani was finally understanding how to read him, how she'd read him as a girl a long time ago without the confusion of adulthood. Commanding his wife to dance with him as Alexandros Skalas was different. He wore a mask as much as she did, only his was unyielding, near permanent, and fused into who he had to be in public.

But dancing with her after he'd admitted, without actually admitting it, that he'd been thrown by all the different facets of her was near miraculous.

"I'd love to dance with you," she whispered, afraid he'd hear her deepest dreams if she said them too loud.

He smiled fully this time and it was like a thousand free birds fluttering their wings in her chest. It felt like a beginning and an ending and Ani smiled back, finding the moment, and him, irresistible. And then he was dipping her deep into a dive, his arm tight around her waist. But she felt no fear of falling, only a weightless floating. And he saw that too.

She gave herself over to the tune, to the rhythm and to him. She lost herself in his tight embrace, in his scent, in the gray depths of his eyes.

He led them around the ballroom with a smooth grace that highlighted the wiry strength in his shoulders, the rock-hard thighs, the innate masculinity of him. But what cast a net around her heart and lured the foolish organ to play once more was his laughter. The pleasure written into his features as she joined in. His hands, his smiles, his moves... they enchanted her, caged her all over again in a new way just when she'd decided she needed to break free.

Applause broke out around them as they finished the dance with a flourish. Flushed, chest rising and falling, Ani looked up to find him watching her with a naked hunger that made her want to sob.

Why didn't he just give in and put them both out of their misery? What kind of a sadistic bastard denied himself what was willingly given and desperately wanted? How deep were his scars that he couldn't let go even in this way?

"Xander—"

"Give me one real thing about you," he interrupted her, dipping his head low until his mouth rested on her pulse. "Willingly."

She shivered at the sudden touch. "What? Why?"

His exhales coated the fluttering pulse at her neck, his fingers drawing lines over her spine. He was seducing her will away from her one word, one caress, one question at a time and he didn't even want her. No, he *wanted* her. He'd just decided he couldn't have her, for some ridiculous reason.

"Because I want to know you, Ani."

Ani... Somehow, his use of her nickname felt intentional, making a joke of the warnings in her head. "I'm tired. I would like to go to bed, please," she said, fighting the lure. But there was something in his tone—a need wrapped in a command—that made her pause.

He pulled back, his gray searching hers with a sudden urgency. "What would make you the angriest?"

"Letting my stepbrother win after everything he did to break me," she said. She was giving up a truth she'd never given voice to before, and suddenly, released into the sacred space between her and Xander, it lost its power; its hold on her.

She thought he'd probe and pick at the wound but the only sign that he'd even heard her was his hands tightening on her arms.

"What would make you the happiest?"

Kissing you. Seeing that desire in your eyes for me. Having you move inside me. Having you claim me for real. Belonging to you.

The answer came as easily and naturally as her breath, and it scared the hell out of her—how deep she was already in.

"Seeing my brothers," she said, going for her second choice. "I'd give anything to spend just a few minutes smushing them. They love me like no one else ever has."

She hadn't meant to say it like that, but she didn't regret the words either. She was tired of being afraid and pretending like she wasn't. She was tired of wanting so much and acting like she needed nothing.

His brow cleared as he nodded, then he walked her to their suite, hand resting at her lower back, and left her standing in the middle of the room, staring at his retreating back.

She couldn't help calling out his name. "Xander?"

He turned and Ani saw something she'd never seen in his face before. Ever. Regret darkened his eyes, leaving his mouth with a bitter twist. "Farce or not, I would not look at another woman, much less touch one when I'm married to you, *matia mou*. When I'm consumed by thoughts of you." He tucked his hands into the pockets of his trousers, his gaze touching every inch of her in a tender caress. "Go to bed, Ani."

She nodded, her heart settling from its mad, rabbiting pace for the first time that day. Because she believed him. And now she could sleep without wondering what about her had driven him away.

CHAPTER TEN

ANI AND XANDER returned to the villa in Corfu, and she slid back into the routine of running and playing her cello and hiding from him when he wasn't actively facilitating the distance between them by working. In front of Thea, their strange, wordless truce easily looked like a married couple settling into domesticity. Because even with the distance they both maintained, the charge between them was always there, striking into a conflagration at the most innocent of touches.

It seemed they were in some kind of holding pattern. His polite kindness and his concern for her were more torturous than all the contempt and dislike she'd faced for years.

Three days later, Ani heard the airborne thrum of two choppers. Dressed in tank top and shorts, she rushed to one of the overhang terraces that provided a breathtaking view of the island. The helipad showed four distinctive figures she'd recognize anywhere in the world.

Screaming, Ani ran down the stairs, barefoot, wet hair dripping thick clumps of water down her back. Excitement and joy swirled through her as she crossed the stretch of green that separated the house from the landing pad.

Ayaan, already taller than her by several inches, threw his lanky arms around her and she thought how much he'd changed in just two months. The middle one, Aryan, shyest of all, waited for her to greet him. And the little one, Ayush, handed her a slimy toad as a gift.

Ani tried—and failed—to fight the tears when Killian enfolded her in his arms.

At the familiar scent of his cologne and the solid comfort of his bear hug, a sob rushed out of her. Burying her face in his chest, she cried her heart out, unable to stop her emotional outburst.

The hairs on the nape of her neck prickled and she turned to find Xander on the highest terrace of the villa, watching them. Watching her.

Across the cliff of the mountain, across the distance—it seemed, across the universe itself—their gazes held. His, offering amends, and hers, desperately wanting but unable to reject it.

"What would make you happiest?" he'd asked, and this was the result. Would he give her what she *really* wanted if she asked?

Maybe he deserved her gratitude, but Ani couldn't see her way past the fear in her heart. She knew she hadn't processed all the emotions he'd been unlocking in her from the moment he'd come to save her at the church. She couldn't even offer him a nod.

He was twisting her inside out, and soon there would be no escape.

Cutting her gaze away, she lifted her young brother who instantly scrabbled over her back like a monkey, threw out a dare for a race and took off running while her two brothers kicked up sand at her heels.

She wondered at how her heart could be so full of joy and happiness and still want more. How she could be surrounded by people who loved her and still miss another. Still crave another. Still need another.

* * *

"You have given her a wonderful present, Xander," Thea said the moment Xander sat down to breakfast with her, three weeks after Annika's brothers had arrived at the villa.

More like an easy way to relieve his guilt, but Xander didn't say it.

Behind them, on the strip of the private beach, they could hear Annika and her brothers' raucous laughter and shouts. The villa had never been witness to such exuberant joy and antics.

Not even before his gentle mother had started drinking to cope with his father's brutal control. Not even before Xander's hero worship of Konstantin had been shattered when he'd found him terrifying Sebastian with a belt in his hand. Because, of course, Xander had been the perfect son, the perfect heir, the perfect firstborn, desperate for Konstantin's love and approval.

It was only when he'd displeased Konstantin by taking him on in defense of Sebastian that Xander had realized the kind of man his father was and how conditional his approval was. They'd never been an emotionally expressive family even before he'd understood just how broken they were.

It wasn't just Annika's brothers that were responsible for the tangible delight that had been reverberating through the empty walls of the villa.

It was her. She had turned a holiday for the boys into treasure hunts and beach races and hide-and-seek games and scary stories at night and sleepovers and early morning swims and excursions to explore the flora and fauna around the villa.

It was everything he and Sebastian had never known as boys, everything boys should grow up with. Everything Annika would give to her own children when she had a family with the man she loved—a future he could see so clearly now, whatever she did with her fortune.

The thought struck Xander like a fist to his solar plexus, knocking the breath out of him. It wasn't like he could banish her from his life forever after this was over, because she was his grandmother's goddaughter and his twin's best friend and she'd be his...*ex.*

Even if he somehow managed to remove her from his life, Xander had a feeling he'd never be able to purge her from his head. From his—

A sudden scream of laughter had him turning around.

Like an outsider watching through a dirty windowpane, he craned his neck to spot Ani carrying her youngest brother—the one she called Bug—on her shoulders and running into the waves lapping at her feet. She ran in and out, not even a little tired at carrying the boy on her back, endless in her enthusiasm for childish play and adolescent games.

In a hot pink tank top that was plastered to her chest thanks to the spray of water, and cut-off denim shorts hinting at the round globes of her glorious ass, she was temptation incarnate.

In three weeks, her appearance had changed drastically. From the suave, sensuous, perfect Skalas wife to this exuberant woman. She was always half wet, in shorts and tank tops, her hair full of sand, her skin tanned, her lips chapped thanks to the hours she spent with "her boys" down at the beach, exposed to the sea breeze.

She'd never looked more beautiful, for joy had etched itself into her features. And Xander wished he could always see her like that, as she was now, happy and surrounded by love. To arrange the very world to suit her needs.

She'd even bedded down with them on the floor with sleeping bags in Sebastian's wing, claiming Bug didn't want to sleep alone in a strange house.

He should have been relieved that there was no need to resist her every single time he walked into his bedroom. His bathroom counters were empty enough to see the gleaming black marble again, and his bedroom excruciatingly organized without her clutter, and his bed was empty and enormous without her spread-eagled on it.

There was no relief. Only a loneliness he'd never felt in his life before. They hadn't even properly slept together and she was already under his skin. He was running out of reasons why he couldn't treat this as a mutually pleasurable agreement.

It had been a valid question from Annika and he still didn't have an answer—not one that he understood and found acceptable. Because what he wanted was more than scratching an itch. More than the mutually convenient farce he'd planned. And that way lay an impossibility. A specter he didn't want to face. A painfully awful dive toward the deepest fear he'd never let surface before.

"Xander?" Thea prompted.

He rubbed a hand over his face. "I was getting tired of seeing a morose, miserable wife, Grandmama."

"I wish you would let yourself—"

"And I wish you had told me how much she suffered at her stepbrother's hands."

Consternation filled Thea's eyes. "Did she share that with you?"

"I surmised enough," Xander said, helplessness fueling his anger. "How could you leave her there, year after year?"

"He was her legal guardian, Alexandros. Still, I did not give up on her. Still, I fought to have her every summer. Annika is a proud creature. For a long time, even I didn't know how he much tormented her."

"Why not ask me to step in on her behalf?"

"Then I would become another person who takes away her choices, who takes away her power over her own life. She told me she didn't want to bring that misery here, that this was an escape. She is as proud and stubborn as you are, Alexandros. I have done all I could, all she would let me do."

"You suggested she marry Sebastian," Xander said, his mouth turning dry with anger and jealousy.

He'd been blind not to see it before now. Of course it had started at Thea's suggestion—a solution for the two people she loved most. He looked away, loath to let her see the betrayal he felt, the strange loss of something he hadn't even known he valued. It seemed now that if he acknowledged the tiny sliver of emotion he felt for Annika, everything else would flood in.

"I did not think you were right for her," Thea said, unflinching in her brutal honesty, saving him from spelling out his disappointment. "Ani deserves—"

Xander pushed back his chair with a hard scrape and shot to his feet. He knew what his young, innocent, strong-as-fire wife deserved.

One look at her was enough to know it.

Ani was the kind of woman men built families and legacies around, the kind who spawned legendary love stories. The kind who would fight for her love, for her children, against anyone, the kind who would spread sunshine wherever she went. The kind who loved from the very depths of their soul.

Having been a stranger to that kind of love meant he and Sebastian had a better awareness and understanding of what it meant and what it demanded and what it took. And crystal clear clarity about their own capabilities in the matter.

"I have a meeting," he said, and was about to leave when Killian Mackenzie and Ani arrived with their arms around each other.

The older man extended his hand toward Xander, gratitude shining in his eyes. "Thank you for arranging this trip. The boys needed it and I'm thrilled to see Ani so well looked after."

Next to him, his stepdaughter bristled at the comment and Killian laughed. "Don't begrudge me my gratitude, Ani."

"We don't have to prostrate ourselves in front of him, Killian. Arranging the trip is hardly more than a moment's effort for Xander," Annika said irritably.

"Hush, love," Killian said. "I'm sorry we've monopolized her so much. I didn't know until just now when Bug told me that she'd been sleeping by him. The scoundrel was taking advantage of her kindness and I'm sure she could have just—" The already ruddy man flushed, realizing what he'd been about to say. "Thank you, Mr. Skalas, for your generous hospitality."

"Please, call me Xander."

Killian nodded.

"Ani's family is ours too. You're welcome here anytime. All you have to do is call my assistant and she'll set up the flights." Xander was surprised to realize he meant the words. In his few dealings with Killian to ensure the smooth transfer of the funds Ani insisted on sending him, he'd learned of the older man's integrity. Understood the extent to which his business had been run to the ground through maliciously targeted actions taken by Ani's stepbrother.

He understood why Annika had fought for so long against Niven, instead of giving up. This man had given her something even her mother hadn't been able to. As was her nature, Ani was determined to pay back a thousandfold the kindness he'd done her.

The little time he'd spent with her brothers had been

enjoyable in a way he'd never known before. Not that her teenage brother had warmed to Xander. Whatever magic Sebastian had spun, Ayaan seemed to be firmly lodged in his twin's camp. Xander felt the most overwhelming urge to win the teenager over to his side. To win all her family members over to his side the only way he knew—by showering them with gifts and lavishing riches on them.

Which was ridiculous because he was a grown man and he didn't even want Annika's good opinion or her trust or anything more. *He didn't*, he repeated to himself.

"I'm glad you seem to know the way to Ani's heart," Killian continued, while Xander could only nod in silence. "It's like she's a completely different person from the Ani I've known all those years," he couldn't help adding.

Only then, finally, after three weeks of evading him, of fake smiles and platitudes in front of Thea, Annika met his gaze. He had no idea what she saw in his but she searched and probed before saying, "This was the best wedding present by far, Xander. Thank you."

The words were stiff, begrudgingly given, and ratcheted up the sudden awkwardness around them, making it tangible enough that his grandmother and her stepfather stared at them back and forth, as if it were a tennis match.

"I hope our presence hasn't created problems for you both. I'd never—"

"Xander and I don't live in each other's pockets. In fact, my husband prefers me not to be demanding and clingy. He prefers me to get my needs met through other means, instead of begging him for attention."

The words landed in the space between them like the gauntlet they were, drawing both Thea's and Killian's attention.

"Behave, Annika. The man let three rowdy, grubby boys

invade his home for three weeks. The least you owe him is a proper thank-you. A kiss, even," Killian said, determined to smooth out the ripples between them.

Raising a brow, Xander let Annika see the challenge in his eyes.

Exhaling on a heartfelt sigh, she crossed the distance between them, walking toward him like a martyr approaching the sacrificial pyre.

Her palm on his chest, she went up on her toes to kiss his cheek and something like the very devil stirred inside Xander. He wanted more than a peck offered under sufferance. He wanted everything.

Annika had shown him the shape of a future he'd never imagined for himself even in his wildest dreams. A future he wasn't equipped for.

For the first time in his life, he felt anger and a near painful powerlessness at everything he'd been robbed of by his parents. Of how much he'd lost by molding himself to be what was required. Of how much he didn't know of what it was to... But he wouldn't lose her. He wanted that future she'd showed him and he'd have it through other means, through every strategy available to him.

He turned at the last second so her mouth landed at the corner of his. Palms on his chest, she flinched, but didn't pull back. Sinking his fingers into her thick hair, he tilted her chin up and dusted away the thin layer of sand stuck to her jaw.

Then he bent and kissed her cheek, tasting sand and water and sun on her skin. He tasted joy and desire—everything he'd never known he wanted, much less needed. Even the acrid taste of fear in his throat couldn't stop him from gathering her tight in his arms.

How he'd missed the feel of her curves in his hands, her

scent in his nose, her taunts and her digs in his head. "If you've further damaged that tendon in your thigh after your adventures, I'll never invite them again."

Despite his growled threat, she settled into his arms with a soft groan, like a kitten coming in from the cold. "I didn't miss physiotherapy for one day."

"But you've lost weight in just three weeks," he said, feeling a strange tenderness well up inside him.

Her eyes widened, something shifting in her expression. Some of her anger melting away, he thought. "I haven't had an appetite since we returned."

He didn't pick up the gauntlet she'd thrown down. He spoke quietly. "Did you have enough time with them?"

She nodded. "Was that my reward for good behavior?" she asked softly, snuggling deeper into him, as if she meant to stitch herself into his skin. "Bringing my family here? Because I could get used to it."

"Could you?" he asked, tempted beyond distraction to promise her the world, to bind her to him with some new deal, to control the outcome of this game before she realized he was playing it for real.

What if that was how he was supposed to bind her to him? By using this inexplicable, relentless need between them, by making all her dreams come true…?

Xander calculated the risks, formulated the strategy, and tried to forecast the outcome. Because one thing he didn't know, and refused to even anticipate now, was losing.

Annika nuzzled her face into the hollow of his throat, knowing Xander was only allowing the intimacy for the sake of their audience. She'd missed crowding him in their bedroom, messing up his stuff in his study, missed being near him. She was such a loser when it came to this battle between them—while he probably didn't even consider it one. Or if he did, he believed he'd already won it.

"I could do this for a long time if the perks are this good. I'd have even come to you first instead of going to Sebastian," Ani added, wanting to thrust her own blade in just a little, wanting to see if this misguided distance was taking the same toll on him.

"Believe me, *pethi mou*. I'm well aware of my strengths and my weaknesses in comparison to Sebastian."

For the first time in her life, Ani didn't like the taste her words left behind. She straightened, shame heating her cheeks. "That was an awful thing to say. I'm—"

Xander held fast, refusing to let her pull away. "I can bear the cuts, Ani. You're used to fighting, *ne*? I'm too, for what I want." He palmed her jaw, looking at her as if she were a puzzle he was determined to decipher. "And this wasn't a reward, nor an incentive. Not punishment, not a deal."

She swallowed at the sudden rush of longing those words unlocked inside her. "To assuage your guilt, then?"

Some new resolve shimmered in his gaze. "No. I wanted to see your happiness."

The cello arrived three days later—one of the most expensive in the world, made in the eighteenth century by a master craftsman. It was even more precious than the one she'd unwisely touched at the hotel in Lake Geneva, and a sign from the universe.

So yeah, she didn't need a thirty-million-dollar cello as a sign, but she'd been considering applying to music college and getting a degree when she was finally free. She could practice on it until she wasn't Xander's wife. Treat it as a once-in-a-lifetime treat. Work on her skill. Be ready when this was…over.

For an hour, Annika walked around the cello, afraid to touch it, afraid even to breathe near it, making perambulations like a pilgrim around a temple. But even the awe in her heart at having access to such a beautiful instrument didn't outlast or outweigh the confused ache she felt for the man who'd bought the beautiful instrument for her.

What was Xander doing and why?

He lavished expensive, thoughtful gifts upon her and yet he barely touched her. In the three weeks since Killian and her brothers had visited, he'd barely been home. He'd had her flown out to meet him for a dinner on a yacht in Morocco for one night, where she'd played her role perfectly. Then he'd sent her home with a polite kiss on her cheek. He might as well have given her a gold star for good behavior.

"I wanted to see your happiness."

He'd said it with such determination and deliberation, but would he ever give *them* a chance? And yet, to her the words were magical because no one had wanted to see her happiness like he did. Every inch of her was beginning to believe that this farce was the realest thing in her life.

Fighting tears, Annika finally lifted the bow and drew it across the strings of the cello. The music she created instantly lifted her spirits, infusing her with a feeling of being alive, with courage and desire.

She was crying when she finished playing a while later, her arms and shoulders sore and tight. The instrument already owned a piece of her heart, as did the man who had given it to her. And she herself felt lighter, her mind clearer, free of fears thrust upon her by her stepbrother, or the secret wish she'd nurtured for years that if she was back with Killian and the boys, she'd somehow have her mom back, or the foolish hope that by protecting the boys, she'd somehow earn the approval of a parent who had left her behind.

Acknowledging the truth made her feel powerful. Ready. For the first time in her life, Annika could appreciate what she had and all the things she could have, all the things Xander would give her if she extended her hand. Her heart. It was all within her power.

The only question left was whether she'd dare do it, whether she could survive asking for everything.

Xander returned to the villa after being away for three weeks. The maximum amount of time he could stay away, while still being in control.

Ani had been beautiful and elegant at that soiree on the yacht sailing along the French Riviera, like a glittering gem with all its rough edges finally polished away. But not an act. Something had changed about her, as if she was finally emerging from the cocoon of smoke and mirrors.

When the cello player of the popular string quartet that had been hired to play for the evening had been absent, she'd stepped in. It was her first time playing in public, her first time sharing her music, and she'd shone. Xander had felt a possessive pride to see her up there, to know that she and her music and her wicked quips and her daring challenges all belonged to him.

A good thing he'd drummed it into his head at a very young age that his business trumped everything else, because it had been near impossible to drop her at the helipad.

And in those moments when he'd stood leaning against the car, watching her walk away toward the waiting chopper, with his jacket around her slender shoulders, her face turned over her shoulder, her eyes speaking to his across the distance, he'd known his plan could work, that the biggest risk he'd ever taken would pay off.

CHAPTER ELEVEN

IT WAS PITCH-DARK when Xander arrived at the villa close to midnight, to find it alarmingly silent. He checked his phone to see if he'd missed a call from Thea about a social engagement but there was none.

He undid his tie and rolled back his cuffs as he spotted a sleek figure swimming laps in the overhang pool attached to Sebastian's wing.

Moonlight sprinkled golden dust over long limbs swishing through the water. Reaching Sebastian's floor, Xander poured himself a glass of whiskey—his twin always had the good stuff—and went to sit by the pool. Beyond the pool, a view of the dark sea stretched out for miles, and the scent of wildflowers hung thick in the humid air.

It was a peaceful spot—something he'd never noticed before.

Annika instantly changed direction and swam toward him. With her usually unruly hair plastered to her scalp, the high cheekbones and her wide mouth came into stark relief. Stripped of makeup and all the armor she usually wore, she looked very young. Definitely too innocent for him. Not that it would stop him from taking what she offered. He wouldn't make that mistake again—not now that he knew all of her. Not now that he had a plan.

He could finally see what his actions had communicated

when he'd walked away from her that night in the ballroom. Not just a rejection of their intimacy or what had already seeded between them, but a rejection of everything she'd overcome. By treating her as fragile, he'd taken away her power. He'd become just another man who tried to control her.

"I didn't know you were coming home tonight."

Something about the casual, almost welcoming way she greeted him threw him. He looked inside the whiskey tumbler, cursing himself for all the missteps he'd made with her. "Is this home to you, Ani?"

He braced himself for a roundabout, flaky answer. She surprised him, yet again, and he wondered at how he could never be entirely sure he knew what she might say or do. But he liked that about her.

Her eyes glowed as she said, "Its allure dimmed for a while, but not anymore. Whatever happens in the aftermath of this—" she waved her hand between them "—it will always be home to me. Even if I'm not welcome here."

"It worries you that you might not be," he repeated, taking that in. "What would you have done when Sebastian and you separated? Or did you think you could really make the marriage work?"

"Anything I would've had with Sebastian is different from this, with you, Xander. There was never anything more than friendship between us. He helped me out and let Thea weave her fantasy about how the marriage might save him. Which is stupid enough because no one knows if Sebastian needs saving, much less himself."

Xander swallowed another gulp of whiskey, resenting the warmth that crept into her voice when she mentioned Sebastian. That he had lost her affection through his own actions wasn't lost on him. In fact, it was a pretty big indicator how the future would shape itself, given who he was. But he'd won before in his life, even when the odds had been stacked against him. And he would this time too.

"I changed my itinerary at the last minute," he said, picking up the question she'd asked. "I have to leave tomorrow morning again, though."

She rested her chin on her arms on the lip of the pool, studying him with an intensity she didn't hide. "I don't like staying here when Thea is away. The villa's too quiet and the nearest village too far to walk to."

"Use one of the cars in the garage."

"I don't know how to drive."

He frowned. "You're twenty-three. How can you not know?"

"I've lived in New York most of my life, and I had chauffeurs and bodyguards to drive me when I lived with Niven."

"I will have someone come in to give you lessons."

She pouted. "If I have to learn, I want you to teach me."

Surprise caught him in a chokehold. "That would not be a good idea, *pethi mou*. I'm not known for my patience. We'll be at each other's throats before we even leave the estate."

"Or maybe we'll rip each other's clothes off. I've never done it in a car. Either way, I'll learn something new."

Xander cursed, loud and long, but it didn't dispel the tension building inside of him.

"I'm not a fragile, wispy thing to be scared away by you, Xander. I've faced a real monster. And I—"

"I'm sorry, Annika." He pressed his whiskey tumbler to his temple, unable to meet her eyes. "I'm sorry that I did not see it."

"Not your fault."

"It is my fault, when you're part of the family."

"More like a hanger-on, you mean. You had no duty toward me, especially when you clearly pushed me away. And I still don't know why."

"Do not look for noble reasons behind my actions, Ani. Hear what they say."

"Not until they tell me what I want to hear."

His mouth dried at all the possibilities she painted with that answer. The minx was luring him in as well as if she were a siren singing her song. "You're stubborn."

"A lot like you. And I always thought we were total opposites."

He smiled then. It was impossible not to when she was in such a warm, playful mood.

"So you do plan to be away this long regularly?"

"I have a few big fires going on right now. Things I need to get in place to convince Thea to make the announcement."

"I never realized how hard you work. Sebastian definitely doesn't."

"Sebastian hates everything to do with the Skalas Bank and the legacy. If he didn't think it would hurt Thea immensely, he would have thrown his share of the pie at a charity a long time ago. Instead, he lets me handle his money and be his proxy in the boardroom."

"And you give him back millions of euros in profit."

"Are you looking for someone to manage your fortune, Ani?"

She laughed then, and he heard a freedom in it he'd never heard before. As if she'd let go of everything that had weighed her down before. "I'm just trying to understand what your life is like. It's not as one dimensional as I thought."

"Ouch."

She giggled this time and there was no way he could resist it. Resist her. He needed the taste of her in his veins, now.

He bent forward from the lounger and caught her mouth with his. She tasted like moon-kissed light and raw, artless desire and the darkest decadence.

She returned his kiss with a fervor he'd come to need as much as her taste. When she climbed out, he brought her into his lap, all the while nibbling away at her sweet lips. Urgency beat at him. Why had he wasted so many days?

He knew the answer, but this time desire beat out everything else.

She laughed against his mouth, drenching him, clinging to him, kissing him, devouring him with her little groans and mewls and demanding nips.

He filled his hands with her curves, need revving through him like wildfire. Her breasts were perfect in his hands, the nipples beading hungrily against his palms. Using his fingers, he pulled down the cups of the bikini top and flicked at the plump knots. She arched into his touch, thrusting them up, and Xander latched his mouth on to one brown nipple. Her raw groan rippled through her body and his.

Water drops from her hair hit him like wet lashes, and he wondered if they were sizzling on his hot, hungry skin. Drawing her deep, he suckled on her breast and she went wild. Her fingers descended into his hair, tugging and pulling, as he lavished the same attention to the other breast. Then she moved up on him, straddling him until they were locked.

"You're so wet," he murmured against the valley between her breasts, wanting to feel warm, silky flesh.

She giggled, dripping water onto his face, then found his mouth. "I'm thinking it's the bikini you're talking about?"

He grinned too. Their gazes met, and something passed between them, something bigger than them both, an unspoken communication. Almost a communion. And the fiery waif that she was, she didn't shy away from it.

Her hands clasped his cheek. A shaky exhale whispered out as she kissed him softly, tenderly, and Xander thought his heart might punch out of his chest. "If you give me two minutes," she said, rubbing her damp cheek against his mouth, "I'll shower and smell minty fresh."

"No," he said, pulling away the thread of the flimsy bikini around her neck. Her breasts fell into his palms, as did a soft gasp from her mouth as he kneaded the soft weight. "Sebastian fills that damn pool with mountain water. As for you..." Pushing her onto her knees, he pulled off her bikini bottoms. From a table next to the lounger, he grabbed a towel and wiped her down.

He took his time with every curve and dip, touching and licking the flesh he wiped dry, learning every inch of her. A sudden breeze drifted over them and she shivered. He pulled her closer while she busied her fingers with his shirt buttons, sudden tension wreathing her.

"Look at me, Ani," he said, trying to make it a request and failing.

She looked up and he thought he could see her heart in those big brown eyes. He cursed himself for not recognizing the bounty she was all these months.

"You're shaking, *agapi mou*," he said, running his palms softly over the goose bumps on her silky smooth flesh. The words fell easily from his lips.

"I can't take another rejection," she said, on a broken whisper. "You're the only thing I've reached for in my life for myself. Maybe I should've told you that instead of playing games. But my life has been—"

"Shh... Ani," he said, gathering her close. Instead of offering empty reassurances, he ran his thumb down her belly button to the jut of her sex. He played with the swollen bundle of flesh that had popped out of its hood and stood proudly, demanding his attention. He traced every inch of her folds and went further down, notching a finger at her entrance.

Damp arousal flooded his fingers. Damn, but she was ready and so was he. Holding her gaze, he unzipped his trousers and freed his shaft. The mere touch of his own fingers made pleasure surge through him. He notched the tip at her entrance, bathing himself in her welcome wetness.

On her knees, she undulated her spine, leaning in and away so that she rubbed herself against him. Playing with him. Teasing him. Casting a lure so wide and so deep that he thought he might never get out of it.

One hand on her hip, he thrust inside her on one of her downward movements and all the world seemed to cease around them. She gasped and closed her eyes.

Breath serrated in his throat, Xander waited with patience he didn't know he had. He pressed his mouth to the curve of her breast, while sending his hands to stroke down her damp back, wanting to soothe her.

She writhed in his hands, moving forward and back, pulling those hips up and down in tiny movements, testing the fit, learning and chasing her pleasure. It was the most erotic sight Xander had ever seen. "You're a natural at this," he said, catching her lower lip with his teeth.

She sank into the touch and nipped him back. "Nah. I researched it. I just need a little more to get used to you. To this."

He smiled. "Take your time."

Lifting her hands to her hair, she stretched like a cat. "This feels good, Xander. So good. You?"

"It's perfect, Ani. You're perfect."

With every slide and shift and slip of her hips, pleasure raced down his spine like lightning, gathering in his balls.

He tightened every muscle in his body against the oncoming spiral, against instincts urging him to move, thrust and pound into her.

"Okay, thanks for your patience. That slight pinch is fading," she said, in a husky voice, rubbing her breasts against his chest, her palms stroking every inch of his taut, muscles. "Now can I have more? All of you?"

He looked into her eyes, his jaw tight, holding on to the last thread of control. "I'll stop anytime you want me to, if it gets too much."

She nodded, pulling farther out of his reach, but he arrested her movement. "I know. Xander, oh, Xander, it hurts not to have you move, not to have you all the way. I want you to take what you want and give me what I want. Hard. Fast. I want everything now."

He took her words for what they were and with an upward thrust of his hips, he lodged himself all the way inside her. She clenched around him like a velvet glove, a pulsing hot one. He groaned at the delicious burn spreading through him.

Hands on her hips, he pulled her up and slammed her down, and they groaned in unison. Again and again and again, until all he could feel was her—her tight sex, her soft groans, her near sobs.

"This is what you denied me last time?" she demanded. "I should kill you!"

He laughed and they were kissing again, and slowly she caught on to his rhythm. She scraped her nails over his shoulders, her breath coming through in soft pants.

"Tell me what you need, *agapi*," he said, pressing his mouth to her long neck. Feeling her pulse between his lips. "What shall I do to push you over?"

"I don't know, Xander, everything feels too good. Don't

stop moving." Then with an artless abandon, she brought his hand to her clit. When he pinched it between his fingers and rubbed, she threw her head back and clenched him harder with her sex.

Xander let her set the pace, drinking in the voluptuous picture she made. He upped the pace of his fingers and when she made those sounds that told him she was close, he nipped at her nipple. She fell apart with a soft scream he wanted no one else to hear and then he flipped her over, until her back hit the lounger and he took what he wanted from her.

He pounded into her, urgent need licking a flame through him, and when his climax came, it was with an abandon he'd never known, with a depth of feeling that mocked all of his strategies and his plans.

Within minutes, her damp flesh turned cold. Xander gathered her to him, wishing he could tell her with words how incredible it had been.

"That was…amazing," she said, sounding awed. "Was it for you too? Or is it always like this?"

"It's never like this," he said, clearing his throat. "Chemistry is inexplicable."

"Oh, good. I did okay?"

He tightened his arms around her, wondering how he'd never seen the self-doubt and the vulnerability in her before. How had he been so blind? "You were better than okay. I've never had sex out of a bed—forget out in the open, by a pool, where anyone can see us. You drive me…insane, Ani."

She giggled suddenly and he wanted to know why. He wanted to know everything about her. "OMG, I can't wait to tell Sebastian what we did to his lounger, by his pool. For once, I can shock the pants off him and not the other way and—"

He covered her mouth with his hand. "I'd prefer it if you didn't remember my brother when you're naked in my arms. Or share details about us with him."

"Are you jealous, Xander?"

"About the ease he has with you, about the affection in your words when you speak of him, yes." He marveled at how easily the admission came. Wondered if it could truly be that simple, at least, on the surface. "I've always been jealous of the hold he has on you."

"He's like a brother to me, Xander."

"A brother you would've married."

"That was an arrangement."

"That could have led to—"

"*No.* I wouldn't have slept with Sebastian. I know you don't get it, but that's not how this works. That's not how any of this works."

Silence descended between them, full of her anger and his lingering doubts. He didn't know how to tell her that it wasn't her he doubted. It was his own flaws. He would always be jealous of whatever she shared with Sebastian because he wanted it.

He wanted all of whatever she had to give. Every smile, every word, every hug, every kiss, every little piece of her vulnerable, generous heart.

"Let's go in. You need a shower."

"I can't move."

"I'll carry you."

"Can we stay here? Please? For two minutes?"

He didn't miss the wariness in her voice. Standing up, he straightened his clothes, grabbed a washcloth and ducked into the shower stall. Leaning one knee on the lounger, he gently nudged her knees open and patted her down with the washcloth.

"Thank you."

He pressed a kiss to her shoulder in reply, settling himself back against her. It was strangely disquieting how easily the intimacy came and how much he craved it. For her part, Annika didn't seem even a little surprised by it.

"Your mother's ring…" she said, a sudden clarity to her voice. "I've left it on your nightstand. I'd apologize for taking it but it wouldn't be honest."

Xander stilled behind her. For weeks he'd wanted to bring up that ring. But whatever outrage he'd nursed against her had fizzled away, leaving only curiosity. "Why did you take it?"

"I stole a few things from the first man Niven forced me to get engaged to. A family heirloom, his sister's expensive bag, a bottle of expensive drugs… It was a way to make them dislike me, to break off the agreement. The next summer, when I visited, you wouldn't look me in the eye. I mean, we were never friends like Sebastian and me, but suddenly you acted like I was dirt."

"Ani—"

"I thought, he loathes me anyway, so let me steal something from him."

"Why the ring?"

"It was the one thing you cherished. I hated the thought that you'd give it to Diana. I hated that you…pushed me to the margins of your life. I wanted to take something from you that held your heart."

Shock punched through his chest, as if someone had defibrillated his heart to wake him up. *"Annika…"* he said, an admonishment and an entreaty rolled into that single word.

"I know what I'm saying, Xander," she said, patting him on the arm as if to soothe him. "I knew your kindness even when all you showed the world was your ruthlessness."

"I do not know whether you are foolish or brave."

"A little of both? You gave me something I've never had."

He whispered something in her ear and she laughed and slapped his arm. Eyes twinkling, she looked over her shoulder at him. "That too, yes. And it was very…mighty and grand and big and thick and—"

"Minx," he said, taking her mouth in a hard, deep kiss that had them wriggling against each other like teenagers in a car.

"Shall I tell you a secret," she whispered against his lips, taunting him, "or keep it to myself forever?"

It felt as if the entire foundation of his life hung on the answer to her question.

Turning back, she nuzzled her back into his chest, and he held her to him, as he'd never done with another soul. "I think I'll hold on to it."

No words had ever made Xander feel such relief and yet such devastating loss.

As incredible as it sounded, Ani and Xander had been married for four months. He still traveled a lot and Ani practiced her cello, and when he invited her to join him for a business dinner or a charity gala or a networking event, she flew to him.

In the last month alone, she'd joined him in Tokyo, Jakarta and Paris. He never let her stay more than one night. They attended whatever important meeting he wanted her to be at, had mind-blowing sex when they returned to their hotel suite and usually he was gone when she woke up the next morning. A scribbled note would be waiting for her.

See you at home, Ani.

Ani had stashed all seven notes written in his hand on the most luxurious stationery from beautiful historical hotels in her keepsake box. It was as if she and Xander were marking a trail of their journey toward each other on the map. As if every city and hotel was standing witness to them. Apparently, beneath all the practicality she'd drilled into herself, she was an incurable romantic.

They had met her stepbrother, Niven, at the Plaza in New York on one such business trip. She'd almost begged Xander not to taint it with that meeting but in the end she had kept silent. With a perceptiveness that still amazed her, Xander had known how disturbed she'd be at the sight of the man who'd tormented her with his mind games.

For the first time in her life, Annika hadn't come away from the meeting wanting to throw up or scratch her nails down Niven's face. Xander hadn't said one threatening word to him. In fact, he'd been downright polite. But Ani had seen the ripples in the power dynamic, had seen Niven realize that he was now facing a much bigger predator.

Then, to her shock, Xander had spent the rest of the afternoon with her and her brothers, throwing a ball and chasing their dog in Central Park. As if he'd known that Ani had needed to shed the fear and disgust from the two hours she'd spent in Niven's company.

She realized how wrong she'd been to think that he and Niven were cut from the same cloth. Not when Killian had confirmed that Xander had already set things in order to personally invest in Killian's business, to give it a boost after the malicious losses of the recent years. She'd buried the truth to protect herself.

All of Xander's actions in the last few months felt personal and her foolish heart equated it to an emotion that she was yet to see enter his eyes or fall from his lips.

She didn't push for fear of fracturing the little they had. It was an intense physical connection and a strange sort of friendship, maybe even a deep understanding of the past that had shaped them. And a commitment to their own goals. It was a strange but satisfying mishmash of things that she wasn't sure were enough to make a relationship last.

But the funny thing was that she was happy. She wanted to see where they'd go from there, if time would deepen the fragile bond that was forming between them despite themselves.

In moments of utter madness, she even found herself hoping that Niven's diabolical mind would come up with some fresh strategy to prolong the delay in releasing her trust fund so that she could stay married to Xander.

CHAPTER TWELVE

THE PRODIGAL GRANDSON returned to the villa one bright July morning as Ani breakfasted with Xander and Thea in the front gardens. Sebastian appeared out of thin air, strolling down the cliffside toward their table, looking as dashing and handsome as ever.

Ani stared, shocked at how different he suddenly seemed. There were a million little details that differentiated him from Xander, and then there was how her heart could be so easy and light with Sebastian whereas with Xander, everything she felt was deeper, brighter, fuller.

Sebastian smiled more, though it was fake. He had a languid ease to his movements that was also fake. Then there was that perpetual mockery that filled his gray eyes.

And through her cataloging, Ani could feel Xander's gaze on her, drinking in her reaction to his twin. She didn't dare meet it, afraid of what he'd see in hers. Pursing her mouth, she picked up her coffee cup and took a sip while Sebastian kissed Thea's cheek with an effusiveness that made the older woman blush, and then gave a nod to Xander.

When Sebastian bent toward her, she pushed her chair away and shot to her feet, terrified that he'd see straight into her heart and declare in his usual mischievous way that she'd finally fallen in love.

She stumbled as the realization hit her with the force of a well-placed punch.

Xander had been relentlessly kind to her for the last two months and kindness always confused her, for she was a stranger to it. He catered to her deepest wishes, and any woman—especially one like her who had never had a real boyfriend or a real relationship—would be drawn in by his attentions. As for the sex, it was phenomenal, but that was chemistry and Xander was a man who never did anything less than perfectly. Didn't mean she was in love with him, did it?

"Still angry?" Sebastian asked, approaching her slowly.

She folded her arms. "You didn't even have the decency to send me a text, you brute."

"But I sent the next best thing. Or should I say, I sent someone better than even me?"

Ani's mouth twitched but she was damned if she would forgive the rogue so easily. "Tell me you weren't rolling around in some woman's bed and I'll forgive you."

He opened his mouth and closed it.

Outraged, she threw a filthy curse at him in Greek—one he'd taught her—and marched away.

He chased her.

Ani ran.

Sebastian ran.

Ani sped up.

He caught her and threw her over his shoulder like he used to when she was a bony ten-year-old forever following him around, and ran like a madman in circles until her head was swimming and she didn't know what was up or down. "Let me go, you brute!" she screamed, half laughing, half sobbing.

He stilled, laughing. Over his shoulder, he watched her

face. "You look like you've been thoroughly and frequently sexed up. It's a good look on you."

Ani gasped and pounded his back with her fists. "You're such a—"

"I think the lady doth protest too much."

"Don't, Sebastian."

"Don't observe that you're practically glowing and while that might be because of frequent good sex, it might be because you're deliriously happy?"

"All that…don't. No games, please. Not with me. Not with him." Her heart crawled into her throat and it wasn't just because of gravity. She couldn't bear it if something Sebastian said fractured the fragile thing between her and Xander. And for all Sebastian had been her only true friend for so long, this was too private, too…precious for her to talk about. "All this is…temporary, mutually beneficial."

"Is it?"

"Yes. I'm having fun, Sebastian. Isn't that what you're always recommending? Live like a twenty-three-year-old? Sow my wild oats? Don't take life so seriously?"

"That's all you want?"

She nodded, burying every fragile wish and hope beneath a false smile. She didn't want either Thea or Sebastian interfering, playing her advocate, and somehow either guilting or arguing Xander into making this permanent. She wanted Xander to want her for herself. She wanted him to want to spend the rest of his life with her because he couldn't live without her.

Sebastian looked almost disappointed. Though that was momentary. "I guess this fairy godmother only brought you good sex, then?"

Firm, strong hands plucked her off Sebastian's shoulder before she could respond. Ani would know the touch in her sleep. Her feet hit the ground, even as half of her clung to Xander's side. She hid her very revealing blush in his chest, loving his possessive hold of her. "Enough, Sebastian. She has a bruise on her thigh that you will disturb if you throw her around like a bag of sugar."

Sebastian watched them, brows raised, not missing anything. "Your wife is no fragile flower."

"She's *my* wife, though. And I would thank you to—"

"She was my friend first. My rights trump yours."

Xander stilled next to her, a sudden tension clamping down on him, and it translated to her immediately. She wished she didn't know him so well, but she did. In his tension, in his hesitation, she saw his vulnerability. His reluctance to claim her, even in front of his twin. His inability to commit to this, even as a joke.

And her heart broke a little for him and for herself.

Ducking under his arm, she slipped out of his grasp. "I'm not going to be the bone you fight over."

Her knees were shaking under her as she returned to Thea, wondering if being in love with him meant the little she did have of him would never be enough.

Thea surprised them ten days later with an impromptu party. Ani and Xander had refused one multiple times, tired of the social circuit they'd been on for almost three months. But Thea had warmed to her and Xander together so much that she had apologized to Ani for interfering in her life, which only made Ani feel doubly guilty and desperate to confide in Thea that she'd truly fallen in love. Except Ani thought Thea already knew it. Sebastian knew it too. Killian had taken to teasing her on the phone. Even her teenage brother Ayaan knew it.

Only Xander didn't, and she so desperately wanted to

tell him, but the thought of losing what little they did have stopped her.

At the announcement of a party, Ani dressed hurriedly in a floral white summer dress that clung to her breasts, put her hair into a loose side braid and perched a flower on the side. When she'd rifled through her drawer looking for a missing tube of lipstick, she found a small green velvet box under her pajamas.

Annika rubbed the soft nap of the box, her heart progressively inching into her throat. She flicked the lid open with her thumb and tears filled her eyes.

It was Xander's mother's ring, a sapphire set in yellow gold, the one she'd returned to him. The foolish, hopelessly in love part of her wanted to put it on. But he hadn't given it to her, had he?

He'd simply slipped it into her clothes drawer and the gesture—or the lack thereof—wasn't lost on her. If she wasn't careful, she'd spend the rest of her life desperately looking for hidden meaning in Xander's actions when there was none.

She arrived downstairs, flustered and hurt, to find Xander waiting for her at the foot of the stairs. He took her hand and it was clear he'd wanted to see his mother's ring on her finger. But before Ani had a chance to demand that he give it to her, Thea beckoned them.

Cousins and family friends and aunts and uncles, most of whom she'd met a few times, greeted her with an extra dose of exuberance that made Ani frown. In the midst of it all, Thea dropped her bombshell, with less pomp and circumstance than Ani would have expected, especially after all the hoops she'd insisted Xander jump through: she announced to the stunned company that she had nominated him as the chairman of Skalas Bank, effective immediately.

Suddenly, Ani understood the deference that was being offered to her. Because she was Alexandros Skalas's wife, the future Skalas matriarch, the woman who could wield as much power as Xander himself could, with their own individual fortunes.

That night, Xander didn't come to bed for a long time. The last she'd seen him, he'd been deep in talk with Thea, so Ani had bidden a thoughtful-looking Sebastian good-night and retired.

Now, having woken up and reached for Xander, she found the bed cold. She was debating if she should go looking for him when she heard the bathroom door open. Right on cue, the shower turned on. Grabbing Xander's pillow, she nuzzled her face into it, chasing his scent.

Just thinking of how he moved inside her, how many times he'd pushed her over, made Ani's body thrum with instant need. Feeling hot under the sheets, she threw them off. Her mind turned back to the evening.

She'd congratulated Xander on his victory, as surprised as he seemed to have been. Clearly, Thea had kept it to herself until the last minute. But Annika hadn't been quite able to parse his mood out. He'd been…less than happy, if that word could be applied to Xander, ever.

Not that any of his family or cousins could read his mood. To them, he was the juggernaut behind Skalas Bank, and he would remain so for their lifetimes, ensuring their stock options and their children's trust funds stayed fat and prosperous.

She knew Sebastian had noticed Xander's strange mood. He'd even probed her for the cause, but for the first time in her life, Annika had avoided her friend's gaze. Whatever troubled Xander, she didn't want to discuss it with his twin.

She felt protective about her husband, which just proved how ridiculous all of these feelings were.

Being in love with Xander was a high and a low and every crazy in between.

Her heart gave a mighty thump like it always did when he came to bed. After all these weeks, she still wasn't quite used to sharing it with him. To having him right there if she extended her arm. To find him pulling her to him in sleep, wrapping his arms and legs around her as if she were his favorite soft toy. To be woken up at all times of the night by his soft whispers and sweet caresses and, sometimes, filthy demands.

If he was insatiable with her, she was even more so with him. Her hunger for him seemed to have no end or bottom, forever filled with an urgency and fear that it might be over soon.

"I am sorry I disturbed your sleep," Xander said in a rough voice.

Ani turned and looked up.

Dressed in gray sweatpants, his chest still damp from his shower, he was watching her. With the moon hiding behind clouds, Ani couldn't make out his expression.

"I—" she licked her lips, feeling his gaze there "—reached out for you. Your side of the bed was cold and that woke me up." Cheek cradled in her palm, she exhaled. "I have gotten used to sleeping by your side. I don't like waking up alone."

His fingers came into her hair, though he made no other move to join her. Ani closed her eyes and sighed as he sifted the strands. "That is not a good idea, Annika. There is a lot more traveling in my future."

He said it easily, in his usual matter-of-fact tone, but Ani heard something else in those few words. A warning. A rebuke. A...hesitation.

But she wasn't ready for this bubble around them to break, for reality to intrude, for all of the conditions and deals they'd made to poison this sweetness. And from that fear came anger. Her spine always came back up when she was pushed. "If nothing else, it's something to put on a future dating profile—Annika Saxena-Mackenzie-Skalas likes sex and cuddling."

The night lamp came on and he moved to block its glare from falling in her eyes. She didn't know what to make of this man who protected her from everyone and everything and who gave her everything except the thing she wanted most. "That mouth needs to be punished."

Desire trickled down her spine like melted honey as images and ideas scrambled her brain. She pushed up to her elbow. The flimsy strap of her silk negligee slipped down, baring the tops of her breasts. His gaze feasted on her, and her own went to where his arousal was now clearly outlined.

And while he watched her like a hawk, Ani ran her thumb over her lower lip and then traced the shape of his erection. "Punishment…reward, *po-tay-to…po-tah-to*," she said, inching upward on the bed toward him until her mouth was near his thigh. "I think the secret to a long, happy marriage is calling it whatever the hell you want it in your head."

He grinned, his pupils already blowing out the grays. "Is that what you want, Ani? A long, happy marriage?"

Ani didn't answer. Instead, she slowly tugged the band of his sweatpants down until her prize shot up toward her. Pushing her hair away, she fisted his hard length and felt the answering dampness at her folds.

Xander stood unmoving but the grunt that fell from his mouth sounded savage in the pregnant silence.

Bracing herself on one elbow, Ani fisted him up and down, just the way he liked. That bloodthirsty streak she had observed in herself when it came to him flowed through her again. She knew his likes and wants and what could break through his ironclad control; maybe she even knew what was in his heart. "I thought men loved blow jobs. How come you've never asked me to do this?"

Lust etched into his features so that Xander looked stark, almost forbidding. He clasped her cheek with a reverent tenderness that threatened to unravel her one last secret. "I wanted it to be your choice."

"I want to go down on you. I want to blow your mind. Will you show me how to make it good? And I don't want any of your gentle bullshit. I want you to use me and my mouth however you need to get off." She licked the soft tip and looked up again. His breath was a sibilant hiss, a melody to her ears. "I want your...destruction."

He cursed. "I can't bear to hurt you, *agapi mou.*"

"You won't. You'd never, Xander." She opened her mouth and closed it over the head of his shaft, and made a humming sound.

Fingers descended into her hair, and his hips thrust forward jerkily, and she realized he was trying to control himself even now. It lit a fire under her. Moving her hand from base to tip, Ani took a little more of him on the second try. This time, she felt his fingers in her hair, pressing in time with his thrust, a curse ringing out from his mouth, over and over again.

She planted her other hand on his abdomen for purchase and felt the clenched throb of his muscles there. On one exhale, she tapped his hard length against her lips and felt his full-body shudder.

"Damn, Ani. How did you—"

"I watched some stuff to see how to do it. Is it working?" Ani took his curse as assent and continued. Her jaw ached and her core ached and she continued anyway because she wanted Alexandros Skalas undone at her hands, at her mouth. For a while, his thrusts turned rougher and jerky before he pulled out of her mouth.

She wiped the saliva from the corner of her mouth, and pushed her hair out of her face. Raking her nails over his abdomen, she held him there. "I want you to finish. In my mouth. I want—"

Leaning down, he kissed her, swallowing away her protest. "Shh, wildcat. I've used you roughly enough for your first time," he said, his voice a warning.

"But I want you to—"

He kissed her cheek and then her temple, his hard length wedged against her belly in a rough brand. Then he pushed her back onto the bed and covered her with his hard body, just the way she liked it. "Shall I do what I want with you, Ani? Shall I go harder, Ani? Take you faster? Ruin you for anyone else?"

For just a fraction of a second, Ani didn't respond. For one thing, it was impossible to respond when her entire body was a mass of sensations with Xander pinning her with his hips and doing that thing that made her eyes roll back. For another, his question had a savage edge to it that she both loved and hated. Loved because she wanted him to see her as an equal here, needed it; hated because, even in the midst of pleasure spiraling through her, she didn't misunderstand the portent of something in his words.

Her hesitation lasted only another breath.

The stubborn, ruthless man that he was, he made her climax twice for all the "hard work" she'd put in with him. Her pleasure had been so drawn out, so acute that she thought she might have blanked out for a few seconds.

Skin damp and muscles trembling, lungs fighting for

breath, Ani fell back against the bed. Xander followed her until his entire weight covered her.

Throwing her arms around his sleekly muscled back, Ani sighed in bliss. She loved it when he gave her this—all of him. Loved being pushed into the mattress by his weight. Loved fighting for breath under his broad chest. Loved when he enveloped her until her world was nothing but him and how he looked at her. Loved it when words trembled on her lips, begging to be released.

She shuddered with the effort to contain them.

Xander rolled away, taking her with him. Ani scooted closer until her back was plastered to his chest and she could hear his thundering heartbeat. His mouth was at her shoulder and his arms held her tightly.

They stayed like that for a long while and it was the happiest Annika had ever been in her life. This was it, her dream of all dreams. And she wanted to hang on to it, wanted to nurture it and build a future on it.

When she looked back at him, a wary shutter fell over his eyes instantly. She swallowed, and rubbed her nose against the bicep he'd curled around her neck. He was damp and sticky and she loved his scent in these moments. "You're in a strange mood tonight."

The same tension she'd seen in him the last few days— ever since Sebastian's return—thrummed through his body. She felt his mouth over her shoulder, his fingers drawing invisible lines on her hip. "I do not have strange moods."

"I prefer your blistering honesty, Xander. That way I always know where I stand with you."

"And you want to know where you stand with me, *agapi*? Does it make you anxious?"

"Yes, well, turns out I'm a people-pleaser in a relationship. Especially with you. After all, you're the giver of expansive, expensive gifts and I like being—" turning around, she waggled her brows suggestively "—on the receiving end."

Laughter lines crinkled out from the corners of his eyes and she wondered if he laughed more these days in general or if she was imagining things the way she wanted them. "You don't care about those gifts, Annika. And the things you do care about—"

She pressed her mouth to his cheek, gratitude and love twining through her in an overwhelming wave. "You're taking care of those."

Something serious dawned in his eyes. "You should not make a habit of depending on me for everything."

Rubbing her thumb against the corner of his mouth, she said, "It's a bad habit, I know. But the thing is, no one's ever done that for me before. No one has ever made me feel like what I want matters and—"

"Ani—"

"Yes, yes, I know, Xander. You're doing all these things because you feel guilty and because you're just naturally a protector and because it's what you'd have done for any woman you'd fake-married. There, did I cover all the bases?" she said, secretly and silently begging him to refute all her claims. Wanting him to tell her that he did all those things because her happiness mattered to him.

"I am unsettled, yes," he said, sitting up against the headboard and dragging her upright until she was half over his lap, half clinging to him.

"You didn't seem happy today. You don't seem…satisfied at Thea's announcement."

He looked at her then, his gaze holding hers but keeping its secrets. "Thea apologized for stringing me along with conditions all these years for the chairmanship even though

I had earned the right more than a decade ago. She told me today's announcement came about because of you."

It wasn't the answer to her question and yet Ani couldn't stop asking. "What?"

"She said you made her see how unfair she has been to me. That she'd always demanded too much of me. 'Dumping the burdens of the family and the bank and the legacy all on his head even though he is no older than Sebastian,' apparently were your exact words."

Heat kicked up her cheeks and she shrugged. "Yes, well. You know my feelings on the subject." She frowned. "You're unhappy that I interfered?"

"Of course not."

Xander pushed a hand roughly through his hair and leaned his head back, wishing for the first time in his life that he was a different man. Wishing that the mindless pleasure of a few minutes ago wasn't the last time he made love to his wife. Wishing Ani hadn't changed him, wishing he didn't see the only way left to him was to give up the one and only thing he'd truly wanted, and needed, in his life.

"Please, Xander, tell me what's going on."

He shouldn't be surprised that Ani could see into his mood so clearly either. "For the first time in my life, I have been caught unawares. For years, becoming the chairman of Skalas Bank was my sole ambition."

"And now?" Ani said, her heart in her eyes.

"Thea has decided to travel for the next two years," he said, evading her question. He didn't know the answer even if he wanted to give it to her. For so long, all he'd cared about was the bank. But now...now that he had achieved his goal, it felt empty. And his twin's probing questions of the last few days had only shaken the foundation of his entire game. And today, finally, he knew what he needed to do. Fear gripped him with its cold fingers, leaching every bit of warmth he'd taken from Ani.

"Thea didn't tell me anything about that," Ani said, straightening, reminding him that he had to tell her without hurting her.

"I found out by accident. She is adamant about traveling and will not listen to Sebastian's admonishment that she is too old." He gently rubbed a finger over her lips. "I think you have caused ripples that even you do not understand."

"Is that a good thing or a bad thing?"

"It's a thing," he said, throwing her own words back at her. And then, because he couldn't bear to do what he needed to do while she touched him, he gently untangled himself from her and shot to his feet.

"Xander? What's going on?"

"With Thea's announcement and her travel plans, and some of the things I'm trying to figure out about the conditions attached to your trust fund, it might be better if you stay with Killian in New York for a few months. That way, you're close by for any legalities regarding the trust fund."

On her knees on the bed, the straps of her negligee loose over slender shoulders, her hair a magnificent mess around her face, she looked breathtaking. Her lips trembled but fighter that she was, she pursed them. "What about Alexandros Skalas needing a wife for all the charities and society galas that Skalas Bank hosts? What if Thea takes her nomination back and—"

"She can't. It is done."

"She trusts us not to…cheat her, right? Not to make a mockery of things?"

"I think we have already done that, *pethi mou*." Coward that he was, Xander could not look at her. "Thea will understand that I don't want to leave you here alone while I travel for weeks at a time. As for the optics of our marriage, lots of high society couples live independent lives. There is no reason you should put your life on hold. Your family, your friends are in New York. You wanted to apply to music college, right? Why not get started on that?"

She laughed but there was no warmth in the sound. "You just told me not to depend on you for everything and you've already made plans for me. And music college was just me rambling."

"Why should it be?" he said, turning around. "Why should you not go after what you want, for yourself and no one else? You are far too talented not to nurture it, Ani."

"What did I do wrong, Xander?" she said, shoulders squared, ready to fight it out with him.

He took her into his arms then. She threw her arms around his waist like she used to as a child and he pressed his mouth to her hair, his entire body shaking. His heart felt like it might punch out of his chest. "You didn't do anything wrong, *agapi*. You never did. Not now. Not then. I am the one who…" The wet splash of her tears against his chest burned him. "Thea's announcement…led to us discussing other things. Things that I have never faced, things I have hidden from Sebastian. Things I have done in foolishness, like pushing you away with the flimsiest of excuses. Things I planned even last month that I…" He looked into her eyes, his hands cupping her shoulders.

"What have you hidden from Sebastian?"

"I never told him that Mama wanted to take him along when she left Konstantin. She had all his stuff tucked away and ready to go."

Her mouth flattened, and a flash of fire sparked in her eyes. "And you?"

He shook his head. "Only him."

Ani pressed a hand to her temple, her lips trembling. "How could she have… That's cruel."

Xander shrugged, as he'd always done, although this time, he knew his indifference was a lie. "There are a lot of things that I told myself didn't matter, Ani. Only to realize I'm a fool."

Suddenly, her arms went around his waist and she hid her face in his chest and he held her loosely, scared that if he tightened his hold, he'd never be able to let go. All his schemes and strategies and risks would mean nothing even if they succeeded, if he didn't have what he wanted most.

"I'll agree," Ani said, pressing her mouth to his chest, "if you swear you aren't just…retreating from this."

"I'm not," Xander said, lying through his teeth, hoping she would forgive him when she learned the truth.

"I want another wedding present if you're going to send me away," she said, nuzzling into his chest.

He laughed then and even to his ears, the sound was a little broken. He riffled his fingers through her hair, holding her tight in the circle of his arms, wondering if he would ever feel whole again. Wondering if she would give him the chance. "What would you have of me, Ani?"

Instead of asking him for anything, Ani simply kissed him and he kissed her, wondering at how doing the right thing could feel like such painful loss.

CHAPTER THIRTEEN

"I NEED YOUR HELP," Xander said, when he finally pinned his twin down. Without Thea and Annika, the villa felt like a graveyard and he'd taken to sleeping at his penthouse in Athens. Not that he got much in the way of sleep once he'd made the most terrifying decision of his life, the biggest risk he'd ever taken. Sending Ani away had felt like ripping his heart out of his chest, but somehow he'd managed it.

"Or rather help from some of your seedier associates."

Whatever he heard in Xander's tone, Sebastian swallowed his usual facile retort and studied him. "The mighty, straightforward Alexandros Skalas wants to play dirty?"

Xander shrugged. "Just some information to bring down Niven Shah. I have most of the things in place to ruin him. Only one last part is missing."

"Ani's stepbrother?"

"I'm not going to make her wait another year until she can access her trust fund. That controlling bastard has put her through enough."

Sebastian's brow cleared. "I always wished I could have done more for her."

"You should have. Or if you found yourself incapable of it, you should have come to me."

"She didn't want my interference, Xander."

"So you leave her to deal with an untenable situation alone?"

"Such sympathy for Ani when you had none for Mama? She was caught in just such a situation."

Xander felt as if his twin had slapped him. Their mother was one topic they never discussed. Never. Their parents had broken them in different ways, and while their father had been a true monster, their mother... Xander had always thought of her as weak. Thought himself and Sebastian better off without her. He was only beginning to realize that this rationalization provided himself a false comfort.

"Annika is nothing like her," Xander said, his throat feeling as if it was full of hot coals. "But it should please you to see she has made me realize how harsh I was about Mama. Not everyone can be strong like Ani. Some women break. Some women run. I don't know if I can forgive Mama ever, but I can wish that she found peace after she left us with him. I mean it," Xander said.

Sebastian swallowed and nodded.

"You should know something, though, Sebastian. Your faith in her was very much returned," he said, gathering the courage to say the words he'd buried so deep that he'd only accessed it again at the prospect of wanting a future with Ani. And knowing himself inadequate to meet it. Only now, when he'd acknowledged how much it hurt to lose Ani, how much he doubted his ability to be what she needed, he could feel this other pain too. "Mama never meant to leave you behind."

His brother stared, stunned.

"I found her traveling bag the previous night. She had your passport and hers and your medication and your art supplies. She had every intention of taking you with her."

A curse spat out from Sebastian's mouth, as if it was poison he had to expel from his system.

"I think Konstantin discovered her plans at the last minute and she had no choice but to leave in a hurry." Xander forced himself to meet his twin's eyes. So alike and yet so different. "I am sorry I never told you that. I was...devastated that she would leave me behind with him. That she didn't think I needed her love and her protection just as much as you did."

"You left that evening and stayed with your friends," Sebastian whispered, his brow clearing. "I can't imagine what you must have felt, Xander."

"Three months ago, I would have said it was her loss." The words came easily. "I molded myself to make that true, to not need anyone ever again. But when I—" he swallowed the abject pain and misery filling his very breath "—when I realized I wanted a future with Ani, a real one, I realized what Mama's thoughtless abandonment has cost me." He was too ashamed to tell Sebastian how at first he'd strategized to win Ani's love and commitment like a game, only to realize that it would shame and taint everything she gave him and everything they shared. That in the end, she'd realize that he'd given her everything but love.

Sebastian's gaze reflected the bitter understanding of Xander's loss. "I'll get you what you need to beat Niven. You're right. It's high time Ani was free."

Xander clapped his brother on the shoulder. For the first time in their lives, that one thread of resentment that had always simmered between them died. The topic of their mother was put to rest.

"Have you told Ani that she'll have her fortune earlier than she imagined?" Sebastian asked as Xander turned to leave. "That you're ruining Niven?"

"No. It is not her burden to carry."

"Not even that you're in love with her?" Sebastian taunted with a raised brow.

Denial danced on Xander's lips but wouldn't take shape. "She should be free, Sebastian. Free to make her own choices. Free to live her life the way she wants. Free to be who she is."

If Xander thought his twin would convince him otherwise, he was wrong. Sebastian simply nodded.

For all that they were different in temperament, in this it seemed they agreed. Or maybe Konstantin was powerful and ruthless enough to cast a shadow on their lives from even beyond the grave. Because more than anything, Xander refused to bind a woman to him when she had no choice. Especially Annika, who should be free to love as she pleased.

As if he knew exactly where Xander's mind went, his twin surprised him yet again. "You're nothing like Konstantin, Alexandros," he said. "You should also know that I would not have left with Mama, not without you. Not for anything."

Xander nodded, knowing in his gut that his brother spoke the plain, unvarnished truth. Despite trying his best to pit them against each other, Konstantin hadn't broken their bond. And it was a thing he had always been glad for. Even if he'd gambled away the one thing he loved most in the world, the one person who showed him what happiness could be, and who he could be.

Annika was sitting under the covered patio in the backyard of Killian's house on a lazy Saturday, watching the boys play, when she got the first phone call from some big-shot lawyer from a fancy law firm in NYC.

It had been a month since she'd traveled to New York. She'd seen Xander only once since then. Once in five weeks and three days, to be exact. And that was only because when he'd told her that she'd have to meet Niven one more time, she'd nearly cried on the phone at the prospect.

Xander hadn't calmed her down or done anything normal like that. No, just as she'd sat down to lunch with Niven at the Plaza, he'd walked in through the doors, kissed her senseless, and spent the next three hours grilling Niven and his lawyer about the conditions for her trust fund.

Ani had spent most of that three-hour meeting daydreaming of him dragging her to his suite and ravishing her to make up for two weeks of no sex. Instead, when the meeting had finished, he'd kissed her again with such tenderness, told her he was expected in Tokyo and walked away, leaving her staring after him like a kicked puppy.

She hadn't gotten it even then.

Now she saw what he'd done, as her phone rang over and over. Thea called and congratulated her on winning a battle she'd fought for so long. Sebastian called and asked how it felt to be free, and an heiress. Niven called and while Ani had barely said anything on the phone, he'd yelled and begged her to stop her damned husband because he was ruining Niven.

Ani fell back against her lounger, shock buffeting her this way and that.

Xander had not only strong-armed Niven into releasing her trust fund months—probably years—ahead of schedule, but he was also destroying ruining him for his sins against her. And he hadn't said a whisper of any of it to her.

"No one will make you do anything you do not want to do ever again," he'd said, cradling her against his chest at the helipad. *"Not Thea, not Killian. Not even me."*

Only now did she understand that he'd released her from their agreement. Because he'd received the coveted chairmanship of Skalas Bank? Because he didn't need the farce anymore? Because her usefulness as the socialite Skalas wife was done?

No, the man she loved was not that cruel, that ruthless, that calculating. Not with her. Was it because he didn't, couldn't, love her? Because he found it easy enough to leave her, like her mother had?

Annika swiped her phone on and her trembling fingers hovered on the call log. Could she sound coherent if she heard his voice on the other end? Could she not beg him to take her back? Could she not blurt out that after everything he'd won for her—her fortune, her revenge, her ability to say goodbye to a battle that had cost her too much—she'd lost the most important thing?

In the end, she chickened out and typed a text instead.

They're saying the trust fund is mine. What should I do?

His reply came back within a minute.

Nothing for you to do. All the legalities will be taken care of. Enjoy it.

What does it mean, Xander?

This time, his reply took forever—or at least the three minutes felt like forever, and the entire time her heart thudded so loudly in her chest that she couldn't hear anything beyond its wild thrashing.

It means you are free, Ani. Of duties and obligations and battles and wounds. Free to begin a new life, free of controlling men. Free to pursue your dreams, whatever they might be. As you should be, agapi.

Annika laughed because it was probably the longest and most grammatically correct text in the history of texting and then she was sobbing because Xander was giving her up and it felt like her heart was breaking into so many shards. He'd given her her freedom and her fortune—everything she'd ever wanted—and still somehow managed to cheat her.

The phone slipped from her hand to the ground with a soft thunk. She pulled her legs up to her chest because it hurt everywhere and she felt as if she was drowning, and even the boys running up to her, anxious and scared and angry and a little heartbroken, wouldn't stop the tide of tears pulling her under.

Because she wanted him—Alexandros Skalas. And he'd told her while calling her his love that he would not give her his heart.

CHAPTER FOURTEEN

THE SUN WAS painting the horizon over the Ionian Sea a decadent splash of pinks and oranges when Annika walked into the first floor of the Villa Skalas on a bright December evening, six and a half months after Xander had sent her away.

Three months after he'd turned her into an heiress and yet robbed her of the one thing she'd held precious. Despite never wanting to step foot in the villa again, she'd taken the first flight Sebastian had booked for her without asking questions.

The first floor was ominously empty and she wondered if something terrible had happened to her godmother, if she was too late. The last time she'd spoken to her, Thea had been in Morocco, but admitted, when Annika had relentlessly badgered her, that she had developed a bout of pneumonia. Ani had instantly told Sebastian. That was three weeks ago. When he'd told her two days ago that Thea was worse, Ani had begged to come home to the villa.

Her heart raced. The entire villa seemed to be empty. She plucked her cell phone out of her bag and was scrolling through it when a tall shadow emerged from the terrace.

Relief and fear warred in her as Ani took a step forward. "Sebastian? How is she? Where is she? Can we go to the hospital immediately?"

The tall shadow took a few more steps further in and she realized her mistake.

It was *not* Sebastian, once again.

It was the man who had broken her heart as easily and effortlessly as he'd once stepped up to marry her.

It was Xander, looking like he'd been dragged under a bus. He had dark shadows under his eyes, his hair was too long and curled around his ears, and his white shirt fell loosely against his lean chest, as if he hadn't been... No, she was not going there.

"What the hell are you doing here?" she said, unable to rein in her temper. Anger had always been her refuge when she was hurt. "Where's Thea?"

He raised his hands, palms facing her as if asking for forgiveness. "Thea is well. I mean, she is still recovering from pneumonia, but she's not as serious as Sebastian led you to believe. She's given up traveling for now and is resting, which is what she needs."

"What do you...?" Ani swallowed and fought the urge to step back as Xander moved forward. "Then why?"

"She *has* been in really bad shape. We didn't tell you for a while because I...didn't want to worry you."

"Because you're the lord and master of everything, right? You get to decide what's right for everyone?" she bit out.

"No, Ani. I'm trying not to be that person. But it's a lifetime's habit."

She tapped her feet impatiently, hiding her shock at his raw admission. "And now?"

"She has been asking for you."

Annika glared at him. "But Sebastian made it sound worse. What the hell is wrong with you both?" She grabbed her bag and turned around, intent on walking all the way to the nearest village if that was what it took to get away from him.

"He didn't want to but I twisted his arm."

Annika's steps faltered at Xander's admission, but she kept trying to put one foot in front of the other. Granted, she didn't cover the entire damn distance to the double doors that opened out into the courtyard, but she was halfway there. Even if her stupid legs and her stupid heart refused to listen to sense.

"Aren't you curious why?"

Ani hesitated, then turned around. As long as she didn't let him touch her or kiss her, she would get away. She would not fall for his comforting lies again. Folding her arms—to hide their shaking more than anything else—she tipped her chin up. "Fine. Why?" she said, using her most bored tone ever. It was gratifying to know that she could still pull it off.

"Why did you ask him for a loan?"

"None of your business. And since Sebastian apparently cannot keep a secret from you, you can tell him I have no use for his money anymore. In fact, tell him I'm done with him too. I've had enough of you both manipulating me."

That her hit had landed was only betrayed by the flattening of his mouth. "Why did you give away your fortune after battling your stepbrother for years? After letting him control you with it for so long? What was the point?"

That was what this was about? "You were right, for once," Ani said, knowing he'd never rest if she didn't answer him. "The trust fund…became a weight from the past. I thought I'd be free if I had it, or that I would have my mother's blessing in some twisted way. That I would somehow have what should have been mine, for once. Instead, it only felt like another shackle."

"So you gave it away to your brothers and charity."

"If you know everything, why are you asking me?"

"Because I'd like to understand."

"Understand what, Xander?"

"Why didn't you at least keep enough for college?"

"Because I got my hands on it through you. You and your favors and your pity would taint any education I used it for. You would stay with me forever, even though you washed your hands off me. I wanted to be free of you too. Not just Niven. I wanted my life, my choices to be my own. Completely. Especially after I realized…how much of a shadow you could cast on my future. I couldn't be beholden to you in any way."

He flinched as if she'd slapped him, and whatever satisfaction Ani had imagined getting out of telling him never materialized. In fact, she only felt an overwhelming sense of loss all over again.

"You're very stubborn and determined, aren't you?" he said, staring at her as if he was seeing her for the first time.

"Not a single phone call, not a text for six freaking months and you've the gall to question me now."

"What do you plan to do now?"

God, the man was relentless. Ani sighed. "I plan to go to college. Which is why I asked Sebastian for a loan. I plan to sleep my way through a thousand guys in college. I plan to live and laugh and make choices that have nothing to do with the past. I plan to live for me. And I plan to live it out of the shadow of the man who made me realize that I had my freedom all along, to make the choices I wanted. I just had to grasp it."

"That is all I wanted for you, Ani," he said, somehow reaching her.

Suddenly, he was close. So close that she could breathe in his cologne and sweat. Could see the swirling storm that deepened his gray eyes. Could see the tension radiating from him as if someone was holding him down and he was thrashing to break free. "The freedom to make a choice."

Tears ran down Annika's face with no warning. Something about his words unlocked the tight hold she'd kept on herself for months. She wiped them roughly with the back of her hand. "You didn't even have the decency to tell me that you're dumping me the moment you had your chairmanship."

"Is that what you think, *agapi*? That I dumped you because I had no more use for you?"

"Your actions speak for you, Xander. And even this…" she ran a hand between them both "…you manipulated this. You couldn't see me in New York?"

"I wanted you home, Ani. I wanted the best advantage. I wanted—"

"What the hell are you talking about?" Ani said, pushing at his chest as he crowded her, beyond incensed now.

"I wanted to be your choice, *pethi mou*. I didn't want you to be mine because you had no choice. Because you needed a husband for that trust fund. Because I was your first or because you are attached to this damned villa and Thea and Sebastian or because I helped you achieve that freedom. I wanted to be your choice when all you had were choices and freedom and fortune and your entire life ahead. I needed to be your choice. Because you're mine, Ani. I knew that, long before I made love to you. I knew, I think, that night at the ballroom, when I first heard you play the cello."

She looked at him as if he was spinning impossible and incredible stories out of nothing. Xander felt her disbelief like a gash in his skin and that was his own fault.

"You didn't even touch me for weeks after the gala. You

lavished me with gifts and the boys' visit and…if you knew you wanted me, for real, forever, you couldn't have waited. You couldn't have kept me at a distance. You don't know what love is if you can do that, Xander."

He rubbed a hand over his face, every accusation hitting him where it hurt the most. "I knew, Ani. I knew and I sat with the truth. I knew and I strategized, calculated the risk, forecasted the outcome. I…planned to bind you to me through any number of means. I—"

"You're a ruthless bastard."

"I am, *agapi*. I knew I couldn't let you go. And I did everything except consider the possibility of loving you. Of telling you what you meant to me. Of telling you that you showed me the shape of a future I couldn't live without."

She pressed a hand to her mouth but her soft cry had already escaped. Eyes big in her angular face, she stared at him with anger and pain and so much love that Xander thought it might shatter him to pieces.

"Before Thea made that announcement, you were so happy with me. Then Sebastian returned and he asked me what I was doing to you and I knew that it was wrong. That it wasn't enough. That night, after the party, I told you that Thea and I talked. I realized how much I…loved you, how I was afraid to tell you that, how I hated the fact that you were mine because you had no choice. I loved you so much that it hurt. I shuddered at the thought of you finding me inadequate. Of failing you. Of losing you before I even had you. I went in circles until I knew what I had to do."

"You manipulated me, spun sweet lies in my ears, and sent me away because you loved me?" she said, throwing the words at him now. Tears running down her cheeks. "You still don't know what it means to love, Xander."

"I do, *agapi mou*. You taught me what it is," Xander said,

covering the last distance between them. "Then and now. I love you so much, Ani, that it—"

"I hate you," Ani yelled, when he clasped her cheeks and pressed a gentle, reverent kiss to her temple. "For six months, every day, I waited for a text, a call. Every day, I waited for one of your fancy lawyers to serve me divorce papers. Every day, I called Sebastian and tried to ask him where you were, with whom, if you had—" She broke as a sob rose through her, and his arms were around her and it was the only place in the world she ever wanted to be.

"I hate you," she whispered again, and suddenly she was airborne as he was carrying her and running up two stories with her cradled in his arms, whispering rapidly enough in Greek that she couldn't half hear his words, and then he was placing her in his bed, *their* bed, and kneeling between her legs which she had automatically parted for him. And then he was kissing her.

Xander was kissing her and Ani didn't care if the universe itself had caved in in that moment.

Roping her arms around his neck, she shamelessly threw herself into the kiss. It was more necessary than air and it was sloppy and messy because she was still crying and then she bit his lower lip because she was so…angry.

"Every day of the last six months has been an eternity," Xander whispered, dragging out a long kiss. His hands and his mouth were everywhere and nowhere enough. "Ayaan told me you were going to parties, dances, nightclubs. Every time he told me you went out with someone again, a piece of my heart was chipped away. But I told myself that's what you needed. That I had to wait. That even if you went to some other man, all that would matter was that you returned to me. It was torment of the worst kind."

Ani stared up at him, feeling his pain as her own. "You're

way too possessive to even imagine me going to another man, Xander."

"I hoped that you wouldn't, *agapi*. But I had to prepare for the worst."

"And if I had, Xander? If I had fallen in love with someone else?"

He took her hand and pressed his face into her palm, tension wreathing his lean frame. "It's strange, isn't it? The kind of conviction you have in your gut when you love someone? I had this…faith—which felt irrational enough at times—that you loved me too. That you would return to me eventually."

"So you tormented us both in the process?" Ani said, rubbing her thumbs over the shadows under his eyes. "I had no idea you and Ayaan were in touch."

"The little fiend is as cunning as Sebastian. He's been texting me with enough details to write a book."

Laughter broke out of her. "Hey, that's my little brother."

"Well, he is a little rascal."

"He knew how much I cried every night. He kept bringing me ice cream. He knew I was pining over you, and all the time you were keeping track of me and he never told either of us."

Xander smiled, feeling as if his heart was beating in his chest again. "You look happy at the thought of me being tormented, *agapi*."

Her brown eyes shone like precious gems, one lone tear still running down her cheek. "I'm bloodthirsty enough to like it. Xander, how could you—"

"Because I love you, Kyria Skalas. I know how much you hate Niven. I know how my father tormented my mother with his need to control and dominate and take away her choices. I… I love you so much that I had to let you go.

When Sebastian told me you asked for a loan, I had my lawyers poke into Killian's affairs. He told me what you'd done, against his objections. For the first time in months, I took a full breath. It felt like a sign. And then, Ayaan told me you…haven't been happy for a single day since I sent you back. And I couldn't bear to be away from you any longer. Thea is desperate to see you. And I am desperate for you to stay."

"Xander—"

"Be mine, Ani," he said, pressing his face into her chest, asking for a benediction. "Give me a chance to make all those dreams of yours real. Build a life with me. Build a family with me."

Ani plastered herself to his chest, wrapping her arms around his broad back. She was still trembling, a scared part of her wondering if this was all a sweet dream from which she would be torn at dawn. "You are mine, Xander."

"Marry me again. Just for you and me. Marry me, Ani."

"Yes, please. But tell me again. Tell me how much you love me."

"Enough to sustain Sebastian's constant mocking. Enough to realize that for the first time in my life, I wondered if my mother's loss had left me whole. Enough to want to be a better man."

"I love you, Xander. I have loved you for as long as I can remember and when you push me out of your life, then and now—"

"I'm sorry, *agapi mou*. Even then, I was afraid, you see. I had realized too late how attached I was to you. How impossible a relationship between us could be. And the thought nearly broke me. So, in my usual way I told myself you meant nothing to me. That you didn't deserve my…" He groaned and Ani laughed. "I was the one who didn't see you, who didn't know you, who didn't deserve you, *matia mou*. But I promise I will do my best to deserve you, to have you and hold you."

"You have me, Xander," Ani said, and kissed him and dragged him on top of her.

And when he looked into her eyes she said yes once again, and he took her away to ecstasy and belonging and a forever kind of love that she'd thought only existed in her dreams.

* * * * *

A DIAMOND
FOR HIS DEFIANT
CINDERELLA

LORRAINE HALL

MILLS & BOON

CHAPTER ONE

JAVIER ALATORRE GOT out of his sleek rental car and immediately stepped into a thick, cold puddle of mud. He scowled up at the drizzling gray sky, then at his now-ruined shoe.

He could not fathom why anyone would live in this isolated, wild place when they could have everything at their fingertips in sunny Spain.

But Matilda had wanted this, and after a rather disastrous series of events, he'd allowed it. As a kindness, as a gift. He had not bothered her while she'd spent three years holed away in this place, and he wasn't particularly keen on doing so now.

But the time for licking her wounds was over. Time was ticking.

He'd known Matilda Willoughby for nearly a decade now. He'd never been able to think of her as a *sister*, though Ewan Willoughby had been an excellent father figure to him in the years he'd been involved with and then married to Javier's mother.

Javier had been sixteen when his mother had begun seeing Ewan. Though his mother wouldn't agree to marry Ewan for another five years, Ewan had acted as a father to Javier almost immediately.

In those early years, Ewan had changed Javier from an angry, potentially violent scrapper into a polished, sophisticated businessman. He'd encouraged Javier to attend university, he had secured Javier an entry-level job at WB Industries before he'd graduated, and then he'd set him on the path to heir apparent. Ewan had polished all of Javier's rough edges, taught him the delicate art of control and turned him into the man he was today.

It hadn't been until his parents' engagement that he'd met Matilda. A shy teen who'd preferred hiding behind her father and spending her years at boarding school rather than concern herself with Javier.

Then the unexpected and unthinkable had happened. Ewan had died suddenly, with no warning, no chance for Javier to prepare. Javier hadn't just lost his father figure. He hadn't just gotten a promotion and a business he had to ensure succeeded for the man who'd left it to him.

He'd become the guardian of a sixteen-year-old. One he'd barely known. He could have counted on one hand the number of times he'd been in the same room as Matilda at that time.

But he'd taken such a strange responsibility seriously all the same, endeavoring to keep Matilda's life as smooth as it had been when her father was alive. He ensured she finished school, kept her incredibly complicated and hefty finances in order, and set her up in a nice house with his mother when she wasn't at university. All while he took the reins of Ewan's company and made it even *more* impressive.

He would not fail Ewan's memory, the man who'd changed the course of his life. He would not allow all the warped ugliness of his childhood to change that. Which was why control was always the name of the game.

He sighed, studying the little cottage Matilda had been calling home instead of his mother's house in Valencia. Part of his control was keeping adult Matilda out of his orbit, for reasons he didn't care to dwell on.

Now he needed to call upon all his control to do what needed doing.

Javier straightened his jacket and moved for the door. If the day were more pleasant, perhaps he could have called it picturesque. But today the cottage simply looked gray and incapable of keeping the cold out with its rustic stones and dilapidated-looking roof.

Much like living in this cottage, Matilda had never made much sense to him. Her obsession with plants. Her sweet, trusting nature. Her preference to be alone. *This*.

Three years ago she'd suffered a great embarrassment, yes, and her inheritance meant that she was *quite* notorious simply for the amount of money she had. But Javier could never understand *hiding away*, just because the man she'd been engaged to had turned out to be a scheming, lying gold digger.

The press had been a bit relentless, and they'd painted her an empty-headed fool, but the daughter of Ewan Willoughby should have had thicker skin, in Javier's estimation.

But he'd done what he thought Ewan might in the situation. He'd allowed Matilda to buy this little cottage in the Scottish Highlands. He'd given her time and space to do what she pleased for the time allotted.

It had been easier with her far away than it had been when she'd been gallivanting about Spain on the arm of Pietro the traitor. Showing up at events he was at, looking every inch a *woman*, and not a child to be guarded.

But those years were long gone, and Javier did not have to understand her to make certain she was taken care of, and now, that she lived out the requirements of her father's will and last wishes. Because he *was* her guardian, no matter how old or anything else she was.

Before he could make it to the door, he heard the sounds of someone approaching from behind. He turned to find Matilda striding up a muddy trail.

She wore layers of wool and knitwear, much of it as muddy as the trail. Her curly auburn hair had likely been pulled back at some point, but most of it had fallen out of the band and whipped about her flushed face.

He had not seen her in person for over a year. Perhaps it was closer to two now. He'd chosen to vacation in Capri rather than return to his mother's home for Christmas where the two women had gathered.

Ever since her twenty-first birthday party, shining and happy on Pietro's arm, Javier had refused to name the thing that wormed through him at the sight of her. Her red hair, her violet eyes, her slim form. She was an attractive woman, and any reaction within him was simply a product of biology.

Nothing more.

She carried a strange basket filled to the brim with plants and she swung it as she walked, humming a little tune despite the wet, dreary day. She did not seem to notice him standing there until she was practically upon him. Then she stopped abruptly.

"Javier." She blinked. She did not smile, as she might have once at his arrival. He immediately saw a wariness in her nearly violet eyes, like she knew exactly why he was here.

Which would hurry things along.

"Matilda. You have been avoiding my calls."

"And emails," she added, somewhat cheerfully. She brushed past him and headed for the cottage door. She unlocked it, wiping her muddy boots on an equally muddy mat outside the door.

So much mud, Javier half feared what would be found inside.

"You needn't have come all this way," she said, stepping inside. She hung the basket on a hook, then went about removing some of her layers.

The cottage was warm, not frigid as he'd imagined. He'd give her that as he stepped inside. It was also…to call it "cluttered" would be a kindness. It looked like a science experiment gone awry, which was Matilda's calling card, in fairness.

"I would have much preferred to stay where I was, warm and dry and all, but again. You were not returning my correspondence."

She sighed heavily, then held out a hand. "Would you like me to take your coat?"

He looked at the hooks along the wall. All hanging with wet and muddy clothes, or baskets filled with dirt and green. "No. Thank you."

She laughed, and at least there was that. She had found her good humor once again out here, instead of being the pale, devastated girl of three years ago.

He had not liked that at all.

"Tea?" she asked, moving into the tiny kitchen. He had no idea how she'd even find a kettle.

"No, Matilda. I have my plane waiting. You may take as long as you'd like to pack." He glanced at the acres of plants. Living, dried, halfway between life and death. "Perhaps we can hire someone from the village to take care of your… garden while you are gone."

"I do not plan on going anywhere, Javier," she said quite firmly as she produced a kettle from who-knew-where.

He didn't care for the firmness in her tone. This was another new piece of her. She had once been quite obedient. Now she'd had too much time alone. Too much independence. Better than being a doormat, he supposed, but the behavior did not suit his current purposes.

"Whether you plan on it or not, you will be returning to Spain with me. You will be twenty-five in six months, so there is much to do to find you an appropriate husband."

She slammed the kettle and glared at him. "You can't be serious with all this."

"I apologize, *cariño*, but *I* do not plan on marrying you. So we must work on finding someone suitable. Six months is not much time."

"Honestly, Javier." Every step of making tea was done with jerky, angry movements. Not the Matilda he was familiar with. "I know my father put that ridiculous term in his will or whatever, but I have no plans on seeing it through. Surely no court would enforce it, and who would sue me for being single?" She glared up at him again. "You?"

"It is what your father wished, so it will be done."

"He isn't here, is he?"

He wanted to be annoyed with her, but he heard enough grief in her tone, even though she kept it out of her eyes, that he tried to maintain some patience. Ewan had always insisted it was a virtue.

Javier had yet to fully accept that, but he was doing his best.

"He entrusted me with this, Matilda. I am sorry I cannot be more amenable to your opinion on the matter. Your father wanted you married, and so you shall be. But never fear. I will help you."

"Not by marrying me, of course. Too much wantoning about the continent to do?"

He smiled at her, a smile that had most women in his orbit either blushing or disrobing. "Precisely."

"I do not wish to be married," Matilda insisted, doing neither, which was for the best, of course. "Even if I did, there is simply no way to ensure that it's because someone loves *me*, not my bank account."

"Pietro was one man, Matilda," he said, with all the limited gentleness in him.

"Do not speak his name in my house." There wasn't so much anger behind that admonition as there was hurt, and Javier had no interest in diving into *that*. He'd never understood why she couldn't find her anger in the situation. Her fighting spirit.

Toward Pietro, of course. Not him.

"We will go to Spain. I will find you a husband who does not have any designs on your money."

"You cannot simply trot me about Spain and expect me to find love in six months."

Javier did not think she needed to find love so much as she needed to find a good match. A partner. Perhaps one who would not look around this cottage and see the horror he did.

Ewan had not *loved* Javier's mother, so much as the man had saved her. It had been…friendship over passion. It was why it had taken his mother so long to agree to marry Ewan. She had not trusted *love*. Love was what had made his entire childhood hell.

Still, Javier knew better than to argue intangibles when he had tangibles to accomplish. "Perhaps not, but you will definitely not find it playing the role of hermit out here."

"I am doing botany."

"I have gardens in Spain. You may do botany there. While you find yourself a husband."

She rolled her eyes, then closed them. She sucked in a

deep breath, then let it out slowly. When she opened her eyes, the unique violet landed in him strangely. An edge of something that he wrote off as frustration that she was making this more difficult than she should be.

Always frustration with her because he would not allow it to be anything else. *Control.* No one did it better than Javier Alatorre.

"Javier. I appreciate that you've taken time out of your busy schedule running my father's company and sleeping your way through Europe, but I am quite content to stay right here. I have no intention of marrying *anyone*, and while I appreciate your dedication to my father's memory, as much as I love and miss him, he was not a perfect man and his decision to put this into his will was wrong. If I ever marry, it will be on my own time, of my own will."

Javier had learned years ago, at the hand of this woman's father, how to control the temper his monster of a biological father had left to him. To contain the roiling anger inside him, the monster inside him, somewhere else.

But she poked at all the lessons he'd learned. He wanted to shout at her. Throw a few of her colorful pots against the wall and watch them crash into a thousand tiny pieces. The kind of battles that even all these years removed from them felt more comfortable than the peace Ewan Willoughby had offered him and his mother.

But he did not give into those old impulses, bred in him by a violent father. He would never unleash such a horror on Matilda. *That* is why he preferred her countries away.

But for the next six months, he would have to muster all his control, all his patience. Because he would not fail Ewan. So he breathed, and he smiled.

"Unfortunately, Matilda, you are incorrect. You have no free will."

* * *

Mattie had lived on this planet for almost eight years without her father, and still she missed him with a deep, throbbing ache. But missing him did not mean she couldn't curse his name for this thing he'd done to her.

Javier Alatorre being the looming guardian who wouldn't go away had never been *comfortable*, but Mattie had never *hated* it until now. Mostly, Javier had been hands-off. In the years she'd gone to university in Barcelona, their paths had crossed more frequently, but Pietro had always been with her. It had felt like a…strange little safety blanket.

Not that she felt unsafe with Javier exactly. Just on edge. Never quite sure where she stood. He could be so…opaque.

It did not matter. Not then. Not now. She had built a life for herself in the ashes of her last one. She was not the same woman who'd had her heart crushed, her humiliated face plastered across every tabloid and website interested in the doings of the incredibly wealthy.

She had thrown herself into studying plants, into creating a life that made her happy. Into a life that kept her firmly out of any public's interest.

Maybe cutting off any friends she'd had *before*, and basically only communicating with her stepmother, Elena, on any kind of regular basis for the past three years had left her a bit…lonely these days, but some ridiculous marriage Javier facilitated was hardly going to solve *that* problem.

She studied him across the little counter filled to the brim with her plants. Some experiments. Some for fun. She was fascinated by how things grew, what they needed to flourish. And what ended up killing them.

And in the middle of all this green and growth and *her* space was the man who her father had allowed to have far too much power over her.

It should have been Elena. Mattie had never pegged her father for a chauvinist, but making Javier her guardian and putting him in charge of all her finances and her entire future reeked of misogyny.

Now Javier was here, throwing his manly weight around like he got to decide. Invading her space with his broad shoulders and fierce dark eyes.

He had always been handsome, even when his shoulders had not been so broad and he had carried a chip the size of Spain itself on them. But there was something under all those good looks, all that easy charm he'd learned how to employ so successfully.

A current of danger. A thread of something…threatening. She did not know what or why, but she had always known it was in her best interest to steer very clear or to have some kind of buffer—Pietro, Elena.

She'd done an excellent job up to this moment.

Now he wanted her to come with him to Spain. To shop her around like she was a prized cow to be auctioned off.

"How do you suppose you will force me to go to Spain, Javier?" she asked, trying to sound like one of her old professors posing a philosophical question to an audience full of people who hadn't lived long enough to have a philosophical quandary.

"I beg your pardon?"

"I do not want to go. You say I have no free will. So how will you take my will away from me? How will you *force* me to do all these things, when I am refusing to do them? How do you suppose you will—legally and ethically—determine who I will marry? Do you have hidden puppetry skills that will make it seem as though I said *I do* to the man of your choosing? Perhaps you've studied hypnotism and think you can get me down the aisle to a stranger that way?"

His gaze was cool, his expression bland, except for the sharp blade of his mouth. He had fixed a mask of bored indifference onto his face, but he was *here*. He was not taking no for an answer. So, it wasn't all indifference.

"I do not recall you being so dramatic, Matilda. Isolation has not agreed with you."

"On the contrary, isolation has introduced me to myself. Isolation has given me *everything*. I have no reason to believe marriage will offer me much of anything. I refuse, Javier. I will not go to Spain with you. I will not find someone to marry. I have a hard time imagining you showing up with a priest on my twenty-fifth birthday demanding I marry *you*. So we are at an impasse."

She had the oddest image of him here now that she'd spoken it. Marrying Javier. Him living in her tiny cottage among all her plants. The dangerous energy pumping off of him, even when he pretended to be relaxed and acting in her best interest, would incinerate them both.

Not that it would ever come to that. Javier might prize her father's memory, bend over backward to jump through every ridiculous hoop he'd set up at his death, but Javier would never marry the likes of her.

So this was all a very large waste of everyone's time. Surely Javier would see that and leave.

"Would you like to stay for dinner?" she asked. Hoping the homey, cozy offer—both things Javier avoided at all costs according to his mother—would send him packing.

But Javier did not relent. He did not soften. He did not turn tail and run. He stood there, all icy expressions and that throb of something hot and angry that was surely a figment of her overactive imagination.

"If you do not do this, Matilda," he said, his voice low and harsh, "I will cut you off. Financially, as is the stipulation of the will. Furthermore, I will cut you out of WB Industries altogether. You will have nothing."

For ticking seconds, Matilda could only stare at him. A strange kind of numbness settling over her. Shock, perhaps. Outrage would come, but she was too surprised to find it in the moment. Because he was forgetting one very important part of her father's will.

"The stipulation of the will is that if I do not marry by twenty-five, *you* have to marry me. You cannot cut me off, Javier. You will have to marry me."

But he shook his head. Because he thought he was in charge. Because he thought *she* didn't get to decide her life, but *he* did.

"You have an hour to pack up your things, Matilda."

CHAPTER TWO

JAVIER CONSIDERED THREATS a last resort, but he was running out of patience. If the woman could not honor her father's memory, then he would be harsh. She might find it unfair, but he considered it the *most* fair.

Would Ewan approve of such methods? Javier did not know. But it was never his goal to be a carbon copy of Ewan. Ewan had impressed upon him the importance of being his *own* man, using his *own* strengths to build an empire.

And protect his daughter.

Who seethed in her little kitchen. Muddy and unkempt and surprisingly unruly when she'd always been quite dutiful before.

"I shall set a timer, if you need one."

Those violet eyes narrowed. He did not recognize this version of Matilda, but it was immaterial to his goal. He'd learned not to let himself get distracted or wound up over the immaterial. Over this woman.

"You can go to hell," she said, but she stormed past him and into a room. Slamming the door behind her.

"This isn't very mature of you, Matilda," he called through the door.

He heard the crash of something. Hopefully her beginning to pack. He did not care if she *liked* what she was doing, as long as she did it.

He could admit in the privacy of his own mind that he was a bit surprised by her reaction. It wasn't as though he thought she'd jump for joy, but he assumed she would understand it was a necessity.

Instead, she thought it was…a joke, he supposed. Something to ignore because a "court" would not enforce it. Well, she was right about that, because he would not be forced to marry her or *anyone*. But he would not disappoint Ewan.

He considered his proposition very fair, considering he was giving her the *choice* of suitors, even if not the time she wanted. She was being the unreasonable one, and she was going to have to start falling into line without these surprising little rebellions.

Speaking of rebellion, he realized it had been quiet inside her room for some time.

Suspiciously so. Javier considered the layout of the cottage, then sighed. Preparing himself for the sting of cold, he stepped back outside.

He was not surprised to find her there, climbing out of the window at the back of the cottage. She'd changed clothes. She still wore dull brown and baggy clothes best suited for hiking, but they were no longer muddy. Nor were the boots she wore. Her wild hair had been bundled up under a cap. She looked like some kind of old-fashioned street urchin.

More so when she turned, stopped abruptly, and scowled at him. In one hand she held a little bag. In the other, a pocketknife.

He raised an eyebrow at it. "What are you going to do? Stab me?"

She lifted her chin, but she'd clearly never had to physically defend herself because she was holding it all wrong to be threatening. He would know.

"Maybe."

"You don't even like to kill spiders, Matilda."

"Spiders aren't attempting to ruin my life."

"Clearly isolation has gone to your head. You are inventing dramatics and not behaving like yourself at all."

"Maybe this *is* exactly myself, Javier."

"A pity then. You were much more marriageable before."

"Well, my goal is no longer to be *marriageable*. It is to be *happy*."

Something about the word *happy* settled in him like fury. But he was not a man who used his fury like a weapon. Not anymore. Because of Ewan Willoughby. "And wouldn't you be happier seeing to your father's last wishes? I would be. Stop acting like a spoiled child. Now, if you don't wish to bring anything else of your own to Spain, that's well enough. You certainly have the funds to buy whatever you need. Let us be off then."

"This is insanity, Javier. I don't know what's gotten into you, but if you'd have some sense and simply let this go—"

He stepped forward. She lifted the knife like her chin, but she didn't know how to hold it to do any damage. She'd lived a pampered, sheltered life of a princess, really. She knew nothing about protecting herself from an attack.

Which made him even angrier. He wanted to reach out and shake some sense into her, but he kept his arms at his sides even as he leaned in closer.

"Your father saved the course of my life, Matilda," he said, every word as vicious as a threat. "I owe him everything I am. So, no, I will not simply let this go. Turn away. I will not give up on this. I will find a way to get you married. Now you can come have a say in it, or I can go find a man for you on my own with none of your input. I will not rest until this is accomplished. Do you understand?"

Her eyes had gotten very wide, but she had not stepped

back. She had not wilted or scurried off...like he expected her to. She stood her ground, even if her eyes were suspiciously shiny.

"I know you loved him very much," she said, her voice a rough scrape against the frigid cold air around them. "So did I, but he was wrong to do this to me." Her lower lip wobbled, but she firmed it.

He did not think isolation had been good for her, clearly, since she wasn't being sensible. But he would give it one thing. The time alone, or maybe the embarrassment itself, had developed a backbone in Matilda.

It would be good for her, something Ewan would be proud of, but that didn't mean Javier didn't curse the bad timing for *him*.

"If it is wrong in his name, so be it." He took a deep, cleansing breath. He straightened his jacket. Then he pasted a relaxed smile on his face. "Now, will you be getting in the car on your own, or do I need to carry you?"

Mattie was tempted to continue the standoff. But she had no doubt Javier would indeed pick her up. And that would require his hands on her body and she...

Well, *she* might have changed a bit over the past three years, but the idea of him touching her still felt...dangerous, for ways she didn't allow herself to fully fathom. It was like looking into a black hole. Peer too deeply and she'd get sucked in and disappear forever.

Much like being married off. But she clearly wasn't going to get through to him with reason. So what could she do?

Maybe she should consider it a...vacation. She'd visit Elena, enjoy some time in Spain and then...figure out how to convince Javier she could certainly live the rest of her days without ever getting married and everything would be fine.

She could be rational and logical, even if *he* could not. At least not when it came to her father.

Though the pocketknife in her hand that she used for cuttings and grafting might prove her logic had failed her momentarily. She folded the blade back and slid it into her pocket.

"Ah, so you're ready to be reasonable," he said, with that easy smile she realized was not quite so easy as he pretended. She'd watched him just now. All that vibrating anger and frustration carefully masked.

No, this man was not the easy playboy she'd always assumed. But he *was* the dangerous man she'd always feared. So she'd be careful.

But she wouldn't be the old Matilda. She would not scurry away from him, or behind other people when it came to the strange reactions he stirred in her. She would face him down. She would be her own protector now.

"Reasonable would be leaving me be, but if you feel duty bound to honor my father in this ridiculous way, I'll go along with it for the time being." She began to trudge after him toward his car. "After all, it's been a long time since I saw your mother."

"You will not be staying with my mother. You will be staying with me in Barcelona."

This put a bit of a hitch in her stride. "But… I always stay with Elena when I'm in Spain."

"Yes, when you are vacationing or summering. But this is not a vacation, Matilda. We have a very short period of time to find you a husband and get you married, and I will be overseeing the entire endeavor. So you will stay with me."

With him.

"I hardly think…"

"Let me stop you right there, *cariño*. You do not have to think. You only have to obey."

She considered pulling the knife back out. Maybe it wouldn't do any damage, maybe she'd never actually bring herself to be violent, but it felt more like power than sparring with Javier.

"Be a good girl and get married off like some medieval princess who has no agency, no power and no say?"

"If that is how you wish to look at it. I happen to see it as a privileged woman having to adjust her expectations for the future, for her own good, rather than any kind of *infringement.*"

"That is because you are a man, and even a lack of privilege doesn't stop you from making the world yours."

Something flickered in his eyes, and she wasn't so naive anymore to fancy it hurt, or even guilt. No, Javier did not have any emotional attachment to *her*—not as stepbrother, not as guardian. She was simply an inanimate extension of her father to him.

"Get in the car, Matilda. I would like to be home by dinner as some of us have jobs and business to attend to. You've enjoyed all this free time to do whatever you please while you bemoan your lack of agency and power, have you not?"

It wasn't fair of him, nor was it fully off base. She *had* enjoyed a life doing whatever she wished because of her father's money these past few years. But only because she had not been able to face any role in her father's—now Javier's—company after what had happened with Pietro.

She didn't think that meant she should have to go along with what her guardian said when she was twenty-four. An adult. Her own woman who could make her own decisions.

No matter what her father had thought she'd be at this

age. Apparently weak and silly and whatever it was that he thought meant she needed a husband as some kind of legal minder.

The thought depressed her, as it always did. Because he was not here for her to yell at him. To demand to know what he'd been thinking. To find answers to why the man who'd always treated her like she was smart, savvy and special had determined that had some kind of shelf life.

And because she was distracted by that feeling, she allowed Javier to usher her into the passenger seat of his rental car. She watched her cottage disappear as Javier drove away.

She knew it was a little childish to pout and sulk, but she thought she'd earned the right to indulge in *some* childishness. As her beloved adopted home passed by outside the car. As all her plants and experiments were left behind.

She had found herself out here. Yes, away from everyone. Yes, *isolated*. It had changed her. Just as Pietro's betrayal had changed her and her father's unexpected death had changed her.

She would not marry just anyone. She wouldn't marry at all. It was ludicrous.

She sneaked a look at Javier. His gaze was intent on the muddy, bumpy roads as he drove. His grip tight on the steering wheel as it tried to jerk this way and that. He was all sleek, controlled power, threat, *danger*.

And she was going along with him. Maybe she could convince him to leave this ridiculous need to see through her father's archaic wishes by virtue of just what she had said to him. She would not go into this worrying about being marriageable, about how the men Javier threw her at perceived her. She would not concern herself with the society manners and hostess smiles she'd been raised to embody.

She would be herself. So firmly and wholly, *no one* would want to marry her.

Maybe then Javier would get it through his thick, grief-warped skull that he did not owe it to her father to make his daughter miserable.

And she would be free once more.

CHAPTER THREE

THE FLIGHT HOME was smooth and uneventful. Javier was a bit frustrated he'd had to make the trip, but it had turned out acceptably. Matilda had come because it had been the easiest course of action and that was the kind of woman she was.

Javier had always thought Ewan wanting her married off *was* a bit old-fashioned and unnecessary, if Javier gave it any thought at all. Mostly, he considered it his duty regardless of his own opinions on the matter.

He certainly wasn't going to marry her. Ewan had put that in there, but Javier knew that it must have been some kind of incentive to find someone else for her. Ewan knew him too well to want him for his precious daughter. So, he wanted someone else, and had been smart enough to put something in there to make sure Javier accomplished this for him.

Matilda's recent behavior made him think perhaps Ewan's instincts had been right on about getting her married. She needed someone to usher her through the difficulties of life, lest she be tossed about like a buoy at sea. She could not always run away and hide when bad things happened. She would need to learn to face life's difficulties now, and perhaps a husband was just the way to teach her that.

Perhaps she would not be grateful to him for ensuring her father's wishes were met, but she should be.

They switched from plane to car once they landed in

Barcelona, and Javier took the drive himself. While he appreciated his staff, and the luxuries money could buy, he prized his control when it made sense to.

He drove them to the sprawling, ancient estate outside of Barcelona he'd purchased a few years ago from some minor royal. He'd never invited Matilda here. He barely even allowed his mother. It was *his* place. *His* world. For him and his small staff. No family. No women.

If Javier ever saw Matilda in Spain, it was at the house Ewan had bought his mother in Valencia. And he'd avoided those little get-togethers because they'd felt...

He had no words for it. When Ewan was alive, the man had felt like a...coach, perhaps. A leader.

Without him, it felt as though Javier was supposed to step into those shoes. To be the head of the family. And every time that thought took hold, he looked down at his hands and saw his biological father's fists there.

He did not look down at his hands on the steering wheel now. He focused on the road, the turn and then the meandering drive up to his house, where he allowed no ghosts of a past he'd banished long ago.

Matilda would have to stay with him now for as long as this took. It was the only way to ensure this went off without a hitch, so that is what would be done.

Javier parked in the front and carried her meager bag for her. Luis was waiting at the door. The man acted as Javier's right-hand man at the estate and was one of the few people Javier trusted implicitly.

He took the stairs, handed Matilda's bag off to Luis, but Matilda did not follow. Javier frowned as he turned to see her inspecting the plant that grew and flowered over the archway at the beginning of the stairs.

"Have her bag put in her room, Luis. We will eat out on the terrace momentarily."

Luis took the bag and nodded, disappearing into the house to instigate the dinner preparations.

Then, keeping his irritation on the back burner, Javier retraced his steps and met Matilda underneath the arbor and the vine she was inspecting.

"Javier, I had no idea. Your mother made it sound… dreary." Her hand trailed over a climbing plant that twisted around the arbor. "It's beautiful."

An odd tension took residence in his chest. He knew his mother found this much space for one man its own kind of hermitage, but she did not understand. The fact Matilda seemed to…

Was irrelevant, of course. She *was,* in fact, a hermit. Naturally she would find little wrong with the refuge he'd built himself. At least *his* choice of isolation was on a paved street, near a populated city, within driving distance of anything a man of his stature could want. And he held a job, dealt with people day in and day out.

He was no hermit.

"I had no idea you had such a green thumb," Matilda continued.

"It is not mine. I have an excellent gardening staff." The amount of plants and whatnot that had come with the house had required such.

"I don't recall you ever having any interest in plants."

"I do not. The house came with them, and so they are well tended." He did not ever spend any time asking himself why he'd been so drawn to the house with extensive gardening needs when he had no vested interest in such things. He certainly wouldn't start now.

"I believe you were complaining of being hungry not all that long ago?" he prompted.

"I always forget my hunger in the face of interesting plants."

"Perhaps you have just been away from good food for too long." He took her arm, a gesture that might have once felt paternalistic, but it was harder and harder to pretend as though she was the teenager he'd first met all those years ago when his duty was to find her a husband.

He had to be able to view her as a woman so he could find the appropriate match for her. As much as his goal was to see her married, it would not be to a scam artist like Pietro, or someone who would treat her poorly. That was definitely not what Ewan would have wanted.

Javier had no use for *love*, and wasn't all that sure that *happy* mattered either. He wasn't sure what Ewan would have felt about either—this was not covered in their conversations in Javier's young adulthood. Still, he knew Ewan wanted his daughter taken care of. Content, if not happy.

So Javier would endeavor to find that for her, no matter how difficult she was about the whole matter. He finally coaxed her away from the plants and inside. He led her through the house to the guest wing where she would have free rein over a series of rooms. He took her through all of them, ending with the opulent bedroom with a terrace where his staff had set up a nice evening meal.

She did a slow circle in the middle of the room as if taking everything in. "Javier, this is...too much."

He raised an eyebrow at her. "You forget I know that your childhood home was essentially a castle."

She sighed a little at that. "I suppose it was, but it was my home. And I was a child. I had no sense of what it took or cost to keep such a space taken care of. Now I do."

"Do not concern yourself with cost. You are a guest. As such, you shall be afforded the best. It is not as if I can't afford it."

She frowned at that, but she did meander out onto the terrace to observe the table of food. She eyed the layout with some interest. "Your mother did say you have the best cook in all of Europe."

"Yes, she should know, as she routinely tries to steal Emil away from me."

Matilda smiled at this. "That does sound like Elena." She eyed the setup, then him across the room, still inside. "Aren't you going to eat with me?"

"I have much to do this evening since I had to waste my day flying to Scotland."

She scowled at him. "You didn't *have* to. You could have let me be."

He waved this away.

Matilda walked back into the room and toward him, still wearing her drab hiking clothes. Her hair once again wild. Those violet eyes studying him with an expression he did not wish to discern. She looked so strange here, in the midst of all his chosen opulence, a dull, brown sore thumb, aside from her hair and eyes.

Which made no sense. She'd been born and raised rich as they came. She could belong in any room she chose. He would not concern himself with why she chose to hide herself away.

Or why those violet eyes on him almost made him uncomfortable, when it was *his* house, and *his* space, and all that lay before him were *his* choices.

"Eat and get some rest, Matilda. It is sure to be a long six months." And with that, he turned on a heel and left her there.

Because nothing got to haunt him here. Not even the living.

* * *

Mattie couldn't sleep. For a wide variety of reasons. She wasn't the greatest sleeper in the best of times, so she was more philosophical about the situation than frustrated at her whirling mind.

The meal she'd eaten by herself in complete silence had been delicious, and she was used to eating alone, wasn't she? Eating alone. Sleeping alone. *Being* alone.

But that was in her *own* space. A space she chose, an isolation she chose. It was not doing all those things alone in a house where someone else resided. A house that wasn't hers. Without the freedom to do as she pleased.

She blew out a breath and sat up in the gigantic bed. Another change. She had nice sheets back at her cottage, but the bed was a narrow little plank to fit the tiny room. This bed might be twice the size of her bed*room* back in Scotland.

Was she really going to play along with this ridiculous farce? She could walk out of here, call for a taxi or something, and head back to Scotland where she belonged.

But she was all too aware Javier would only follow. Badger, demand, threaten. It was not in Javier's nature to take no for an answer—ever—but most especially when it came to her father's wishes.

She thought of her father now—something she tried to avoid so as not to get mired in the grief of loss that hung around her even all these years later. She'd had a good relationship with him. It had been the two of them for so long after her mother's death, which had happened before Mattie remembered. She hadn't minded going to boarding school as a teenager because she knew her father was doing it *for* her, to give her the training he couldn't. Because she'd never wondered if he loved her, even when they didn't agree on the best course of action.

She hadn't minded him marrying Elena, and by extension bringing Javier into their lives, because the woman and the young man to mentor had made her father happy.

Mattie was not so good as to have not ever felt *some* jealousy toward her father's mentorship of Javier. Or when on their weekly calls when she'd been away at school he would brag on his impressive stepson.

But Ewan Willoughby had been a good man, a good father, with love and wisdom to go around. So while sometimes she'd felt some envy that as a girl—interested in plants and science more than business and money—she could never quite have the same relationship with her father that Javier did, she had never felt Javier, or her father for that matter, didn't deserve the relationship.

In a way, she had a similar experience with Elena. Finally there was a woman in her life to teach her how to do her makeup, or what to say to a boy when he was especially rude that would have him crying to his mother rather than snickering to his friends. It had taken some time, and most of their relationship had developed after her father had died, but still Mattie was grateful for her stepmother.

What she sometimes could not figure was how the warm and giving Elena had raised such a hardheaded son. One who could charm the whole world and never share even a *drop* of it with his mother.

Or her.

No, he'd always treated them as a duty. Not cruelly. Not completely devoid of warmth, but always a responsibility more than…than…family. Even in those years when she'd been on Pietro's arm, running in the same circles as Javier, he had watched her from afar—she'd always *felt* him doing it—but he'd never gone out of his way to engage.

This whole ridiculous scenario was a case in point. She

was just an item on his to-do list. A responsibility handed to him by her father.

Mattie scowled at the window. The drapes were drawn so she could not see the night outside, but she wanted to. She wanted to be *outside*. In those gardens Javier seemed to have no care for. They'd just "come with the house." This ridiculous monstrosity for *one* man.

She all but threw herself out of bed. Maybe there was no point going home when Javier would only follow and badger, but there was no reason to be some dutiful little child about the whole endeavor. She was an adult. She got to do as she pleased, and she *pleased* a nighttime tour of the gardens.

She stormed out of her set of rooms and began exploring the dark hallways full of twists and turns and doors. She could remember how to get out of the front of the house, but she wanted to see the back.

One of these doors had to lead outside, but she opened thick door after thick door only to be met with dark rooms. Dens and sitting rooms and empty bedrooms.

Honestly, the size of the place was ridiculous, and she did not know how his tiny staff took care of it.

She moved into another hall, found a promising-looking door. Old and heavy, the kind she would have thought made for an exterior door. But once again as she opened the door her gaze landed on an interior room. A bedroom.

Javier's bedroom, if the scowling man standing next to a giant four-poster bed was anything to go by.

The scowling *shirtless* man. Like he'd been in the middle of taking off his clothes. And she was frozen to the spot— hand on the doorknob, head peeking in. At the impressive ridges of pure muscle, at the odd play of white scars against tan skin, at the fascinating trail of dark hair that disappeared at his pants' waistband.

She could scarcely breathe. Like being caught out in a wild storm, all lightning and wind and icy lashings of rain. Dangerous. She did not understand her internal reaction, but she knew everything in this moment was *dangerous*.

And yet, she didn't run like she should.

Because you are not a coward, and this is nothing.

She cleared her throat, hoping to find some port in the storm inside herself. "I was trying to find a door out to the gardens," she offered, irritated at the squeak in her voice, but glad she hadn't said something worse. Like *Where did you get those scars?*

"Instead you found the door to my bedroom," he replied blandly.

"I'm sorry." And she was, mostly, because as mad as she might find herself with him in the moment, she knew how he guarded his privacy. "I suppose I should be relieved I did not walk in on anything terribly tawdry," she offered, trying to sound worldly and unaffected even as she felt her face grow hot.

"I do not bring women back here," he grumbled, grabbing the button-up he'd had on earlier off his bed and pulling it back on.

His comment caught her off guard considering his bedroom looked like luxury and sin personified, wasted on a man alone. "But it's so lovely."

He looked up from his buttons, his eyes direct. Intense. "And mine."

Yes, he'd always been fiercely protective of what he viewed as his. She should bid him good-night and return to her rooms. *To safety*, something inside her whispered.

Instead she stood there, held immobile by his gaze like some kind of bug pinned to a board, her heart galloping in her chest. Stupidly. When she should excuse herself. When she should escape this thing rioting around inside her like a gale.

"Come," he said, holding out his hand.

Her heart leaped to her throat. She struggled to take a breath and her entire body felt as though it was on fire. Surely he didn't mean...

It was a ridiculous thought. Javier might not be choosy when it came to his many, *many* romantic partners, but he'd certainly never looked at her twice—*and never will*, she told herself fiercely. *And you don't want him to.*

She didn't particularly want to touch him either, but to admit that would be to admit that her mind had gone somewhere it very much shouldn't. So she swallowed down all those jangling feelings she knew better than to have and lifted her chin.

She was no longer the scared little girl who'd been conned into believing a man might love her or care for her. She was an adult now, and she did not let foolish fantasies betray her. Her being anything more than a responsibility to him was neither what she wanted, nor even remotely possible.

She was done believing in the impossible.

So she stepped forward and took his outstretched hand. Hot, large, calloused when she couldn't picture Javier doing physical work, let alone having time for it. But he had scars on his torso, like once upon a time he'd done something other than sit in boardrooms in expensive suits and lead her father's company to soaring profit.

He led her to a pair of doors. With his free hand, he pushed them open and pulled her outside into the dark night. A beautiful balcony stretched out and around to a stone staircase that led down into a moonlit garden straight out of a fairy tale.

The dark earthy scent washed over her, the leaves and

flowers whispering those amusing secrets plants had. So beautiful, so surprising, she forgot her hand was in his.

Until he dropped hers, and it felt like a loss. She looked away from the gardens, back at him, but he jerked his chin toward the staircase. "Enjoy, *cariño.*"

She decided that was the only thing to do.

CHAPTER FOUR

JAVIER STEPPED ABRUPTLY away from Matilda. Something... odd was happening to him, and he needed to find a good thing to blame it on because it certainly couldn't be *her*.

She walked down the staircase into the moonlit garden like she had always belonged there, in the warm night and lush dark. A little spark of flame in a dark he never spent much time looking at...because it tended to wrap inside him like feelings, and he didn't see the point in that.

Matilda certainly wasn't afraid to wade in. To show her enjoyment on her moonlit-gilded face with a bright smile and wide eyes. She no longer wore the drab brown hiking clothes, but the baggy pajamas weren't much of an improvement. Though the fabric did look soft...

He didn't realize he'd moved forward until he found himself at the top of the stairs, watching her reach out and trail her fingers over long, velvet leaves. Such joy over something as simple as plants. The way she touched them like...

Well, it didn't do to think what *like*. It didn't do to think of her gaze taking a tour of his bare chest when she'd poked her way into his bedroom.

But why would it not? He knew the effect he had on women. Why would she be immune? And wary, which was good. For everyone involved.

Such basic...reactions were normal, and nothing new

to him when it came to the opposite sex, so why it should sweep through him like some kind of thunder was beyond the telling.

It was just that she had invaded *his* space. *His*. These were his private quarters where no one was allowed. He even limited the staff who entered these doors. Because it was his and his alone.

What had possessed him to invite her to explore the back gardens? While he did not spend much time enjoying them on his own, and thus did not feel quite so possessive of them as he did his bedroom, he did not like how much it looked like this was exactly where she belonged, unwelcome fairy sprite that she was.

He let her walk around, but he stayed put on the balcony. Maybe he tracked her every move with his gaze, but he did not move. When it seemed as if she had inspected every plant for five long minutes apiece, at least, he sighed.

"*Some* of us have early meetings and cannot gallivant around all night. The gardens will not be any different in the morning."

"That is where you're wrong, Javier. They will be entirely different in the morning. Some flowers will bloom in the sunlight, some will droop." It sounded like she was reciting some kind of poem. "A leaf will unfurl. The whispers will change in the heat of day. Everything will be different in the morning."

He did not like how that felt like some sort of dark premonition inside him. Because nothing changed without his permission these days.

"I warned you to get a good night's sleep, did I not?"

She tilted her face up to look at him. He might have believed her some statue of a goddess if her hair did not gleam in the moonlight, if she wasn't dressed so shabbily.

"I am not a child, Javier," she returned. "I know you may view yourself as my jailer of a guardian since you dragged me here against my will, but I am a grown woman."

He wanted to scoff at the idea of *grown*, no matter how possessed and adult she seemed in this moment. But he focused on the reality of their situation—as this was the only important thing. Ever. "What a tragedy you have endured to be brought to a beautiful home with delicious food and have your every need met," he said drily.

Her lips firmed into a scowl. "Every need except the need for independence, freedom, agency." She ticked off all these things on her fingers. Like they were needs, when at best they were wants.

At. Best.

"And," he continued, ignoring her, "I do not recall *dragging* anyone. This penchant for exaggeration does not suit a grown woman."

She let out a little sound then—not quite a laugh, not quite a scoff, but it gave the impression of both. And more…more he could not put his finger on.

Wouldn't.

But she climbed the stairs, with one last wistful look at the garden below. Then she came to stand in front of him on the balcony, rather than scurry off to her room as she should. She stood there before him and said nothing. Just looked at him as though she were looking *into* him. He had to curl his hands into fists at his sides to resist the urge to reach out and touch the burnished flame of her hair.

"I am here." She gestured at his house. The grand house he'd purchased himself. Lived in *himself.* The house that was a symbol of all he controlled, and always would.

"You have won this round," she said, so seriously and with a sadness in her eyes that twisted something painful inside of him—though he refused to name what. Then she plastered on a smile before brushing past him. "We shall see about the rest." She strode inside and out of his bedchamber.

He did not watch the door she quietly closed behind her. He did not stare out at the gardens. He looked down at one fisted hand. *Your father's fists, naturally.*

He shoved this thought away. He would win "the rest" as she called it. For Ewan. For his own pride. And for *her* own good, whether she could see that or not.

But clearly, that was going to require some distance. So he set about to create some.

Mattie was awoken the next morning by a knock on the bedroom door. Disoriented by the big bed, the strange darkness in the *huge* room, and how dead asleep she'd been, she simply lay there for a few moments, blinking and wondering what was a dream and what was real.

Before she could react in any way, the door opened. And a woman Mattie had never laid eyes on once in her life entered. She was all quick, brisk movements.

"Good morning, Ms. Willoughby."

"Uh…good…morning." Mattie pushed herself into a sitting position in the bed, watching as the woman crossed her bedroom and tossed open the curtains and let the daylight in. Which was when Matilda realized just how much light they'd been keeping out. Outside the windows, a bright sunny blue-sky day dawned.

"What time is it?" Mattie asked. She *never* slept this late. "And who…are you?"

"I am Carmen Perez. I will be acting as your assistant for the next six months or until you are married." She eyed Mattie still in bed, a blank expression that didn't do much to hide the woman's disapproval. "Mr. Alatorre has a strict schedule for us to follow the next two days leading up to the ball, so it is time to get up, Ms. Willoughby. It is nearing eight thirty and we have much to do."

Mattie tried to get her brain to engage. Usually she was a morning person, but that was in her cottage in Scotland puttering about *alone*. Not being bossed around by a stranger. "We...do?"

Carmen tapped the screen of her tablet tucked in the crook of her elbow. "You will dress immediately. Then breakfast. We then have some appointments to find you a gown for tomorrow night. We don't have much time."

For a moment, Mattie just sat in her bed and wondered if this was all some very realistic bad dream. From three years of total independence to just...being ordered around. All because of her father's ridiculous will.

No. No, that was not going to work for her. She fixed a smile on her face. "You're just going to stand there while I get dressed?"

"I can step outside if you need privacy, Miss Willoughby." This was said with a clear side of derision.

One Mattie pretended not to notice. "I'm afraid I'll need a little more privacy than that. I will meet you down at breakfast in thirty minutes."

Carmen's mouth firmed. "We do not have thirty minutes."

"I'm quite certain *I* have as much time as I want."

"That is not the case. Mr. Alatorre has filled your day, and tomorrow as well. The schedule is strict and has no leeway. Perhaps if you'd woken at an acceptable hour..."

Mattie attempted to breathe through the spurt of temper that wanted to explode. She kept the bland smile on her face. Javier had not once discussed a schedule with her. Or an assistant or *any* of this. "If Mr. Alatorre has determined this schedule, then why is he not here?"

"He is a busy man. It is my job to ensure you follow the schedule and are ready for the ball tomorrow, and so I shall."

Mattie supposed it made sense in a way. Javier wasn't going to take her shopping. But why hadn't he warned her? Why wasn't he here making the introductions? Why was he *avoiding* her and flinging this woman at her with no warning?

Mattie didn't know what to make of it, but she knew she didn't like it. And she was hardly going to hop to Javier's—or this stranger's—direction.

"I will meet you at breakfast in fifteen minutes then. But I will not get ready with you standing there watching me or standing outside my door like some kind of guard. I am no one's prisoner, and I will not be treated as such."

Carmen did not roll her eyes, but somehow gave Mattie the impression that's exactly what she'd done. "As you wish, Miss Willoughby," she said coolly. "If you are not downstairs in those fifteen minutes, though, I'm afraid we will be forced to skip breakfast altogether."

"That *would* be a shame," Mattie replied with a smile, but she did not budge from the bed. Just held Carmen's cool gaze. She would not be bullied into Javier's schedule, Javier's plans.

No, she got to have *some* control. If Javier wanted a battle of wills, then so be it.

Finally, Carmen turned and left the room, clearly irritated with Mattie already. Not the best first impression for the woman who was going to act as her assistant for the next few months. But she wasn't really *Mattie's* assistant. She was little more than Javier's hired enforcer.

The thought made Mattie scowl, then hurry out of bed. She pulled on some clothes quickly, knowing time was of the essence.

Because she wasn't following anyone's plan but her own.

Maybe she would go to that ball tomorrow, meet the men Javier wanted her to meet, but she would *not* follow his schedule. She would *not* be ordered around. She would do what *she* wanted to do.

And what she wanted to do was get dirty.

She hurried out of her room, going in the opposite direction Carmen likely would have gone to the dining room. Mattie poked around until she found a side exit, then walked the property enjoying the warm sunshine. Quite a difference from a Highlands morning.

But her walk had a purpose as well. She hunted down the gardener. At first, he was a bit standoffish—until she proved she did in fact know what she was talking about. Eventually, he relented, furnishing her with tools and agreeing to a little plot of scraggly plants he'd been set to replace today. She discussed the options of potted plants he had ready for planting and explained what she wanted to do with the section.

"Mr. Alatorre is quite particular about wanting things to look very neat. Clean lines. He's not fussy about what kind of things we plant or how we care for them, but he does like a uniform look."

"Don't worry, Andrés. I will handle Mr. Alatorre." Mattie flashed him a sunny smile as she finished piling everything she wanted into a wheelbarrow, then left Andrés in the little gardening building before he had a chance to change his mind about letting her handle things.

Practically giggling with delight, she pushed the wheelbarrow over to what she was determined was *her* patch of land. Because she would not be denied gardens for even a week, let alone six months.

She settled her tools, the pots, then got to work at removing the old and dying plants that needed replaced. It was a warm day and she worked up a sweat just clearing the area. When she took a break, she looked back at the house. She was on the back side of the building, and she recognized the stairs that curved down to a patio just a little way in front of her. She'd come down those stairs last night to enjoy Javier's gardens, though she'd gone to the left rather than the right last night.

But this meant Javier's bedroom balcony was right above them. It meant if he stood there and looked out in the daylight, he'd have to see *her* progress on this little patch of land.

He likely wouldn't ever do such a thing, but it gave her a perverse kind of joy to design a very abstract planting—instead of Mr. Alatorre's preferred "straight lines"—where there was a chance he would have to see them.

She looked back at the patch of soil. No, this wasn't the right space for straight lines and rows at all. It needed something a little wild. Big fat blooms and vibrant, seductive greens. She'd talk to Andrés about adding some kind of arbor. A trellis maybe, with a little bench.

Yes, she was going to make this space all her own for as long as she was here.

She wasn't surprised when Carmen finally found her, though she'd been hoping to be a little further along with her planting when the woman stormed up to her.

"I have been looking everywhere for you, Miss Willoughby. This is *not* what we agreed upon."

"Did we agree upon something? Because all I seem to recall is you ordering me about like Javier Jr."

The woman's pinched face only tightened. They were not starting out on the right foot, which Mattie felt a twinge of guilt over since it wasn't Carmen's fault Javier was an ogre. But still. Lines had to be drawn.

"If you are quite finished, we need to go shopping," Carmen said crisply, her eyes traveling over Mattie's dirty hands in horror. "I have very strict instructions from Mr. Alatorre about what you are allowed to wear tomorrow night, and this is not something that can be put off."

Allowed. This really was getting out of hand.

Mattie shook her head, kept her focus on the plants. "No, Carmen. I'm not finished. Nor do I plan to be any time soon."

"We have a schedule."

"*You* have a schedule. Given to you by Javier. One I was not consulted about, and therefore have no plans to follow. Now, if you'd like to discuss a schedule for tomorrow, with *me*, I'd love to sit down and do just that. Later. Once I'm finished here. But it will be *my* choice, not his."

"*You* are not my boss, Miss Willoughby."

Mattie speared the trowel into the dirt with perhaps more force than necessary as she stood and turned to stare Carmen down. "And you are not mine. Nor is Javier, no matter what he might think or what he might have told you. *I* will have some control over my life."

And somehow, someway, she was going to get that across to *someone* here.

CHAPTER FIVE

JAVIER RETURNED HOME from work earlier than usual in a blazing foul mood he knew he needed to get under control before he faced Matilda. Still, he did not retire to his room or get himself a drink like he should.

He stormed through his estate, having a pretty good idea of where this impossible woman would be.

Carmen's report had *not* been favorable. He knew Matilda had developed this frustrating rebellious streak when it came to him, but he had assumed she would have listened to the commanding Carmen.

Apparently, that had not been the case and now he needed to waste his time lecturing her like an unruly adolescent. When the entire plan was to maintain as much distance as possible.

She was upending *everything*. After he'd been so kind as to give her three years to herself, she couldn't give him six months to get this accomplished?

A kindness, or self-serving?

He ignored that thought as he stormed his way through the house and out the back entrance. Once outside, he followed the sound of humming.

She was kneeling in the dirt, surrounded by tools and plants and complete disarray. She was dirty and sweaty and looked happy as a clam.

Too many things slammed through him. The fury, dark and potent, had already been there, but something new added an odd cracking fissure of pressure at the center of his chest. A swell of something that felt as though it could take him out at the knees.

All of it wrong. All of it unacceptable.

He fumed at her back, but he knew better than to let that explode. He would not be his father. No matter how many of those instincts lived inside him like ticking time bombs, *he* was in control and always would be.

He kept his voice as bland as he could manage. "Carmen informs me that you delayed your shopping trip."

She didn't look over her shoulder at him, didn't jump in surprise at his appearance, but he did see her spine stiffen. "I was tired."

"Lying doesn't suit you, Matilda."

She looked up from one of the plants she'd just deposited into the dirt. All defiant violet eyes. "Fine. I didn't want to go on a shopping trip I was given absolutely no warning about. I, in fact, refuse to do anything that I'm not consulted about first."

"You were being consulted about what kind of gown you would wear. Now you will not have a say in that either."

She sat back on her heels, looking at him with something that appeared too close to disappointment to be real.

Why should *she* be disappointed in *him*?

"You will go first thing in the morning," he continued. "Carmen will choose the dress and ensure it fits. You will spend your day preparing for the evening's ball and following Carmen's orders."

"And if I don't?"

"I have already explained to you what happens if you do not find a suitable husband."

"Yes, but you did not lay any threats about me spending every second of every day the way *you* want. So I suppose you'll have to come up with a new punishment if you expect me to be your little robot blindly following orders."

She got to her feet, brushing dirt off her knees, shaking her wild hair back behind her shoulders. When she turned to face him, it was in something of a battle stance.

He did not want to battle her or anyone. He wanted things to go as they should.

"You should have been there this morning. *You* should have introduced me to Carmen. *You* should have consulted me about this schedule you want me to follow. I am not your prisoner. I am not a child."

"I know nothing of fashion or gowns, nor do I plan to," he returned, purposefully misunderstanding her.

"I did not say you should have taken me shopping, Javier. I said I should have some say in how my days go, and who assists me. *You're* the one wanting all this to happen. You should have been there."

"I am a busy man, Matilda. Perhaps you recall the responsibility of running your father's company, and the fact that I had to take an entire day out of my responsibilities to collect you from Scotland."

She shook her head. "I am only surprised you didn't send someone else. But I have been thinking on this all day. Why did you, the man who handles everything so carefully, handle this so badly?"

He could only blink at her. He could not recall the last time anyone had accused him of handling anything remotely badly. And this would have gone perfectly if she did as she was told. Like everyone else in his life did.

"And the only conclusion I can come to is that I think you're afraid."

That at least was amusing enough that he raised a derisive eyebrow. "And what, pray tell, do I have to be afraid of?"

"Me."

For a moment, just a strange split second, he felt as though he'd been pierced through. A bright light shining on all he kept shadowed.

Then she kept talking.

"I honestly can't understand why. Maybe it's because if you have to spend time with me, have to admit I'm flesh and blood, you might have to come to realize how ridiculous this farce is. Maybe somewhere deep, deep down Javier Alatorre is capable of feeling guilt."

"I would not bet on it, *cariño*," he returned darkly.

"Have dinner with me then. Let us sit together and discuss this as adults, without assistants thrown at anyone. Stop foisting me off into empty rooms or onto your staff and deal with *me*."

"I dealt with you last night, did I not?" Which somehow sounded and felt darker and more threatening than it had been. He'd shown her the gardens. The end.

Color bloomed on her cheeks, as though she also felt a dark intent that had not at all been there.

"I am not one of your employees, Javier. I will have some say," she said, recovering admirably. "Carmen can't just sweep in and tell me what to do any more than you can."

It frustrated him that she had a point. Because he wanted to control this and her, but there was no reason for her to simply sit there and take it. She didn't earn a salary. Didn't need his good graces. He wanted her to fall in line because it was easy, but aside from holding her finances over her head, there was no reason for her to capitulate.

It set his teeth on edge. So instead of continuing the argument and risking losing any more of his temper, he turned and walked away without explaining what he was doing. Which maybe was exactly the kind of thing she was talking about, but she did not get to call *all* the shots.

He found the kitchen staff and gave them instructions to bring dinner out to the gardens. Then he returned to her. She'd spent some time tidying up the area, but not herself.

He could tell she was surprised he'd returned. Even more surprised when the kitchen staff brought out the meal and began to set it out on the patio furniture nestled in the curve of the stairway that led up to his bedroom.

"Let us eat dinner then and discuss all the *say* you'd like to have." Because he wasn't afraid of her. Not in the least. If he had any concerns about spending time with her, she wouldn't be here. He wouldn't have fetched her from Scotland himself.

Satisfied with that line of thought, he settled himself at the table while she washed up. She came to sit next to him with dirty knees and wild hair. She'd clearly gotten some sun today—she must have spent most of the day out here.

He turned to survey her work as she filled her plate. The entire space was filled with small new plants, all different shades of green, a few with tiny blue blooms. He frowned at the lack of lines. The way the plants seemed to cluster together in a mishmash of shapes.

He frowned. "This is not how I like things."

"Well, you are wrong. This will look much better." She looked over at the space of land, and then smiled. A real smile, full of joy and contentment. "Just picture it." Then she went on and painted a picture of what she wanted the space to look like in between exuberant bites of food. Excitement flushed her cheeks as she spoke of trellises and blooms.

He didn't care about plants, but he found himself wanting to know the difference between the two Matilda had been planting. Because she spoke with her hands, broad gestures that gave away her enthusiasm. She smiled, her eyes twinkling as she explained her process.

The way she explained it reminded Javier of planning a business merger. The way she discussed what plants would benefit from each other and which needed more space. More sun. More shade. So many things to consider to make it all work.

She looked over at him, all bright and happy, and it struck him he could not remember ever seeing her this way. Unless he allowed his mind to go back to when she'd been on Pietro's arm.

Which was neither here nor there and certainly not the task at hand. He'd asked her enough questions about plants to get them through dinner before he realized it.

Unacceptable.

He cleared his throat, refocusing on what was important. Which was not her enjoyment, and certainly not her beauty. "While your plans are quite lofty, you will not have the time to redesign my entire gardens. That is why I have a gardening staff."

She frowned at him, all that joy melting off her face and twisting deep inside him like pain. "You forget, Javier, I have lived the life of wealthy socialite before. I should have plenty of time to do whatever I please."

"That was when you had a fiancé on your arm. Now you are in search of one, and your time is mine until that happy occasion."

Any easy contentment was gone now. From both of them. Which was good because this was about business. Not enjoying each other's company.

"You will go shopping first thing in the morning with Carmen. This is nonnegotiable. If you wish to have more say in your schedule after tomorrow's ball, that is between you and Carmen. As long as you see to your duties." He didn't like how much that felt like a compromise, but what did it matter what she did with her days as long as she was prepared for the events that would allow her to meet her future husband?

She studied him for a long moment and then she smiled. In a way he did not trust. "Very well."

He was not sure what was worse. Arguments or easy agreements. Arguing gave him a headache. He didn't trust her acquiescence at all. "You will find an appropriate wardrobe for the next six months. Gowns. Elegant clothes befitting your station. No more of this drab hiking wear."

"Naturally," she agreed, far too easily. She wiped her mouth on a napkin, settled it over her plate.

"*I* am in control here."

Her mouth curved as she stood. "Why Javier, what would make you think otherwise?" Then she sauntered off—*sauntered*, all hips swaying and mature confidence. As though she was yanking and unspooling all of his control.

And he was left staring at a little patch of overturned dirt, little clusters of happy plants tumbling over each other. Not controlled. Not precise.

Ruining everything. Just like her.

Mattie did not want to go shopping. Not alone and certainly not with Carmen, but the next morning she got ready. Not to be dutiful. She had no plans to do that. But she would attend all her appointments.

Even if she had her own plans.

Javier might not admit it—to her, to himself—but he'd compromised last night. He'd eaten with her, discussed what he expected of her, and even asked questions about her garden.

She refused to acknowledge the little fluttering in her chest at the way he'd looked at her. Because it had been brief, and probably in her imagination since the minute their eyes had met his expression had shuttered.

And he'd turned back into business Javier.

Still, she would honor the compromise by making some of her own. She would go dress shopping with Carmen.

But that did not mean she needed to *buy* anything.

They arrived at a beautiful little shop that she remembered from her younger years. When she'd been attending events on Pietro's arm, she had shopped here on her own. Quite happily.

It soured her already precarious mood considerably.

"We've pulled some appropriate choices for tonight's event," Carmen said briskly, gesturing at some shop people as they entered. "The sooner we make a choice, the sooner the gown can be altered to be ready in time."

Mattie was led through the store, into some private, luxury dressing rooms. Had there been a time she'd enjoyed this sort of thing? When she'd been Pietro's little jewel? *Pietro's little fool.*

Carmen gestured toward a shop employee who rolled out a rack of glittering gowns that made Mattie's frown deepen. "We will start wherever you'd like," she said.

"I appreciate the effort, and I'm sure these are all lovely pieces." Mattie attempted a smile at her stern taskmaster. "But I think I'll just wear this tonight," she said, gesturing toward the linen pants and loose T-shirt she wore. "I'd be happy to look at some gardening clothes."

Carmen and the shop woman stared at her, mouths slightly parted. "*Perdón*, miss. What you are wearing is in no way appropriate for a ball."

"I know Javier wants me to get all glittered up for the

ball, but I'd rather be comfortable than poked and prodded into a too-tight gown with too much makeup and uncomfortable heels." Memories of a life she'd purposefully left behind. "We can add a necklace, I suppose, but otherwise I think I'm quite comfortable as is."

"Miss," Carmen said, her voice firm if still befuddled. "This is… You cannot wear *pants*."

"Whyever not?" Mattie asked.

"It isn't…done. It's a *ball*. You cannot show up in these… these…*pajamas*. I will not allow it. Nor will Mr. Alatorre."

"Mr. Alatorre is not in charge of me." She refused to let him be. "And this is a nice linen trouser, *not* pajamas."

"Ms. Willoughby, I'm sure we can find a compromise," the shop woman said, her voice a little high as though she was nervous. She eyed Carmen, then Mattie, before offering a bright smile. "Something that makes everyone happy."

I only care about me *being happy*, Mattie wanted to say to the both of them. But that made her feel spoiled and silly, like all those tabloids had once accused her of being. So she had to find some sort of…center of calm. Of *reason*, in this very unreasonable situation.

"Carmen, I realize Javier has asked you to help me in this endeavor, but there is really no point in getting involved. I will handle Javier. I will handle my outfit. I will handle everything."

But Carmen was shaking her head before Mattie even finished. "My job this morning is to procure you a gown, Ms. Willoughby. You can choose to be difficult, of course, but there will be a gown purchased this morning. Whether it is your choice or mine is up to you."

Which was just like Javier and his demands and poked at Mattie's temper. "You could pick out a hundred beautiful gowns, Carmen. *I* will not be anyone's doll. I will not be married off. I *refuse* to be treated like cattle."

"Very well," Carmen said, and her voice was calm and officious, but her eyes were ice. "We will not obtain a gown. You will attend the ball in this getup. And you, and Mr. Alatorre by association, will be a laughingstock. Your picture, in these...*pajamas*...will be splashed across every society page. Of course, you have experience with that so perhaps it is your goal."

Mattie felt the color drain from her face. She hadn't thought about Carmen knowing about the whole Pietro fiasco, but of course the woman did. And clearly knew Mattie's Achilles' heel.

Mattie had no desire to do Javier's bidding, but she had even less desire to be the butt of any more jokes. No more front pages. No, she didn't want to relive *that*.

"*Or*," Carmen said, pointedly, "you can go inside the dressing room and try on what I hand you. You can choose appropriate attire for the ball and find another more reasonable and adult way to express your displeasure over Mr. Alatorre's choices."

Embarrassment slithered through her, the heat filling her cheeks. She had been put neatly in her place, and it seemed she deserved it.

"Do you have a suggestion for a reasonable and adult way to get through to Mr. Alatorre?" Mattie asked through gritted teeth.

Carmen's mouth curved ever so slightly, like she might actually smile. "I would *not* recommend running headfirst into a brick wall, miss. You will have to find another way around."

Mattie sighed, knowing Carmen was right. So she allowed herself to be led into a dressing room and then was handed a hanger with a deep purple gown on it.

On an irritable sigh, she set about disrobing and pulling the dress on. Except it wasn't a dress. It was pants. Sort of. The top had all the makings of a strapless ball gown. A deep purple with intricate beading around the sweetheart neckline that then vined down her abdomen to the skirt—which opened to reveal slim-fitting pants.

Carmen barged in without asking. Much like her actual boss, she seemed wholly unconcerned with Mattie's reaction. But Mattie could see this for what it was. A compromise. An *effort*.

And that's what she was after. With this woman. With Javier. With her life. A compromise between what was demanded of her and what she wanted. Maybe the adult thing to do was try to find the best compromise, instead of stamping her foot like a child and being difficult *just* to be difficult.

"Ah, see? *Hermosa*, no?" Carmen fluffed out the skirt, tilted her head back and forth as she studied Mattie. Then nodded. "This will do."

Mattie turned to look at herself in the mirror once more. They *were* pants, and maybe that made the kind of statement she wanted it to even though they were elegant, feminine and with a kind of open skirt that hid the fact they were pants if anyone was looking at her from the back or side. Certainly not an outfit made for embarrassing herself.

Mattie touched a hand to her bare shoulder. "Is there something with straps? A sleeve? I feel…exposed."

Carmen tutted. "You have beautiful shoulders, but we will leave your hair down and it will ease any concerns about modesty." She bustled behind Mattie and undid the clips and hair ties that held her hair back. She artfully fluffed out Mattie's hair, arranged it around her shoulders, and she did feel slightly less exposed even if she didn't like the woman she saw in the mirror.

Because it reminded her of who she'd been when she'd been in love with Pietro. Happy to shine herself up, to glitter like a jewel for all to see. Because back then she'd thought that mattered.

Now she knew better. The glitter just hid lies and emptiness. It warped, and it made a fool out of people.

She would not be anyone's empty jewel ever again.

But Carmen had a point about being a laughingstock. Going full opposite—refusing to dress to suit the situation—wasn't actually proving any point. It was just drawing a different kind of attention.

That was not the goal. The goal was to avoid marriage. She didn't have to dress like she did back home to do that, she supposed. She just had to be herself no matter how she looked. She could *look* as though she fit in, *look* as though she was attempting to accomplish Javier's "duty."

But it didn't mean she actually had to be doing it. No man would want to marry a woman who wanted to live in a cottage in the Highlands. No man Javier introduced her to would be interested in listening to her prattle on about botany. Maybe Javier could find a man to be interested in the outside package, certainly her fortune, but never *her*.

This was going to be a vacation, she reminded herself. Enjoy Spain for a bit before Javier realized she was fully unmarriable.

"Very well. This will do."

Carmen smiled triumphantly—the first time she'd shown an emotion other than disapproval and outright chastisement. "*Perfecta*, Ms. Willoughby. Now, onto shoes."

CHAPTER SIX

JAVIER RETURNED HOME early for the second day in a row and cursed himself for it. But his concentration had been shot. Carmen had not updated him on Matilda's progress, which he assumed was good.

But he needed to be certain.

Because this ball was important. Because he had introductions planned. She could not fail him on this, so he would ensure she wouldn't. He went straight to his rooms rather than deal with Luis or any other staff members. He needed some quiet. Some solitude. Yes. That.

He dropped his briefcase on his bed, loosened his tie, then without thinking the move through walked out onto his balcony. Because it was a pretty day.

Not because he was looking for her.

But there she was. Down in her little patch of dirt. She wore a silly-looking hat the size of Spain itself. He could not see her face, but occasionally, she would turn her head just so and he could catch her profile.

For too long, he simply watched her. He could not imagine anything so simple, so quiet, so *mindful* bringing him the joy it brought her. It made him want to go down there and ask her more questions about her plans, about why clean lines were so wrong, about how plants might complement one another.

He was walking toward the stairs down to her before it

occurred to him what he was doing. Losing himself. Forgetting himself. And that could lead nowhere good.

They had a ball to attend, a husband to find for her, so she was once again shirking her responsibilities by being out in the garden instead of getting ready. He would have to go down there and chastise her for this, lecture her once again and—

Carmen stepped into his view. She said a few words to Matilda, who sighed, then began to clean up. Then they disappeared inside together. No doubt to get ready for the ball.

Well, good. It was all…good. And now he had time to respond to a few more emails before he had to get ready himself.

Yes, this was all…fine. The odd restlessness inside of him, the off-kilter feeling, was simply someone invading his space. Ruining his garden. Changing his schedule.

He did not like it. He *hated* it, in fact. But it was six months, and he could endure anything for six months.

He'd endured worse, certainly.

So he got a few more work tasks done, though not with his usual razor-sharp concentration. He dressed for the ball himself, doing everything in a silence that usually calmed him but today made him feel more and more tense.

When he was ready, he headed downstairs, expecting Carmen and Matilda to already be there waiting for him.

They were not. He scowled. He was not used to waiting on people. He was used to making fashionably late appearances to events, of course. But this was when the woman accompanying him was his date. When they were late because they had gotten up to something untoward before the festivities.

He was not used to standing stiffly in the entryway of his own home waiting for a woman who was *not* his date to appear. He did not *wait* on people.

He glanced at his watch once more. If Matilda was trying to get out of this, she would be sorely disappointed.

He would go fetch her now, and if she was not ready, well, then he would change tactics. He'd thought he'd been very kind to arrange balls and events that allowed a low-pressure meeting environment for his chosen suitors. But if she would not behave, he would bring them here. One by one. Uncomfortable dinner after uncomfortable dinner until she chose one.

Yes. Because *he* was in charge. He moved for the stairs, ready to storm his way to her quarters, but stopped short. Because she was there, already halfway down the stairs. A red and purple vision.

He wouldn't call her polished. She seemed as wild as she'd been when he'd seen her back at her cottage. A windy Scottish gale all on her own. But she was not muddy or hidden behind droopy layers of fabric now.

No, this was a sleek storm. Lightning and pelting rain. The fabric of the bodice dipped between her breasts, glittering and vibrant like an arrow determined to showcase the alluring curves of her tall, slender frame. Her hair was down, a riotous mess of curling red, and she wore makeup as smoky and dangerous as this feeling curling in the pit of him.

Her lips were redder than her hair.

His body hardened. An absolute betrayal of all that he was. All Ewan had given him. It was one thing to have the passing thought that she was beautiful, to be *momentarily* affected by the color of her eyes, the radiance of her smile or the way she smelled of plants. It was another to be gripped by something darker.

Too close to need to fathom.

"You are late," he said gruffly, needing something to be an anchor and if it was his own anger, so be it.

She adjusted the satin gloves on her arms. They should be ridiculous, as pointless as they were, but they seemed to draw out the delicate ivory of her skin, making her glow. Like a pearl.

"Carmen said you're always late, so it was of no matter," she replied, fussing with her outfit and not meeting his gaze. "I swear they spent hours on my hair alone."

"You are wearing pants." It was an utterly pointless observation to make aloud, and he could not quite believe such banal words had come out of his own mouth. But it was such a strange little ensemble, one that showed off impossibly long legs, encased in purple fabric though they were.

Her gaze lifted to his, a glowing violet as if the purple of her outfit eradicated all the blue from her eyes. "So are you." She arched a brow, but her mouth curved, which did nothing for the clawing fight against his body's reaction to her. "If you object to my outfit, I can gracefully bow out and let you attend the ball on your own."

He decided everything would be best if he ignored her. Focus. Control. The task at hand. "I have three men to introduce you to this evening," he said, turning and striding for the door without offering his arm.

He would not touch her if he could help it.

"Three?"

"We are playing the odds. Whichever ones you like, we'll arrange another meeting with. We'll discard the ones you don't."

"Discard? Like waste?"

"If that's how you see it," he offered. He would not jump to the bait and argue with her. Not tonight.

"And if I like none of them?"

He held the door open for her, waited for her to step out into the balmy evening before leading her down to the waiting car. "I have three more lined up for Friday's charity gala."

"Quite the meat market."

"You haven't given me much time to work with."

"I suppose it would have been easier for you if I'd just married Pietro so you could wash your hands of me. No matter what he might have done to me, as long as I wasn't your responsibility."

He knew she was poking at him on purpose. It was the kind of jab leveled at him in business all the time—meant to hit where it hurt, meant to make him feel poorly for his behavior. Javier had thought he'd eradicated his need to explode in response, but her accusing him of such a thing when he'd bent over backward to be good to her poked at all he was endeavoring to control.

Fury pumped through him. That rage he kept buried deep because he knew whose rage it was. Knew what would become of him if it won. Who he would become if he let it consume him.

When he turned to look at her, she took a step back, eyes widening in something too close to fear. There was no triumph in frightening her. Only that sick feeling that always twined with anger.

This is who you are, a dark voice whispered.

And he knew it was the truth, but he also knew how to control it. Even if he couldn't seem to control *her*.

When he spoke, he made certain his voice was ice over the fire that must have shown in his expression. "*I* was the one who saved you from that farce with Pietro, Matilda. It would do good to remember it and how much worse it would have been had I not intervened. It would do good to remember that I act *only* in your father's stead. Behaving the spoiled brat does neither of us any favors. I am being beyond reasonable by affording you the chance to choose yourself. By giving you these opportunities to do that which you would not do on your own. *I* have bent over backward to give you the gift of *choice*."

She retook the step she'd retreated from. Now it was anger that flashed in her violet eyes, instead of fear. "You are delusional if you think flinging me at random men and demanding I marry one of them because of some archaic decision my father made is a *choice*."

Javier waved off the driver and opened the back door of the limousine for Matilda himself. He waited until she was close enough that he could speak quietly, in little more than a whisper. "Perhaps I am, *cariño*. But if you find yourself a husband, you can be rid of me and my delusions forever." And it would be forever.

Once she was married off, he would make certain he never laid eyes on Matilda Willoughby again.

Mattie didn't say anything on the drive to the event. She wanted to be angry. She wanted to be indignant. But she was just getting tired. Tired of conflict. She wanted to go home to Scotland and hide from all this…upheaval.

This morning she'd told herself she was going to be an adult about this. She'd had plans to plaster on a smile, do whatever she liked, and prove to Javier that no one would be interested in her.

Then she'd walked down those stairs expecting some kind of reaction from him. She hadn't fully realized she'd been holding her breath waiting for him to say something. Positive or negative. She'd stood there waiting for *something*.

But he'd only commented on the time, when Carmen had assured her he wouldn't mind being late. He'd commented on her pants, but without approval or disapproval. Then jumped straight into the business at hand.

Wiping his hands of her, no matter how she felt about it. He'd made it abundantly clear—even if he *had* eaten dinner with her last night and asked her what felt like insightful questions about gardening—that he wanted as little to do with her as possible.

And she felt strangely crushed, which made no sense to her. So she'd fallen back into the bad habit of poking at him, seeking that reaction she didn't want, but couldn't seem to stop seeking out. She kept reverting back to a fight.

Maybe that wasn't all that strange. Javier *had* acted as her guardian for the last few years of her schooling. Elena had been the actual parental figure, but it was Javier who'd had the control.

So maybe the rebellion was natural, but she needed to find some kind of maturity in the face of him. He was a formidable opponent in this strange war they found themselves in.

Mattie had to be smarter.

But it was a bit lowering to realize that running off and living an isolated life hadn't actually given her power or maturity, only the illusion of it. For three years, she'd held on to the belief that she'd built herself into a woman she could be proud of.

For the first time, she wondered if that were true. Or if she'd just…run off and hidden. It was her first reaction, even now. Not to find a way to deal with him, but to run away.

When the car came to a stop in front of the event venue, Javier made no move to help her out of the car, or to take her arm as they entered the big, crowded building. He stayed close, but he did not even lay a finger on her. She didn't know why she should notice such a thing. They were not on a date. He was acting as her guardian. But it seemed odd there wasn't even the faintest touch of the elbow to guide her this way or that. She just had to follow him.

The large ballroom was packed with people in tuxes and sparkling gowns. Some people's gazes skipped right over her and landed on Javier—women's eyes in particular. Some people did the kind of double take that made her shoulders tense because she knew she was being recognized from her infamous broken engagement, from the knowledge she'd fallen for a schemer like Pietro.

She wondered in this moment how she'd been thrust back into this world. Surely she should have found a way around Javier's stubbornness back in Scotland. Thrown herself to the ground and demanded he carry her, force her. Maybe instead of maturity, she needed to lean into childishness.

"Ah, here is your Option A," Javier said, his voice low and gravelly in her ear, causing a strange little fissure of electricity to move over her skin.

Nerves, likely. "Is this how we'll refer to them?" Mattie asked, disappointment in herself making her feel tired, her limbs heavy. "I can't wait to see what you have up your sleeve for X, Y and Z."

"His name is Clark Linn," Javier said, ignoring her. "Your father worked with him when he first started at WB and quite liked him."

"Are you setting me up with men old enough to be my father, Javier? I may have issues, but I don't think I have daddy ones."

He sighed. Heavily. "It was an internship while Clark was at university when he worked with your father. Clark is thirty. Is this an acceptable age for you, *cariño*, or would you prefer man-babies?"

Mattie didn't bother to respond to that as Javier led her

over to a man leaning against the bar. When he spotted Javier, he straightened and flashed a very white smile.

He was dressed as fashionably as Javier, ruthlessly styled. His shoes gleamed. His blond hair was slicked back without a lock out of place. But something about his polite smile left her feeling…gross.

"Clark Linn," Javier greeted. "Good to see you this evening. I wanted to introduce you to Mr. Willoughby's daughter, Matilda."

Clark held out a hand and enthusiastically shook Mattie's. She noted his other hand didn't let go of the nearly empty glass. "Nice to meet you."

"You as well, Mr. Linn," she greeted with a smile, since it wasn't this man's fault Javier was an unreasonable gargoyle.

"Oh, you'll have to call me Clark or my dad is likely to appear in a puff of dark evil smoke." He laughed heartily at his own joke.

Javier didn't even smile. "If you'll excuse me, I have to speak with Mrs. Alonso. I'll be right back." Javier slipped away and Mattie turned her attention to Clark, trying to dream up something to say.

Something other than *I have no idea why I'm here, why I'm engaging in this farce, or why anyone ever does.*

"I rather enjoy these charitable things," Clark said, gesturing around the ballroom. "Makes you feel like you're making a difference and all that." He took a sip of his drink, looked her up and down quickly before flashing another very white smile. "I'm *very* involved in charity."

"Oh? Which ones?" Mattie asked, standing awkwardly next to the bar. She thought he might suggest they move to a table, or at least out of the way of people trying to get service, but Clark remained parked right there, signaling the bartender to refill his drink.

"Oh, my mother handles the specifics. I'm on the board of one." His eyebrows beetled together. "Something about blind children, I believe? You'd have to ask her."

Mattie tried very hard not to frown. To keep her smile in place. His *mother*. And Javier had scoffed at younger people being man-babies.

"I'm very busy, you see," he explained. "I'm a senior analyst with WB."

"Naturally."

He blinked at that, as if uncertain that her response was positive or negative. It was decidedly negative, but he shook his head as if shaking the possibility away.

"I knew your father. He was a good man." Clark lifted his refilled drink, took a long sip.

"He was," Mattie agreed. And his *mother* certainly hadn't been in charge of the charities her father had aligned himself with.

"We used to go golfing together when I was interning for him. He'd gone to uni with my father, naturally. But I always beat the son of a..." Clark trailed off, cleared his throat. "Well, you know, he insisted on using these old clubs. I'm very interested in science, of course, so I have state of the art." He started prattling on about golf clubs of all things.

On and on and on. Mattie could only stare at his mouth. No words penetrated. They were too boring. But his lips kept moving and moving and *moving*. Like an animatronic robot.

He hadn't even taken a breath to give her the chance to get a drink for herself—since he didn't offer, though he kept signaling for refills of his own. She'd about kill for a drink right now, but he just kept *going*. Until she thought she was either going to scream or run away.

But that would be embarrassing, for the both of them,

so she blurted out the first thing she could think of once he took a pause to take a drink. "Would you like to see a photograph of my garden?" she asked brightly. Because if he could go on and on about *his* passion—even if she didn't understand how anyone could be passionate about *golf clubs*—why couldn't she go on and on about hers?

"Erm. Well, certainly."

"It's back in Scotland. That's where I've spent the past few years. I have a keen interest in botany, so I've done some experiments." She pulled her phone out of her purse and pulled up a picture of her experimental garden back at the cottage. "I used spikenard, it's a native plant to the Highlands. You see, this was the control section." She pointed at the center square. "Then I tested different kinds of fertilizer in these other squares. All on the same plant with the same sun and water."

"Fertilizer," he repeated, as if he couldn't quite believe that's what they were talking about.

And that's what gave her the idea to go in fully, because she certainly hadn't understood why he'd been talking about golf, but he'd gone on and on and on. So now it was time for some golf club payback. "Yes, and there are so many different options to choose from, but much as I anticipated, my experiment showed manure really is the best option."

"I beg your pardon."

"I mean compost, of course, but nothing beats what nature offers of its own accord. Luckily my place in Scotland is near a lot of farms. Now, worm castings are also an interesting option. I had some success there." She smiled up at him, truly enjoying herself and the way he looked like a deer caught in headlights.

It was wrong, probably, but maybe maturity could wait. "Let me tell you about worm castings, Clark."

CHAPTER SEVEN

JAVIER COULD NOT fathom why his gaze kept going back to Matilda, particularly when Valeria Ortega was talking to him, and he knew exactly where that could lead if he let it. A *very* pleasurable evening with absolutely no strings.

His favorite kind.

But she was talking about some beach, and it all felt very superficial when the important goal of tonight was Matilda finding a man she could potentially marry. So she could get out of his house. So she could be out of his orbit forever.

She still talked to Clark, and they hadn't moved from the bar. Clark had not gotten her a drink or invited her to dance, but they seemed to be engaged in a great and deep conversation.

She was *grinning* at that idiot. It awoke something dark and ugly inside him, and he could not fathom why. He ground his teeth together. Clark had seemed like an acceptable option days ago. Javier didn't often second-guess himself, but watching Matilda chat with him, her whole face lighting up with entertainment, seemed to point out all Clark's many faults that Javier had not considered before.

What had once seemed something in common—wealthy families with lots of ties to WB—now seemed to highlight what an ineffectual result of nepotism Clark really was. What Javier had always considered a bland kind of uselessness now seemed like a dangerous brand of ineptitude. When Matilda needed someone…stronger. A man who would take care of her. Who would steer her in the right direction. She did not need to be married off to someone who she would have to play *mother* to.

"I thought she was your ward or some such," Valeria said at his side.

Javier didn't startle, nor did he look at the woman who spoke. Not when Clark was leaning his mouth toward Matilda's ear. "She is," he practically growled.

Matilda had been against this whole thing and now she was cuddling up to Clark Linn of all useless people? This just proved she needed a guardian. If her inner compass was really this off then—

"Then why are you staring after her like a scorned lover?"

Javier whipped his face around to look at the woman. Her eyes widened and she startled back a little, no doubt at the fury on his face.

Like father, like son. In the blood.

Javier took a careful breath and wiped any trace of anger off his face, even though it still leaped and twisted inside him. A mark he'd never be free from.

But he would control that mark. Always. And much better once Matilda was situated. When he spoke, he spoke in a low, bland kind of tone making sure he gave the woman in question a carefully crafted expression of gentle recrimination.

"I can see how you might be confused, but it is my responsibility to ensure Ms. Willoughby's future is taken care of. This is not a responsibility I take lightly."

"Ah, I see."

But it was clear she did not. So Javier made his excuses. Whatever might have happened with Valeria was of no matter anyway. He had crafted the image of a playboy, and sometimes it was easy to *be* that image, but sometimes things took precedence over the mindlessness two people could find in each other.

His focus had to be Matilda, not his baser urges.

It was clear she had no sense when it came to men. She was showing Clark something on her phone, and she looked as happy as he'd seen her in her little garden plot this afternoon.

Javier had to make a conscious effort not to scowl. He plucked a flute of champagne from a passing tray and then made a beeline toward Matilda, ignoring anyone who hailed him along the way.

And he ignored Clark as he approached as well. "You look thirsty," he said to Matilda, handing her the glass.

"Oh." She frowned a little, taken off guard, but took the offered drink. "I am, thank you." She pointed at Clark with her free hand. "I was just telling Clark about my gardens."

"Extensively," Clark muttered into his glass, with another word that sounded alarmingly like *manure*. Then he brightened. "Oh, there's my mother. Excuse me, won't you?" And he beat a hasty retreat.

"Did he say…manure?"

"It's the best fertilizer option in a garden. Particularly when dealing with native plants and Highlands soil." She sipped her drink, then smiled up at him, with such fake innocence he felt the very strangest sensation that he wanted to smile back. Clever, she was that. Always had been, even when she hadn't been able to wield it quite so sharply.

But it was at cross purposes to his goals, so he could not enjoy it. Would not.

"You can try to scare off every suitor, Matilda, but it will not change the necessary actions required of you."

She sighed and rolled her eyes. "Javier, he spoke of nothing but golf clubs. He couldn't even tell me the charity he was on the board for. Talk of manure felt only fair."

Javier hid the wince. For some reason, even though he understood her position, he couldn't quite admit his error. Even as relieved as he felt that she had not been charmed by the likes of Clark Linn. "Your father liked him."

"That just makes me depressed. He's a pompous fool. At *best*. My word. Do *you* like him? Because I'm not sure what's worse. That you enjoy his company and think he's someone I could ever consider marrying, or that you're just flinging me at anyone with a pulse."

"There is nothing wrong with Clark."

"Perhaps not. But I'd rather talk about worm castings than golf. I'd rather talk about the digestive tracts of rats than listen to another man ever discuss his putter." She scowled into her drink that *he* had supplied. "It wasn't even a euphemism."

Javier did not care for the disappointment in her tone, as if she would have preferred the man make crude mention of his...putter.

"Javier, you can't really expect this to work," she said, turning to face him, her violet eyes full of exasperation.

"It was one man, Matilda. I have many more lined up." Of course, as he went through his mental list, he was wondering why he'd included most of them. They all had something wrong with them, and picturing Matilda laughing with any of them made him feel...off.

Her gaze surveyed the room. "Lucky me," she said darkly.

"The next one is Diego Reyes. He is a controller at the botanical gardens. This should spark your interest, no?" Something in common. That was why he'd chosen Diego. He could give her something she wanted.

Why that felt like acid in his gut he would not consider.

"What on earth is a controller?" she asked, sounding exasperated.

"Finance, *cariño*. He comes from old money here in Barcelona, and while his profession might be dollars and cents, he has an interest in the gardens themselves. He may even care about worm casings."

"Castings," she muttered.

"We will find him and I will introduce you."

"Or I could go home. And I don't mean *your* home."

"Do you really want to be alone in that tiny little cottage forever?" What she really wanted was of no matter, of course, but he did not understand her choices. Her wants. Clearly some people remembered her little stint with fame, but most did not pay her any special mind. Years had passed. She could go back to the heiress life she'd had without much problem.

She'd enjoyed herself back then. How she could go from enjoying that to enjoying a Highlands cottage made no sense.

"I don't know, but I'd rather be alone than be chained to someone I can't stand. I know you think our parents did not love each other, so I won't argue that point, but I know they enjoyed each other's company."

He had no wish to discuss that. She had been young and naive. *He* had been old enough to understand all their parents had found in each other was comfort. Not love.

Never love.

"So, we wipe Clark off the list," Javier said, focusing on the important task at hand. "And we give Diego the time of day. You cannot expect to find an enjoyable companion when your only companion is plants. If nothing else, I do this for your mental health."

"Oh, yes, of course. You are a selfless saint, Javier. Everyone knows this about you."

No, he did not consider himself selfless, but he did consider himself in charge. Someone who knew what was best for her, as her father would have wished it.

So he hailed Diego from across the room. "Let us move on to bachelor number two."

Diego did in fact have an interest in plants, Mattie found. He even told some entertaining stories about the botanical gardens and made her eager to visit. For a few fleeting moments, she thought maybe… Maybe she could suck it up and do as Javier wanted and maybe in all this ridiculousness, she could find someone who might not be odious.

She had no plans to marry *anyone* in six months' time, but that didn't mean she had to be completely close-minded to the beginnings of a relationship, she supposed. Diego was handsome and charming and they shared a common interest. He didn't even flinch when she mentioned worm castings—she was considering that a sort of litmus test for all these men Javier threw at her.

She glanced around the room, not fully realizing what she was doing until her gaze landed on Javier. He stood—about a head taller than the two other men he spoke with. He was smiling, nodding. He looked…not relaxed, she supposed, but far more…calm than when he was with her. What did that mean?

"What possessed you to wear such a terrible outfit this evening, *querida*?" Diego asked, bringing her attention back to him.

He was aiming that charming smile at her so that the words she thought she'd heard made almost no sense at all. Maybe she'd misunderstood his question.

"I beg your pardon?"

But he reached out, gave the little flare of fabric that

began her skirt a derisive tug. "Surely you can do better than this."

She could only blink at him for long ticking seconds. This man was looking at her very nearly adoringly and yet... criticizing her. Her *clothes*?

"You are very amusing," he said, somewhat apologetically, all the while smiling. But there was something in his dark eyes that didn't match the smile as he continued. "But I could not be seen with such inelegant style. The hair alone." He grimaced. "Such a terrible color."

Mattie tried to find words, but she was rendered mute. Flung back into that old place of sheer embarrassment. Mute from criticism. She had never encountered much of it, admittedly, until the broken engagement had been splashed all over the papers and internet—thanks to Pietro.

This was more private than public, and yet she still felt that same awful shame sweep through her. Because she'd thought he was charming for a moment. Because she'd actually thought she might let him take her out on a real date.

And then this.

"I know what Javier's about," Diego said conversationally. "We all know what he's about. Many of us are quite on board with something of an arranged marriage, but I would need to see some effort."

"Effort," Mattie repeated. Dumbly.

"To be seen on *my* arm, I'd need a woman who understood the allure and importance of femininity. A delicate laugh, instead of whatever that thing you trotted out was. Somewhere between a seal and a dolphin. Darker hair, for certain, which can be accomplished in the appropriate salon. Better posture wouldn't hurt. And this *immodesty*," he said, gesturing at her *chest*, "would be ours and ours alone."

He said this like she should nod along, and she almost

did. Except it was the stupidest thing she'd ever heard anyone say. It made Clark opining about golf clubs seem like high philosophy.

She dreamed about dumping her entire drink over Diego's head. Or punching him square in the nose, if she had any idea of how to punch and do damage. But something that created a scene would only make this just like the *then* these awful internal feelings reminded her so much of.

She refused to be that girl again. Elena had taught her how to handle rude men. And he *was* being rude, and completely ridiculous. Worse than yammering on about golf clubs.

She carefully set her drink down so she wasn't tempted to throw it at him anymore. Looked him dead in the eye, and calmly delivered her takedown. "Diego, I do not know what you think of me, what you expected from me, but you are a rude, shallow ass, and the idea that I would ever consider marrying you is so ludicrous I cannot imagine how you came up with it. I talked to you as a *favor* to my stepbrother. I think he was worried that you had no friends."

She leaned forward, reached out and patted his arm as his mouth dropped open. "I am *so* sorry you're confused, but I think we're done here." Then she flashed him a smile and carefully turned away, making certain it looked casual and not like a flounce or a storm.

She didn't walk toward Javier. She walked toward the exit. She had to get out of here. Reevaluate what strange twists of fate had led her back to this same awful place she'd left.

You mean ran away from?

But she didn't want that much self-reflection right now. She just wanted *out*. So she didn't head for Javier's car that would be waiting—and wouldn't take her without Javier.

But a rideshare app would.

CHAPTER EIGHT

JAVIER KNEW BETTER than to let his anger simmer. Simmers turned to boiling turned to explosions, but none of his normal calming techniques worked on the drive home.

She had left. *Left.* Without telling him anything. Not where she was going. Not why. This had not been a part of his plans, and it enraged him.

He had never worked so hard to help someone so determined to waste his help. His protection. His guidance. And to be blamed as though it was all his fault when he would have been happy to leave her in Scotland *forever.*

Spoiled heiress did not begin to cover what she was. *Unacceptable* did not begin to describe her behavior. He had not thought he would have to lay down rules like she was still a teenager, but it was clearer and clearer to him that her isolation had not helped her be anything but an ungrateful brat.

He would not accept this. He would exert his control in whatever way was necessary. She *would* be married, if he had to handpick the groom, and force them both down the aisle. If Ewan had wanted something different, he should have lived. He should not have put such stipulations in his will.

Because one thing was for certain. Under no circumstances would Javier himself marry Matilda. He had no wish

to marry *ever*, as Ewan no doubt had known and added to
his will as incentive.

Javier would not put the stain of his father on another
generation, and if anything made that clear to him, it was
the white-hot fury that he had been so sure he'd eradicated
from his life. Packed it up in a deep, dark box he never let
around people.

Only Matilda tested that.

How *dare* she.

A thought that repeated in his head the entire ride home,
no matter how many mantras he repeated to himself, no
matter how he used the breathing techniques Ewan had
taught him. It seemed some twisted poetic justice that the
man who'd taught him how to control his temper would have
a daughter who would test it with every breath she took.

Javier was practically out of the car before it stopped. He
should take his time, find some calm and center, but he did
not. He went tearing through his house, determined to…

Something.

He found her in one of his studies—the one he liked
best and used only for personal pursuits. No work, nothing
stressful. This was his personal oasis.

And she was sitting there in his favorite chair like she
knew, when she couldn't possibly. She was back in her hideous pajamas, hair piled atop her head, curled up in *his*
chair, reading *his* book and sipping *his* brandy.

It wasn't rage, heavy and twisting and impossible to
breathe through, inside him, though it should have been. It
wasn't anything he recognized squeezing every last atom of
air out of him. Just something too big, too uncomfortable.

If he had a scalpel, he would use it on himself this moment, cut his aching chest right down the middle and eradicate whatever this was.

Matilda looked up as if sensing him there. She did not have the good sense to look guilty or apologetic. She went right back to reading his book. "Good evening, Javier," she said casually, as if anything happening was just normal. "I didn't expect you home so early."

"Odd how I felt the need to make a hasty exit when my companion for the evening disappeared."

"I didn't disappear. Your entire staff knew where I was once I arrived home some…" She looked at her watch. "Half hour ago, I suppose. Let's not get dramatic. If I recall, you find such behavior *immature*."

Javier could count the times he'd been shocked into silence on one hand. This was one of those moments. He could find no words.

She had accused him—him, Javier Alatorre, survivor and beyond successful businessman—of being immature. When she was the one who could not follow a simple instruction.

"You knew that I had one more person to introduce you to. You knew that I would not approve of your early departure, and that is why you did not approach my driver. Or *me*. You knew what the expectations were, and you did not meet them, Matilda." He did not growl these words and he considered this a feat of his impressive control.

"What are you going to do about it, Javier? Play daddy?" She rolled her eyes. "Punish me?"

For a moment, it seemed the earth simply tilted. Fire lit from within. A terrible, awful need.

All these years he'd ignored this, hidden it, argued it away as something else, but it had been simmering. And for some reason in this moment, he could no longer deny.

But how could he want her? Why did he want her? It made no earthly sense. Nothing in this moment made any sense and he had to reach out to the wall to hold himself upright. To breathe through too many terrible things battering him.

And she just kept talking.

"News flash, Javier. You do not have the authority to ground me or anything else."

He had not been thinking of grounding when she'd mentioned punishment, but she was moving on—thank goodness. He could too. With careful breathing. With a reminder of all he'd risen from and would not go back to.

"And partly it's my fault for allowing you to steamroll me back at my cottage," she continued. "But tonight made it clear that this needs to end. We need to find a compromise."

Compromise. He did not *do* compromise, but it was enough of a business word he could call on some of his usual cool and calm demeanor when allowing people to think they were getting a compromise when they were getting anything but.

"And what do you suggest?"

"For starters, I will not be flung at man after man at these events. Your taste in men is appalling."

"I suppose that is why I focus on women."

For a moment, he thought she might laugh. He waited for it, but her mouth only barely curved. Why did it disappoint him to not hear that sound? It shouldn't. He couldn't let it.

"And just what was so wrong with Diego?" he demanded instead, lest he find himself continuing to wait for said laugh.

Something flashed in her eyes, almost like a strange vulnerability, but clearly he was imagining things as it disappeared and she lifted a defiant chin.

"He insulted me."

"Perdón?"

"He said that I had a lot of work to do before he would

even consider having a kind of arranged marriage with me." She made a vague waving motion with her hand as if to encompass all she was. "My style was wrong. My hair too bright. My laugh too loud."

A different kind of fury twisted in Javier's chest. Not at Matilda, but *for* Matilda. That anyone would say such outrageous lies to her.

Perhaps her style was different, but it was not wrong. Her hair was gorgeous. Her laugh…

"I'm sorry you had another stag waiting to mount," she continued, not sounding the least bit sorry. "But I simply could not bear another conversation with another insipid… *jobby.*"

"I do not know this word."

"Good."

Javier was tempted to pinch the bridge of his nose as something dull and pounding began in between his eyes. A stress headache, courtesy of Matilda Willoughby. Perfect.

"Perhaps if you wished to be so choosy, you should have not hidden away for three years," he offered, though if Diego had truly said the things Matilda claimed without any of her worm shenanigans, he was an even bigger fool than Clark.

She shrugged, unbothered. "Perhaps," she agreed readily. Too readily for him to believe it. "And perhaps if you did not have such a warped sense of duty, I would not need to choose. We could go down a million *perhaps* roads, Javier. Oddly enough, they all hinge on your determination to see this through."

"Your father's wishes? Yes, what an ogre I am."

She sighed. Heavily. Which was his go-to, and he frowned at her using it on him. She set the book—*his* book—aside, and the drink—*his* liquor. Then she stood, crossed her arms over her chest and met his gaze.

He wanted to touch her. *Inhale* her and the way she made this room smell like flowers and earth instead of the usual mix of lemon and wax.

He wanted to burn the world down over what she was doing to him, no matter how little he planned on letting himself act on such atrocious impulses.

"It seems as if my worst-case scenario is that you are forced to marry me in six months, and likely ship me back to Scotland so you can live in peace. I'm finding this less and less of an appalling option, Javier. You would make a fine husband as you would not want to spend a moment with me, and I could go back to my old life."

The very idea was like an ice water bath. *Never.* Never would he betray Ewan in such a way, since he knew that could never have been the man's intent. All that was warped within him anywhere near his precious daughter? This was bad enough right here.

And she needed to get it through her thick skull he was not an option, shipping her back to Scotland or no. "Your worst-case scenario is that you marry no one, and I cut you off from everything. There is no *old* life, Matilda. There is only your father's will."

Some of her defiance slumped. "Would you honestly do that to me, Javier? Because that is not the term of my father's will."

"It is if you cannot fall in line. I will ensure it."

She searched his face with too much openness, too much vulnerability showing there in her expression. "I will never understand you, Javier," she said so quietly it was almost a whisper. "How hard you are when it comes to your mother and me."

"You know nothing about my mother, Matilda. You know nothing about me, and it is best we leave it that way. Now,

Friday night we will attend a charity gala for the Coalition of Rural Safety. You will attend and not escape early. You will behave yourself as I am the president of the coalition, and your behavior is a direct reflection on me. I will not *introduce* anyone to you if that is the compromise you desire, but you will be required to speak to some men of your own accord."

"Required?" she replied. Then she laughed, but there was no humor in the sound. "What does this charity you're president of do?"

"They help fund and expand rural safe houses, protect domestic violence victims and transition them into new lives. Among other things."

"I'm glad you know the name of the charity, Javier. That speaks well of you when compared to the awful men you think are suitable to be my husband."

"I am only providing you options, *cariño*. I never said you had to marry either of them. Feel free to find your own." He knew he should not say the next, but it seemed the only way to escape this hideous, inappropriate, inescapable lust. "But we know your track record on that score."

"Yes, we do," she said quietly, that same flash to her eyes that looked too close to hurt to name.

And since he wanted nothing to do with that, he turned on a heel and left.

Mattie sat in the cozy study but only felt a chill. She had known Javier had it in him to be harsh, but she seemed to bring out a meanness in him that made her heart twist.

Her "track record" was appalling. Because it was only Pietro and that had been an unmitigated disaster, and maybe she could admit here in the silence of an unfamiliar room that she wasn't over it. She didn't trust herself.

Oh, it was easy enough to pick out a Clark or a Diego as being a bad fit. But she *had* been charmed by Diego. Then he'd pointed out all her flaws. Easily noting all the things she worried about internally, like he could sense them.

Or like there really *was* something wrong with her. And isn't that what she'd feared? Isn't that why three years of isolation, though lonely, had felt like a reprieve? Because she didn't have to worry if she was all wrong. Whether it be *her*, or her ability to determine if someone was a good person or not.

Funny that she could look at Javier, who was so irritating and overbearing and *rude*, and yet she knew...with no doubts...that he was a good man. Not just because her father had loved him, but because he took his responsibilities seriously. Because Javier had loved her father—for *him*, not his company, or his money, even if he'd ended up with some of both.

It would be easier if she could paint him the evil monster, but she knew at worst he was just misguided. And probably had never really dealt with his grief over her father. He'd probably buried it under work and women.

Women. So many eyes had followed him around the room tonight. And he had smiled at some of them, touched their arms or shoulders. Spoken to them and laughed. He could have any of them, and she could not fathom why that made her stomach hurt.

So she wouldn't spend another minute thinking about it.

She thought about going to bed but knew she'd only stew. She could go walk the gardens, even work on her little plot if she could hunt up some kind of lantern. But as much as those things brought her peace, they didn't eradicate frustrated thinking patterns. They tended to allow her to dig into them.

So, she did what she did when she was back in Scotland and struggling with loneliness. She called her stepmother.

She pulled out her phone and dialed Elena for the first time since she'd arrived in Spain. When her stepmother answered with enthusiasm, Mattie figured she could not possibly know what was going on.

"It is good to hear your voice. How is Barcelona treating you?" Elena asked in her usual warm cheeriness, at total odds with her son's usual icy distance.

So Mattie decided to jump right into it. "Do you know what he's up to?"

"Well." There was a long, drawn-out pause. "Yes."

Mattie's mouth dropped open, even if Elena couldn't see it. Because Elena said nothing else. Offered no commiseration. She was just *silent*. Like she agreed with Javier.

"I know you have your reservations about the situation," Elena said. "But it is not such a bad thing to be taken care of, *mi niña hermosa*. I know Javier is going about it in his typical rigid fashion, but I'm certain you can make the best of it."

"Best of being marched around like goods to be sold?" Mattie could hardly believe Elena would suggest such a thing.

Elena was quiet for a moment. "Mattie, you know I love you. I think you're a beautiful, smart, sweet woman. I also know that you loved your little cottage."

Mattie could not begin to understand where this was going. She just had a feeling of dread settle over her, like bad news was on the horizon. Like this would not be the comfort she'd sought. At all.

"Perhaps this is not the exact situation I would have chosen for you, but I'm glad you're in Barcelona. I'm glad you're not hiding any longer."

"Hiding? I wasn't hiding," Mattie replied, a knee-jerk reaction. "I was *finding* myself."

"I know this is what you told yourself, but… Trust me. A person does not find themselves by refusing to engage with the things that hurt them. I have been trying to slowly encourage you to that realization yourself."

Mattie thought back to the visits she'd had with Elena. The invitations to stay longer, to move in with her. Suggesting she get another degree, a job. Never as pushy and demanding as her son, but… Yes, she supposed Elena had been urging her toward something.

"I was happy in Scotland."

"Perhaps. Or perhaps you were just comfortable."

Mattie sat a little straighter in the chair she'd been lounging in. Those words hit…hard. "I…" She had no easy argument. She found no words to insist otherwise.

She had been more comfortable than happy, and it was a shock to realize it here. Now. When she didn't want to be *here*.

"Isolation can be a wonderful thing, but it is no good for you when you are hiding. That is not solitude. It is…well, cowardice. I have done such, my dear. It is why I took so long to marry your father. I was afraid of all my past mistakes. All that was wrong with *me*. I was a coward, and it took time and healing to be brave enough to say yes to him."

Mattie frowned a little, wondering what confident and nurturing Elena might have ever doubted herself over. But she supposed it didn't matter. The thing was she'd gotten over it, married her father. "I am glad you did."

"Me too," Elena said, her voice tight with grief. "And I know you are not a coward, Mattie. That is not you. Not at your heart."

Mattie had to swallow the lump in her throat. She felt

chastised, though she knew that wasn't Elena's intent. But it was something… It felt like something her father would have said to her. She would have argued with him. Scoffed at how little he understood her.

Then, eventually, realize he was right.

Wasn't this the realization she'd been butting up against in her short time here? She had loved her isolation, but that was because it had been safe. Because she didn't have to worry. She had convinced herself it was honorable, but…

She *had* been hiding. From all her pain. All her doubts. It had *felt* good, but she did not know if it had been good *for* her. As a person. As a mature adult. Perhaps it had even kept her from wonderful things.

Still… Javier's plans did not feel like the right course of action to correct that.

"Do you honestly think I should let Javier take me from event to event, flinging terrible men at me?"

"You must do what I always do when my son thinks he's right about something foolish. Play along. Agree with him whenever and however—externally. Then, do whatever you feel is best regardless. You do not need his approval or agreement."

"And yet *you* think I should go on this ridiculous husband hunt?" Mattie demanded, because regardless of all the mistakes she'd maybe made in hiding away, she was certain this was not what she wanted. "Being married is not the be-all and end-all for me."

Elena sighed audibly in the phone. "Nor should it be, *mi niña*. But being alone is not good for you, no matter how much it feels as though it is. Your father knew you had a tendency to withdraw when faced with…discomfort. And he was right. Perhaps you do not find the man for you on this journey, but you should *try*. Put yourself out there. Allow for possibilities. Possibilities are what life is made of. What is the harm?"

That had been what she'd told herself when she agreed to go with Javier. *What is the harm*? But she saw it in all the ways it reminded her of three years ago. In the way she couldn't trust herself. It reminded her of all that hurt, and it made her want to…

Well, as Elena had said her father thought. Withdraw. Hide. Because… "I… I really thought I was in love with Pietro, Elena. How could I…put myself out there again knowing how bad I am at this?"

Elena made a considering noise because she was always good at this. Listening, and not responding so quickly, so decisively that Mattie felt honor bound to resist advice. She gave the questions, the concerns space.

"Let me say this. Something I have never shared with you for a wide variety of reasons. Before your father, I survived a terrible marriage. Not because I was forced to marry, but because I fancied myself in love with a man who could not love at all. Not me. Not his child. This was my choice, and a wrong choice I stuck with for far too many years. Then, with your father, I held back. For too many years. Afraid of making the same mistakes when I knew he was nothing like the first man."

Mattie was shocked. She'd never heard Elena mention her previous husband, who Mattie could only guess was Javier's father. Mattie had always known it was not a topic she could broach with either of them. Part of her had always assumed—clearly naively—that he had died, and that the loss was too painful to bear, much like it had been for her father with her own mother. Mattie had never wanted to be the cause of such pain, so she'd never broached the subject with anyone.

But now… So many things fell into place. The scars on Javier's side. The charity gala he was so serious about. His lack of sympathy for her situation when he'd actually been through some kind of hell, not just an uncomfortable situation.

"I had not yet given myself the chance to heal, to grow, and when I finally did your father was there. You were there. Even this terrible mistake I made for far too long was not the end of my world, my life. You cannot think mistakes are the worst thing that can happen to you, *mi niña*. You must learn to have some grace with yourself."

Mattie closed her eyes. Those words seemed to cut deep even though she didn't feel like she'd been especially hard on herself, kept herself from things she enjoyed because of something she'd chosen.

But maybe…

"I was seventeen when I married this man. And you were just as young when you thought a scheming *actor*—who did all he could to fool you—charmed you, while you were still grieving. Now you are older and wiser. You will make better choices, and some will be mistakes, but that is part of life."

Mattie gripped the phone. She wanted that to be true, but… "Are you so sure?"

"Positive. I married a monster, Mattie. And I stayed for far too long. Your father was a bright light in our lives after much darkness. It is why Javier is so devoted to his memory. Ewan was the only one who did anything right by him."

"Elena. You—"

"No, it is true, much as I hate to admit it. So, do me a favor. Play along. *Try* to find someone. And I will be very surprised if you do not find someone who'll be very good to you by the end of six months. But if you do not, I will stand up for you to Javier, for what little good it will do."

Mattie felt as if she had no choice now. She would do anything for Elena, and perhaps... Perhaps this would be better for her than continuing to hide. Not that she thought she'd find anyone. Just that... Well, she didn't have to fight so hard against it.

But that did not mean she would be *grateful* to Javier. "I hope that doesn't mean I have to be sweet and accommodating to your son."

Elena laughed, low and husky. "Ah, of course not! You must make his life hell, sweet girl. You know, you are not so different. Javier might give the illusion of being in the middle of things, but he is just as withdrawn in the middle of people and business and that haunted estate as you were out in Scotland."

Which Mattie saw for the truth, and it made her heart hurt for him. Especially now that she understood... Elena had called his father a monster, and Elena was not one to exaggerate. His childhood must have been very difficult indeed.

"That being said, I don't think either of you fully understands what a soft spot he has for you, Mattie. He plays the cool, aloof taskmaster, I know, but underneath is still a complicated man with feelings, no matter how little he likes it."

"There is nothing soft about Javier," Mattie muttered.

Elena made another considering sound, but she did not press the topic. "Come now. Tell me about the gardens."

So Mattie settled in and did just that, and when she went to bed she did not stew or fret or rage. She went to sleep content.

But when she dreamed it was of monsters and little boys with dark eyes and soft hearts.

CHAPTER NINE

JAVIER ATE HIS breakfast alone as he did most mornings. He was relieved when Mattie did not show up to join him but instead slept in or ate in her rooms. The distance and living of two different lives, with the exception of events, was paramount.

Last night had been... An aberration. He was not going to beat himself up for being attracted to her. She was beautiful. Attraction was a bodily function, and while he had no control over its existence, he had every ounce of control over what he would do about it.

Which was *nothing.* He would marry her off—the sooner the better—and never think of her again.

He wasn't totally inflexible, of course. He'd gone back over his list of potential suitors and set into motion even deeper investigations of the men. He'd never intended to fling just *anyone* at her. But originally, he'd only looked at their finances, their press reputation, external things. Now he would know everything about any man who came within Matilda's orbit at his behest.

He would find her a husband no matter the time, effort or cost. And if this unchecked fervor struck him as odd, he merely pushed the wriggle of doubts away.

This was how you won at life.

"Good morning," a cheerful voice greeted.

Javier looked up from his plate and scowled. She was a *scourge*. And not dressed in any of her frumpy, brown, hiking wear. This morning she looked fresh and ready for... well, a trip to the office. A slim black skirt. A frilly top in a color blue that downplayed the violet in her eyes. Her hair was pulled back and ruthlessly styled into some kind of concoction that hid the wild curls.

He did not repeat her greeting, because she'd made his morning—usually spent alone and in silence—decidedly *not* good.

"Are you planning on going into the WB offices today?" she asked, taking a seat at the table. Next to him. When there were plenty of chairs to keep space.

It was of no matter. He focused on his breakfast and finishing it so he could leave. Not an escape. Just a need for solitude. Just *his* life, *his* schedule, *his* rules. As he liked everything.

"Yes," he answered, attacking his omelet.

"I would like to go with you."

He looked up from his plate. "Why?"

"I *do* have a stake in WB. And there are people who were very kind to me after my father's death that I should not have cut off so wholesale after...everything." Emil himself came out of the kitchen and put a plate in front of Mattie. They smiled at each other as Mattie thanked him.

Javier's scowl deepened at the effect she seemed to have on everyone who was supposed to be devoted to him. "What brought all this on?"

"I spoke with your mother last night."

"Is that so? I know my mother couldn't possibly have taken my side on anything, so you'll have to explain."

"She actually did take your side. She said I'd withdrawn and hidden myself away rather than deal with my problems for the past few years." Matilda slathered jam on a piece of toast, but then she lifted her gaze and skewered him with a pointed look. "Much like you."

He should have known his mother would find a way to support *and* betray him at the same exact time. "I do not have any problems."

She took a bite of toast, chewed thoughtfully. She'd put on makeup, and it sparkled around her eyes, brought his gaze to her mouth, the color of raspberries.

"Maybe you don't, but I think it strange. Your mother began bringing you around my father's house...what? Ten-ish years ago? And while we weren't really in each other's orbit until they married, and even then minimally, that's still about a decade of my life I've known you, and your mother, and been under the impression that your father had passed away."

"I beg your pardon." He could not believe she'd just spoken the words. In all these years he'd never had to explicitly state his father was an off-limits topic. He'd thought it clear.

What had his mother done?

"All these years, I'd always assumed he'd died. Not that he was, in your mother's words, a monster."

Ice skittered down his spine. Memories he'd long ago erased threatened to pop out of the ether. He very carefully set his fork down. When he spoke, he made sure his voice did not resemble his father's at all. He was quiet. He was calm. He was control. "I will not, under any circumstances, ever discuss that man with you or anyone else. Do you understand?"

Her eyes were soft, far too soft with too much compassion he didn't want. "I think I do."

"You could *never*."

She nodded. Perhaps the first time in these few cursed

days where she didn't argue with him. Didn't try to mount a counterpoint. She just set herself to the task of eating.

Javier was no longer hungry. He got to his feet and strode for the exit, but she spoke before he could fully leave, because of course she did.

"Even if you leave me behind, I'll show up at WB today."

He didn't turn. He didn't even look at her over his shoulder. He stared at the long hallway in front of him.

He wondered if she had any clue the war she was waging inside him. If she would persist in being so *her* if she had any idea where his thoughts continued to dwell no matter how hard he worked to keep her off his mind entirely.

She would run if she knew. Hide. He wished he could let her.

But she needed a husband first.

Mattie didn't bother to attempt to make conversation as they rode to WB's Barcelona headquarters. Javier was angry with her, and for this one, she couldn't blame him.

She thought by addressing his trauma, he might let her in, and that had been so foolish she wondered what was wrong with her. Of course he'd shut her down. He'd shut her down for much less most of their acquaintance.

And still, she could not let it go. What did "monster" mean to Elena? Had he hurt them? Were those scars Javier had from his own father?

Clearly, he did not wish to speak about it, to share with her about it, and she didn't blame him for that, but she couldn't stop thinking about it. What it meant. The way it changed who he was in her eyes. It gave context to his edges and made her feel like that sheltered heiress the press had painted her. Hadn't it been spoiled and self-centered to never have guessed he might have gone through something terrible?

She sighed and watched as the WB Industries building came into view. It was a strange experience. In Javier's home, or in the grand ballroom last night, she hadn't seen the Barcelona she remembered growing up, but this building had been like a second home.

They'd moved to Barcelona after her mother had died, and she had no recollection of their home in London before. Her entire childhood had been here. And much of it spent in these offices.

The driver pulled to the front and Javier got out. He came around and opened her door, but she could tell the move was grudging and simply so no one who might happen by might witness him being rude.

She followed Javier inside, again without saying a word. It was a strange sensation to be back here, to see so much that was familiar and so much that had changed. To watch as people reacted to Javier in much the same way they had reacted to her father.

Respect and even reverence.

She didn't have to ask anyone to know he was a good boss. She could see it in the way he was treated. And again, this gave more insight into the man he was under all that armor.

What made a good man so closed off? So…hard when he wanted to be? It would be a complex and likely painful answer, and for the first time in her life she wanted to… go down a road of complexity and pain if it meant understanding him.

Javier did not stop to talk to any of the people they passed, but judging from the somewhat surprised looks on people's faces, that was rare. So she had to blame herself for that.

They took the elevator to the floor her father's office had been on all those years ago, and intellectually she *knew* Javier had moved into them a few years back, but she'd never *seen* it, or imagined it.

It settled uncomfortably in her. Yet another sign Elena was right. She hadn't just gone to find herself in the Highlands. She'd withdrawn—away from everything and everyone. And while she had learned *some* things about who she was and gained some newer sense of independence, none of it could really be tested until she left that safe little cottage.

And faced her past.

They stepped off the elevator and a woman Mattie recognized looked up, then back down, then up again in a double take.

"Oh!" The woman's smile brightened, and she hopped to her feet. "My goodness, I wouldn't recognize you but for your hair." She grabbed Mattie by her shoulders, smile wide and eyes bright. "Aren't you a beauty?" Her gaze moved to Javier. "Isn't she a beauty, Mr. Alatorre?"

Javier only grunted and strode for the door to his office.

"Would you like me to rearrange your morning?" Mrs. Fernandez—who had once been her father's administrative assistant—asked after him.

"That won't be necessary. Matilda can entertain herself." Then he strode inside the office.

Mrs. Fernandez shook her head. "Someone is grumpy this morning," she said, with all the opposite cheerfulness. "It is so good to see you. So grown. We have missed seeing you around the offices."

"I never did anything but bother you all," Mattie replied, but with a smile because she had never *felt* like a bother. Her father had created what had felt like a second little family out of his team at WB. "Which I plan to do today.

Do you have some time at some point to take me around to anyone who's still here? I... I have been remiss in staying away so long."

"Oh, most of the team is intact. The changeover to Javier was smooth enough, though we all miss your father terribly. Even now, I sometimes show up expecting to see him at his desk. All these years later."

Mattie nodded, a little lump appearing in her throat since she knew that feeling well. She swallowed it away.

Mrs. Fernandez checked her watch. "Give me fifteen minutes, and then we'll make our rounds, yes?"

Mattie nodded. "I'll just wait with Javier." Which he wouldn't appreciate, but part of her felt like she had to see Javier in her father's place to fully accept all these changes.

She stepped through the door, then came to an abrupt stop. So much outside the room had changed, she expected it to feel different in here too.

It didn't. It was still a huge room, with all the same office furniture her father had chosen. Maybe the carpet had changed, and the computer and phone equipment had modernized certainly, but *so* much was the same she half expected to see her father walk in behind her. To smell the familiar scent of his cologne, hear his raspy voice greet her cheerfully.

There's my Mattie girl.

She fought very hard to blink back tears. Javier stood over the desk, booting up his computer but not taking a seat. He was backlit by a giant window that looked out over Barcelona. Mattie had always loved that view. She wondered if Javier ever turned around and looked out it and made up stories about the people walking below, like she and her father had.

She almost asked him, but then she saw the picture on a

bookshelf. The same exact picture in the same exact place her father had kept it. It was the only photo of them all together. On her sweet sixteen.

Her father had died a week later.

"You gave me a necklace," she said. Her voice felt like a throb in her throat, and she shouldn't poke at these old wounds lest she begin crying. But…sometimes the wounds healed better if you gave them a little poke.

Wasn't that Elena's whole point?

Javier looked over at her, then at the picture. "My mother picked it out and put my name on the card," he said, but he did not sound quite as stiff as he had this morning. There was *almost* a hint of warmth in his voice, even if his words weren't warm at all.

She'd known even then Javier hadn't had any part in that necklace, and still part of her had liked to think the gesture had been genuine. Even knowing better. Wasn't that her problem? Blind to the fact someone might not be who she wanted them to be.

The tears in her eyes wouldn't blink away no matter how she tried to fight them. It was too much. The realization these past three years hadn't been what she'd thought, the desperate ache of missing her father, how inadequate she felt in the face of Javier, now understanding that something awful had shaped him.

"You did not have to come here."

She shook her head, meeting Javier's gaze. He looked properly offended at her show of emotion, and that almost made her laugh.

"No, I did." A tear slid over, and she brushed it away quickly. "I had to see it. I didn't think it would hit me quite so hard, but that isn't a bad thing. Some days, I can go almost the entire time without thinking of him. And some days, it hits me so hard out of the blue. How much I miss him. How much I wish he'd had more time."

A little sob escaped, and she was embarrassed, but at the same time, she couldn't lean into that embarrassment. Her father had *died*. She was allowed to cry about that, even all these years later. "But these aren't bad thoughts. That's just the…nature of grief. I'll always love him and wish he was here, and that might hurt, but it's also beautiful."

Then the tears just flowed. She didn't even try to stop it. She needed to get it all out. The grief, the regret. Over everything from then until now. And once she got it out, she'd clean herself up and decide what step to take next.

But for now, she let the release claim her.

She didn't stop when Javier approached. She didn't look at him, but she didn't cover her face either. She just stood there and let herself cry.

His arms came around her. Warm and strong. In all the years they'd known each other, he'd never done such a thing. If he'd ever witnessed her cry—something that had only ever happened around the funeral—he'd always gone in search of Elena to comfort her.

But today it was him. And she remembered what Elena had said last night, about soft spots for her when she was so sure there were no soft spots at all.

"He would not want you this upset, *cariño mio*," Javier said quietly.

Mattie nodded into Javier's chest. "I know, but I needed to be. For a few moments." She took a deep breath, the worst of it subsiding. She leaned into him, grateful that he was here. If she was back at her cottage, she would have found something to do to distract herself, to disassociate, but there was something far more comforting about standing here in the middle of it, leaning on Javier, as she slowly came down from the emotional upheaval.

When she finally had control of herself, she pulled away. He handed her a handkerchief and she mopped up her face. She took a deep breath, then managed to smile at him. "I know that was probably very hard for you to witness, but it was a good thing for me."

For the longest time, Javier said nothing. He just stood in the exact place, his arm still half outstretched as if he'd never moved it after handing her the handkerchief. When he finally spoke, the words were so quiet she nearly didn't hear them. "I think of him every day."

Mattie nodded. It felt like a strange step *toward* something, even though it was an obvious admission. He was working in his office. How could he not? Her throat threatened to close again. "He would be so proud of all you've done for WB." She looked back out at bustling Barcelona. Those people who could have any lives she could dream up and more.

And she'd hidden away for three whole years. All because some man had fooled her. "I don't think he'd be very proud of me."

"He was proud of you no matter what you did or didn't do. And always certain you would find your way."

"So certain he put forced marriage into his will?"

Javier sighed, but before he could admonish her for yet another complaint about the ridiculous clause, she waved it away.

"It doesn't matter. We don't know why he did it, but we do know—*I* do know he loved us both. So, from here on out, I shall endeavor to give him what he asked."

Javier looked at her suspiciously. "I am going to need that promise in writing."

She laughed, surprised to feel that laugh ease the last little aches in her chest. "I didn't say I'd be *agreeable* about the whole thing. Just that I'd try to do it."

His mouth curved, ever so slightly. A strange warmth unfurled inside her, starting low and spreading out. But before she could really think about what it was, what it meant, his phone rang, and his smile was gone as he moved to answer it.

CHAPTER TEN

JAVIER WENT THROUGH a set of meetings, out of sorts and unfocused. Even in those strange first days after Ewan's unexpected death he had been able to focus on business. On maintaining Ewan's legacy. It had seemed more imperative than anything swirling inside him.

How had Matilda put him so off course in so few days? *Nothing* was going as planned and he could not seem to stop thinking about her. Everything was all her fault, of course, but her crying jag made it hard for him to muster up his animosity.

Clearly, it was not her fault. She was a bit of a mess. He on the other hand...

Matilda's words from this morning came back to him. *She said I'd withdrawn and hidden myself away rather than deal with my problems for the past few years. Much like you.*

Hidden? He scoffed. He was the only one in this family who dealt with the logistics, the reality of the situations in front of him. Every problem that landed on his desk was one he dealt with. He'd been the one to uncover Pietro's lies. He'd been the one to deal with the fallout of the canceled wedding. He'd allowed Matilda the purchase of the cottage, the withdrawal from life. And he'd kept WB going.

When Javier finally made his way back to his office at the end of the workday, he found Matilda in the lobby. She sat, an array of people around her like she was holding court. Ewan's stalwart employees, most of whom had personally helped Javier with the transition to full-time leader, looked at her adoringly. Their little princess.

And the thing was, she sat there, listening to them all, appreciating them all. People who weren't connected to her at all, but who'd worked for her father. Who saw her as an extension of a man who'd been good to them for many years.

He thought of what she'd said about Diego criticizing her, and he could not for the life of him understand what was wrong with the man. She was the most beautiful woman in any room, and while she tested his patience on a moment-by-moment basis, he did not know anyone with as good and sweet a heart as Matilda Willoughby.

Which was why he needed to keep his distance.

Darkness poisoned light.

None of the men he would introduce her to tomorrow night were near good enough. He would have to go back to the drawing board. Find her someone…perfect. As good as her. Or close, anyway.

She laughed at something Mrs. Fernandez said, then glanced up, catching sight of him. She smiled. That warmth, that light.

He needed escape.

Much like you, his mother had said to her.

But escape wasn't because he was a coward, because he was hiding, it was because he knew better. It was because he was *saving* her. Yet again.

When would any of the women in his life thank him for it?

"If you are not ready to go, I can send the car back for you," he said, not sure why his voice sounded so rough.

"Oh, no. That's all right." She stood, then went around to

each person in the room and said something to them, then hugged each of them.

When she walked out of the building with him, she seemed...different. They'd been at odds since he'd picked her up in Scotland, but today every encounter they'd had was something else. She had been sad, happy, determined and in the midst of all those emotions seemingly perfectly at peace.

What must that be like?

"Thank you for letting me tag along today, Javier. I'd like to do it more often, but I want some kind of position. Nothing important. Business and numbers are *not* my thing. But I can hardly just sit around for the next six months waiting for a husband to pop out of the woodwork. I need to do something."

"You are rich as sin, Matilda. You could do whatever you wished. Include sit around."

She shook her head. "No. I want to...participate. Carry my weight. I can deliver the mail or something. Clean offices. Just *something*."

He opened his mouth to argue with her. He could hardly have the daughter of Ewan Willoughby delivering mail, but he understood too well the need to carry weight. "I will see what I can work out."

She nodded and settled back into the car seat. "Good."

"I trust you had a good day then."

"It was like...coming home. Before I went to boarding school, they were like my extended family. And they always kept in touch. When I was going to uni, they were all there for me. Kind to Pietro even when he wasn't particularly friendly to them. They always reached out. And then just because Pietro made a fool out of me, I cut them out of my life." She shook her head. "I never realized how im-

mature and hurtful that was. So busy with my own pain."
She shook her head. Then she straightened her shoulders.
"But no more."

Javier had to look away from her, out the window as they
rode back to his home. He had no desire to catalog all the
ways she'd changed in three years, all the ways she was
changing right before his eyes.

When change was only ever the enemy. A detriment to
the control he wielded over everything.

Except her, something inside him whispered.

Well, soon enough she would be someone else's problem. He'd get straight to work on finding her a suitor she
couldn't refuse.

When they arrived in front of his estate, he got out of the
car and strode up the front steps to do just that.

But once again, Matilda didn't follow. She stopped under
the arbor, lush with purple blooms that reminded him of her
eyes. "Your home really is beautiful, Javier. You should take
a moment to enjoy it."

He looked back at her, there under the arbor. The sun
danced in her hair, teasing out the reddest strands that had
worked their way loose over the course of the day. Untamable, just like she was.

Just like this thing inside his chest felt. "And how do you
suggest I *enjoy* it?"

She sighed, shaking her head before climbing the stairs.
But she did not go inside with him. She took him by the arm.

"Take a breath," she returned. She led him back down
the stairs so that they both stood under the twirl and riot
of vines and flowers. The sweet smell of the flowers and
Matilda herself. She looked up at the arbor and the way the
fading sunlight filtered through it.

He could only stare at her. The curve of her mouth, the

unruly strands of curls. If their lives were different, there would be no conflict. He would have bedded her already. That detrimental need didn't claw at him now. It twined along his limbs, whispering curses and lies.

You could have her. What would be the harm?

Lies because their lives were *not* different. She was Ewan's daughter, his ward, and too good for the depth of dark in him.

But when she looked up at him, it almost felt as though she shone some light into that void inside. As if opening up to something good, he could somehow make amends of the past. Heal those old scars he'd hidden away. Boxed up. Kept contained and locked away so that they only ever touched his soul. No one else's.

But any light was a fairy tale. Maybe his mother had believed in it. Maybe it had worked out for her aside from Ewan's untimely death.

But she was not related to the monster she'd married. His father had been Elena's choice, mistake. And this was a stain, yes, but it was not the same.

That monster was Javier's blood. And it wasn't just trauma that made him feel that way. He'd read study upon study of the cycle of violence. Of how hard it was to stop. He understood the science, the psychology of it all. He was marked.

So his only chance at stopping that cycle—something he would do everything in his power to do—was to keep himself apart from any chance at perpetuating it.

And still, they looked at each other, gazes locked, heated. Usually now was the time she looked away, scurried off.

But tonight, she did not.

He could kiss her, in this moment, and he had no doubt she would not stop him. He had no doubt he saw a flare of interest, curiosity in her gaze. This was not a one-sided betrayal of her father's memory. There was a chemistry that sparked between them, brighter with each passing year.

What would be the harm?

It must have been the devil himself who whispered such terrible words in his mind.

But the devil was a devil because temptation was so very hard to resist.

Mattie was breathless. Off-kilter. Something had…changed. In the air around them, in his gaze, inside her.

He was…close. He was…intent. As though his gaze itself was a touch, as if he could see through her. As if he wanted to.

And something that had always seemed…terrifying— his full attention, any harmless touch, breathing too much of his air—seemed less so in this moment where she felt herself changing.

The idea of him as a *man*—not her stepbrother, not her guardian, but a beautiful, intense *man*—was uncomfortable, but not in an awful way. If she breathed passed that initial knee-jerk reaction to flee, to hide from what felt like danger like she always had in the past, to set it all aside, she found herself…curious.

Was it really danger? Or was it just…one of those complicated things she'd been running from for years? *Hiding* from.

She was done running and hiding, so she leaned in instead, though it went against her initial instinct. Though it made her heart scramble in her chest and heat rush to her cheeks. But in the moment of choosing discomfort, she began to realize there was nothing to fear here.

Maybe she'd lose—make one of those mistakes Elena had

insisted were part of life. Maybe she'd win—find what was on the other side of this strange new territory. But at least she'd stood her ground for once.

Javier didn't move, but his gaze dipped. From her eyes to her mouth.

Heat shot through her, making it hard to catch a breath. Every sensitive part of her felt heavy, needy. She knew what this was, even if it was foreign. Even if she'd never felt it quite like this with that dangerous edge, with such *force*.

This was desire.

"Some of us have responsibilities, *cariño*," he said, and it came out like a growl even as his expression remained remote. "And cannot spend our day smelling the roses. If you'll excuse me."

"They're not roses, they're bougainvillea," she muttered after his retreating form.

He didn't even pause to acknowledge the correction. He walked away as though she was nothing.

It made her want to…yell. Stomp her feet. But she just stood under the arbor, throbbing, for the first time in her life truly understanding desire. Because she had never felt this wild, dark, thrilling thing with Pietro. He had always been so…kind, gentlemanly. She'd fancied him a romantic because he'd always been so careful with her. Even though they'd dated for two full years before their engagement, he had been clear on waiting to do anything more than kiss her on the lips until they were married.

She had thought it romantic at the time, *safe*. Now she realized it was the words of a man who couldn't muster up the fake interest to want her even though he could muster up acting as though he loved her.

And now that landed in her worse than before, because clearly… No, there was no *clearly* when it came to Javier.

She did not know what that moment was. Not *faked* interest—he'd all but run away. So, whatever that moment meant to him, he wanted nothing to do with it.

Perhaps he found her attractive now that she was more age-appropriate, but he did not *like* her. He'd made that clear.

Well, he had comforted her in his office this morning, that little soft spot his mother had mentioned. It was not Javier's natural state to comfort, so he must care in some way. But it was likely only as an extension of her father's wishes.

Which meant he'd never act on anything that arced between them. He'd always see her as Ewan's daughter. Nothing more. Nothing less.

She blew out a frustrated breath. He had looked at her mouth. And oh, how she wanted to know what it would feel like. Javier Alatorre's lips on hers. The thought alone sent a shiver through her in this humid evening air, and for a moment she could almost imagine what it would feel like to have his hands on her bare skin.

This heat, this need that curled inside her was so new and different from anything she'd ever felt. Anything she'd ever *allowed* herself to feel.

Because she always played it so damn safe. Pietro hadn't been, but she'd thought he was because he'd put up a safe front. He hadn't made her conflicted, even if it had all been lies.

Well, she'd give Javier something. He'd never felt safe. It was just now, for the first time, she thought she might want a taste of danger.

He'd never give her that. *Ewan's daughter.* Nothing more. That settled inside her like such a loss she had to...do something. Prove something. *Be* someone more than just a man's daughter.

Well, Javier wasn't the only man in the world, was he?

Maybe she'd never felt desire before, but now she had. Now it enveloped her. Other men had fierce dark eyes, harsh, unsmiling mouths. Other men were tall and broad-shouldered and handsome.

She could have desire for someone else. She *would*. At the charity gala, she would find someone who looked at her the way Javier just had, but a man who would *act* on that look. Even if she didn't marry him. Even if he was a terrible person. Even if it was a mistake.

She'd survive.

After all, isn't that what Javier did? Slept with anything pretty that moved?

Friday, someone would want her. And she would want them right back.

CHAPTER ELEVEN

JAVIER FOUND HIMSELF waiting again. He would claim it put him in a foul temper, but he'd already been in one. One that had darkened his door ever since the moment in front of his house two nights ago.

He had been far too close to letting his baser thoughts win, and he had yet to find a way to combat the temptation that was Matilda. Getting her out of his orbit quickly was key, he knew, but it was a delicate situation.

He had to find some better way to…

All thought left his brain as she appeared at the top of his stairs. Siren-red dress. What little of it there was. Acres of pale skin. Her eyes sparkled like jewels, and her hair was loose and wild.

Every part of him tightened, *yearned*. He would burn himself on all that flame, and it would be surely worth it. He nearly reached out for her when she reached the bottom of the stairs. Nearly jerked her to him, to devour her on the spot.

He could. Taste her. Take her. Right here. Right now.

"Is everything all right?" she asked. All innocent-eyed while standing there looking like sin incarnate. There was a high neck to the top, giving an illusion of modesty, but the sparkling fabric displayed her curves as generously as if it was skin itself.

It took great effort to speak. "This is quite a different ensemble than your last."

She looked down at the dress. "Is it? Because there aren't pants?"

"Because there is so much skin, *cariño*. I'm not sure this is an appropriate choice for a charity function."

"Carmen disagreed. She insisted I wear this one. And I saw plenty of women at the ball the other night in dresses much like this one. Besides, if I am to be married, I would want the man to find me attractive. Apparently, some find me *too much*, so I shall endeavor to find someone who does not find red hair and a loud laugh such an abomination. I feel like this ensemble goes with that goal."

Rage twisted along all that desire, so many sharp edges he felt as if he was being attacked from the inside. "If you let that *fool* in your thoughts for more than a second, then I do not know what to tell you. Nothing he said was true. If I had to guess, it was some warped attempt at control. You are better than falling for that."

"Am I?"

"You are older and wiser, Matilda. Behave it. Believe it."

"I shall try." Then she smiled up at him, practically beaming. She linked arms with him and began to walk toward the door. He curled his fingers into his palm to keep from sliding his hand up her bare arm.

"Who do you have in store for me tonight?" she asked cheerfully. Another change from the other night. Her attitude about the whole thing. He should be happy and grateful. Eager to introduce her to the man he had lined up for tonight.

A man he'd investigated extensively. Finances, business. He'd even had his investigator interview people he'd had relationships with—without him or anyone knowing he was doing such or why. There was no hint of scandal. While not everyone had sung his praises, no one had spoken ill of him.

But the idea of introducing her to him when she looked like *this*... "No one."

She stopped and raised an eyebrow. "I don't understand."

He pulled her along to the car. Once they were in the car, she wouldn't be this close. "After the first event's...issues, shall we call them, I did some deeper diving into my potential grooms. I've culled the list."

"And not one person on this culled list will be at this event?"

"No," he lied. Not certain what possessed him. Except... he could not introduce her to anyone when she was looking like this. Like an invitation.

One he couldn't accept. Because in the car was not better. Her perfume settled around him like a spell. Like poison.

"So why are we going?" she asked, turning toward him in the darkened back seat of the car.

Excellent question.

He was tempted to tell the driver to stop right now. So no one but him got to see her looking like a treat to be licked up, savored, enjoyed.

But he was very worried about what he might do if he allowed them to turn back now.

So he lied more. "You said you wanted some say. Take a turn around the room and see if you can't find a man of your own choosing. We can always do something of a background check on him after the fact if you so wish."

"How pathetic," she murmured, leaning back against the seat, looking sad. "Why can't I be normal?"

"Because you're rich, *cariño*. It is a price you pay. It is not something you should take personally. It should simply be something you accept."

"Oh, just accept it? Well, of course. Why did I not think

of that?" The sarcasm dripped from her words, but she smiled at him all the same.

He could reach out, slide his hand up the length of her leg. He could lean forward and set his mouth to her neck.

He closed his eyes. *Naturally*, he should want the one thing perfectly and clearly off-limits. No matter how well Ewan had thought of him, under no circumstances would he approve of any of the thoughts Javier was having now.

Her beneath him, naked and his. Taking him deep. *His* for the taking.

So he was a monster after all. But he'd learned how to chain those tendencies. He'd been so sure of it.

Before Matilda.

Mattie would admit, in the privacy of her own mind, that this event was much more enjoyable than the last. Because she *chose* to enjoy it. Or maybe because she had a goal in mind.

Perhaps she wished Javier would have stayed closer to her side since she didn't know very many people. But she was asked to dance by many a man. Offered drinks. She found a woman who'd known her father and had a lovely chat about the coalition, what it did, and how she might be able to volunteer in the future.

It was not so hard to put herself back in the public with a goal in mind. Yes, some looked at her sideways and no doubt whispered about the whole Pietro fiasco, but it had been *three* years. Plenty of the rich and famous had been involved in far more interesting scandals since then.

She was beginning to come to the conclusion that a lot of her anxiety about the public eye was…all in her head. Part of that withdrawing Elena talked about.

"Ah, there you are."

She turned toward an unfamiliar voice from where she

stood on a balcony looking over a large garden she'd been considering exploring. After all, she might be determined to meet a man, but she still loved a garden.

She smiled politely at the approaching form, but she didn't recognize the man who'd come up to her. Should she recognize him? "Oh. Hello," she offered, racking her brain for some memory of who he might be.

"You don't know me," he assured her. He was a nice-looking man. His suit fit him perfectly and was clearly expensive. He had pretty blue eyes and his blond hair was a bit shaggy but styled well. He was tall, broad-shouldered. Handsome enough.

"I think your stepbrother had plans to introduce us this evening, but he seems to be avoiding me," the man said, and he held out his hand. "Well, he's busy ensuring the coalition gets all the donations it needs."

Matilda's brows drew together, and she looked past the open doors of the balcony and searched the interior room for Javier. He had said there was no one to meet tonight, but maybe he hadn't realized this man would be here. There must have been some crossed communications somewhere along the way.

She spotted Javier in a crowd of people. There was a woman dressed *far* more scantily than Mattie herself, considering this woman's skirt was just as brief but the neckline was a deep vee showing off generous breasts. All but *smooshed* into Javier's side. His hand was on the small of her back. He had that charming smile on his face and looked perfectly relaxed. She hadn't seen that relaxed posture from him the whole time she'd been in Spain.

She didn't know why that hurt.

So she looked back at the man and took his offered hand and shook, offering him her best flirtatious smile. He was handsome. Maybe she could cozy right on up to *him*.

"Matilda Willoughby. But call me Mattie. Please."

"Vance Connor."

"You're not from Spain."

Vance smiled. "No. London born and bred. I moved here to work at WB a few years ago, then moved away from corporate finance and into helping those less fortunate."

"Oh, do you work for the coalition?" Mattie asked. She knew working for a charity didn't mean he *had* to be a good person, but she wasn't worried about his personhood, was she? She was worried about finding some heat. Some release.

"I meant artists." He said it deadpan for a moment, then his mouth curved into a charming smile when she'd only blinked. "A joke, I'm afraid. A bad one. I work for the art museum here in Barcelona in the finance department."

"Well, clearly I have a terrible sense of humor, because that *is* funny."

The blue of his eyes deepened. "Well, we'll have to work on that. Can I get you something from the bar?"

Unlike Clark from the other night, he did just that. Got her a drink, found her a seat. They talked. Of WB. London and Barcelona. He even spoke of some volunteer work he'd done for the coalition—organizing some of their finances.

She mentioned her gardens, and he had good questions if not much knowledge. Which felt fair since when they talked of the art at the museum where he worked, he clearly had much knowledge and interest in art and her very little.

He asked her to dance. He was very gentlemanly. No wandering hands. He danced well, smelled nice and of expensive cologne. He gave her his full attention.

She tried to give him hers, but occasionally she found her gaze wandering to find Javier in the crowd. That woman always at his side. Which would cause Mattie to double her efforts to pay attention to Vance.

It managed to feel a bit like a first date, a good one. She did not feel that same punch she had under the arbor with Javier, but she didn't know this man as well. Perhaps her lack of reaction stemmed from those old fears about being tricked. Just because she wasn't hot all over didn't mean a kiss wouldn't be enjoyable.

"Since you're such a fan of plants, why don't we go take a tour of the gardens?" Vance said after their second dance. He offered an elbow. "I can show you around, and maybe you can teach me something about flowers." For the briefest moment, his gaze toured her body. Almost unrecognizable. Not slimy. More an expression of interest she could accept or refuse.

She tried desperately to have some semblance of the reaction she'd had when Javier's gaze had dropped to her mouth.

And failed.

But she took his arm and let him lead her out to the garden, because there was a chance here to do what she wanted. She would power through. If Vance tried to kiss her, she would *enthusiastically* kiss him back. She would make it very clear she was up for anything tonight.

She wouldn't worry about marriage or forever. She wouldn't worry about if he was as nice as he seemed or a hidden scammer. She wouldn't think of Javier at all.

She would focus on lust. Doing something she'd never done before. Jump into whatever danger she could find.

Because she was done running.

Or she'd thought she was.

"Matilda," a dark voice said from the shadows behind her, and *that* voice sent all that sparkling heat cascading through her veins. She turned to find Javier standing behind them, something edgy and sharp in his expression.

"I'm afraid we must take our leave."

"Is everything okay?" she asked. Had Elena had some kind of accident? Maybe there was a fire somewhere.

But he stepped forward, his expression cold. And focused on her arm tucked into Vance's.

Luckily, Vance did not drop her arm. He smiled genially at Javier. "I can bring Mattie home later if she'd like, if you've pressing business, Mr. Alatorre."

"No," Javier said firmly, before Mattie could speak for herself. "I'm afraid I'll need to take Matilda with me."

"Why?" Mattie demanded, a sinking feeling in her chest that this was not something *bad*, it was Javier…being over-protective.

"The car is waiting."

Which did not answer her question. She did not understand what he was doing.

"I'll get your number from Javier's assistant and call you," Vance said quietly in her ear. "How does that sound?"

She nodded and smiled up to him. "I'd like that," she said. He gave her arm a gentle squeeze before releasing her, and she stepped forward toward Javier.

His expression was inscrutable, but there was something in his eyes that reminded her of depictions of hell—flames and tortured souls. And it was something about the thought of him being tortured that had her finally moving, following him through the gala, offering goodbyes to people with fake smiles until they reached his car and got inside.

She didn't say anything at first as the car began its trek back to Javier's estate. She suddenly felt…tired. "Why are we leaving, Javier? What could possibly be so important? When if I recall you chastised me about not leaving early."

"I saved you from something embarrassing again. There

is only one reason a man walks around a dark garden with a woman."

Mattie blinked. He could not be serious. He could not be…stopping this. When she'd made a very conscious decision to do…something. And now here he was? Playing overbearing guardian?

It made no earthly sense, and any exhaustion fled as anger took its place. "Yes, Javier, why do you think I was there?"

If possible, his expression got harder. "Well, I thought you had better sense than to whore about on public property. In the midst of a busy *charitable* gala. Silly me."

The words nearly sucked the very breath out of her, but the sheer hypocrisy of what was happening was too great to be bowled over by. She had to defend herself. "Because you've never done such a thing? Were the women you deigned to touch whoring about, Javier? What about the woman shoving her breasts at you in the *middle* of the party?"

"I beg your pardon."

"I deserve to have my fun too."

"You should have had it before this deadline then. But you chose to have isolation instead. I've half a mind to send you back to Scotland and pick your future husband myself and march you down the aisle in a damn mask."

She laughed. Bitterly. "You might be the most delusional man on the planet," she said. Why had she gone with him? At some point, she needed to find a way to stand up for herself.

She remembered Elena's advice. Go along with him in word, but not in deed. So, she would find Vance's phone number herself. She would call him tomorrow and set up a date.

If Javier had a problem with that, well… It didn't matter. He wanted her to find a husband at all costs. Why should he get in the way when she was finally getting along with someone? Even if her purpose was not marriage, Javier didn't know that.

The car pulled to a stop in front of Javier's estate. He got out, and this time did not open the door for her. It was a petty little slap, and she didn't know why it made her want to laugh. Maybe it was just the knowledge he was angry with her.

But *why*? It made no sense. As far as he knew, she was doing just what he asked. Trying to find herself a husband.

She got out of the car. "Explain this to me," she called after him. "Explain what the hell we're doing, because I am in the dark."

He stopped there at the foot of the stairs, underneath the pretty arbor with all its riotous blooms. He kept his back to her, but he was framed so perfectly by the exterior lights and the flowers. She felt a deep ache and pain in the center of her chest, because…

This was the man she wanted, and she didn't know what to do about it, how to make that happen. It all seemed so impossible.

"You don't find a husband by making poor decisions in a public place."

"Taking a walk is a poor decision?"

He turned then, his expression all patronizing. "If you truly believe that's all he was after, you have much to learn."

"Maybe I wanted what he was after."

"You do not know him."

"Did you know the woman you had your hands all over?" she demanded, stalking toward him. "Because Vance and I *talked*. We had a normal first date conversation, and he seemed to be under the impression that *you* had meant to set us up anyway. So I can't fathom why you'd stop it."

"This is not about me."

She laughed. Bitterly. She wanted to…to…poke him. Shove him. *Do* something to him. But he stood there, stiff and unmovable, looking down at her with anger in his eyes. The sweet smell of bougainvillea washed over her. The blooms seemed to sparkle silver in the moonlight.

And then there was him. Tall. Impressive. Angry, but that only seemed to stir something within her it shouldn't. Why did he have to be so handsome? Why did he have to make her feel like it didn't matter what he said, or did, as long as he looked at her in that way—all heat and need. Maybe that wasn't what *he* felt, but that's what his expression made *her* feel.

"Fine. You are not my prisoner," he said, his voice low, shivering through her like some kind of caress. "If you are so determined to behave recklessly, have the car take you back. Spread your legs for whomever you choose."

She did not understand why in the midst of this ridiculous argument, when she didn't even like him very much right now, her body's response seemed to be: *I choose you.* That she wanted to lean into him instead of slap him or storm away.

His dark gaze dipping again, to her mouth, her breasts. Like he couldn't help himself, because he turned on a heel. "Good night," he said.

Through gritted teeth. With harsh strides. Like a man who could not admit to himself he was running, but, *oh*, he was running.

From her. From what he felt. From this heat.

Because he felt it too.

CHAPTER TWELVE

JAVIER KNEW HE was out of control. He knew all the signs. It was why he removed himself from Matilda and went into his home gym. He punished his body for every last thought he'd had of Matilda, until he was slick with sweat, his muscles quivering and spent.

And still he was hard. For her.

This was an abomination of so many things, and yet he could not control it. Any more than he could seem to control his reaction to her in that garden.

She had been ready to throw herself at some stranger. In the middle of the gala. She might be doing such at this very moment. Letting Vance Connor put his hands on her. Kiss her. Make her inhale with that little shake that made it so clear she was affected by the heat between them.

And he could admit it was hypocritical to have engaged in the exact same sort of behavior before and find fault with her for wanting to engage in it now.

Then a hypocrite he was. He had found nothing wrong with Vance Connor, had been certain he would introduce them, and that Vance would be a very strong possibility for Matilda's future husband.

But this was not about Vance.

It was about Matilda. In that dress. The way she'd smiled at Mrs. Fernandez. The way she spoke about his mother. The way she petted plants like they were puppies. It was about visualizing—very much against his will—what she might have done with Vance Connor in that garden.

It all sent him into a fury he could not control when he had learned to control *everything*.

But he'd left her outside to go track Vance down rather than insist she stay safe in her room. It should *feel* like control, but it didn't. The only thing that he could think would soothe this savage fury inside of him was his hands on her skin.

An abomination.

The workout did nothing to ease the tensions inside him. The riot of emotions he labeled fury even if they were more complicated than simply anger. He stormed to his bathroom and wrenched the shower on. Cold as it would go.

And still, his body ached for simple release.

The water was icy, pounding down, but nothing could erase the heat coursing through him. Hard, heavy. Painful. Something must be done, so he took himself in his own hand. He told himself not to picture Matilda.

He failed. The wild flame of her hair. The way her eyes deepened when she was angry. That earthy scent that seemed to follow her wherever she went like she was some wildflower plucked from her beloved gardens.

He wanted her mouth on him. He wanted to sink into her. To touch that velvet ivory of her skin, to make her scream with pleasure, pulsing around him and—

He heard the creak of a door. *His* door opening. He froze. Surely…

"Javier, we need to talk," she called. As if she didn't know she was walking into his bathroom. She peeked her head in, her gaze landing on him behind the glass of his shower.

He didn't move, didn't take his hand away from what he was doing. For a moment, he was frozen, too many things fighting in his brain to react.

He had not felt such a way in many, many years. He wanted to rage for that alone, but she just stood there. Her cheeks red, her eyes wide. She was still wearing the dress from the gala, but she was barefoot, and she'd washed her face clear of the makeup.

But she did not flee. She stared at him, and there was no doubt she could see *all* of him, what he was doing. And still she stood there, eyes wide and locked on where his hand wrapped around his thick shaft.

It was wrong. He knew this, in his bones, and yet the need roared in his head eradicating all reasonable thought. To order her away. To stop this madness. It could not go on.

But the madness won, the need, the monster inside. So he watched her, and stroked himself, just to see what her reaction would be.

She did not look away. Her breath caught and she stepped closer, her cheeks pink and her mouth hanging just a little open. Then stopped as if she hadn't meant to move at all, as if she didn't know what to do.

"Close the door, Matilda," he ordered through gritted teeth. But he didn't specify which side of it she should be on, and perhaps that was his mistake.

Or his goal.

Mattie tried to find some grip on reality. She'd been so angry, so determined to actually say her piece that she'd been determined to find him at any cost. Even barging in on his shower. At least *there* he couldn't run away from her.

She hadn't expected to *see* anything, or maybe she just hadn't thought at all. She had just known he'd have to face her. Deal with her.

The air was thick with moisture, the room oddly cold, and she could see him through the paned glass of his expansive shower. There was no steam as there should have been if he was taking a hot shower.

Water pounded down on him, rivulets sliding down his impressive, muscled form. But it wasn't the bulge of his arms, the size of his quadriceps, the smattering of hair over his body. No, she couldn't take in any of that. Because he held the hard, thick length of him in his own hand as if he'd been....

Then he slid his hand down it, and up again until everything inside her was flame. He *had* been. She was shaking, wanting. She *throbbed*. Every inch of her body. A need building higher the longer she stood here, watching him touch himself.

Everything about why she was here forgotten. There was only him.

"Close the door, Matilda," he ordered.

And without thinking, she pulled the door closed behind her. Her heart was beating so hard, she could barely hear the pounding of the water.

But she heard him, clear as day.

"You have three choices, Matilda." His voice was low, sharp, demanding. It skittered over her skin wreaking havoc and goose bumps. Choices?

She did not feel a choice at all. She only felt the desperate need to watch him. To see where this led. To hear his voice say her name in that dark, delicious rasp that was so new to them.

"You may run away, as you should."

No. No. No more running away. On this, she was clear. Since she couldn't find her voice, she shook her head.

His gaze seemed to darken there, even shrouded by the rivulets of water and glass separating them. "You may watch."

She let out a shaky exhale. His voice was dark, lulling. *Watch*. Watch...what exactly? Everything? Would he...?

"Or you may disrobe and join me."

She felt as though she'd run a marathon and she couldn't catch her breath. She couldn't find solid ground.

She wanted to touch him. She wanted to *taste* him. All those wants she couldn't quite muster with Vance back at the gala were here, alive and bright. And this was what she'd been after tonight, right?

Lust. Maybe it was dangerous to mix Javier and something so fleeting. Maybe it was wrong on a hundred different levels.

But he was the source of it all.

She had never felt this before. Never *wanted* danger before. Now she could not think for wanting it. She couldn't turn back. She was intrigued by the idea of watching him, but it left a strange little cocoon of safety, and she couldn't allow herself that any longer.

It was time she learned how to weather disaster.

She reached behind her back and pulled the zipper of her dress down. She watched his hand tighten on the hard length of him, and it was if he squeezed her deep inside.

She let the dress fall to the floor. So that she was only in her bra and underwear. Such a strange sensation with Javier's dark eyes intent on her. He had not changed positions at all. He could have been a statue.

If she did not see the way his breath sawed in and out of his chest, she might have believed it.

"The rest," he ordered.

She had never been naked in front of anyone. Not like this. Not *for* this. She had never wanted to be, and she supposed that was why she obeyed. For the first time, she wanted. And Javier wanted her too.

That was why he'd stopped her and brought her home tonight. Maybe he hadn't planned on acting on his wants, but he hadn't wanted her to do anything with Vance either. Jealousy. Possessiveness. Whatever it was, it streaked through her like heat and gave her the confidence to get completely naked.

In front of Javier. Whose beautiful form was naked and wet inside the shower. The impressive muscles, the faded old scars that must have come from childhood trauma. The man she'd told herself she hated.

But she did not hate him in his moment. No. She wanted him. All of him. First or last, it did not matter if he solved this aching need inside her.

He opened the shower door.

Mattie licked her lips, swallowed and then called on all her bravado to step forward and into the shower with Javier.

She squeaked at the ice-cold spray, wondering who would do such a thing to themselves. But he turned her so that it was him taking the icy punishment of the water. He pressed her to the cold wall with one hand on her shoulder, then reached back with the other and flicked the water to hot.

Then their eyes met. She was shivering for so many reasons, the cold probably the least of them.

"This is a mistake," he growled.

"I don't care." Because she didn't. She'd make this mistake a hundred million times if she got to know what was on the other side of all this want. All this *feeling*. Because she was done being afraid.

His gaze slid down the length of her body, slow and intent. She wanted it to be his hands, but for long, ticking moments he just looked. So she looked right back. All that muscle, all that control.

He reached and dragged his thumb across the underside of her breast.

She whimpered. From so little. From so much.

"You should not have chosen this, *cariño mío*. You should have run away."

"I'm done running away." And to prove it, she leaned forward. She pushed off the wall and onto her tiptoes, crashing her mouth to his and flinging her arms around his wet shoulders with more desperation than grace.

Then he was kissing her. Finally. It felt like she'd been waiting for this for *years*, when it had only been days since she'd finally begun to accept that she was attracted to him. That she might be curious to see where the heat in his gaze led.

Naked. Wet. Aching, deep inside. His hands molded over her curves. Big, hot. His mouth devoured hers, tongue and teeth and a need so sharp she didn't know how much more she could stand before she burst.

She needed something. So much. "Please," she said, even though she wasn't quite sure what she begged for. Only something more.

And he gave it to her, his large hand sliding between her legs.

Where no one else had ever been, and somehow, someway, it felt exactly right that it should be him. For all his sternness, the way he blocked himself off, she trusted him. Always had, even when she'd been afraid of what she'd felt.

He touched her there, expert fingers gliding her toward some new plane of existence. All heat and joy. She moved shamelessly against his hand. She would have done anything to chase the feeling he was giving her.

"Greedy," he murmured. "My greedy little flame. Look at you. Wet and desperate. Lose yourself, Matilda. Lose yourself on my fingers."

It was his dark voice, the twist of his fingers, the hot water spraying around them. It was all of it that had her exploding over some new edge, some new world. Into a storm made up only of sensation and the dark, dark heat of Javier's eyes.

She shook, nearly lost her footing, but he held her upright. Held her there as she tried to find some internal balance when everything inside her had shifted, changed, brightened into something different than she'd ever expected.

Had it always been him? She'd convinced herself he was dangerous, something to withdraw from, but maybe all along she'd known this existed on the other side of her fear. And she hadn't been ready for it.

Until now.

His hands moved over her, up her abdomen and over her breasts, his gaze following along until one hand slid up her throat, then stayed there, as if he needed to pin her in place when he only needed that fierce dark gaze to do that.

She did not know why it felt like her entire life centered there on his hand. She did not know why this storm raged inside her when the move should feel threatening.

But it didn't.

It felt like her power up against his.

And she was winning, because he was giving her what she wanted. Almost. *Almost.* "Javier. Please."

"What is it you beg for, *cariño mío*?" he murmured, his palm at her throat, his thumb and forefinger tracing the line of her jaw.

She didn't have much more than the simplest words for this act she'd never done. Never felt the need to. Until him. "You. Inside me."

The noise he made was nearly feral, all growl and wild. He lifted her leg, opening her for him. Lifting her to the exact height she needed to be to take him deep within.

And then he was inside her. So big, too big. Not painful

so much as a weight she couldn't make space for, couldn't accommodate, though she wriggled in place to attempt to do just that. To find something other than this great stretching.

She sucked in a breath, let it slowly out. His groan rumbled through her, a riot of sparks. His chest brushed against her taut nipples, and she arched, pressed, slowly accepted all that length.

The water pounded around them, the air heavy with moisture, and Javier Alatorre was inside her, holding her there. His eyes fierce, his grip tight, and then he moved. All that *too much* shifted into a need for more. Much more. All the more.

They moved together in some dance she'd never been taught but it felt familiar all the same. As if this had always existed inside her. Inside *them*. Tension twisted, built. So many sensations overwhelming her. Hot water, coarse hair, slick skin.

Until it was impossible, this height to which he'd taken her. So high, so achingly wondrous she cried out as it all crashed over, wave after wave. It rattled through her. Not just a storm, but an entire cataclysmic event, because she could feel him shudder as he thrust deep one last time. She could *feel* that he hadn't just brought her to some mind-melting state, she'd brought him there too.

His breathing was rapid, and she could feel tension slowly come back into his body. "This means nothing," he said darkly, all foreboding promise. "It will never happen again. *Never.*"

His words were harsh, ragged. *Desperate.* Because he had to know. He'd changed her, inside and out. Bright and new and his.

His.

No matter what he said about *never.*

CHAPTER THIRTEEN

THE REASONABLE THING to do would be to send her on her way. Javier had made himself a promise there, deep inside her beautiful form.

Only once. Never again. Not his. Just the release of a pressure valve so they could go on through the rest of the next few months by putting this behind him. It was better this way. No wondering would haunt them, tempt them, destroy them. Now they knew.

He wished he'd never discovered that sex, something he had always quite enjoyed, could be different. Could be less about the brief hit of pleasurable dopamine and more about the entire experience.

About the woman, so beautiful, so open, so very much his.

No. Not *his*. That was the whole point. He'd put his hands all over Ewan's perfect daughter and now he had to atone for such a mistake. A onetime mistake.

They would need a businesslike distance to move forward. But first she was standing in his shower, dripping wet and shaking from release. That needed to be taken care of. He turned off the water, retrieved two towels. He tied one around his waist and bundled her up in the other and carried her to bed.

Where he never allowed anyone. *His* space. *His* world.

It should have been unfathomable, but he laid her down in the middle of the large mattress and knew, deep in places he didn't like to look, she was exactly where she was meant to be.

She stretched out on his bed, eyes closed, wrapped in the white towel, her red hair darker wet. She sighed, all sated contentment. And he knew how he *should* feel: horrified, repentant, guilty and damned.

But no matter what he knew, he could not seem to work up those feelings. Not when she looked so happy. Nothing dark and heavy slithered through him. He felt light and...

Things he couldn't name for fear they'd sneak under all his bands of control, for fear they would *win* and ruin everything.

Matilda opened her eyes, fixed him with that beautiful violet gaze, her mouth curved. "How long have you thought of me this way, Javier?"

"I wish I had never thought of you this way," he replied quite honestly. Because she should never have any doubts where they stood. He didn't want to actively hurt her. Maybe his honesty would, but it was better than lies and deceit. He had been up-front from the beginning and would continue to be.

"That doesn't answer my question," she returned. "I was thinking...sometimes, in the old days, you'd touch my hand and I'd feel this...*thing*. It felt dangerous, so I shied away."

"You should have continued to do so."

She sighed, not in exasperation exactly, because she smiled when she did it. But the feeling was close. "So you say. But I quite enjoyed myself, Javier. And you seemed to as well."

Enjoyed was not the word. It was far too simple. Far too

tame. And he could not answer her question, because he did not know and did not wish to.

Sometimes, those times he'd seen her during the three years she'd dated Pietro, he had felt an odd prickle at the base of his skull. A frustration with Pietro's hand in hers. A searing pain at the way she looked up at the other man so adoringly.

It was that which had led Javier to look deeper into Pietro in the first place. To find out all the lies the man had told her, fooled her with. To find out his true intentions.

He'd tricked himself into thinking it was just the due diligence that Ewan would have requested of him. But now, in this moment, he knew.

He just hadn't wanted the marriage to happen. And he'd never know, if Pietro had been completely innocent, if Javier wouldn't have concocted his own reason to stop the wedding.

A terrible, concerning thought.

"Are you going to stand there scowling at me all night?" she asked, smiling indulgently. Like she could read every last thought in his head. Like she knew this weakness inside him.

But one thing she clearly did not know was the darkness. She did not understand that she'd opened herself up to it. That he had to stop all this lest the cycle continue.

He opened his mouth to tell her that she should get dressed and return to her own quarters. To *dismiss* her. Certainly, he had no intent to slide onto the bed himself.

So he had no idea how it turned out that this is what he did. Gathered her against him and tasted her once more. Kissed her until she was writhing against him, until he was hard again, until she murmured his name, wanton and pleading.

But it was she who broke the kiss, who pushed him back though not away. Her gaze traveled down his body, and she wriggled her way down his chest, planting kisses and featherlight touches that had whatever he'd been about to say or do or feel evaporate.

"Cariño mío—"

But she waved him off. "I want to know everything."

It was a strange way of putting it. He didn't like to think of her with Pietro, but they'd been together nearly three years. Surely she'd done "everything" with that slimy bastard. Though she likely hadn't had any male companions during her stint in Scotland.

But he forgot all about Pietro, and everything, when she touched him. Her hand, followed by her silky mouth. Greed over seduction, curiosity over experience.

It did not matter. The sight was too much. She was too much. He was hurtling into a hell that felt too much like heaven. He knew it was a lie, a trick, his own personal downfall, and yet he didn't stop her.

He watched her. Encouraged her. Those violet eyes meeting his. Her mouth full with him. It would haunt him all his days. The pleasure. The pain. He tangled his hands in all that wild flame of her hair, guiding her.

Never again would come tomorrow, and tomorrow would be here soon enough.

Mattie woke up Javier's bed, warm and cozy and a little sore in places she had never once been sore in before. But even in that ache, there was a delicious satisfaction.

She inhaled deeply and let it out slowly. She knew she would not roll over and find him smiling, happy, interested in seeing where all this heat could go. There would be no cheerful or excited plans for where a future could lead.

He'd said *never*, and she did not doubt him for a moment. She was not a fool. Or maybe she was, because she wanted to understand *why*, and had no doubt any attempt would be thorny and painful.

A smart woman let this be this—a wonderful experience to keep her warm and satisfied all her days—and walk away. Maybe she should settle for Vance. Maybe now that she knew all two bodies had to offer each other, she could… replicate it in some way with another man.

But even having never had another experience like this, there was no way to have it with anyone else. Javier meant something to her. It was complicated, and not something she'd fully worked out yet, but it was there.

She turned to him. He lay very still, but his eyes were open. His expression was harsh, closed off, and he held his whole body tense. But he did not say a word, did not attempt to send her on her way.

He just *lay* there.

She studied the scars that marred his muscled frame. Some were jagged, some were small, but they were all there on his torso. She thought of what Elena had told her, and how obvious these scars existed only where they could be hidden away.

She wondered if Javier would tell her…or if he would lie.

She reached out, brushed her fingers across the longest one. "Where are these scars from?"

If possible, he tensed even more. "Where do you think, Matilda?"

"Your father?"

"Indeed."

He didn't need to say much more for her to finally understand in full why her father had meant so much to Javier. Why he felt such a debt to the man. It wasn't just that

Ewan had been kind to him, that her father had supported him in university and business.

It was that Ewan had offered him and his mother peace and safety where they hadn't had any before.

Mattie couldn't even begin to imagine the complexity of feeling that must come from that situation, and she doubted very much she would ever get Javier to speak of it. If she did, it would certainly not be *now* with her naked in his bed.

So she changed the subject, tucking this one away to a time he might be more receptive. "Everyone who knows me calls me Mattie. Except you."

"And so it shall be always."

"Why?"

He rolled off the bed on a sigh. He did not look at her when he said the rest. "Because we are not friends, Matilda. And we will no longer be lovers after you leave this room."

She knew he felt that way. Considered agreeing. It would be the easiest course of action. But much like running away, she wasn't doing that any longer. Easy wasn't always *good*. Sometimes the good things were very, very complicated and hard.

"What if I endeavored to change your mind on that score?" She flung the blanket off of her. Naked and spread out on his bed.

Heat leaped into his dark gaze, nostrils flared, and he curled those large hands into fists. Who knew she would have this kind of effect on a man like Javier? This kind of *power*. It was a heady thing.

Perhaps he didn't want to want her. Perhaps he fought all those impulses when it came to her because of her father or whatever other reasons he might have, but he *had* those wants and impulses. There was something about her that tested this man's impressive resolve.

"You will lose," he insisted. But he didn't prove that statement. He grabbed a shirt and began to pull it on. To get dressed and no doubt storm out.

All these times she'd thought him angry at her for something. Thought him turning away from her was designed to hurt, but she saw it for its truth now. Him walking away was never about her.

"I always thought you were so strong. So brave. Not afraid of anything. Certainly not the kind of coward who is always running away," she said, still quite comfortably naked on his bed. Maybe she should find some embarrassment or shame or timidity, but with Javier...with everything he'd done to her over the course of the evening, she couldn't muster anything other than a smug kind of confidence.

And a new understanding of the man she'd for so long misunderstood.

He stopped abruptly in his retreat, his spine stiffening as he turned to face her. His expression was fierce, and still every inch of him tense and ready for some kind of attack. As if he couldn't quite believe this was just...nice.

"Cowardice." Then he laughed, low and bitter, making her...well, have a *few* doubts about what she'd said, what she felt.

"*Cariño*, I could spend the next few days using you up. Discard you once I've have had enough. It is a kindness that I walk away from you. Time and time again. Perhaps, for once in your life, you should have the good sense to accept my kindness."

She wouldn't let his harsh words get to her. She would focus on the fact he had considered "using her up" at all. "I quite enjoyed the kindness you showed me last night."

"They always do." His smile was mean then.

But it was a mask. It was meant to hurt her, or at least

throw her off. But she could hardly be jealous because she'd had no claim on him before.

Well, if she thought too much about it, perhaps she felt a twinge of jealousy, but not in the way he seemed to think she would. Not in a way that would hurt. It wasn't a bitter envy. It was more a wistfulness that they could not have found each other sooner.

But they could not have. She understood this fully, regardless of what happened from here on out. She had needed these past few years. She had needed her heart broken and to realize just what she did when she failed. She needed to understand her own cowardice, and now that she did... It just didn't seem all that hard to be brave.

It was quite possible he needed more time, and she considered she might even be able to give it to him. But she wouldn't be a coward while she did.

She went ahead and climbed off the bed herself. But she did not worry about her clothes—they were in the bathroom anyway. She simply tugged one of the soft blankets off his bed until she could wrap it around her body.

If he wanted to engage in games, two could play. "I suppose I will see if Vance has messaged me then." She made to set out into the hallway and down to her quarters, though admittedly she prayed she wouldn't run into any staff naked under but a blanket, but if she could make a dramatic exit, she'd risk it.

He grabbed her by the arm instead, stopping her forward movement. "You will not play games with me, little girl." His eyes flashed.

But she understood the anger that radiated off him was not at her, or even her attempt to make him jealous. It was all about whatever was going on inside him. And that...that she couldn't heal for him. He would have to figure some of it out himself.

"It's not a game, Javier," she said, very calmly. "I am endeavoring to give you what you want. I offered myself, you have refused." She lifted her shoulders, attempting to keep her voice calm and vaguely patronizing. "I will not beg."

"You did last night."

She smiled at him. "So did you."

His scowl deepened as he dropped her arm.

Which brought her *immense* satisfaction. This entire strange turn of events did. Perhaps because as left field as it might have seemed if someone had told her this would happen even a few days ago, it felt perfectly right.

Like they'd always been walking toward this moment—whether either of them liked it. Well, Matilda liked it. She liked *him*, for all his faults. But at the core of all those faults was something good. That good thing had just gotten... warped somewhere along the way.

A need to protect. Her. Himself. A need to control likely born out of a childhood where he must have had very little. Because no doubt if Javier's father had *scarred* him, the man had also hurt Elena. And Javier would have borne witness to that.

Poor little boy. Poor Elena.

How long had he held on to those scars, those fears, those traumas? Held tight and polished into something he could bear.

She had never felt particularly protective toward Javier. Never understood that underneath all that...self-assured armor was someone who clearly just needed someone to... care. To *take* care.

She knew he wouldn't welcome that from her, but that

didn't mean she couldn't offer it all the same. And solve some of their problems while she did.

"Here is what I think, Javier. We know and like each other, most of the time. Clearly, we have chemistry. I don't know why I'd bother throwing myself at a parade of men when *we* could be married and likely be quite happy at it."

"Happy? You still believe in fairy tales after everything that happened to you, Matilda?"

"I don't believe happiness is a fairy tale, Javier. I think I've learned that it's a choice. And I think it's one you're afraid to make."

"You would speak to me of fear again?"

"Yes," she replied simply.

"You are terribly misguided, Matilda. And hear me now. I will never marry you. No matter what circumstances arise. I will never, *ever* marry. Not you. Not anyone."

So vehement. So sure. Clearly a decision he'd made long ago. But she could not fully fathom why marriage was such a non-starter to him. Particularly if he considered it a fairy tale when it could also be a friendship, a business arrangement, a facade.

She tightened the blanket around her but didn't cower. She smiled up at him with all the compassion whirling around inside her and asked the simplest of questions she knew he would not want to answer. "Why?"

CHAPTER FOURTEEN

JAVIER DID NOT know why the question struck some deep chord within him. A vibrating, painful ache. When the answer was simple, and something he'd always known.

She shouldn't question it. She was delusional. Whatever experience she'd had with Pietro must have been subpar at best and she was rendered a little senseless by what an exceptional lover could do.

That was all.

So there was no need to go into the reasons he would not marry her. He was Javier Alatorre. He no longer explained himself to anyone. He simply *acted*. He demanded. He *commanded*.

But no matter how certain he was he should not answer her question, he still stood here. Looking down at her. The push and pull of an internal argument inside him.

He should not tell her. He should shut her out.

But if she understood, perhaps she would stop pushing. Perhaps she would stop…

She would never stop. He could not afford delusions about her now. Now that he had done that which he'd sworn never to do. Now that he had to…regain control of the situation.

Because perhaps he had faltered, but he would not fail. He would not simply tear into pieces because he'd taken one misstep. Allowed one misguided *want* to derail that which needed to be done.

Matilda. Married to anyone but him.

So he would make it clear. This wasn't about all that *fear* she kept accusing him of having. It was about all the things someone like her could never understand. Should never understand.

"You know what I come from now, Matilda. I shouldn't have to explain why marriage is impossible."

She got that look in her eye, all determination mixed with something he didn't know how to label. There was a softness to her determination, a vulnerability. The fact that she did not yet know how to hide those was infuriating.

She should be stronger. More in control of herself. She should wield better armor so he could not pierce it any more than he already had.

"But it is not impossible. You've just decided you don't want to do it. And if it's not solely about me being Ewan's daughter—which would still not make it impossible. Actually, the opposite, if I really think about it. But if it's about *ever* marrying *anyone*, I am going to need an explanation."

"I owe you nothing."

"Does everything have to be a debt?"

She was talking in circles. In riddles. Like she was running about digging up all the foundations that kept him upright, so that he was crumbling.

But Javier Alatorre wouldn't crumble. Never again.

"My father was a monster, as my mother told you. He caused the scars on my body, because he was physically abusive toward the both of us."

That softness in her settled in her violet eyes as they deepened with care, concern.

He wanted none of these things from her. They made

him feel weak. Small. Like the little boy who'd cowered in a corner hoping never to be found. Hoping to avoid the blows. Sometimes even wishing it would be his mother in his stead—the monster was her choice, after all, was he not?

And those thoughts, those memories, made him certain of his choices. It made him certain of everything.

It wasn't just the man he was biologically connected to who was a monster.

It was Javier as well.

"It is very clear. Scientifically. Statistically. Children of abuse are more than likely to repeat the cycle. To be a danger to anyone and everyone they come into contact with. I could be selfish. I could gather up anyone and everyone I wanted. I could procreate however I pleased. God knows, plenty do."

Matilda nodded, as if she understood. As if she could. And it made him angry. It made him shake, deep within, with all that violence he'd been handed down. Perhaps he had learned how to control it, but he would never take the chance he might take it out on someone.

Particularly Matilda.

"But I looked at the studies, I looked within myself. I decided to break such a cycle. To let it die with me. So there will be no marriage. There will be nothing. The monster dies here."

Matilda did not nod. She did not cry. She did not agree. She looked confused. "But you are not abusive, Javier."

"Just because I have not used my fists on you, *cariño*, does not mean you know what I am or am not." Who could know?

"You are *not* abusive," she insisted. Missing the point entirely. As he'd known she would. This was why he should not have tried to explain it to her. Explanations never led

anywhere safe, controlled. They never led to anyone understanding that which he *knew*.

So he said nothing. After a while she sighed and shook
her head, but she did not leave. She stood here in his space,
in what was his, and infused it with her scent, with her soft
voice, with too many memories of last night and what she
felt like under his hands, under his mouth, clouding his
mind.

"You speak of studies. Data. But did you ever speak with
someone?"

"I interviewed—"

"No, Javier. Did you speak with anyone about what happened to you? Your mother? A friend? A therapist? Have
you dealt with your own experience in any way? Or did you
simply find the potential effects and decide to control the
universe, so they did not happen to you?"

He pictured icy waters. He envisioned the entire room
encased in it. To fight the tide of hot, dangerous anger. She
needed to leave. Even in his anger, his fury, this uncontrol-
lable thing that felt too close to panic, he would never *show*
her what he was.

That was the gift of control Ewan had given him. "I have
done that which I thought best," he said coolly, envisioning
himself in a boardroom. Giving a speech to his team. Not
her. Not in his room, his sheet.

"That is not healing, Javier."

Healing? Why would he want that? "And you would
know? With your silver platter and perfect father?"

"He wasn't perfect. Nor was being a motherless child.
No, I cannot imagine it left the same scars as what you went
through, particularly with the cushion of wealth, but let us
not pretend my life has been so perfect I could not possibly
understand pain that needs healing."

"It is of no matter, Matilda. I have made my decisions. I will not change my mind. I apologize if last night gave you a false sense of—"

She barked out a laugh, standing there wrapped in his blanket—which should be so utterly ridiculous not alluring in the least. "Oh, Javier. Do not pretend. To apologize. To know what I feel. You do not even know yourself."

"And you do?"

"Not completely, no." She moved forward then, and he held himself still. An iceberg himself. Nothing and no one inside. Just cold. Just ice. Even when she put her soft, warm hand on his chest. "But I would marry you, and I would take care of you. And I would never, ever fear you." She inhaled deeply, watching him with those soft violet eyes. Her exhale danced across his face.

She might as well have stabbed him clean through with the sharpest blade she could wield.

"I do not think you are a monster. For all the ways I have been angry at you, frustrated with you, confused by you, I have never been scared of who you are as a man. I know you would not hurt me in any of the ways you fear, and I know that… It must be very hard to believe that about yourself. I wish I could do it for you. But accepting that you are a good man worthy of anything is going to have to be something you do on your own."

"I will not."

She nodded, a little sadly, but certainly not as she had years ago when she'd found out about Pietro. Hollow-eyed and lost, like a bombing victim. *That* had torn her to pieces, and that tearing had been what had allowed herself to hide away in Scotland for so long.

He'd always told himself that. He'd given her time because of the great hurt she'd endured. He'd never allowed himself to consider he'd allowed it because her far away from him was easiest. That distance put to bed any temptation.

He shook that thought away. It didn't matter if it were true, if what he'd told himself was at odds with his true motivations. All that mattered was that Pietro's betrayal had destroyed her.

His refusal of her suggestion they marry didn't even put a dent in her. Didn't that prove everything he needed to know right there?

"For as long as I'm here, my bedroom door is always open to you, Javier. And the potential that we marry and attempt to make something of whatever exists between us as well." And with that, she left his bedchamber, his own bedsheet trailing behind her.

Opening too many doors that should remain shut. That *would* remain shut. He would bolt them himself.

But her words stuck with him for too long. Like a thorn in his side, this possibility that wasn't a possibility. *I would never, ever fear you.* An impossible little flight of fancy. Perhaps she would always have it, but he would not.

But perhaps she was right about one thing.

He controlled the universe.

So he arranged for Vance Connor to come to dinner here. He would push her toward him. The man she *could* marry.

And would have to.

Mattie returned to her room. She felt a mix of so many things it was a bit exhausting. There was a certain amount of selfish joy that she'd finally shared her body with a man, and it had been beautiful. Wonderful.

Pain enveloped her when she thought of all the good things that Javier could not see in himself. Frustration that he'd block any chance of happiness away because of *statistics*. Because instead of getting help, he'd determined locking his true self away was the only safe option. His fear—

No, she realized. Like everything else, this was simply an excuse. He wasn't afraid of being a monster. He thought it was true. Whether he'd ever lifted a hand toward anyone or not, he saw the man in the mirror as a monster. As the father who'd abused him.

Mattie did not know what to do with that. She was no therapist, no mental health professional. How did you reach beyond someone's trauma to their heart, and all they could be if they believed it?

She had no clue. More, as many doors as she'd opened with Javier last night, she also understood that this was...a tangle. They'd started with sex instead of understanding. Maybe even beyond that, Javier couldn't meet her with understanding until he extended some to himself.

She considered calling Elena but did not know how to talk to the woman about having sex with her son, or about this without admitting to that. It was too delicate and tricky.

But that left her no one to really talk to and that struck her as sad. Pathetic, really. But she only had herself to blame, because she'd cut everyone else off these past three years.

She let that sobering thought depress her through the duration of her shower, but by the time she got out and got dressed for the day, she'd made some different choices.

The past three years had been anchored by wallowing, disassociating with plants, and isolating herself from every hard discussion, decision or feeling she possibly could. She would not repeat those steps here. She had to find different ways to cope.

So instead of gardening today, she called one of her old

friends from school and set up a lunch get-together for later in the week. She left Javier's home—only informing Luis of her plans because she could not find the driver and did not have her own car here. She went into Barcelona and let herself wander, participate in life around her. Enjoy. She went to the botanical gardens and spent an hour befriending a volunteer there—an elderly man who listened to tales of her garden with great interest and showed her things he thought she'd like.

She did. All of it. She went to lunch by herself, chatting with the quirky waitress at a charming little bistro. She stopped by Mrs. Fernandez's house with a bouquet of flowers and was invited in for lemonade and conversation about her many grandchildren.

She wished there was someone she could speak to about what was going on with Javier, but this was the next best thing. *Life*. Not isolation. Not fear. Just life.

As her father would have wanted for her.

This thought led her to take a little stroll in the Parc de la Ciutadella, as she'd once done with her father in the summers. And she didn't feel angry for his ridiculous will stipulations. She just missed him, and felt him there, walking with her, as silly as that was.

When Matilda returned to Javier's home, she felt like a new person. Maybe it wouldn't last, all these epiphanies, all this optimism, but she was going to follow it for now, and try to carve out this new idea of how she wanted the next few years to look.

Not isolated *in* Scotland, though not isolated from it either. Balance. Somewhere, she had to find some balance.

And so did Javier. She couldn't do that *for* him, but maybe she could find some way to nudge him in the right direction.

She barely opened the door to her rooms when Carmen pounced.

"We must get you ready," Carmen said, disapproval of what Mattie had chosen to wear on her afternoon out written all over her face.

"For what?" she asked as Carmen tugged the bags from her hands and set them down on the ground.

"For dinner."

"I have no plans for dinner."

"Mr. Alatorre is having guests over, and your presence is required."

"Required." Mattie sucked in a breath. What would *this* be about? Something designed to irritate her, no doubt. She considered being petulant and refusing, but Carmen already had clothes—ones Mattie had not brought from Scotland or anywhere—laid out on the bed.

"You may choose yourself," Carmen said as though she were making some great peace offering when the choices were both nearly identical. A simple black dress with sleeves, or a dark navy dress that was sleeveless.

Mattie would have preferred some color, so she grabbed the navy and disappeared into the bathroom to change into it. It fit perfectly, of course, even though it wasn't from *her* wardrobe, and she had no idea who'd procured it or when.

She let Carmen choose her jewelry and fuss with her hair. Mattie did some minimal makeup herself, much to Carmen's chagrin.

"With eyes like that, you should use what makeup offers as a weapon."

"With eyes like mine, I don't need weapons," Mattie replied cheerfully. She didn't let herself think about what guests Javier might have invited. She refused to let the little wriggle of anxiety win.

Carmen studied her. "You seem different, Miss Willoughby."

"Mattie, as I've repeatedly told you. And I feel different, Carmen. I feel really different." Different enough to march downstairs full of confidence and bravado and only a little tickle of uncertainty. She followed voices into one of the sitting rooms.

She stopped short, recognizing the man standing next to Javier at once. "Vance."

Vance turned to face her and smiled. Standing here in Javier's home, in Javier's orbit. She didn't know why it struck her as so wrong, only that after the events of last night she didn't know quite how to behave around him.

Which was ridiculous. They'd shared a few dances and some conversation over the course of one evening. She certainly shouldn't feel any guilt for what had happened with Javier last night, or any discomfort that they were now all in the same room.

He crossed and took her hand. "It's good to see you, Mattie."

Mattie. Because he'd listened to her request and filed it away. Unlike Javier, who wanted to keep her at a distance.

Maybe this was the kind of thing she needed to be paying attention to. Maybe this was all the sign she needed. Vance was willing to put forth an effort. Javier was not.

Vance brushed a kiss over her knuckles. It should have been nice. It should have been welcome. But her gaze moved over to Javier.

He inclined his head. As if to say *your move*.

And she knew there would be nothing *nice* about this evening Javier had set up. Particularly when a stunning woman—the same woman from the charity gala—entered the room apologizing for being late and brushing a kiss across Javier's cheek.

A clear sign, or perhaps *shots fired*.

But Mattie had no need for a battle. She understood his need for one stemmed from fear, and she wasn't afraid of him.

But he was afraid of her, and that was something to hold on to.

CHAPTER FIFTEEN

JAVIER HAD TO grit his teeth to keep from snapping at Ines. She kept yammering on and on about the artwork on the wall of the dining room and Javier was far more interested in hearing what Mattie and Vance were chatting so intently about down at the other end of the table.

As they should be. As was his intent. And regardless of anything that had happened last night—because it would be best if they both forgot the happenings altogether—she seemed to enjoy Vance's company.

He tried to focus on Ines through dessert, but knew he failed. He could feel her displeasure radiating from her and yet his gaze could not seem to be ripped from the couple at the other end of the table.

It felt so much like those years Matilda had been with Pietro, those times he'd been forced to share their orbit at society functions...until he'd finally figured out how to know if she and Pietro planned to attend.

He didn't like the clarity now. That all those years he'd convinced himself it was just some...protector instinct, developed only for Ewan's sake, in Ewan's memory. But it was jealousy. Plain and simple.

As though a few years had matured him enough to see past all his own excuses. No matter how he tried, he couldn't convince himself this roiling frustration inside him was distrust or distaste of Vance. He couldn't seem to believe these feelings were about protecting her.

It was about *wanting* her. Damn his soul to hell.

So he was taking care of it. Vance here for dinner, ensuring they made more plans to be together. He would ensure they spent all the time together needed.

But next time he wouldn't be here to witness it. His hand clenched into a fist under the table as Vance leaned over and whispered something in Matilda's ear that made her laugh. Those violet eyes sparkling for another man.

He wanted to bash the man's perfect teeth in. He could picture it. *Feel* the slap of bone against bone. His heart raged for that physical fight he had no right wanting.

Because he was a monster. Violence was his blood. Who else would imagine fighting a man for simply talking to the woman he could not seem to excise from his being? Who else would have to hold himself back from storming across the room and taking that which he wanted?

Her. Her. Her. Last night in his bed. In his shower.

He was a tangle of too many sharp feelings, and this was the perfect example of why he would find a way to get her married off to Vance before the month was over.

For her own good. Her own safety.

"Javier?"

Javier blinked, looked over at Ines. Her mouth, usually curved in some kind of flirtatious expression, was a straight line. She touched a hand to her temple. "Unfortunately, I'm coming down with a bit of a headache. I should take my leave."

"Of course." He knew etiquette demanded he walk Ines outside and tuck her away in his car to have his driver take her back to her apartment in Barcelona proper. But he hesitated, because he hated the idea of leaving Vance and

Matilda alone together, even though that's exactly what he should do.

Ines stood abruptly, the chair scraping back with enough force both Vance and Matilda looked up from their oh-so-intimate conversation. Ines threw her napkin on her plate and began to stalk out of the room.

"If you'll excuse me," Javier muttered at Matilda and Vance's surprised faces.

He followed Ines out of the room and told himself it was good to have an excuse to leave. To stop having to witness Matilda's red hair tilted toward Vance's perfectly straight white teeth.

But the minute he was out of the room, following Ines's retreating form, he wondered what they would do now that they were alone. Would Vance put his hands on her? Would she allow it?

It became harder to breathe. Impossible to focus on anything but the idea that Matilda might press that beautiful, lush mouth to anyone else's mouth. That she might let another man's hands touch her perfect, velvet skin.

Fury boiled inside him like the inherited disease it was. He could control anything, the whole world, but this was the ticking time bomb inside him. *She* was going to be the thing that finally detonated it and he could not allow it. Would not allow it.

Ines had stormed all the way to the front door, though she did not exit it right away. She turned to him then, not looking the least bit pained from a headache. Her expression was all anger. "What was tonight all about?" she demanded.

He blinked, trying to bring his thoughts away from Matilda and to the woman before him. "It was a casual dinner. As I said when I invited you."

"Are you really this...delusional? I don't need to be

your wife, Javier, but I won't be your plaything when other women are involved."

"There are no other women involved," Javier replied darkly.

She laughed, but it was not her usual laugh. Carefree. Seductive. No. This was harsh. A sign he'd miscalculated greatly when he never did. Especially with women.

Still, she did move toward him in what he might have termed a seductive move. She put her hand to his chest, tilted her chin up to meet his gaze. "Then kiss me, Javier."

He looked down at her. Offering her mouth to him. It wouldn't be the first time he'd kissed Ines. The time they'd spent together had been enjoyable enough. He rather liked her when he wasn't...distracted.

"I thought you had a headache," he said instead, and knew it was perhaps the lamest response he could have managed.

Her hand dropped. Her expression turned to icy anger. "Have your driver meet me out front. And do *not* follow me outside." She wrenched the front door open, but offered one last parting shot before she closed the door behind her.

"You need to figure yourself out, Javier."

Then the door slammed shut, the sound echoing through the large entryway.

But there was nothing to figure out. Not for him. And once he got Matilda out of his home, he could go back to his normal life. He would have control of everything that raged inside. The monster would be leashed once more.

He just had to get rid of Matilda. Once and for all.

Mattie walked through the gardens with Vance at her side and wished he was someone else. No matter how nice, how handsome, she could not seem to eradicate thoughts of Javier for him.

The entire meal she'd felt Javier's gaze on her. Not Ines. Not his meal. *Her.* And though she had tried very hard to focus on Vance, had sometimes even succeeded, far too often her thoughts had drifted to last night.

She talked about the gardens with Vance a little bit, about some of the art he was interested in. They had nice conversations.

Everything was *nice*, and a few years ago she might have leaned into that. Been happy and satisfied with that. Because there was nothing *nice* about what she felt for Javier.

But that sharp, edgy, dangerous thing Javier offered had altered her. She could no longer settle for nice. For safe. She needed to face the dragon, so to speak.

"Why do I get the feeling I'm in the middle of a game I don't know the rules to?" Vance said quietly.

"It's not a game." Mattie sighed, feeling a mix of guilt and frustration. "Not that I know *what* it is, but it's not meant to be a game. Vance..."

She stopped walking and so did he. She looked up at him. He was so nice. He was exactly the kind of man she *should* want. But all she could think of was Javier.

"I'm sure it's complicated," Vance offered, kindly. So kind. She nodded.

"I prefer simplicity myself."

"I used to think that too."

"What changed?"

"I'm not sure exactly. Maybe I stopped hiding from myself. Maybe my life just can't be that simple." She wanted to give Javier a taste of that simplicity. She wanted to give him all the kindness he didn't think he deserved. She wanted... him. Plain and simple. So it wasn't fair to pretend otherwise with Vance. "I'm very sorry. This was never meant to be some kind of...leading you on."

"I think I understand that." He lifted her hand, much as he had when he'd greeted her. Brushed a kiss across her knuckles. "I'm sorry it couldn't work out, but I wish you the best of luck, Mattie."

"You too, Vance."

"I don't suppose you could introduce me to Javier's date?"

She laughed. "I'll see what I can do, but I have faith that you can secure your own dates."

He shrugged, his expression amused. A nice man, and she couldn't even pretend to want him. What was wrong with her?

"I'll walk you out," she offered.

Vance shook his head. "No need. Goodbye, Mattie."

"Goodbye."

She let him leave on his own, because there was just not enough pretending in the world. She wanted Javier. Both physically and as a man. She wanted to…help him. He clearly had things he needed to work out that he was refusing to, and she wanted to somehow lead him to a place where he dealt with his trauma so he could… So he could understand he was not doomed to follow his father's footsteps.

What a sad fate he'd given himself.

She found a bench, much like the one she planned to put in her section of the garden eventually, and settled herself onto it so she could enjoy the smell of flowers, the nighttime whisper of plant life. She considered if this was some misguided need to change him or was it a more honest wanting to help because she cared about him.

Had she simply latched onto Javier now because he was in a strange way safe?

She laughed to herself in the darkened garden. No, nothing about Javier felt safe. He made her forget herself. He made her want things she didn't fully understand. He frustrated her beyond reason and made her say and do things that felt like someone else.

These were not bad things. In fact, for *her*, in this moment, they were good things. Not that long ago she'd viewed a loss of safety like a loss of life. But that was a sad, isolated way to live. To never risk. To never try for something that scared her.

She was done withdrawing or isolating from that which felt too scary. She was realizing there was no reward without risk.

Would she have ever realized that if Javier hadn't made her come here? If Elena hadn't pointed out her withdrawal tendencies?

She wanted to believe that she would have, but maybe sometimes people came into your life to teach you something, and maybe she could teach Javier something in the same vein. All his control, all his personal belief he was a monster, was only his own version of withdrawal.

He needed to be brave. She nearly laughed again. He got so offended when she accused him of cowardice, but he was *made* of it.

"What are you doing out here?"

Mattie had to squint at the dark to make out his outline. Standing there. As if he was afraid to get close. "Thinking," she offered.

"Why did Vance leave?"

Mattie let out a long sigh. "He is not a stupid man, Javier. Any more than Ines was a stupid woman."

"What does that mean?"

She got up off the bench and walked over to him. He stayed in the shadows so she couldn't quite make out his expression, but she could all but *feel* the war inside him. Stay or retreat.

Either would make her happy. Because both responses were about how he felt about her. He wanted her, no matter how little he wanted to.

"They both knew that all we could think about was each other. No matter how hard we tried to do otherwise."

"Do not fool yourself into thinking you know what was going on in my head."

She laughed. Probably too loud as that man she'd already forgotten the name of had accused her of doing.

"Oh, so you weren't thinking about the shower last night? My mouth on you in your bed? You weren't chastising yourself for wanting Ewan's daughter? For this foolish notion that you're some kind of monster like your biological father?"

"I was dreaming of beating your date to a bloody pulp," he said, so darkly. Clearly so certain that would shock her.

But it didn't. Because he seemed to not understand a very basic tenet of life she'd learned when she'd been a little girl. Struggling with how she felt about the fact she couldn't remember her mother, or that her father wanted her to go to boarding school, or those first few difficult months testing out Elena as a stepmother and what that meant. Or even these past few days, being so angry at her father for leaving her this ridiculous will stipulation.

"But you didn't even lift one finger to him, Javier. You did not hurt him, threaten him. What does it matter that you thought of it? Thoughts aren't actions."

He shook his head, there in the dark, so she kept moving toward him. Until she was close enough to touch. She wanted his hands on her, his mouth on her. She wanted the wild ride of last night again because she'd never felt quite so free, quite so herself, as she did when he touched her and made her forget everything.

Safety. Danger. Grief. Fear. Worry.

It was all burned to ash when he was inside her.

She reached out, put her hand to his chest, and said things she never would have dreamed she'd have the courage to say to anyone. "I want you. I can't stop thinking about wanting you. Your hands on my body. The way you taste. The way you make me feel."

"I told you what I am, Matilda," he growled. And she understood that growl was him attempting to control himself.

But it was a *fight*.

She realized he thought it all the same. *Any* impulse was wrong, would lead him down the path of his father. So he fought them all, used his control as armor. It was why he wanted no one in his space. Why he kept himself in his own controlled little worlds. Why even his gardens had to be neat, tight rows. To hide this monster he thought he was.

But that was not him, or he would not have hugged her in his office the other day. He would not have taken care of her finances, devoted himself to her father's wishes, kept everything she'd run away from going while she'd been off in Scotland.

No, he was no monster, but she did not know how to prove that to him. Except this. And maybe that was selfish.

But she didn't care.

"You think you're a monster, but I don't. I guess you'll have to show me."

He reached out, tangled his hand in her hair, then fisted it. "Do you think I won't?"

His grasp on her hair was tight, and perhaps she was some kind of monster too, because it sent a thrill through her. Deep and throbbing. "I hope you will."

CHAPTER SIXTEEN

SHE WAS POISON. She was life. She was his downfall and when his mouth was on hers, he could not find himself. There was only want. There was only her.

She pressed against him, and he held his hand curled in her silky hair so that he could move her mouth at whatever angle he pleased. So he could move her head out of the way, so he could set his mouth to her neck, use his teeth.

And it didn't seem to matter that he let go of every scrap of restraint. That he was rough with her, desperate and lacking all control. She did not stop him, did not push away, did not tell him no.

She egged him on. She kissed him back with teeth, held on to him with nails. And then…she begged him. Explicitly and desperately so that he didn't even concern himself with the fact that they were outside.

He pushed up the skirt of her dress, pulled down the underwear she wore. He settled himself on the bench, moving her with him and then settling him on her lap. He thrust inside her, no finesse, no seduction. There was no time. Only the roaring of everything cascading inside him. War. Battles.

And she accepted him so easily, so perfectly. He'd barely moved at all when she came apart like she was as desperate, as lost, as big a fool as he.

He pulled at the bodice of her dress until he freed her breasts, naked to the air and him. Dimly he heard the fabric tear, but it did not penetrate, because she was begging. Making little noises that snapped any last hold on control he had. He feasted on her while she writhed against him, rode him. Hard and wild. Her skin glimmered in moonlight like water. Her pleasure played out over her face, the river of her hair like magic all around them.

She shattered again, and still, he didn't stop. She slumped against him, his name on her lips, but he simply shifted her, until she was splayed out on the bench.

She was flushed, her eyes seeming to glow here in these shadows. Watching him. He should go. Escape now. With what little glimmer of sanity he had left.

But she trailed her own hand down the length of her body, arched her back and made a long, contented sound. Her eyes never leaving his. "More," she whispered.

More, more, more.

It echoed in his head, a need he could not resist. He gripped her hips, settled himself inside her.

"Do not hold back this time," she said. "Give me everything, Javier. *Cariño mio.* Everything."

So that everything he'd ever known, ever held on to, ever believed evaporated, and there was only the tight, perfect glide of her body against his. The ecstasy of letting loose and letting go, pounding every last ounce of emotion into her until she was screaming out his name, and he lost himself in the sound of it. In her. Emptying himself until there was nothing left.

He *shook*, there on top of her. Outside, where the air seemed to slowly cool around them as his breath, as his mind, as his *sanity* returned. He withdrew from her, his head ringing.

She had ruined everything. Fully now. There was no recovering from this.

"Well," she said, somewhat cheerfully, as if anything about this moment could be *cheering*. She sat up, tried to smooth her dress back into place, but the bodice was ripped. Her hair was a riot, impossible to tame. No one would see her and not know exactly what had happened to her.

A flame within tried to fan to life again, but he quashed it. He'd ripped her dress, been rough with her. Perhaps it had not been unwelcomed, but she did not understand. She… She…

She confused everything. Crumbled walls he'd crafted over *years*. He could not let her get beyond those walls and dig up his foundations too.

He stood, tucking himself away. Trying to find something to hold on to. Some grip on control.

She ruined everything, so she couldn't be here anymore.

"You must leave, Matilda." How could she not see that? How could she think this could continue and not be the ruin of everything?

"Where would I go? Back to Scotland?"

"You should go find Vance. Apologize. He seems a good man. I have not been able to find anything wrong with him. You should do what you can to make that work."

"But I only want you."

He had never felt quite so cleaved in two, quite so many emotions batter him. It was pain and it was…longing.

No matter how little he should, he only wanted her too.

But it could not be. It would not be.

"You are mistaken," he said, trying to find the icy control he'd once known.

She laughed. "I know you are the only man I've been with, and I know I'm supposed to think that's childish, but it isn't. It's just the way things—"

But none of the words after *only* seemed to penetrate. A low, dim buzz began in his ears. "What did you say?" he rasped. "I am not the only man. I... You and Pietro were together for years."

Her brow furrowed. "We were, but we never shared more than a kiss. He did not...want me in that way. He dressed it up in many different things, waiting for marriage and what-not, so we never... Javier, you are it for me."

He felt like a soldier on a battlefield struck by a bullet. Like he might simply keel over, dead, at any moment.

This could not be. Too many things tried to crowd in on him. Her initial discomfort in the shower, the inexpert way she had touched him at times. But he had ignored all those things because she had not given them any credence. Be-cause...because... He had known it couldn't be. He had just assumed Pietro had been useless in *all* things.

It couldn't be. But she'd said it so offhand. It made...too much sense. And made so many things immensely worse.

He had broken a sacred trust already, but he had not known...that he would have...debased her in such a way when she was innocent. She'd come to him untouched, and he'd marked her, stained her, ruined her.

Monster.

"If you will not leave, I will."

"Javier..."

But he did not hear anything else she said. Could not. He was striding for the house. Was he running? Everything in-side him was galloping. Wrong.

This was so wrong, and he needed to escape.

Mattie sat on the bench in the garden for so long she was shivering by the time it occurred to her to stand up. She did not understand what had just happened, and she certainly did not know how to fix it.

He'd run away. Actually *run*. It wasn't even cowardice this time. It was fear, straight through. Like she was some kind of threat. To his very life. From the look on his face, she might have thought she'd stabbed him clean through. But all she'd done was told him what she'd assumed he'd already known.

Honestly, she could not fathom why that made anything different. Whether she'd ever had sex with Pietro or anyone else or not, what changed?

"Men," she muttered. Honestly, that was the only explanation for that one.

She walked back into the house, quietly slipping back into her quarters. She wasn't quite certain how she felt. The moment had been glorious. The aftermath had been…confusing. All that being glad she'd pushed him to the edge now felt…sadder, somehow.

He'd run away. Like a boy. She did not wish to hurt him—not with what they'd done, or what she'd said, but how could she have predicted it would have such an effect?

When she got to her room, she didn't bother to change out of her ripped dress. She just sat on the bed and tried to work through…anything she was feeling.

Part of her wanted to run back to Scotland. Hide in her plants. Withdraw from all this complication. It was a tempting safety.

But she had changed. Because even as she felt that wistfulness for isolation and safety, she knew she could not choose it. It would not solve any of their problems. And Javier was a problem she did not want to ignore.

She wanted to fix whatever issue was between them. If only she fully understood the issue.

It was such a strange feeling, to be so new at bravery

and not hiding away, and now see someone do...exactly what she'd once considered a mature, healthy move. Javier wouldn't likely hide the way she had, but he would run. And run and run, until he came up against something that made him realize the truth of what he was doing.

She couldn't help but have some concerns he never would. Her experiences had been so tame if she compared them to his. Didn't that mean he'd need a much bigger and scarier wall to run into him for him to realize anything?

He'd told her to go. Should she? She wouldn't go cuddle up to Vance. It wasn't honest or fair to a nice enough man. But she *could* give Javier the space he so desired. Leave him to figure it all out on his own.

That is what he'd given her years ago, and even now, knowing it hadn't been the healthiest choice, she was grateful to him for it. Just as she was strangely grateful for him seeking her out, being so bound and determined to see her father's wishes seen to.

Sometimes, time did heal, or help the healing process along. Sometimes, time was needed to fully change, mature, to be ready for the changes and maturity that waited.

But she didn't want to give Javier time. *That* was selfish, she knew. What she didn't know was what the right choice to make was.

But maybe there was someone who did. She called Elena. And she told her...not everything, but enough. Not that she'd engaged in a physical relationship with Javier, but that romantic feelings had been introduced. Not that Javier thought himself a monster, but that he had misgivings because of...so many things.

"He told me I had to leave, and I... I don't want to, but shouldn't it be about what he wants? I don't want him to be unhappy. I don't want to the source of...this pain."

"You aren't the source, *mi niña*. You are the wall you speak of. He has hit it, and now he must make a choice. Change, as he should. Grow, as he should. Or close down even harder. So, you must stay put," Elena instructed. "He will expect obedience, and you must not give it to him."

"So what *do* I give him?"

"Do you love him, Mattie?"

The question was asked gently, but Matilda felt as though the gentleness was for Javier, not herself. She had been very careful not to use the word *love* with Elena, with Javier, even in her own thoughts.

But it had hovered there. Just another fear she wanted to ignore. Because love still scared her. She had thought she'd loved Pietro, but it felt nothing like this. She had thought love was safe, easy. Not scary, not painful.

"I know you were happy with my father. I know he loved you very much. Javier does not think you loved my father," Mattie answered instead. "Is that true?"

"Of course not," Elena replied. "Javier saw... He saw the misgivings I had about *myself* as misgivings I had about loving your father. He cannot separate the two, and he would not let me explain it to him when I finally understood it."

He cannot separate the two.

Mattie thought on that. On what she'd seen out of her father and Elena. It did not *look* painful and conflicted, but she had been too young and kept out of it to know how they'd been together in the beginning.

"Your father was very patient with me, because he loved me even when I did not love myself. Oh, Mattie, I hope you'll be patient with Javier if you love him. He needs it."

Mattie realized Elena was giving her an out, not forcing her to answer the question she'd avoided. Maybe she should have told Javier first, but part of her felt as if she owed the truth to Elena here and now, because she was his mother, worried about him.

"I do love him, Elena," she said, though her voice shook. Not with doubts. With worries that she wasn't strong enough to be as good and patient as her father had been. But she would try.

Because for all Javier's faults, she loved the man he was. His strength, his dedication. The way it felt as though they were equals, as though they could help each other be better versions of themselves.

She could be his safe place to land if he let her. He'd already been hers. Even when she hadn't fully realized it.

"Then that is what you give. You cannot control him. You cannot change him. These are changes he will have to decide on his own. But if you're there, if you refuse to let him convince you otherwise, then maybe he can find the safe space to finally…face himself."

"And…what if he doesn't?"

"You decide how deep that love goes, Mattie. You cannot decide anything *for* him. Only for you."

Mattie thought of those words all night, and then all through the next day when she couldn't find Javier. And when finally one of his staff members told her he'd gone and would not be back for some time, she realized she had a lot of choices to make.

For herself. Once and for all.

CHAPTER SEVENTEEN

JAVIER HAD LEFT. Not just his estate, but Barcelona. He could not bear…any of this. Whether Matilda listened to him and left as well, whether she was stubborn and stayed, he could no longer be in this place that he'd cultivated as a sanctuary.

She'd ruined it.

He wasted no time packing, telling Luis to book a flight. First, he flew to London, convinced he would do some business at the WB offices there. He spent the entire morning making mistake after mistake.

It was of no use. He could not seem to find his control, his focus. Everything was scattered in a million pieces.

She'd ruined him.

He left the offices before the day was out. He briefly considered another WB office but knew there was no point trying to work. He could go to his holiday home in Capri, but what would he do there? Fume. Pace. *Think*.

No, it would do no good. So he flew back to Spain. But not Barcelona.

Valencia. Where his mother lived. He did not know what possessed him, felt even more confused when the driver pulled up to her smaller more traditional beach house, surrounded by luxurious modernity.

She could have had a bigger house, a staff. Though much of Ewan's wealth had gone to his daughter, the man had made sure both Javier and his mother would always be taken care of no matter what. Javier had built on what he'd been gifted, creating his own dynasty.

His mother had seemed to be content with what was. Demanding something small, artistic and cozy right on the water, until Javier had given up trying to talk her into something better.

He paid the driver and got out. The night air was warm, and he could hear the water crashing against the beach, though the dark and houses blocked any view of the gulf from here.

He stood in the front yard, staring at the way it *did* exude coziness, here in the dark. A few lights on in the shadows, wind chimes tinkling in the breeze. He had avoided this as much as he could. Often going to great lengths to convince his mother to come to Barcelona if she wished to see him.

Why? He asked himself now when he'd never questioned himself before. Why had he insisted she come to his estate, and why did he suddenly understand every complaint she'd leveled against it? Too big. Too cold. A *mausoleum*.

This too was Matilda's fault. These realizations he didn't want. Making everything he knew to be right feel wrong. Breathing life into the gardens of his estate if nothing else. Understanding the beauty there and refusing to see the lack of life.

Because she was the life it sorely lacked.

Javier marched up to the door and knocked. He would demand Elena handle this. Talk to Matilda. Get through to her. Stop…whatever it is she was doing to him. He could not, clearly, but Elena could.

His mother answered the door. Her mouth went slack with surprise. "Javier." She looked behind him as if expecting someone else to be with him. Her gaze returned to him on her porch. "What are you doing here?"

And all his demands, all his certainty, just seemed to evaporate. He felt lost. A child again. When they'd finally escaped that monster and there had finally been peace and he hadn't known what to *do* with it.

So he'd gone to the streets and found war. Until Ewan. Until a man had looked at him and seen potential instead of a curse.

"I did not know where to go," he managed to say. Because it was true. He had no idea where to go, to be. No idea how to solve this horrible pain within him.

She made a tsking noise, then pulled him inside. All the way to her cozy kitchen, which was much nicer than anything they'd had in the slums of Madrid, and yet it reminded him of being a teenager all the same. Coming home after a fight, bloody and bruised and surly.

She spoke to him in Spanish as she had then, words of encouragement and endearments as she fussed in the kitchen, preparing tea, even though he had not told her the problem. Back then she would have patched him up, begged him to find some good instead of some bad.

He realized back then she had been desperate, afraid. And that was gone. She was calm and collected as she made tea, as she assured him all would be well even without knowing what was wrong.

He had convinced himself he'd come here to have his mother set Matilda straight, but the minute he'd seen her, that had changed. And now, in her quiet and supportive chattering, he realized what he really wanted. Needed.

Matilda had opened up some small kernel of hope inside him, so he'd gone to the one person who knew enough to help him quash it. His mother might have infinite hope in him achieving bigger and better, but she knew him. She knew what it was.

The hope had to be extinguished. That was the only possibility any of them survived.

"Do you remember my thirteenth birthday?" he asked, interrupting whatever she'd been saying about better days ahead.

Elena paused in her movements, before straightening her shoulders and turning to face him. He could tell that she did. That it lived in her head as it did in his.

"I need you to explain that to Matilda. She will not listen to me."

But his mother's expression turned to one of confusion. "Explain what?"

"What I am."

"Javier, *mijo*, I don't follow." She crossed to the table, a mug in each hand. She put one in front of him, then sat across from him with her own. Javier knew from the smell alone it was Ewan's favorite blend.

That old familiar pang of loss rippled through him. Too much to bear under all the rest of this upheaval.

So he had to quash it. By remembering the day he least wanted to. By reminding himself, his mother, *everyone* who he was underneath all the control he'd built inside himself.

"My thirteenth birthday. When you tripped, and you dropped the cake you had made me. Even though he'd told you not to. I was so angry that I couldn't have even that. So I… I was going to hit you."

"You did not hit me," his mother said with vehemence. The same kind of vehemence she'd once used to insist his father had not been wrong.

Because they were the same. She would defend him as she'd once defended his father. "I raised my hand to you. You knew what I intended. You saw what I was capable of."

"Is that what you think?"

"It is what I know." He had seen the horror in her eyes. He had seen everything in her change. He had seen himself then. Fully clearly for the first time.

As bad as the man he'd come from. Evil. Bleak. Lost.

"I was not scared of you, Javier," his mother said so sincerely.

But she was wrong. Misremembering, lying. *Something*.

"I did not think you would actually hit me. I lived with an abuser...my whole life. My father hit me. Your father hit me. It was all I knew. It is why I stayed so much longer than I should have. I thought it normal. I thought...he was right, *they* were right. This was how someone learned."

She had never told him that before. That her own father had also hit her. But this just proved his point. Abuse was a cycle. She had been born into it, chosen it. Then she'd left—escaped. Because the only way to break it was to remove yourself from it. She'd removed him from one part, and he would remove himself from perpetuating it in the future.

He just needed someone to explain that to Mattie.

His mother leaned forward, placed her hand over his fisted one on the table. "When you were very young, your father only hit me. But as you got older, he became more focused on you. It was all I'd known, so I did not stop him, but it...it felt wrong. I did not trust my own feelings then, so I simply lived with that wrong. I did not know better, and still, I carry that heavy burden of guilt everywhere I go. I do not know that I will ever forgive myself for this, but through therapy I have learned to give myself some grace." She managed a shaky smile. "Ewan was part of that grace."

He made a move to get up, to remove her hand from his. To escape this talk of...*grace*. But Elena's grip tightened.

"That day, when you lifted your hand to me. So angry, so upset. Because yes, you couldn't even have this small thing.

You were a young man who had so little. But that was the moment my eyes were opened, Javier. Not to...whatever it is you think. That you are some kind of monster? No." She said this with a kind of disgust that pinned him to his spot. Almost as though...she'd never thought that of him.

When how could that be?

"It is when I saw you...so conflicted. So horrified by your own actions that you *did not want* and did *not* act on. It was an impulse you controlled, at thirteen. Something your father, a grown adult, had never done. My father, also a grown man, had never stopped himself from doing. You did not swing that hand. You did not yell at me. You lifted that hand in a spark of fury, and then you dropped it the next instance as if your entire world had ended. Right there."

Javier tried to find the words to tell her she was wrong. She misunderstood. He'd wanted to hit her because his blood was tainted. Because he was in an inescapable cycle unless he kept everyone at fist's distance.

But he remembered that moment too well. The riot of feelings inside him. Disgust. Horror. He had not wanted to hit her. It had been a spurt of anger and the only way he knew how to deal with anger at that time was violence.

But no part of him *wanted* it.

What did wants matter? If he was capable of lifting a hand to his mother, even if he'd resisted the impulse, he had all the potentials of a monster inside him. Of this, he was sure. Until his mother kept speaking.

"I knew I had to get you out. I had to leave. I did not understand then what physical abuse could do to a boy. What it had done to me. I thought it was all normal. But I understood in that moment the emotional abuse we were putting you through, and I spent the next six months planning our escape so that it would not continue. We owe everything that came after to that moment. So I remember it. Clearly. As the turning point that saved us. *You* saved us, Javier."

"You planned the escape." He had never given his mother enough credit for that. Partly because he had not understood the depths of…trauma she must have faced, the way her world had been warped before she had a chance.

And if he gave his mother grace… He shook his head. This was too much. She was…muddling everything in his head. He wasn't here about the past. Even if it informed his future. It didn't have to be about the cycle he would no doubt perpetuate. His mother just didn't understand.

"Javier. What is this all about? Just what isn't Matilda listening to you about? That you're some kind of villain? You have been a fine guardian to her. I know she wasn't pleased about leaving Scotland, but it ended up being good for her." His mother paused, her hand still on his. "Javier, I think *you've* been quite good for her."

That was the breaking point. He pulled his hand away from his mother's grasp. Stood. Paced. It was clear Matilda had told his mother *something*. And neither of them understood. But there was something they both needed to.

"Ewan would have never wanted me for her. It is a disgrace to his memory. It is a *disgrace*."

"Did it ever occur to you that this is exactly what Ewan wanted? For the both of you."

Javier stared at his mother for a good full minute, possibly without drawing a breath. "No," he finally managed. "No, of course not. That is…that is insane."

"Is it?" Elena asked, sipping her tea. "The stipulation is not that Mattie should marry *anyone else* by the time she was twenty-five. The stipulation was that if she did not, you would have to marry her."

"Yes, but…"

"There are no buts. He put that in there because he always thought about what a fine full-circle thing that would be if you two found each other when you were both old enough. I know he'd hoped to have been here, hoped that the will would never have been used in such a fashion. But don't for a second believe that if he *was* here, he wouldn't be finding clever little ways to put you in each other's orbit. He never would have forced your hands, pursued it, if it was clear as adults you didn't suit, but do not for a second think he wouldn't have wanted it. I *know* he did."

"That cannot be true. He... He must not have known about... He could not have known that I..."

"He knew everything about you, Javier. And he loved you all the same. You know this or you would not be so dedicated to his memory. His wishes. But if you are dedicated to the ones you understand, you must also be dedicated to the ones you don't. You are the only one who fancies yourself a monster. You are the only one who is worried you are not good enough."

"I am *not.*"

His mother studied him for the longest time. In silence. For a few moments, he thought she finally understood. That she would finally agree. That he could be free from this vise in his chest. This pressure and pain and loss of control.

"Do you know why it took so long for me to agree to marry Ewan?"

Javier did not understand this change of conversation. "You were friends. You needed money. A better future for me. You... It was a marriage of friendship, of convenience."

She laughed. Threw her head back and *laughed.* "*Mijo*, truly, you have been so dedicated to these fictions you've created. I loved that man. Deeply. And he loved me. But I was afraid, and I was traumatized, and it took time to work through that. I wish I hadn't let my fear of facing it win for so long. We could have had more years together, but I cannot go back and change it."

Javier shook his head. No. It was not love. They'd had an affection for each other. They had been *friends*. For years his mother had resisted Ewan because…because…

Afraid and traumatized.

He didn't know why he was so committed to not believing they loved each other. Only that it made everything inside him more complicated, more confusing.

But he could see the way Ewan had been around his mother. They were not overly affectionate in public, no. But there'd been an expression Ewan's face had gotten when his mother entered a room.

It reminded him of Matilda. The way she'd looked at him under that arbor, or in his office that had once been Ewan's when she spoke of the locket he'd given her for her sixteenth birthday.

Elena took his hands, like she was imploring him. "Don't make my mistakes. Do not resist love because you think you're not good enough. Do not resist trying to find healing because of the amount of hurt it takes to get to the other side. Don't waste time, Javier. I wasted so much time. But those years I had with him, really had with him, were worth everything. If you have feelings for Mattie, you must deal with them. And it has little to do with me, your past or Ewan. It has nothing to do with being 'good enough'—whatever that means—it has everything to do with your heart."

"I do not have a heart."

"I once thought that about myself. That it had been beaten to pieces. Burned to ash. I failed you for thirteen years. How could I deserve love? I was wrong, Javier, and so are you."

He wished he could argue with her, but that heart he did

not want ached in his chest. A foreign thing, soft and vulnerable. He wanted to shore it up with all the armor he'd learned how to build since he was a child.

But he couldn't muster it. Not with his own mother's regrets laid out between them.

And still there was so much fear. Matilda was…light and…

"What if I…? What if I hurt her?"

"You will. In ways you can't predict. And it will hurt. No amount of control can take away the fact that we're human. Hurting each other doesn't make us monsters, it makes us fallible. What matters is that we apologize, that we seek to make amends. I have never not seen you do this, Javier. You can be a hard man, but you are not a cruel one. No matter what you've convinced yourself of."

"You do not know…"

"You are my son. I know."

He wasn't sure he'd ever heard his mother speak with such certainty. Except maybe her wedding vows to Ewan. A man she'd loved. Not just used as a means to escape poverty and struggle.

Javier did not know what to do with any of this. He wasn't even sure of who he was anymore.

But he supposed… He got to choose. He was in control. And if that was the case, maybe he would choose…

Not to be a monster.

If Ewan, if his mother, if Matilda could not see the monster within him, then maybe…maybe it was not something to be quite so scared of.

CHAPTER EIGHTEEN

MATTIE HAD STAYED put in Javier's house. She had spent the days of his absence deciding what she wanted her life to look like. As much as she loved her cottage and gardens and experiments in Scotland, it wasn't a *life*. A vacation, maybe. But she needed…more.

She went to a volunteer training for the Coalition of Rural Safety. It would require some travel, some fundraising, but it would give her something to do and feel quite useful doing.

Beyond that, she'd thrown herself into her garden. She'd ordered a trellis and bench, discussed obtaining some new plants with Andrés. She would leave her mark on these gardens if nothing else.

Every time she thought of leaving, finding her own space here in Barcelona, she came back to what Elena had said.

You decide how deep that love goes, Mattie. You cannot decide anything for him. Only for you.

The choice to leave was not for herself. It was for him.

When she thought of leaving, she realized the aim was to make him more comfortable, to punish him, but never because leaving was what *she* wanted.

So she stayed. She was elbow-deep in soil, plants, her newly constructed trellis and contentment three days after he'd disappeared when she heard foreboding footsteps approach. She didn't turn right away. She didn't want to get her hopes up, and she wanted to have some control over herself if it *was* the man she wanted to see.

When she felt steady enough, she looked over her shoulder. "Ah, so you're back."

He said nothing, just stood there all brooding and beautiful. She looked back at the dirt on her hands, then decided to finish what she was doing. He would have to determine the course of the conversation if he was just going to walk up and tower over her like this.

For a few minutes, all was quiet. She could tell he hadn't left, but he said nothing, and she continued her work, humming quietly to herself.

"Is this the clematis you were wanting to plant?" he asked by way of greeting.

She stopped what she was doing, looked up at him again. Was that some kind of…peace offering, remembering the plant name she'd brought up that evening they'd eaten dinner out here?

He took a deep breath, slowly let it out. His gaze was fierce, his hands curled into fists, but there was something in him that made her hold herself very still. For good or for ill she did not know.

"We need to talk, Mat… Mattie."

A jolt went through her. Surprise and a spurt of joy she immediately tried to tamp down. Just because he'd used her nickname didn't mean…anything.

But of course, it did.

She sucked in an unsteady breath. He had said, very emphatically and not that long ago, he never would.

Carefully, she tugged the gardening gloves off her hands, then got to her feet. She turned to face him, trying to find some look of impassive disinterest—until he explained what this was. "About what?"

182 A DIAMOND FOR HIS DEFIANT CINDERELLA

"I have been visiting with my mother."

She frowned a little, confused by this admission. "In Valencia?"

He nodded.

"But you almost never go there."

"I did not originally plan to. I went to London. I tried to work. And then I went to my mother so that she would tell me, tell *you* in a way that would get through to the both of us that I am no good for you."

Mattie snorted in derision. "What a fool's errand, Javier."

"Yes, it was. She did…quite the opposite, I suppose."

Mattie blinked. What was the opposite of that? *Being* good enough for her? Wanting to be?

Javier stepped forward, closing the distance between them. His dark eyes glittered with something she could not quite read, but he took her hands with a gentleness they had not often shown each other.

"I cannot control myself when it comes to you. I wanted it to be only physical, but I have never felt this way before. I have never been haunted, poisoned, *obsessed*."

"These are not nice words, Javier."

He made a sound, almost a chuckle. And it warmed her, even if those words hadn't. Because he did not chuckle easily. He did not do any of this…easily.

"I have controlled everything in my adult life, except the loss of your father, and except for how I feel about you. Years ago, when you came and told me you had said yes to Pietro, I suddenly realized… I wanted it to be me."

He said this like the confession had been beaten out of him. Like it was potentially one of the worst things he'd ever done. When it settled in her like warmth. Like joy. Back then, when she'd been so young and foolish, he'd wanted it to be him.

"I did not know how to… It felt wrong. When you were my ward. When Ewan had entrusted your future and safety to me. I had no right to you, even if I was a good man, and I very much did not feel as though I was."

She freed one of her hands so she could cup her palm to his face. "I have never thought you a monster, Javier. I cannot imagine I ever will. Maybe not perfect, but who is?"

His gaze met hers, dark and fierce as always, but with a searching intent she'd never seen there before. "I cannot bear the thought of you marrying anyone else. Now or six months from now."

She beamed up at him. "Then I guess you'll have to."

"We could forgo the stipulations. If you wished. You were right, back in Scotland, there is no real legal ramification if you refuse. I will not hold you to this. I want you to be happy."

For a moment, she worried he didn't want to marry her. That she was misunderstanding. But that was fear. He was here. He was saying these things. "I don't wish. I would be happy to marry you."

His mouth curved. "Just like that? You would marry me? No reservations. No concerns."

"I have known you my whole adult life, Javier. I spent years being afraid of or uncertain of what feelings you brought out in me. But I don't hide anymore. I don't run away. I know the man you are, and I know the woman I am. We will have our issues, no doubt, but I have faith that we can sort them out."

He dropped her hands, framed her face with them instead. His gaze tracked over her features, something like awe in his expression that made her feel…perfect. Like every moment had led her here. Where she belonged.

"You know, my mother even suggested that…that your father might have wished it this way."

Everything inside of her went cold. Her *father*. She thought it was about her, about them and… And it wasn't at all. She thought her chest might cave in.

She pulled out of Javier's grasp. This wasn't real. It was all about her *father*? What a fool she was. What a fool she *always* was.

"What is the matter?" he asked gently.

She took a step back. The words were too hard to find, and if she ran…she could just turn and run. Go back to Scotland, not face this. This horrible, horrible hurt. She would refuse him and never have to marry anyone and—

But she was not that woman anymore, so she fought the urge. She lifted her chin, met his gaze. "Now that you think it has my father's blessing, it's just okay? You don't have to love me, care about *me*? As long as you're fulfilling *his* wishes? Well, no, Javier. I won't marry you to make my father happy."

She blinked furiously at the tears welling up as she whirled away from him and started to storm away. Inside. She would pack everything up right this minute and—

"I would marry you to make the *both* of us happy. Me. You."

She stopped abruptly. Had she heard those words correctly? Her heart was galloping, and there were tears in her eyes and she felt…so many different things.

"I love you, Mattie. I have loved you for a very long time. I have endeavored to control you, control the environment when I was around you, and it worked when you were afraid of me—"

She turned to face him then, and a few tears spilled over. "I was never afraid of *you*, Javier."

"Very well. Afraid in general. What I feel for you, what I want our lives to look like, has nothing to do with your father. But knowing he might have approved...knowing he *would* have approved means something to me. I cannot deny that. Your father was...something of a true north for me. In a childhood of pain and suffering and what felt like wrong choices from everyone, he always seemed to make the right ones. I know he was not a perfect man, but he endeavored to be a good one, so I endeavored to...to mimic it. I am naturally not a good man."

"Stop that."

"I do not *feel* as though I am a good man, but I would like to...to work toward feeling that I might deserve you. Work toward deserving each other. And your father's blessing, according to my mother, is part of that. I'm sorry if that hurts you."

He used those words so infrequently. *I'm sorry.* Sounding so sincere, like he truly was.

She took a breath, trying to separate her fears from his words. Her *fear* was that he could only want her because of her father, but she knew better. Everything about the past few weeks should have taught her better.

She managed to shake her head. "No, it doesn't. I...worry that you could not love me for me, Javier. That is *my* fear."

He nodded. Did not invalidate her fear. Just nodded. "I will endeavor to show you every day. I do not want you to go, Mattie. I want you to stay. To marry me. To love me, and if you need time—"

Time? When she knew time was so fleeting. She cut him off by all but throwing herself at him and pressing her mouth to his. When she said those words for the very first time, she said them against his mouth, her arms wrapped tightly around his neck.

"I love you, Javier."

He held her there against him, tight and perfect.

"I want to stay. I want to marry you. Tomorrow, if you'd like."

His laugh rumbled through her like joy. Like a peace they both had found together. "I think my mother will want to be here, but we will do it. Soon." He pulled back a little. "I am still…working on all this. A work in progress."

She gestured at the spot in his gardens she had made hers. "Good thing I love those."

Then he swept her up in his arms and took her to his room—*their* room. In *their* house. And loved her into *their* future.

EPILOGUE

IT TURNED OUT to be a rather good thing they both agreed on a quick marriage, because Mattie soon realized that they had not taken any of the necessary precautions those first few times they'd come together, so tied up in their own issues. The push and pull of what they allowed themselves to want.

They were still learning things about each other. Still working through things. She and Elena had finally convinced Javier to see Elena's therapist in Valencia. The wedding was set for next month, and all was well.

But Mattie did not know how Javier would feel about a child *now*. Even as she felt ecstatic for a future as a family. Nerves. Joy. Hope. She could have kept it to herself for a while longer, seen a doctor to be sure before telling him.

But Matilda Willoughby, soon to be Mattie Alatorre, was no coward.

She found him in his study, frowning at his computer. "One moment, *cariño*," he murmured when he glanced up at her entrance.

She tried to wait. She really did. But she was nervous, and didn't know the right words, so she simply blurted it all out. "Javier. Those first few times we were together. We did not use any protection."

"I assumed…" He stopped what he was doing, looked up at her. "What are you saying?"

"A little bit earlier than planned, I suppose, but… We discussed having a family." Sort of. She had been quite clear that was a goal of hers, and he had not argued, though he'd said very little. He was still working through it and now they were just…

"Are you… Mattie." He skirted the desk and crossed to her. He took her hands in his, as gently as he had that day a few weeks ago when he'd finally told her he loved her. "Mattie," he repeated.

"I will need to go to a doctor, but one of those at-home tests confirms what I've been wondering."

He didn't say anything. She wasn't even sure he breathed. He didn't look devastated, but they had been working on him sorting through his feelings, verbalizing them and not beating himself up for the negative ones.

"You don't have to be happy right away," she said emphatically. "You can be conflicted. We have time."

He shook his head, but she wasn't sure what he was refuting. "Matilda, you must promise not to let me…" His voice was rough, and he couldn't get the words out, but she understood him now. More and more every day. The worry he carried, about cycles. About what he might be capable of.

But he was working on it, and she had no doubt he would be an excellent father. She had no concern for him hurting anyone he loved. Not in the ways he worried he would.

"Every promise I have is yours, Javier. I know you will worry, and I will likely find things to worry about as well, but you will make an excellent father. We will do our best as parents."

"I had a good example."

Mattie nodded, trying not to feel sad that her father was not here to see them be parents. Together. Javier pulled her close, kissing her cheek and stroking her hair.

"I have loved you too long, *cariño mio*," he murmured. "And even in that I could not have dreamed you would be the answer to everything. That you would open my future to everything." He laid his hand over her still very flat stomach, wonder and joy in his expression even with all that worry. Because joy was not the absence of concern, bravery not the absence of fear.

They had learned that together.

"Love is never too long, Javier." Love was everywhere and everything. The tie that bound them. The thread that tied them together and into a future.

Where they filled their estate with a family, full of love and laughter and tears and always the promise that, no matter what, they would love.

* * * * *

COMING SOON!

We really hope you enjoyed reading this book.
If you're looking for more romance
be sure to head to the shops when
new books are available on

Thursday 25th
April

To see which titles are coming soon, please visit
millsandboon.co.uk/nextmonth

MILLS & BOON

MILLS & BOON®

Coming next month

ACCIDENTALLY WEARING THE
ARGENTINIAN'S RING
Maya Blake

Abstractedly, Mareka registered that they'd cleared the building, that they were out in the square with a handful of people milling around them.

But she couldn't break the traction of Cayetano's stare. His heavenly masculine scent was in her nose. The powerful thud of his heartbeat danced beneath her fingers, his breathing a touch erratic again after his gaze dropped to linger on her mouth, his own lips parted to reveal a hint of even white teeth.

And just like that she was once again thrown to that night in Abruzzo when this foolish crush had taken a deeper hold. When the only thing she'd yearned for, more than anything else in existence, was to kiss Cayetano Figueroa. Who cared that she'd sworn to be rid of this madness a mere...half an hour ago?

Half an hour ago...while she'd been choosing the engagement ring he intended to give to another woman.

Her eyes started to widen. He sucked in a sharp breath.

A camera flash went off, dancing off the diamond ring she'd forgotten to take off and illuminating their expressions for a nanosecond before immortalizing it in life-altering pixels.

Continue reading
ACCIDENTALLY WEARING THE
ARGENTINIAN'S RING
Maya Blake

Available next month
millsandboon.co.uk

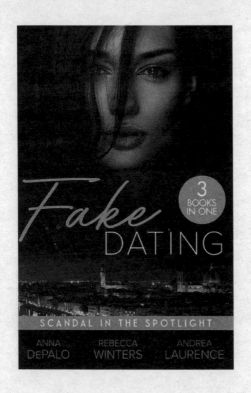

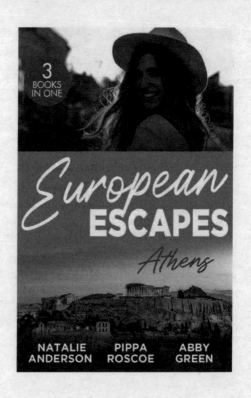

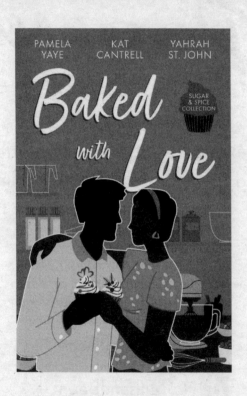

LET'S TALK
Romance

For exclusive extracts, competitions and special offers, find us online:

f MillsandBoon

X @MillsandBoon

⊙ @MillsandBoonUK

♪ @MillsandBoonUK

Get in touch on 01413 063 232